BLOOD BOUND BOOKS

Copyright © 2017 by Drew Stepek
All rights reserved

ISBN 978-1-940250-29-8

Edited by Andrea Dawn

Interior Layout by Black Heart Edits
    www.blackheartedits.com

Printed in the United States of America

First Edition

Visit us online at
www.bloodboundbooks.net

For Lisa.
The one who keeps me Drew...
grounded somewhere between Andy and RJ.

CHILDREN *of the* NIGHT

Children of the Night is a private, non-profit, tax-exempt organization founded in 1979. They are dedicated to assisting children between the ages of 11 and 17 who are forced to prostitute on the streets for food to eat and a place to sleep. They have rescued girls and boys from prostitution and the domination of vicious pimps, and they provide all programs with the support of private donations.

They are making a difference in the lives of hundreds of children each year. Their commitment to rescuing these children from the ravages of prostitution is shared with a small but committed group of detectives, FBI agents, and prosecutors in Los Angeles, Hollywood, Santa Ana, Anaheim, San Diego, other areas of California, Las Vegas, Portland, Billings, Montana; Seattle, Washington; Miami, New York, Minneapolis, Atlanta, Phoenix, Hawaii, and Washington D.C.—all stops on the child prostitution circuit. And their numbers keep growing as more and more dedicated individuals become concerned about the welfare of these desperate children.

Child prostitutes require specialized care for effective intervention. Most of the children victimized by prostitution were first victimized by a parent or early caregiver. Most have been tortured by treacherous pimps, and many testify in lengthy court proceedings against the pimps who have forced them to work as prostitutes.

In most cases these children do not have appropriate homes to return to, and the only relative who is a suitable guardian may live far away from the child's hometown. For many the only option is an out of home placement, college dorm, maternity home, or mental health program. For those who reach 18 and need additional time to prepare to enter the mainstream society, independent living programs are recommended; special education programs are advised for those who need extra help with school, and alcohol or drug recovery homes are suggested for those with substance abuse problems.

Children of the Night is in demand to assist other agencies across the country and around the world to develop similar programs.

www.childrenofthenight.org

Up to 10% of the revenue from Knuckle Supper will be donated to Children of the Night.

FOREWORD

I'll never forget my first encounter with a punk vampire. I was about thirteen years old at the time, and I'd found an only-slightly-battered copy of John Skipp and Craig Spector's 1986 opus *The Light at the End*. (I also managed to get my hands on a copy of Ray Garton's *Live Girls* around that time, but that's a story for another day.) Back then I was consuming vampire literature with a hunger that bordered on rapacious. I had already burned though more titles than I can list, including Anne Rice's *Interview with the Vampire* and its grislier heir apparent, S.P. Somtow's rock-'n'-roll bloodsucker yarn *Vampire Junction*. Both of those novesl primed the pump for Skipp and Spector's gory trip through a gritty and surreal New York City underworld, but the vamp that lurked in Light's pages was far removed from Rice's introspective Lestat and Somtow's charismatic Timmy Valentine. Rudy Pasko was a Nosferatu for the age of splatterpunk: an all-too-human predator who lived on blood but thrived on degredation, rape, and brutal, frenzied murder.

So I'd like to think I was more prepared than most when I picked up Drew Stepek's *Knuckle Supper* back in 2011. I didn't know much about the book before I read it—only that it was about a punk vampire in Los Angeles, and that it was a response to the *Twilight* novels and their ilk. I assumed Drew didn't care for the brooding neck-botherers that were rubbing their sparkly bits all over the bestseller list, and that he meant to put the bite back in vampire fiction. What Drew saw in those books, though, was something far more upsetting. The problem wasn't that we'd romanticized vampires, he argued. It was that we'd turned them into pedophiles.

Knuckler Supper, then, pushed vampire literature into territory that was far more disturbing than any bloodsucker tale I'd experienced before. It wasn't the gore that I found so unsettling—I cut my teeth on *Faust* comics and other underground horror fare in the '80s, so *I've seen some things, man*. What got me about *Knuckle Supper* was the desperate plight of the characters at its center: a murderous vampire junkie named RJ Reynolds and a twelve-year-old, very human prostitute known as Bait. If you're reading these words, it's probably not a spoiler to say that Bait's story didn't end well. RJ, though… well, RJ is complicated. He might still have a shot.

I won't condescend to warn you about the gruesomeness you're going to encounter in Knuckle Balled. If you've found your way here, I think it's safe to say your taste in horror runs considerably left of center, and you've probably got a stomach to match. The same goes for profoundly disturbing content; it is, after all, a story about unspeakable abuse visited upon children. Most of that is kept off the page, but a few lines land like a kick in the teeth (as they should). Drew looks into the darkest corners you can imagine, and he doesn't flinch.

And yet—you knew there was an "and yet," right?—RJ's story isn't entirely one of degradation and despair. I'll admit I've lost my taste for horror that doesn't offer at least a few thin rays of hope and humor, and you'll find both running through Knuckle Balled. RJ is no Lestat, but he's no Rudy Pasko either. His novelty in the world of counterculture vampire fiction isn't that he's a remorseless, bloodthirsty killer, or that he's a monster struggling to maintain some semblance of his humanity. It's that he's both.

~ April Snellings / Rue Morgue

Just 'cause you got the monkey off your back doesn't mean the circus has left town.

~ **George Carlin**

1

VOICED

My name is RJ, and I'm a drug addict.

Like a shitty Nar-Anon meeting on some preachy episode of *TJ Hooker*, that's the way my nightmare always began. My subconscious was forcing me into rehab to face the consequences of my choices. These choices—the ones that resulted in Bait's death—ate away at my body from the tip of my toes all the way to the longest strand of hair sticking up on my head.

I'm a bad man. I'm a selfish man. Although I'm not technically a vampire, who's to say that I'm not some form of vampire? By form of vampire I mean a Hail Mary abortion kept alive by a perverted Catholic sect called The Cloth who crossed their arms and shook their heads at my junkie mother's right to choose.

The fact was this: I was alive. I needed blood… and heroin.

In the dream—which I'm not sure I can call a dream because I'm not technically certain I was asleep—I would find myself planted in the middle of a circle of plastic junior high-quality assembly chairs. The meeting didn't take place in a junior high, however. It took place in the torched remains of the gymnasium where I was brought to life by way of an incubator, steroids, and a constant drip of narcotics. That was how the lovely cunts at St. Matthews fed me to instill my addiction.

I grabbed tightly onto the chair that seemed to be ass fucking me as I pinched my finger on a screw that was coming loose. It felt like the center of the seat contained a makeshift dildo fabricated from the same uncomfortable plastic utilitarian chair materials as the base.

I cleared my throat, making certain that everyone heard my plea for forgiveness.

Ahem. My name is RJ, and I'm a heroin addict.

Everyone in the circle around me just seemed angry. The dream cast always featured a filthy assortment of assholes and unfortunate collateral damage who had turned my walking abortion life upside down.

To my right was a dirty pig of a man in a Roman Catholic vestment masturbating into the face of a little boy in a sailor outfit as he chugged fetuses from a giant beer stein. To my left was a cracked-out slut who was birthing lifeless children from her gash, one right after another, strung together by umbilical cords as if she were processing macabre sausages.

My conscience had a funny way of grabbing a bullhorn and yelling into my ear, *Hey, dickhead, you're worse than every living and unlikable piece of shit in this room. Remember, this is the room where you were crapped out of your druggie mother's ass. This is the room where you were sentenced to walk the earth as an unloving and uncaring shell of normality.*

I pleaded for acceptance into their cult of sobriety. Still, no one responded. I wanted to be welcomed into their world of the living. Surely I wasn't as bad as Father McAteer, who was located halfway around the circle, and was much more preoccupied with polishing and placing a diamond ring onto the skeletal finger of his latest victim. I mean, he brought me and all the other abortions in Los Angeles to life because he wanted to stop the mass prostitute abortions on the streets of L.A. That's pretty bad.

Again.

My name is RJ, and I'm a heroin addict.

I tried to stand up and extract revenge on them for ignoring me. Who were they to sit and judge? I was better than all of them. I didn't have a problem. Unlike them, I was *forced* to live like this. I didn't ask for it. If I had my way, that piece of shit mother of mine would have shoved a vacuum up her twat and sucked me out before I fell into the care of McAteer and The Cloth.

How dare they look down their noses at me. Sure, I've killed several hundred humans, including half-vampire people. So what? And yeah, sometimes I killed people for the fun of it, but mostly I killed because I needed that sweet warm nectar in their bodies. I needed to stay alive... and get high. Killer or victim? Which one was I? After literally crawling out of a dumpster in my teens, the only way for me to stay alive was to feed my hunger.

My hunger... my everything... my loving heroin... the only love of my sad half-life.

The itches and sweats intensified as they continued to ignore me. I felt so debilitated in the dream that I vomited cotton balls, then tried to pound them back into my corroded mouth with my fist.

Ashamed.

I was ashamed of my existence. Not even those derelicts who sat on their high horses would get the chance to point and laugh at what was left of me. Broken into a thousand pieces of waste on the inside and filled to the brim with darkness, regret, and sadness. That was what was left of RJ Reynolds. Badass vampire, heroin addict, gangster motherfucker.

"I got your back," a baritone whisper vibrated my ear drum.

I turned to see King Cobra standing next to me. His voice was warped by one of those awful steel collars that The Cloth used to control us when we were in captivity. It was just a week ago, but it felt like years. They forced us to eliminate all the other vampire gangs in L.A. I escaped the vise of the collar. Cobra didn't.

I wanted to tell him how much he meant to me. He was the biggest threat to my drug dealing operation and I despised his fascist rule of the streets. Thing was, I never got the chance to enjoy the alliance we formed after we were kidnapped by The Cloth because—

"*Adstringo gutter!*" A voice screamed from the other side of me.

Because that happened.

The dream and the wish of getting the chance to spend more time with King Cobra left me as the collar tightened and squeezed the contents of his head out all over my shoulder.

I knew who spoke The Cloth's magic phrase. It was The Habit: the awful teenybopper actress who had outlived her appeal, turned heroin addict and then nun mercenary for a pack of vampire exterminators.

She lifted her repulsive nun's habit— "It's a *habit*. Get it RJ?" —and started fingering herself. Small fetuses dropped to her filthy toes. "I know you want to get inside this shit."

There might have been a time when I wanted to fuck her, but that was long ago. Mostly I wanted to keep off the streets by living in her heroin den. Now even that house was gone.

"Too bad none of you vampire scum can get a hard-on," she reminded me.

That was the truth. A lot of us cheated the fact that we didn't have enough blood in our bodies to get aroused by using a syringe full of blood and some crushed up Viagra.

She limped away into the dark, leaving a trail of unborn babies in her wake.

And then, just as I stood up and was about to grab an arm bong and my rig and leave those dreadful monsters, another familiar voice rang out like a news story sound bite from a murder scene.

"She's dead, motherfucker. I kept her alive because I knew you'd be back. I wanted you to see me kill her, you piece of shit."

I sat down and closed my eyelids. I didn't want to look up and see who was sitting across from me in the circle of horrible creatures. I told myself it was only a stupid dream. But the voice fought louder than my attempts to reel myself back to reality. It spelled out my greatest failure. It reminded me of the worst thing that I had ever done that sat on top of a mountain of blood-drained corpses. The failure waved a flag from atop its mountain and insisted that there would never be a way to correct this wrong. It was beyond a lack of judgment. It was beyond taking the left path to damnation rather than the right one toward salvation. It could never be fixed and it could never be rewritten. It was worse than taking human life for pleasure.

With my head down, I sat there and debated whether or not to further confront the demons that I conjured up. For some reason, all I could think about was killing that lump of human feces to my right—the pedophile priest—and sucking what was left of his barren existence from his knuckles. After all, that was my justification for killing pimps, gangsters, child molesters, and the accumulated dirt on the streets of Los Angeles. Wasn't it? They didn't have any right to live.

A rat scurried by my bare feet. Rather than looking up and facing myself in a mirror of misery, I watched it circle around my legs in a figure eight. I refused to give any further attention to the pedophile or the welfare check assembly line on the other side of me. And I definitely didn't want to catch a glimpse of the horror tragedy across the room from me that I had created. I snatched up the rat. Trying not to draw attention to myself, I rolled open my leather syringe case with my calloused heel. Using my big toe and broken and bent second toe, I clinched onto a needle's plunger and pulled it out of the case. With my other foot, I exchanged direction. The toxin gleamed a strawberry milkshake color, a sign that it contained both heroin and blood. The vermin dug his fangs into the meeting point of my thumb and index finger. I flicked him in the face with my other hand. I didn't want him dead before I bit into his hairy spine like a snack cake.

He released his teeth just as my left foot—accompanied by the vessel brimming with my eternal love—slid up my inner thigh. Slowly, I grabbed the syringe with my hand. The rat looked up at me with his dingleberry-sized eyes. He knew what was coming. He could see a cloud of death rolling into the decrepit assemblage taking place in the gymnasium that he called home. From the corner of my eye, I caught a peek of the yellow caution tape that guarded my birth secrets and the evidence that The Cloth had committed crimes in the eyes of their God. It reminded me that, like it was for that rat, this was my home.

Starving for a fix, I pulled back on the plunger and dragged my now wet tongue across my dehydrated and busted lips. The rat squirmed for a second. Then, he stopped, looked up at me and gave up.

From across the circle, I heard another familiar voice. It was the voice of my conscience again, only this time it had the tone of thirteen-year-old runaway and wannabe prostitute, Bailia Jenkins. Bait.

"Make me like you." It was the voice of my failure. I finally looked up. "Bite my neck." She pleaded with me. "You can make me live forever. You're a vampire."

I dropped the rat and the scag, looking away from her. As the lights dimmed in the room and the horde of wrongdoers—the NA equivalent of the Legion of Doom—collected their kids, their hatchets, their fetus-shooters, and slung bronzed baby shoes around their necks, I lifted my head again and saw the truth. My truth.

In front of me was a sneering Dez, lightly patting another me on the head as if I had just inched out a win at a spelling bee. I was the one who saved him from the streets when he was left at the dump by the fucking priests. And he repaid me by taking away the closest connection to humanity that I ever had, the cure for my loneliness and pain. In the arms of my duplicate, in my other mouth, and literally all over the other me was what was left of Bait. I didn't know whether Dez killed Bait out of jealousy or if he, like almost all the creatures like us, was indifferent to the lives of humans.

It didn't make sense to fully blame him for killing Bait. He may have tortured her and delivered the final blow, but I was just as much to blame for bringing her into my wreckage. If I could have bitten her neck and brought her back to life, I would have. The fact is, that was just romantic fiction, and no matter how many times I told her that I didn't have any miraculous powers beyond my super strength, fast healing, and sensitive hearing, she refused to believe me.

For some reason, I stood up from my uncomfortable nightmare chair and walked across the circle to the welcoming arms of the traitor, Dez. I bent down in front of him and the other me. Then I shared in the feast of the thirteen-year-old girl who taught what it meant to feel alive.

1
MISPLACED

The buzzing of a prepaid cell phone that Eldritch picked up for me at a 7-Eleven woke me. It vibrated against my face and dusted up some pebbles on the balmy Texas asphalt where I guess I had passed out. We had spent a few days on the run, hiding out in abandoned buildings around the outskirts of Austin, and it was enough to force anyone into an alley for a nap. You'd never know when you'd find something comforting like a pissed-on throw pillow that lived a second life beyond the giveaway bin at the local Salvation Army.

I scrapped some eye boogers off my lashes and yawned. Coming off of half a week on "poor man"—Eldritch's fun time concoction of Rottweiler blood, eighty percent meth and twenty percent heroin—was an unmatched spiral to the bottom of the heap. That is, of course, when the buzzing paranoia and face-picking turns the corner to exhaustion. I looked at the phone display.

Where are you?!?!?!?! Are you still on 6th? You've been in that alley for over an hour!!!!!!!!!!!!

I'm not sure if I could see clearly enough to process all the exclamation and question marks at the end of his text. However, I was sure his intention was to convey a sense of urgency that he normally reserved for the editors who spew out his dick-suck-worthy acting reels and his crack team of antique furniture delivery men who couldn't seem to get that unique, Eighteenth Century armoire to his ten-thou-a-month Bat Cave quickly enough.

Trying to keep my two-ton eyelids open long enough to grab the handset with my post-amphetamine shake fest jumping bean hands, I wrote back.

Fuck you. Taking a nap.

I scratched at the crown of my head; I came up with a handful of dead hair rather than relief. The phone buzzed again.

Good God, man. Need I remind you that for every hourglass grain that passes, constables are running Amber Alerts on television!!!!!!!!!!!!!!

The over-use of exclamation on the second text made me dizzy. I propped myself up from my fetal meth position and sucked in the hot, polluted air of Austin. I tried to shake my eyes straight and the refuse in my hair loose. That was a mistake. Immediately, I found my head between my bent legs, hurling up the single-serve bag of Peperoni Pizza Combos that I swiped from a gas station during my ill-fated journey through the streets of this white-trash knockoff of Los Angeles. The only real difference between this asshole of a town and the cesspool of my formative years is hipster, indie ball-licking music taking center stage in front of the washed-up whores-turned-DJs that I had become accustomed to. Oh, and of course the fact that street people in Austin were lowered to wearing the secondhand fashion statements of two years ago that the Lost Angel pricks delivered as care packages to brighten the hopes of the excrement that filled the streets of South by Southwest.

I had been so totally out of it since we left California—stopping only in Peoria, Arizona to take care of some business involving a child molester and his accepting wife—that I didn't really have time to pull myself through the pain of downtown Shitville. To Austin's credit, it was a lot like Silverlake and Los Feliz. The same D-bags exchanged their cardigan sweaters for knit caps and ironic Donkey Kong wristbands. As if my confessional nightmare wasn't crummy enough, it was followed by waking up in the center of an aiming-low star fucker nirvana.

Playing to my predicament, I tried to get all the speedy, rancid bile out of my stomach. Luckily for me, the delicious pretzel outer shell of the Combos provided my tongue with flavor and my throat with buffer.

A hand tugged on my shoulder.

"Hey, friend. You okay?"

I picked out a piece of Combo stuck between my teeth with my tongue and spit it onto his custom, limited edition Adidas. That was when I noticed his shirt. It said "Funky Cold Medina".

"Really, dude?" I blurted out like a fortified wine-drenched vagrant. "'Funky Cold Medina'? That's the best you could do?"

"Whatever, you piece of shit," he said as he threw a handful of loose change in my face.

The phone buzzed again, causing it to shake off my knee and onto the ground. I picked it up as my vision crossed planes between blurry and borderline dyslexia-like symptoms. Before I took the time to focus on the new message, I realized why Eldritch was quiet for a few moments. It wasn't because he wanted me to collect my thoughts or get my shit together. Rather, he wanted to produce a manifesto detailing our situation in flowery Shakespearian dialect.

I closed my left eye because it was agitated by the LED-lit display and held the phone in path with a street light. As if that made any sense or resulted in any difference whatsoever. It read:

No response? That is what could be expected from a shrewd individual of your character. As the sun creeps up on us such as the plague of our fathers, you have simply forgotten the situation you have delivered onto us. My trusted carriage...

I think he was taking about his retarded hearse...

...is the suspected kidnappers and killers' transportation. If you cannot commandeer a more formidable mode of transportation, then I must no longer participate in your folly of misguided and dangerous actions. Simply stated, I will be leaving you to your own devices and dropping off the child at the nearest constable house. In an agreement we made, you promised full participation in helping to veil us from those who find us the despicable demons who took the lives of an innocent suburban couple and abducted their sole living offspring. Am I incorrect to expect your aid? Please advise on your progress and respond with due diligence. Regretfully, if your complete participation in this matter is met with tom foolery, then I am out of—

His fancy pants words strung together as a blob of nonsense, but it was all too obvious that he was preoccupied with the kid to finish his text, to which I replied:

Don't end a sentence with a preposition. Bad English.

One. Two. Three.

Just get the fucking car, RJ.

I hadn't really seized the opportunity to laugh at myself in recent weeks, so I took a second, licked the barf off the back of my teeth and giggle a little. I slid my drained body up a brick wall and typed.

On it.

Eldritch was right about one thing. The night was coming to end. As SXSW scenesters started stumbling out of their new favorite clubs where they discovered their new favorite bands, I inched along the sidewalks, being bounced around like a racquetball by drunken, coked-out corduroy.

My path drove me further and further from the action. I needed to find a less conspicuous vehicle than the overwhelming lot of refurbished rockabilly posers' classic Ford pickup trucks and roadsters that lined the afterhours parking spots on 6th Street. Beyond that, I needed to find something more practical for two people essentially allergic to sunlight and a pre-teen girl, who, unfortunately, needed to be tied up and gagged.

Kind of a funny thing about me saving Bait's little sister, Pinball, from the atrocities of the doublewide where she grew up is that she only understood what she saw. Acting on nothing but vengeance for her sister, I didn't make a good first impression on her. As a matter of fact, our introduction was the ripping apart of her stepfather and mother. In other words, I was the monster who killed her loving parents and took her away from her life.

You can never know how a child interprets abuse. Maybe my victims, Thomas the child rapist and his glutton of a wife, told her they did what they did out of love. It was either that or she simply couldn't differentiate between having a middle-aged man's testicles in her mouth and getting a loving hug for doing well in school. So, if me being a monster in the eyes of a child for the time being meant that Pinball didn't end up as burnt pieces in the remains of a meth lab in the Salton Sea like her sister… then so be it.

Despite my recommendation to leave her in Peoria, Eldritch insisted that we take her with us. I don't know why. The last thing that I wanted was another kid to worry about and take care of.

My knees popped as I stopped at the window of an electronics store and took a good look at myself.

"I don't think I know you," I said to my reflection.

My bushy mess of a hairdo shot out sideways, overgrown at my ears. It was still kind of blonde, but all of the blood and dirt that clumped onto it since I last showered at Eldritch's loft in Los Angeles just made it look like someone sprayed shit on my head every morning. Even worse, the hair acted as lights leading into a landing strip that drew all attention to the drooping and bagged craters that contained my eyes. The eyes were sometimes blue and sometimes green. Rarely did others get the opportunity to gaze into my peepers—my best quality—because my pupils were constantly dilated. So, if I ever had to describe myself to anyone, I would play it safe and say I had black and red eyes. The older I got, the more my cheekbones tended to push at the bags. It was a constant fight between what seemed to be living material and the death spreading across the center of my face.

I dug around the edges of my nose with my index finger and my thumb. My large nostrils were so dry that the flakey skin created a path of irritation right into the top of my lips, which seemed to have a constant cut near the middle of the top. I curled my lip and threw my arms over my head, doing my best imitation of Billy Idol. I quietly wailed like Billy but came up embarrassingly short; my "Rebel Yell" was more of a "Careless Whisper". My boney arms dropped to my sides and I slapped on my atrophy-mutated belly. The drugs tore down our bodies but combined with blood, they helped us live. The body was just a shell in a constant state of hyperkinetic rejuvenation. Unfortunately, my organs didn't self-build muscle, but they never stopped layering bandages on top of bandages.

I bent over to a puddle by my feet, wiped the sewage across my face and the stood up again to look at the piece of shit that stared back at me. The water was refreshing but did little to mask my junkie features. At that point in my life as a career degenerate, I could dip my face in paint and make cool Misfits' shirts. I dragged my tongue across the roof of my mouth that was coated with yuck mouth plaque. I licked some scum water off my cheek and tried to swoosh it around. I guessed my breath was always shit.

I stuck out my tongue. It was bumpy and blue as if it was the first thing that a couple of wisecracking TV detectives noticed after I had been fished out of the wharf. It matched the color of various unseen parts of my body, like my armpits or the raw area on the insides of my thighs around my balls.

I slapped on the stomach a few times and then spit out the sludge I used as mouthwash. Then, I stretched my neck closer to the electronics store and smiled into the window. My teeth were fucked up. The naturally crooked, street-cultivated ivories struggled to stay attached to the root. The years of drugs had browned each of them around the gum line and cracked them around the rim in back. If I licked my teeth, I could feel the broken-down damage and poverty of being a gross addict. On top of that, I was a grinder when I slept. So, the irony of being a vampire with teeth that could barely break down a piece of steak was never lost on me. It was my reality, and it wasn't like I could swing by a dentist's office, even if I had the money or insurance to do so.

I bobbed my head back and forth and lifted up my ratty t-shirt as I started dragging my hand up my torso. My fingers wobbled in and out of my ribs that stuck out in weird places. I did have the power to heal but nothing ever grew back perfectly. Wherever there was a break at some point in my life, there were little balls that ranged in size from BBs to golf balls. Like I said before, my body was comprised of bandages layered over bandages. If something broke, it would tie itself off like a water balloon or sprinkle a little glob of superglue onto the fracture. My body never finished the job by sanding over protrusions so jagged edges and bumps were common.

I knew my body was torn up, but I had no noticeable scars. The only plus of being a vampire—or an aborto-fiend—was the healing part. The sensitive hearing was kind of useless. The super strength was cool, but it wasn't like any of us used our powers for good. As a whole, at least judging from the things like me that I had met, we were pretty much a society of psychotic boobs.

It had been a long time since I looked at myself, so I pulled my shirt over my head and inched even closer to the window to see if I could catch a glimpse at any remaining ink from my Faction Batman tattoo. It was eroded off of my chest by acid when I was kidnapped by those awesome Catholic priests that always seemed to guest star in my nightmares. No dots of ink or even a scar remained. I rubbed at the section where it used to be over my heart, maybe hoping that some skin was covering it up. Stupid, really. According to Cobra, The Cloth did me a favor by removing it from my body. At the very least, no more Batman or vampire/bat jokes for the rest of my life. I certainly wasn't going to replace it. All that said, being semi-bulletproof didn't beat being covered in a bunch of scars. The scars on the inside hurt worse and didn't look as cool.

I pulled my shirt back down and tried to pull myself out of my hypnosis by hopping up and down a few times. My actions caused my dick to jump in my saggy jeans. I didn't have a huge penis, but it was bigger than a lot of the dicks that I had ripped off of other dudes. I was so blessed. My soft dick was bigger than a bunch of guys who knew that they were about to be killed. Nothing gives a man a hard-on more than knowing that he is seconds away from not breathing. I rolled my eyes as I flicked the front of my jeans. What a useless apparatus. We couldn't get a fucking boner unless we shot ourselves up with Viagra and blood. Most of us couldn't have kids—as if we'd ever want that—and it still hurt to get punched in the balls. The Cloth should have done us all a favor and just hacked our cocks off. It probably would have made us a more streamlined army of insects. I never got to ask Father McAteer why The Cloth decided to circumcise us rather than going all in. It must have been the natural secondary process after they sterilized us and preparation process before discarding us in dumpsters.

All that time studying my broken body in the electronics shop's window came to a halt when I noticed a news flash come on a TV in front of me. It was about this dude Eldritch was in love with named Stephan Rodderick. He was the star of a popular kiddie vampire movie series called *The Nightshayde Chronicles*. As we heard days earlier, on our way to Peoria, he OD'd on heroin but didn't die. Eldritch assured me that he was one of us: a vampire.

I watched closely as they displayed his headshot on one side and showed clips from the melodramatic turds that little girls called cinema. My eyes shifted focus back to my reflection. If they only knew what vampires *really* looked like. I doubted that he was one of us. His teeth, his eyes, his cheekbones, his hair, and his body were all too perfect.

As I fixated on his perfection, anger grew inside of me. If he was a ghoul like me, why the fuck did he have it so good?

A flash of light bounced off the window, blinding me.

"What the fuck?" I yelled as I covered me eyes.

I spun away from the window to see a blurred figure taking a picture of me with his phone. It was my "Funky Cold Medina" friend from the alley.

"Hey asshole," I said. "Why are you following me?"

He didn't respond. Rather, he touched the screen on his phone, threw it into his backpack and started running away.

I hobbled along after him, calling out, "Are you with The Cloth? Who the fuck are you? Why are you taking pictures of me?"

Follow him. He HAS heroin.

Dammit. "The Gooch" again. It had started while Cobra and me were imprisoned by Fat Mac and The Cloth. They had used methadone to curb my heroin cravings. It was the voice that whispered in my ear, tugged on my arms, and ripped at my scalp. The Gooch never invaded my heinous dreams. It just came out when I was feeling alone. Feeling hungry.

So in addition to finding a replacement car so we could ditch Eldritch's hearse, my other mission was to find heroin. The simple truth was, scag shut The Gooch up and I didn't like being reminded what a stain on the world I had been since I was brought to life. So, I followed the Medina guy because I wanted to be alone in my head.

III

SILENCED

I tried to track the Medina dude as I scraped my toes against the concrete, making it further from the dimming lights of last call in downtown Austin. I knew that the closer I got into the world of scrap heaps, pawn shops and tow yards, the closer I got to securing a less conspicuous vehicle. In Eldritch's defense, he didn't know that following me into the war to save Bait would result in us making our way to Austin. However, I couldn't excuse him from spinning around in a hearse with a chrome Platinum Motorsports customization emblem on the gate, emphasized by a license plate that read NSFRATU. The lengths that guy went to were painful. We might as well have run over a reporter covering the death of Bait and Pinball's gross parents in a Wonder Bread truck and whipped out our dicks for the camera man. But hey, it's all hindsight, right? When I originally went to save Bait, I had no idea I would end up in Peoria and then Austin, either. He said he had a plan and he saved my ass several times. It was dumb to kidnap the kid, but I owed him.

The streets got darker as the businesses became sparser and more beaten down. Medina had long since disappeared beyond the shadows of the buildings in front of me.

My phone buzzed in my back pocket.

I shook my head, pulled it out and turned it on.

Please tell me you found a vehicle, RJ.

And just like that, I had forgotten about the dumbass Medina taking a picture of me altogether.

I looked up from the phone without responding and, as luck would I have it, in the economic urinal of Austin, I saw a car lot. Well, it wasn't exactly a car lot *per se*. It was more of an animal shelter. At the moment though, it seemed to provide the perfect solution to my dilemma. I could steal a dog catcher truck. Eldritch and I could roll in the front and we could put the kid in a cage in the back. The police would never suspect a dog catcher mobile in Austin to answer for the murders of two scumbags in Peoria.

I shook off the spins and looked up the chain-link security fence until my eyes reached the razor wire that rolled ominously across the top. Although I didn't quite understand why such security measures were in place for a building that housed mange-infected pets that nobody wanted except for some hippie giving their dumb kid a first taste of responsibility, I figured scaling it would be a piece of cake.

I cracked my knuckles and then my neck. I blinked really fast twenty times, wiped a little bit of spit off the corner of my mouth and then jogged in a circle. Ah, the art of procrastination is an area of life that I had mastered. It wasn't so much that I felt I couldn't tackle a ten-foot barrier as much as I was pretty burned out. Compound that with the fact that I was desperately in need of blood and heroin and you have a formula for defeat.

THAt's right, friend. You Need HeroiN.

I managed to creep up the shaky fence with relative ease. That was, until I reached the razor wire. Remaining as steady as I could, I propped my legs up to the highest point and extended my body upright. This maneuver allowed me to shift my left leg over the death trap as I supported my weight by grabbing onto two razor-less strands of wire. It would have been nice if I had clippers.

"Wait a minute," I said to myself. Why was I bothering to climb the fence at all? It would have been much easier to simply open an entrance for myself at the bottom. After all, I did have super strength. I was being such a dipshit.

As I pulled back my leg and prepared to hop down and start over with plan B, a bright light flared on behind me.

"Fuck!" I lost balance and nearly swallowed my tongue. I fell backward and upside down, tangling my legs in the razor wire. A little bit of piss squirted out of me and a sharp pain bit into my ankles. "Dammit!"

I figured the cops had me. I slowly peeked out of one eye into the glare, expecting to see a patrol car's spotlight blazing on my face. There were no cops standing in front of me with guns drawn, however. The light came from the marquee of the rundown cinema across the street. I hadn't noticed it when I was jogging in circles like a fucking idiot. I kind of wished I had.

Before I sat up to untangle myself, I tilted my head sideways to read what was playing. I figured it was probably some late night rubby theater for perverts who didn't believe in home video.

CHAPLINS, the marquee read. Well, it was supposed to be CHAPLINS, but for some reason the N was hung backwards. I didn't know if it was a piss poor attempt to be alternative or subversive or if the pock-faced usher who hung it was just stupid. I decided that my first assumption was correct. The great lengths that the Austinites went to being perceived as counter-culture was exhausting. "Funky Cold Medina," I said, remembering the dumb hipster who threw change at me. "What an asshole."

The double doors of the building flung open. From the blackness inside, a figure appeared, spinning a cane. Under a black bowler hat waddled a man with a white face, Hitler mustache and dirty, crumpled suit. As he reached the front of the theater, the humming neon of the marquee illuminated and blinked so I could see his full get-up. The cane stopped spinning and as if it was controlling him like the winding key on a toy robot. He stopped right before he reached the curb and stared at me.

Still inverted, I grinned out of the side of my mouth and pointed at my legs. "I really wanted a dog." I gave an uneasy laugh, unsure where this encounter was headed. "Right?"

The man didn't respond. He blinked a few times, then he bent down, the bowler hat toppled from his head and landed in his palm as he took a bow. That was a good sign. I mean, it was queer as hell, but it was much better than half of Austin's cops surrounding me at gunpoint. He rolled the hat up his arm and back onto his dark, greased-back hair.

He continued to gaze at me. After a minute of us uncomfortably making eye contact, I attempted to bend my body upward and unlock my legs. Unsuccessful, I dropped back down.

Two other figures appeared on both sides of the Charlie Chaplin impersonator. On his left stood a thick-bodied sheik guy in a turban with his arms crossed. He nodded. On the right was another guy in a bow tie and a gray-striped jacket. He tried to pull a pork pie hat onto his head and it popped up into the air above him. Frustrated, he pulled it down again to the same result. All three of them, their faces painted with bright foundation, thick eyeliner and black lipstick, remained dead silent.

"So, are you guys in a ska band or something?"

The silence continued. They didn't even smirk at my attempt to lighten the mood. The marquee caught my eye again. CHAPLINS. I slapped myself on the forehead. "Oh, I get it. You guys are supposed to be Buster Keaton and Rudolph Valentino." Surprisingly, I knew a lot about pre-talkie movies from living with that washed-up-kiddie-star-turned-junkie-nun, The Habit. At the time, she was trying to get her career on track by playing Mary Pickford in a Lifetime movie. They laughed her out of the building during her first audition. She may have brought a bunch of heroin home for both of us, but in hindsight I should have killed her when I had the chance.

"You boys playing dress-up tonight?" I joked.

And yet, they still didn't respond.

I nodded and looked up at the sparse blood in my body running down my legs. Defeated, I looked back at my new friends. Their numbers had doubled. Some fat fuck in a bigger bowler, kerchief, and thick bacon-sized suspenders that reluctantly held up his enormous pleated pants appeared behind the sheik. Another sharply dressed guy with a top hat and a cane tucked under his arm was joined by some woman with greasy-ass hair who I guessed was supposed to be Garbo. That is, if Garbo had a meth face.

I scratched at my thigh and covered my hand with blood. "Okay. I'm sorry," I pleaded. "I shouldn't be breaking in here. Can you give me a pass this time and help me down? I'm gonna bleed the fuck out." I brought my hand to my mouth and licked it, trying to refuel my body with whatever I could.

Still no response.

I exhaled, deciding that these clowns were going to sit there and watch me die. What a way to go. Fucking idiot. And just when I decided things couldn't get any worse, the centerpiece, the Tramp, flipped his cane and held it straight across his chest. Spikes popped out of Chaplin's cane, and the rest followed suit by arming themselves with various weapons. Fatty Arbuckle bounced a bat off his foot as Valentino unsheathed a half-moon sword from behind his back. Speed-scarred Garbo snatched two blades from her garters. Another new member in a Sherlock Holmes get-up—either John Barrymore or Basil Rathbone—lit a match and fired up a deep-bucketed pipe.

I tugged on my legs with my pelvis, trying desperately to somehow shake myself free. The razors dug into my shins, scraping into the bones with their points. My body started to grow a little cold. I bounced my back against the fence and almost said, "Come on guys, this isn't funny anymore," but it was never funny and I would have sounded like a pussy.

And then, as the neon of the marquee popped and blinked, the now ten-person 1920s horror show started walking toward me. Chaplin led the way, twirling his death cane.

"Fuck me." Knowing if I didn't get free that I'd become a living piñata, I reached up and began tearing apart the razor wire that was crippling me. I was becoming increasingly dizzy as I started grabbing furiously onto wire wherever I could to snap it free. The blades thrashed my hands. I looked at the cast of terror. They had made it half way across the street. They closed in on me in a tight half-circle, with the Tramp moving to the back center.

My left leg finally broke free. Knowing time wasn't on my side, I tugged the right leg free, tearing some wire down with me. I managed to shift my body and bend my head to the side so I could land on my shoulder instead of my head. I pushed myself up quick and faced them.

"Okay, you fucking weirdos." I wiped my hand up my body, trying to capture as much blood as I could. I drenched my face. "The time for talking is over."

I jumped toward them as they took to defensive positions, raising their weapons. "You guys don't want to fuck with me!" I swung the razor wire like a whip and they folded back a bit to avoid contact with the spikes. There wasn't enough slack from where the rest of the wire still connected to the fence though, and my only weapon was pulled back from my hand and clattered to the ground.

"Fuck it." I put my fists up and stupidly jumped into the center of the posse, swinging away.

From my right eye, I saw Fatty lift his baseball bat to swing at my face. I caught the end in my palm and tugged it free from his grip. I flipped it over to my other hand and plunged it into heinous Gretta Garbo's nose. She didn't scream or cry. Rather, she went cross-eyed, and as she dropped to her back, she latched onto my belt loops and slid under me, cutting into my heels with her daggers.

As I ducked down and jumped backward to avoid the rapier of Douglas Fairbanks, I managed to catch Garbo by her snatch. Disgusting wharf-like fumes materialized in my nostrils. Her eyes shot wide open as the smell made me vomit on her, then pounded my heel into her throat, snapping all the bones like a box of crayons. Trying to hold my breath so I wouldn't get sick again from the smell of her lady juice, I set my thumb on her clitoris and shoved my four free fingers into her hole.

Before she had the opportunity to fight me off, I held down her thighs with my other foot and tore her plumbing from pelvis, up to her gullet, and all the way through to her heart; plowing through her organs and opening her up like a body bag. I smashed a hodge-podge of her insides into my mouth and used my tongue to squeeze the nectar like a sponge.

Vampire blood. There were vamps in Texas. There were *girl* vamps in Texas.

With my strength returning, I nabbed the bat off the ground and swung it savagely, completely knocking Fairbanks's head off his neck. The body stood for a second and then went limp, falling on top of Garbo. Without taking any time to assess my situation, I jumped on Arbuckle as Valentino started to make his move with the Sinbad sword. I dug into Fatty's jugular and ripped it free from his sweaty, clammy flesh.

To avoid Valentino's sword, I spun lard ass around by his neck, using him as a shield in front of me. The blade split his head down the middle of his skull as he gasped for air. I shoved his jugular vein into my mouth and leapfrogged over his shoulder, trapping Valentino's arm between my thighs. I clamped his forearm tight, and as he released the handle of the sword, I spun around and broke the arm in half. I kicked him down and hammered the bat repeatedly into his clavicle and sternum. Trying to remain focused on the movement around me, I clawed his chest open and had at whatever organs I could get my hands on.

It was about the moment when I swallowed Fatty's jugular vein and shoved Valentino's liver into my mouth that I realized these motherfuckers were on some pretty heavy drugs.

THAT'S NOT heroin.

I didn't know which drugs they were, however, because an unfamiliar tingling throbbed in my head, causing me to become disoriented. Seconds were dropping from my vision and everything around me became choppy. The world seemed to melt as I tried to shake off the feeling. The marquee blared into my eyes and zoomed in and out, becoming more and more faded and losing focus. Everything went hyperactive.

Before I had the opportunity to take a breath, piano wire snapped about my neck. I whirled around to find myself only millimeters from Sherlock's pipe. The synthetically-laced tobacco smoke blinded my already fogged eyes. I palmed the pipe into his mouth and, catching him off guard, I bent down under the now loosened piano wire and headbutted him in the chest. As he doubled over, I knocked off his deerstalker hat, seized the back of his head, and pounded him face first into a pile of rocks. His arms shot out cartoony and stared flapping around like a breezy geezer at a car dealership. I planted my knee into the back of his head, flattening his face into the concrete. I shifted all my weight into my knee until I crushed his cranium, exposing his brain. I huddled over him and dug my teeth into the hole. I could have sworn his brain was talking to me. Maybe The Gooch had made a telepathic connection.

Pleased with my meal, I looked up to see the lesser known stars retreat into the theater. Chaplin, however, swung his cane around and pointed it at me. His faced stretched horizontally, opening holes in it that flickered like film grain. I was having massive hallucinations. The marquee shined from behind him and lit up his black outfit. He looked like Hitler combined with Christ.

I stood up, brushed myself off, and walked toward him. He stood his ground, and then, in a moment of breaking character, he ran at me with the cane in front of him. Clicking another button as he closed in, he released a massive switchblade at the cane's tip. Distracted by the terrifying hallucinations unfolding everywhere around me, I fell backward. Before I realized it, Chaplin was on top of me. I turned sideways, catching the blade in my right arm. I looked at my arm. It looked like my foot. He shoved his hand in my face. It also looked like a foot. He secured the dominant position on top of me and for some reason, he started slapping me in the face.

Realizing that wasn't damaging anything other than my pride, he tried to gouge my eyes out. My body was so jumpy and wired that he couldn't hit either target. I slipped my arms under his knees, breaking off the blade from the cane which was now deeply lodged in my bicep. I latched onto his trunk and pulled him close. The white makeup on his face smeared into his black hair as eyeliner cascaded down his cheeks like tears. I locked my arms together around his back. He sucked in, trying to gain the air coming from my mouth.

That's when I sat up, snapping him inversely over himself. He hacked out some blood and bent back onto his legs like a folding chair. I don't know if I was afraid that he was going to crawl away, but before I got back up I pulled my arms out from under him and wrenched his head off.

His shirt buttons popped open and much to my surprise, it said "Funky Cold Medina".

"Why were you taking pictures of me?"

I stared into the horror of his dead eyes for a few seconds, expecting him to say something. He didn't. So, with my fingers, I moved his lips and started singing. "So, I gave some to my dog when he began to beg, then he licked his bowl and he looked at me and did the wild thing on my leg."

I tossed the head aside because I became preoccupied with my hideously deformed hoof hands. I started picking a hole into my hoof hands.

"Ha. 'Funky Cold Medina'. What a fucking awesome shirt."

My body pulsated as the marquee went dark.

You're wet, The Gooch said.

And he was right. The Chaplins were filled with the strongest PCP I had ever taken.

IV

POISONED

It took me awhile, but I was almost back to the abandoned barn and fire pit where I'd left Eldritch and Pinball. As soon as I saw their silhouettes bouncing off the fire, I gunned the dogcatcher truck. If I timed everything right, I figured the truck would drift to a halt directly in front of them. Then I'd kick open the door for them to get in. Of course, piling in would take them time since the shock and awe of my stunt man-inspired entrance would leave them dead fucking silent for a bit, and they would, of course, have to shake off the dust that I sprayed all over their faces first.

The way I envisioned it—mind you, I was on enough PCP to make the entire 70s' student population throw themselves from a high school roof—when I kicked open the passenger door, I would hear a sad trombone sound effect as if God were supplying the score and Foley work for my every living move. I would tip my black felt cowboy hat up, if I were wearing a hat. Covered from head-to-toe in the desert's salt of the earth, foolish Eldritch would open his eyes and then throw his Texas sheriff's hat on the ground and stomp on it. Deputy Pinball's eyes would suddenly appear behind a mask of dirt. She would remain still for a couple of seconds and then begin shaking. *BOOM!* Tears would burst from her face. Then, at the very end of my dazzling automotive ballet, after they realized that I had gotten the best of them, I would wink.

Fuck, I wished I had that hat. I decided that the hat wasn't as important as a toothpick. I needed a toothpick. Wink and toothpick. The toothpick would surely go down as the icing on my cool cake.

So, yeah. It didn't quite go down like that.

I gunned the truck, at the same time I started flicking my high beams and honking the horn. It was then that I noticed that the steering wheel look less like a steering wheel and more like a doughnut.

I finally looked up at Eldritch. As expected, his eyes bugged from his dumb face like a wolf in a Tex Avery cartoon. Maybe not. I don't know. He nabbed Pinball by her collar, popped her under his arms and started running from the fire pit. I quickly recalibrated my mission as Eldritch leapt like a bitch of a billy goat and headed toward the abandoned barn in the distance. I told him hours earlier that we should take refuge in the barn, but he wouldn't listen to me. He insisted that it gets cold in the desert at night and that we would need to build a fire. He argued in way too many words that the years of sun on the old wood was a certain fire trap for loose embers jumping from a campfire.

I tried to roll down my window but my broken wrist prevented me from success. So I just used that hand and mashed it through the window. "That's right, assfucker. The barn is good enough for you now," I screamed. "Yeeee hawwww!"

My margin of opportunity was closing. Seconds before he reached the entrance to the barn, I decided it was time to spin the custom steering wheel—which my warped brain still saw as a cruller—and perform the money shot. My heart raced in my ear as I ground my teeth in anticipation. I spun away. Spin wheel. *Spin.* The race car drift sequence began as planned, but I overcompensated for the turn and whirled the wheel off the console with my super vampire strength.

"Oh shit!" I cracked in my best southern twang. Actually, it was more of a southern drawl, I think.

The dog catcher truck oscillated about one hundred and eighty degrees before it began rolling.

About three and a half revolutions later, the truck came to a stop on its side. Some obnoxious alert sound buzzed in my ears as if the door was ajar in my brain, signaling that I was in imminent danger. There was still a fifty-fifty chance that when I untangled myself from the truck, Eldritch and Pinball would be covered head to toe in dust and that the only real casualty would be the truck that had taken me around six to seven hours to commandeer.

I unfastened my seatbelt and lifted myself through the passenger-side window above. "Please don't go off," I begged the airbag. I coughed a bit and counted to five to make sure that all the pieces were in play for the big reveal. I decided that I would end the scene with an incredibly astute statement like, "Need a ride? You might want to clean yourselves up first."

I fully lifted myself from the truck and turned to face them. But it was too dark outside and since they were no longer in front of the fire, I had a difficult time making out whether or not they were blanketed in dust. I adjusted my sight. They didn't move. I cleared my throat. They remained still. I waited another second or two. It might have been a minute or two. I couldn't really gage time lapsing because the entire world was spinning and dissolving around me still from the PCP.

I cleared my throat yet again. Eldritch took a step toward me. Pinball hid behind his leg.

He cranked his head to the side as if he was disorientated, a good sign he'd been sandblasted.

I rubbed off some blood from my right ear and ate it. "You guys need a ride?"

I winked but they stood silent. I jumped to the ground and lifted my hands over my head briefly, to suck in more air, their lack of expression was killing me. I breathed too hard though, vomiting bile all over myself. I doubled over from the smell and was reminded that not only was I not wearing pants, but I had shit all over myself in the truck. I wiped my forearm on my ass cheek to make sure I remembered the soiling correctly. I had.

Amazingly, I caught Pinball's eyes as she peered out behind Eldritch's legs. She was crying.

Unfortunately, it wasn't the type of crying that I was expecting. In my mind, her crying was expected to be akin to a conquered grown man. I was fully expecting something along the lines of Junior in *Smokey and the Bandit*. Nope. Her crying was the result of witnessing absolute horror, then feeling absolute terror.

I looked down at my body. My left arm was dangling. My chest was caved in so badly that I could see a crater in my sternum. Both of my legs were completely shredded from the razor wire that surrounded the animal control lot. I bent down and tore off the passenger side mirror and took a closer look. Blood was gushing out from every open hole in my face. I looked worse than most of my Chaplin victims back at their theater.

Eldritch let Pinball go from the protection of his leg. She darted forward then veered off toward the barn. He remained quiet and lowered his head. The more I thought about it, the more I realized that he was more disappointed than terrified by everything that had gone down. He wasn't ever easy to scare, but his inability to say anything spoke volumes.

Pinball unlatched the decaying barn door and slipped inside. Nausea washed over me and I collapsed under my own weight. I puked again. I guess I was actually poisoned by all the PCP in my system. When I finally managed to get to a relative stable stance, I began to shuffle and drag myself toward the barn.

"RJ! No!" Eldritch shouted.

I got close enough to him to realize that he wasn't covered in dust or sand or anything dirty whatsoever.

"Let me handle this, please," I said.

I grabbed onto the door latch, closed one eye in an attempt to focus and stretch myself back to full height. My bones, which were only partially broken, cracked and shattered inside my stumbling carcass. My body was drowning in its blood, which was pushing me into shock. Unluckily for me, the power of lethal dose of amphetamines inside my body was like dumping recycled water over my head, waking me up.

I heard Pinball whimpering under Eldritch's hearse. He'd parked it in the barn because even though we were nowhere near the street, someone in Peoria likely spotted it and the cops were on the lookout. It's not a stretch to say that you could see it from the moon.

I lugged myself closer to her. "It's okay. I'm really sorry. I didn't mean to scare you. It's just me, RJ. Remember?

I went on. "It's me, the friendly vampire guy." My right kneecap cracked and I dropped down to one leg. I could hear her, but with my senses booming different signals from all directions, I felt like the compass in my head was gyrating all over the place. Add the pulsating visuals of the PCP and I might as well have been Snow White in a wheelchair trying to escape an evil batch of forest creatures out for revenge.

I heard a scuttle to my right and my head snapped toward it.

"It's okay. I'm the good guy who saved you."

Scurrying out from under the hearse, she plowed past me again. As quick as I could, I reached back behind me to catch her, only to rip out a strand of her hair. I fell onto my back and smacked my head on the corroded bumper of the dead car as her entire head of hair flew into my face.

"Jesus!" I screamed, thinking I'd ripped her entire head off her body. Stunned, I threw the hair ball on the hay on the ground trying to shake it off me like a spider. It certainly didn't feel heavy enough to contain a head. With my eyes squinted, I picked it back up and surveyed it. I turned it over, hoping not to see Pinball's mangled scalp inside. Instead, I saw a tag. A tag from a wig.

Completely perplexed, I looked over to see the dome of Pinball's bald head behind Eldritch's legs.

As he petted her hairless head behind him, he breathed, "She has leukemia."

And then, everything went black... including my ugly soul.

V

BLACKENED

I rubbed my forehead. It was drenched. "How long have I been out?"

Eldritch handed me a rag to wipe my head. "You have only been unconscious for about—" he looked at the face of his phone, "—two hours. Now, however, I am the one who is exhausted."

"Two hours?" I threw the rag back at him. "That's nothing."

He looked up from the hay beneath his legs. He was sitting Indian-style on the floor of the barn. "You have been out for two hours." He snapped a small twig between his fingers. "I have been subduing you for two long days and nights."

"What do you mean?"

He picked up the rag again, folded it, and delicately placed it in my lap. "I mean you had ingested such an elevated-level of angel dust—among other things—that you needed to be restrained throughout much of your two-day flight through the world of insanity." He pointed at the rag and then dragged his finger across his right eye. "What in the name of Odin happened to you?"

I took his signal and wiped my left eye, tucking the Odin comment into the back of what remained of my pulverized brain for use at a later time. "Let's see…" My body felt undone and bent like I imagined it would after freaking the fuck out for two days after fighting a gang of vampires and getting in a horrible self-inflicted car accident. The more I tried to remember what happened, the more I felt the stinging of a migraine.

"Hmmmm. Well, I remember texting with you when my heart finally stopped trying to escape from my chest as I was coming come down off the poor man shit you fed me. Then, I almost beat the dick off this stupid hipster cunt wearing a 'Funky Cold Medina' shirt. He was taking pictures of me so I followed him." I threw the rag back to him again.

Eldritch cleared his throat and grabbed me by the chin with his palm. He stretched one of his metal talon fingers up to my forehead and with the rag, he wiped my face. "Please don't ever sing that melody again. Nothing beyond that chorus has blown from your lips for the past two days. I believe Paulina…" He stopped rubbing my face.

"Paulina?"

"The female youth. The one you call Pinball. Paulina."

I propped myself up onto my elbows and looked around the barn. "Where is she?"

"Not to worry. She is outside by the fire. I barred her from any further exposure to this madness." Eldritch yanked a cigarette out of his pouch and cut a small slit in his tongue with his metal finger. A small bubble of blood gurgled on top. He licked the end of his cigarette and snapped his fingers to produce fire as theatrically as always. He lit it and sucked down a huge barrel of smoke that he then blew toward me. I felt the thick sting of cloves invade every unhealed scrape on my face. The sores tensed up and rejected the hideous exhaust. I would never forget that atrociously sweet smell multiplying and potentially further damaging my lifeless body.

I rolled my head back to try and avoid it. "Come on, you dick. If you're going to smoke those pussy, goth cigarettes, please don't blow the smoke in my face."

He ashed the cig. "Cloves are a natural antioxidant."

I lofted the smoke back at him. "Not when you smoke them. Aren't they used to get rid of moths?"

He blew another drag in my face. "I think you're confusing them with mothballs. I believe the smoke will accelerate your healing process. I have never seen anyone that forspillan."

I spit out a big chuck of flesh that was hanging from my gums. "Forspillan?"

"I believe you would call it 'wasted'."

"Whatever, Eldritch, like you've never been fucking wasted."

He gripped my chin again, tighter this time, and dragged the talon from my forehead to directly above my left eye. "There is no whatever. What happened next?"

I saw the campfire outside the barn reflecting through holes in the rotted wood. "Let's see. I made my way out of downtown Austin." The migraine continued to bite at my head. "And then I found us a car. The truck."

The tip of his metal blade dug into my eyebrow. "That would be the constable truck for animal authority."

I took him by the wrist and slowly pulled his fingers away from my face. "I think it's called a dog catcher truck, but yeah, I figured we'd tie Pinball up and throw her in one of the cages or something."

"The lass's name is Paulina Jenkins."

His unsteady hand began to shake and move back toward my face.

"Godammit, Eldritch. I think there's a fucking hole in my face, asshole. It's isn't a blood smear or fucking chocolate."

His talons folded into his lap like a peacock fanning its feathers as he calmly said, "The hole in your face rejuvenated two days ago. However, you may continue your story."

"Thank you. So, I was climbing this fence to get into the dog pound and I was completely fucked up... lack of blood, still tweaking my brain out. Well, I managed to get my legs tangled up in this gnarly razor wire. Then, I got jumped by a gang. A fucking vampire gang, dude. Did you know there were vamps here? Did you know there were girl vamps?"

"Which gang?"

"Are you kidding me? Is there more than one? How the hell did they know I was one of them? I'm sure they wouldn't have brought out their full arsenal of silent movie shitbags if they thought I was some drunk dildo who stumbled away from South by Southwest. I followed that guy who was taking pictures of me there. He was the leader of the gang." Blood started to dribble from the hole in my cheek.

He nodded. "They call themselves the Chaplins. Just so you are aware, there are many more supernatural beings in Austin than in Los Angeles."

"What? You're killing me. Answer the question. How did they know I was a vamp? Why was he taking pictures of me?" I swabbed at the hole like my finger was a Q-tip.

Eldritch swatted my hand away. "They must have put the Amber Alert and our arrival together." Then, he shoved the rag back into the hole. "The rag is clean."

I held the rag on my cheek. "That doesn't make any sense."

Eldritch nodded his head, approving that I finally decided to use the rag. "Did you speak with anyone while within Austin City Limits?" He smirked.

"I bet you're real proud of yourself with that one, huh, dick? I told you I spoke to that fucker in the 'Funky Cold Median' shirt. About fifteen minutes later, he was behind me taking pictures of me. Then, I followed him. Then, I was attacked. I didn't know he was a vampire."

He raised an eyebrow. "Didn't you?"

His voice electrified my headache. "I don't know, shithead. No."

"Are you sure you didn't know?"

I threw the rag back at him. "Jesus fucking Christ. I thought he was some pervert."

He looked down at the now disgusting ruby towel in his lap and whispered, "The one thing that I do know is that the Chaplins only dress theatrically for combat. I was very good friends with them. Unfortunate. Maybe, this Funky Cold Median you spoke of is a new recruit. You once told me that you can smell other in-humans. I believe I can as well. It would not be outside the realm of possibility."

"The only thing I smell right now is your patchouli and it's making me want to barf."

He ignored the comment. "Could you smell them?"

I ran my nose across my arm. "I smelled like vomit and Combos. Now, I smell like vomit, Combos, and B.O. meets diarrhea casserole. Do you think you could have hosed me the fuck down while I was losing my mind for two days?"

"Alas, we are in the moisture-less desert, RJ."

I felt the drip start again. I snatched the rag out of his lap. "So, yeah. Maybe I followed this guy back there unconsciously because I suspected that he was a vampire. It doesn't matter; even if he led me back there to his dress-up buddies in makeup and suits, I still smeared those assholes all over the pavement. I was like a super fighter. I was like an evil superhero cage fighter or something."

I would have told Eldritch that The Gooch instructed me to follow the guy, but that would have opened up another can of worms, and I didn't feel like breaking *that* seal. If he learned of me hearing voices that drove me to heroin, more than likely it would lead to him trying to exorcise it out of me using some Wiccan ceremony.

Eldritch brushed a piece of hay off of his mesh tank top. "Judging from your condition over the past two days, I am going to speculate that you are delusional. Scratch that: either you are delusional now or you were hallucinating heavily when you faced these veiled foes. For God's sake—"

"Don't you mean 'Odin's sake'?" The corners of my mouth curled up, revealing my teeth.

Before I got the chance to laugh, the flat end of his hand collided with my face. "I should have let you perish. What kind of man are you to consider putting a child in a cage? A child who recently witnessed the slaying of her parents at your hands? A child recovering from a malignant form of cancer?"

I polished the bridge of my nose as I shoved his hand away from me. "What do you mean cancer?" I then remembered the unpleasantness of the barn and the wig. "Oh."

"Yes, RJ. The child is recovering from leukemia."

I never claimed to know anything about regular people diseases. And even though these sicknesses never really affected my kind, I do know the words *cancer* and *AIDS* equate to *bad* and *death*. "How bad is it?" I asked.

"Children's leukemia is never a good thing. However, to answer your boorish question, she has been in remission for over a year. It seems she is much stronger than she looks. From what she has shared with me, her parents shaved her head purposely to garner attention from their community."

"You're kidding, right?"

"I am not." He rubbed his finger across his leg. "I find her inability to comprehend the magnitude of her ailment concerning."

"Meaning?"

"She understands that her hair fell out from the medication and treatment and she partially understands that she is sick. I do not, however, believe she understands the disease or what could happen if she neglects it. I am suspicious that her guardians failed to explain it to her, and I am sure that she understood very little of what the doctors explained to her." He rubbed my face jizz off his palm. "It is our duty to escort her somewhere free from danger. That somewhere will be without you."

"Why? And why just me? You're twice as dangerous as I have ever been."

He proudly swung his black hair out of his face. "Thank you."

"It's not a compliment, you vagina. We saved her from them. Those filthy fuckers raped her. We saved her from people who think it's okay to rape children with cancer. I seriously cannot in my wildest dreams think of anything worse than that."

He opened his mouth to fire back, then closed it and huffed from his nose.

"Do you know why Bait called her Pinball, Eldritch?"

He shook his head.

"They called her Pinball because that pedophile of a stepfather of hers made a game out of pinning her down and making her lick his nuts while her mother watched and laughed."

"She's terrified of you, RJ."

I clasped my hands together, the cliché for begging. "Please let me speak with her. I need to *make* her understand. I did it because I promised her sister I would."

"But you slew her parents and seized her as if she was your property."

"Step back, asshole," I grunted. "You're the one who said we should take her. I wanted to leave her there."

He shook his finger at me. "We could not leave her there."

"I don't know if I agree with you or not, but I didn't take her. That was

28

all you, Eldritch."

"As far as she believes, you killed her sibling as well. Shall I also remind you that you attempted to devastate us in a truck while screaming nonsense and drenched in blood. You took off your britches and your frame was scantily held together by strings."

Was it possible that unlike her sister, Pinball was afraid of me? Was she afraid of vampires or whatever undead drug abortion we were? I needed to make this right. If not solely for me and my conscious and my haunting dreams, then I had to make it right for Bait.

"Okay, Eldritch," I finally agreed. "What do you propose?"

"The most difficult part will be you speaking with her and attempting to make her understand why *we* removed her from her home."

"Sounds easy enough," I said, remembering my long talks with Bait. As far as I knew, I was great with kids.

"It will not be. She is not her sibling. She is not the hardened soul you kept so close to your side. Whether or not we believe maiming her parents for the injustices they committed was honorable, they are all she has ever known. Her father having carnal knowledge of her and the reality of her declining health are two things she only understands in part because that is all there ever was for her. From what I have pieced together, she understood fornication with her father as a gift of love and the disease as her punishment for her not loving him back enough." Eldritch's voice was sorrowful and his eyes twitched. For some reason, he related to the girl. She was a familiar pain to him.

"It's okay, man." I put up my hands to relax him. "We—you and I— we can make this okay. What do we need to do?"

He wiped a tear off his left cheek. "Sadly, I believe that we have come to the end of our passage. We must release the child."

I scratched the tip of my nose. Turning Pinball over to the cops made me feel like I was having an allergic reaction. "Here's maybe a better idea. Who do you know in Austin?"

"I worked with Stephan Rodderick on the second *Nightshayde Chronicles* film," he bragged.

"That's lame. Come on, star fucker. Someone who isn't *that* guy."

He hammered his fist into his palm. "He *is* one of us, RJ. I told you when we escaped from Los Angeles. He is a very trustworthy and beautiful soul."

"Didn't we also hear that he just OD'd on heroin?" I shot back. "Think of someone else."

"He did OD, and is recovering, which makes this a beneficial situation." He got up, walked to the barn door and flicked his cigarette outside. "He will be looked at as a hero during his darkest hour, and we will safely be able to liberate the child."

I ran my fingers through my hair, or at least tried to. It was hard to plow through due to all the gunk in it. "Fine. How do we get in touch with this *Nightshayde* bitch boy?"

Eldritch picked his phone out of his back pocket and walked back toward me.

Sweet, I thought to myself. This was going to be as easy as ringing him up and dropping the kid off at the pool.

Then, he showed me the screen. Apparently Eldritch called him several times in the past few days, including when we were in Arizona.

I grabbed the phone. "Amateur, Eldritch. Did you leave a message?"

"Several."

"And you don't think that was the reason I was attacked by those Chaplin guys?"

Eldritch raised his finger. "He is an actor. A performer."

I threw the phone at him. "And, if you're right, he's a fucking vampire. Which means he really is a drug addict, and what follows drugs and vampires? Gangs, you shithead. What are we going to do?"

"We need to go into the city and retrieve some medication for Paulina. There is an emergency letter in her purse. She has been complaining a lot. It might not be anything serious, but we will need to embezzle it from the appropriate apothecary. We just need the medicine to control her recovery and prevent her recovery from derailing. We will speak with some of the local organizations—"

I interrupted and stood up. "Gangs."

"Gangs." He pounded his fist in his palm again. "They will escort us to Rodderick."

"Why bother? Why can't we just go get an Austin star map and go to his house? He's your boy."

"I do not believe there are star maps in Austin." He looked at his phone and began typing.

I pushed his hand away. "He's an actor."

"Yes, an excellent artist and—"

I grabbed him by the wrist. "And?"

"*And* he's the biggest narcotics dealer in the Southwest of these American States. If your friend King Cobra were three people, they would not control as much as Rodderick does."

"That can't be true." I released his arm. "He's a dumb actor, just like you said. He makes shitty vampire lovey-dovey crap movies."

He looked back at his phone and swiped down. "He controls more than you could possibly comprehend."

"I can comprehend quite a lot." I swatted the side of his head. "And

30

this is your plan to save the girl? Hand her over to another crummy gang leader?"

"You asked me if I knew anyone in Austin and if I had an alternative plan, good sir. He needs something positive to divert the press away from the overdose. The only other choice is to turn ourselves over to the authorities."

"Let me talk to Pinball and see what she wants. There is no way I'm just going to hand her over to this D-bag. Besides, what is going to prevent him from killing us to prove to the cops that the cretins who did this to her parents are dead? Don't you think that a show of bravery will be much better for his career than turning over some little girl? Once I talk to her, then we'll decide on step two."

Strangely, even though this part of our adventure was one hundred percent on his shoulders, Eldritch reluctantly agreed.

VA

ADORED

I delicately pushed the barn door open, still feeling the disgusting sting of Eldritch's clove cigarette pollution tightening my lungs and agitating my wounded face. Yes, we heal at a superiorly rapid pace, but when you get as ravaged as I had over the past few days, the process takes a tad longer than it should. Damn off-the-grid Catholic slits. They got us halfway there with their illegal super-steroid. I wish they would have gone a step further and created a drug that completed the healing process instantly.

To my annoyance, the hinges on the door screeched like an alarm. Pinball, who had been napping by the fire, jolted awake. She might have given herself an unguarded minute, but Eldritch was right: she was scared out of her mind.

I put up my hands. "Shhhhh. I'm not going to hurt you, Pinball."

She wriggled to her feet.

"Take it easy," I said, offering assurance that I came in peace. "Take it easy. I really need to speak with you."

She desperately clutched a stick she had been using as a teddy bear. Her eyes centered on mine. If she was her sister, she would have made a comment about my current crumbled state and then bashed me in the nuts fifteen times with the stick; the stick, most likely, scorched from the fire and dowsed in glass. I had to learn quickly that she was not her sister. Rather than go on the offensive, this one expected the worst and waited for that to play out.

I kept my hands in the air. "I really need to talk with you. I just had a conversation with our big friend in there." I pointed to the decrepit barn as I took a straggled step toward her. "We have every intention of doing what is best for you."

Her index finger rubbed on the stick for a second, then she loosened her grip and batted her eyes. Her actions seemed like a greenlight, so I shuffled two steps closer.

Before I had a chance to take cover she yelled, "Monster," and hurled the stick at me. Immediately, she spun around and peeled out like a dune buggy.

"It doesn't have to be like this," I tried to assure her as I took the thick side of the stick on the bridge of my nose. "There is nowhere to run to, Paulina." I ran after her to the best of my ability.

She pumped the breaks on her ballet shoes and stopped. She didn't turn around.

"Paulina, right?" I asked in my most relaxing voice. It was difficult for my voice to sound like anything other than years of smoking, hard drinking and heroin abuse, but if I pitched it correctly, it didn't sound like Tom Waits with an aluminum can stuck in his esophagus. "That's your name, isn't it? Paulina?"

She looked at her shoes that now showed the wear and tear of being abducted and forced into the hot southwestern desert.

I focused on the shoes in an attempt to build a sense of trust. "Those are pretty cool shoes. Are you a dancer?"

She continued to stare into the darkness.

"My name is RJ," I continued. "Like I told you before."

She brushed sand out of her eyes with her forearm and mumbled, "My momma got 'em at K-Mart." Her voice sounded like Bait's baby talk voice that she used when she wanted something.

"What was that?"

"My momma got 'em at K-Mart. They ain't real." Her voice quieted. "I wasn't s'pose to dance because when I tried, I spit blood all over them other kids."

I swiftly decided that ballet, dancing or anything fun that normal kids did probably wasn't the best thing to point out. I changed the conversation. "I'm friends with your sister, Bailia."

Pinball half turned her head back toward me. Then, she looked back down at her shoes.

"Do you remember your sister?"

"I hated Bailia," she finally shouted back. "Cause a' all the bad things she did, I got sick."

Eldritch was right. She didn't understand her illness at all. That buzzard's cock of a stepfather of hers led her to believe that she was being punished for all the bad things that happened in his life. I'm sure if he couldn't pay the rent on his trailer, it was her fault and resulted in his pants being unzipped.

"Paulina, that isn't true." I kicked at a rock. "Bailia loved you very much."

She half-turned back to me again. "Then why'd she leave me?"

Selfishly, I wanted the conversation to end. I hated what an insensitive shit I had become. In my defense—or so I told myself—I had never been qualified to speak to children about the repugnance of the world. Going beyond my inherent lack of compassion for anything beyond getting a fix, I was, after all, a serial killer, a junkie and a monster.

I turned my head back toward the fire, hoping that Eldritch managed to teleport behind me and offer his support. No luck. He needed me to suffer through this laborious exchange on my own.

Thinking back to the home invasion in Peoria, I didn't know if I expected Pinball to be a carbon copy of Bait to replace the empty feeling I had when I saw her die, or if I just wanted another pet to wait for me to say *sit, stay, rollover*. The mobile dog catcher's truck I hotwired pointed to the latter.

Again, I took a few short steps toward her. "Bait—ummm—Bailia left because your father was doing some very mean things to her."

Her legs popped together as if she was preparing to do a jumping jack. "He does 'em to me, too."

Not anymore, I thought.

"He does them things 'cause he loves me." She began braiding her wig on the side. "He doesn't want me to be sick anymore because I cost too much money and he wants to spend that money on dolls for me. He never did buy me a doll."

As I managed to creep up closely behind her, she turned around to fully face me. Her pasty cheeks had turned red and her eyes turned downward. I don't know exactly what remission from leukemia entailed, but this child looked like she had just fought every second of her life to be standing in front of me.

Her wig tilted slightly to the side. I wanted to reach over and fix it, but I didn't want to alarm her again or point out that she didn't have any hair. That pissed me off. Her mongrel parents kept her head shaved to get attention from the community. They were probably trying to sue the doctors who saved her life.

Pinball took two steps away from me to get to what she considered a comfortable distance to continue the conversation.

"Paulina, that's not true. What your father… stepfather… did to you is a really, really bad thing."

She put her hands in the pockets of her magenta pants and blew her uneven bangs off her forehead. "Is Bailia gonna meet us out here? That's what the other stranger tol' me."

Fuck you, Eldritch, I thought. He could have warned me before sending me on this journey into heartache before I started trying to chum up to her.

I sneezed into my hand and I tried delicately to drive around the subject of Bait's death. "I'm sorry, Paulina," I said. "Bailia couldn't make the trip with us."

Her face crumpled up for a second like a rotten apple and then exploded outward with tears. "Is Bailia dead, too?" She began side-stepping, as if she wanted to take off again but her legs got tangled and she tripped on her K-Mart ballet costume shoes.

I hopped toward her, immediately offering my hand to help her up. She smacked my hand away and the flavored jewel on her Ring Pop broke off into my palm. She squirmed on her butt, unable to brace herself to stand on an unstable patch of Texas ground.

I held the oblong gemstone from her Ring Pop out as an offering of peace. "Please. Let me help you."

She spit at my hand and yelled, "Why'd you kill my mommy and daddy? Why'd you kill my sister? You're a monster." The constant stream of watery hatred on her face mixed with all of the sand and ash from the fire that had built up over the course of the last couple of days. As she gasped for air, I noticed that one of her front teeth was missing. The combination of her muddy, gaunt face and her missing tooth made her look like a rotting pumpkin. She howled and rammed the top of her head into my nuts. Maybe she was more like her sister that she let on.

I buttoned my eyes closed, dropped to my knees, and lifted my hands together, praying for forgiveness. "I didn't kill your sister," I said, then regressed to lying between breaths. "She told me to rescue you." It wasn't really a lie, but it wasn't true, either. I was positive that if Bait had lived, rescuing Pinball would have been our next mission. I opened my eyes again to see the wig between my knees.

Pinball grabbed the wig and haphazardly tried to reconfigure it onto her little bald head. The bangs hung embarrassing and sideways over her left ear. Acting on impulse, I unclasped my hands and reached out to straighten the wig again. She stepped back, grabbed the two sides of the fake hair like hoses and slipped it back into a sufficient position.

I crawled toward her. "Please, Paulina. You have to let Eldritch and I help you. I know that it wasn't a good thing to kill your parents, but I do want to help." I spoke for Eldritch, "We *need* to help you."

She scuttled to a rock, sat down and readied her legs in a launch position, warning me that another ball-ramming was in the works. "I hate you! You're a monster!"

"I know. I know you don't understand. I will stay as far away from you as you feel comfortable. But I need to protect you. Eldritch wants to protect you, too."

She began crying again.

"Do you have any grandparents?" I asked. "Do you have any aunts? Uncles? Is there anywhere we can take you to be safe?"

She stood up from the rock and started stomping her feet. "*No!*"

Oh boy. I certainly didn't prepare myself for any part of this conversation.

"Okay. Okay. No to grandparents and no to aunts and uncles. Can we take you to a friend's house?"

"I don't have no friends," she wailed. "They all call me 'Ugly Head' and spit on me at the bus stop." The cycle of misfortune came full-circle as Pinball's confessions mirrored the awfulness that Bait left behind when she escaped bullying to enlist herself into the glamorous world of prostitution. "Bailia used to protect me. And she left me alone. And then... and then... and then," she stuttered. "And then, all my dumb hair fell out 'cause God was punishing me for letting her leave. And then... and then... and then you killed my daddy. He was the only one who ever loved me."

It was time for me to step up and set things straight. Time to explain my rude interference into her life. Even though I was still wishing that Eldritch had handled this rather than me, I needed to feel the lifting of my guilt as I told her the truth. My head rang like it was in the mouth of a gigantic church bell at midnight. I realized that I hadn't done anything for this kid. I did it all for me. I was nothing but a selfish derelict who felt so much guilt for letting Bait get killed by Dez that I took it upon myself to kill her parents.

I rubbed my fingers across my eyes to dry them up before I broke down during my confession. "I can't take back what I did. What I did was a horrible thing." I stood over her and gently moved a strand of her synthetic locks that had strayed across the part back into place.

She batted at my hand and got back up. "I hate you," she whimpered as she ran back to the barn.

"I don't think you have an ugly head," I called out to her as she slammed the door shut, leaving me alone again in the middle of the desert.

I sighed. I had no idea what our next move should be, but I was making no progress with Pinball. Eldritch was thinking clearer than me at least. If he decided that making this actor prick a hero would draw enough media attention to make Pinball the feel-good story of the year and get her placed into a loving new environment away from the shit world of fake vampires, then I had no choice other than to comply. I figured that the child was sick and needed proper care. It was wrong to take her from her those fucking reptiles. As much as I didn't yet trust this Rodderick guy, and as much as

I hesitated to hand her over to another bag of feces drug addict, I had to believe that someone, someday would smile on me for doing the right thing. Eldritch needed to take the lead on this, making right of my mistakes, and I needed to trust him as well. Pinball seemed to trust him, and he had come up with the only idea that didn't compromise who and what we were.

VII

PLEDGED

"Try to get some sleep, Little One," Eldritch whispered as he waved goodnight to Pinball and closed the barn door. He crept over to my seat near the fire and sat next to me. "She has been sleeping on the back seat of my automobile."

I took a swig from a bottle of water and swished it around in my mouth, trying to dissolve some of the dried blood around my gums and cheeks. "I got that."

He looked at me. He must have detected the agitation in my voice. When you're a junkie and you don't have heroin, everyone either annoys you or makes you want to punch them. That is unless they are getting you high. For example, Eldritch calling Pinball "Little One" made me want to step on his throat.

The thing is that the meth and heroin combination that he gave me back in the Salton Sea and the two days of tripping my nuts off on PCP only made me feel worse. There never was and there never will be a replacement for the taste of heroin. Stimulants like speed and synthetic hallucinogens like angel dust only make you tired and sick. Putting anything besides the devil's honey in my body is like having a mosquito bite you on top of a chicken pock. It only makes the itch that much worse. The Gooch was my internal reminder that there was only one drug, and nothing even came close to satisfying me like it.

"I think that the girl is very sick," he said.

"You think or you know? I thought that she was in remission."

"She has been holding her stomach and groaning. You are shaking." He handed me his jacket. "Please, take my cloak."

I looked at the black plastic trench coat and waved it away. "I see you brought your costumes with you." Even out in the middle of nowhere with just him and a little girl, I would never have put that thing on.

He pulled it back and carefully draped it over his lap. "Whether you appreciate the fashion or not, it will keep you warm."

I hugged myself and rubbed my arms. "I'm not shaking because I'm cold. I'm shaking because I'm buggin'. I hate fucking meth and I hate sherm more. For the past week, all I have been doing is coming down from both and it's exhausting."

"The angel dust was all your doing."

"My doing?" I got up off my seat and kicked at a log at the bottom of the fire. "You're kidding me, right?" I flicked my finger in his face over the crackling flame. "You are the one who called your pal and told them we were in town. You sent me in front of a firing squad, Eldritch. You fucked me."

He scoffed. "I think that the accuracy of your confrontation with the Chaplins is grossly exaggerated."

"Grossly exaggerated?" I paced around the fire. "Oh, fuck you, dude. I did what I said I would and got us a vehicle."

He pointed to the remains of the dogcatcher truck. "That is not the appropriate form of transportation for us. Paulina is not a pet and neither was her sister. We need to speak about what is important."

"I don't know what you mean. Heroin is important." I pried my eyes open with my fingers to show my hunger. "I need heroin and I need it now."

DAMN STrAight.

"That is exactly what I am talking about." He folded his hands over his coat. "You need to decide if saving Paulina is more important than that."

I put my elbow on my knee and put my head in my hand. "I told you we shouldn't have taken her. Why did we even take her? And we left the dog there."

He softened his tone. "Someone will take in a dog before they'll take in a child. We took her because you slew her guardians. We took her because I have a way to give her a better life."

"I killed her parents because they were fucking scumbags." My face remained in my hands as I scratched at my twitching right eyebrow.

"As you are not to blame for Bailia's demise, I do not believe that they were either."

I peeked out from behind my fingers. "Don't bring up Bait, asshole. I tried to save her because she reminded me of me. On the shitty streets. No parents. No anything."

He threw the jacket over his shoulders. "But she is why we are here, correct?"

"Again," I repeated, "This is different."

"It is only different because you created this predicament."

"Do you have any handcuffs in your wardrobe?" I half-joked. "Why don't we just handcuff her to the railing outside the police station and then track down the real assholes responsible for her sister's death. It's pretty obvious that I can't take care of a kid, and unless you raised a litter of wolf pups, I don't think you can take care of a kid either."

He closed his eyes and cracked his neck. I was wearing him down.

"Why aren't we trying to find Dez?" I argued. "Where's The Habit?"

He changed the subject. "Do you remember back in Los Angeles when you told me that you wanted to save Bailia because 'it was the right thing to do'?"

"I did say that," I admitted. "It was different. Bait wanted to be with me. As for Pinball, we didn't have to take her. They would have found her a home. She's a tough kid."

He rotated his neck the other way and cracked it again. Maybe I wasn't wearing him down, after all. Maybe I was just pissing him off. "She has leukemia, RJ."

"She *had* leukemia," I reminded him. "Her perverted parents kept shaving her head after she beat it so they could fleece people for money and sympathy."

"I suggest you do not go down this road," he muttered. "You need to decide if saving this child is as important to you as it is to me."

I backed down a bit. "What do you need me to do?"

"Unfortunately, she is not fond of you. We need to go into the city and find passageway to Rodderick."

I grimaced and tossed a piece of wood into the fire. "Yeah, well he's still a fucking druggie."

"As are you. How do I know that you did not go into Austin while looking to commandeer *that*—" he pointed to the dogcatcher truck again, "—and found someone to sell you PCP? Or did you kill someone for PCP?"

"This again? I tore those weirdos to shreds. I'm sure it's all over the news. Turn on the radio in your Batmobile."

"It will not be in the news," he insisted as his eyes followed my restlessness. "It will never be in the news. They cleaned it up *if* it happened the way you say."

I strutted in front of him and bent down so I was looking him straight in the eyes. "Who is 'they'? Is The Cloth here?"

"The Cloth is everywhere." He stared right back at me. "They are in every city where beings like us walk among the living. In Austin, they are called the Minutemen."

"How do you know so much about them?" I could hear my teeth chattering, so I started warming my arms again with my palms. "And don't lie."

He shushed me and pointed back to the barn.

I walked back to my log and sat back down. More quietly, I asked again. "What do you know that I don't? I saw my file at The Cloth's church. I have to be the only one of us who knows exactly what I am. Reminder: we aren't vampires. We're walking drug addicted abortions."

"You do not remember?"

"Remember what? The Cloth? Sure I remember."

"My father was a Lutheran Pastor in Duluth," he began.

"Aha!" I shot back up and clapped my hands. "I knew it! I knew that you were from Duluth and I didn't just imagine you telling me that when I was wasted. Raised by wolves. What a crock of shit."

He put his head down. "That is the thing, RJ. I have told you all this several times. It would seem that nothing about me is important enough for you to remember. If you must know again, my mother had cancer and died before giving birth to me. My father prepared for such an event. He was aware of the acts of the Catholic Church that led to your birth, your life. The Cloth was at my mother's death bed and I was prematurely born. Then, as I am sure is the same case as with you, they brought me to life."

I deflated.

He stood over me. "Do not concern yourself with my past. I have come to terms with what I am and how I came to be."

"So, the wolves, the mountains, Canada?" I asked as I looked up to him.

He smirked. "All myth."

"Eldritch, why are we doing this? We both know better."

"Because, it is the right thing to do." He sighed as he started to head back to the barn. "I believe you when you tell me that your vengeance in Peoria was justified. I believed you when I followed you to the Salton Sea that you wanted to save Bailia. I am glad you are choosing to follow the right path."

The freezing terror of withdrawal grabbed me by the tailbone and tugged. "Easier said than done."

"Hold it over the fire." He pointed to the log next to me. He'd left a rig filled and pre-mixed with blood. "It will get you through the night."

I picked up the syringe and using the fire as a nightlight, I looked at the contents. "This doesn't have meth in it, does it?"

"I already said that I do not want to kill you. Goodnight, RJ. I recommend you sleep outside. The Little One has had enough trauma for one day."

"Hey," I called out before he closed the door. "How's the weather up there in Duluth, anyway?"

He smirked. "As bad as the weather in the mountains of Canada."

I sat by the fire for a while and injected the drugs into my arm.

It's methadone, idiot. Not good enough.

VIII

CORRODED

After charging our phones and ditching the hearse in an alley outside of town, we turned onto Rundberg on the East side of Austin. I looked around for a second, noting the Starbucks. "This is hardly a fucking ghetto."

"Fortunately, there aren't any real public squalor areas in Austin," Eldritch hummed as he posed under a street lamp. "They have done quite a magnificent job sanitizing the city."

"You told me that a gang runs out of here. When I hear inner city gang, I expect a shithole. You know, like Los Angeles."

He pointed to a real estate advertisement on a bus bench. "Shall I commandeer agent Tom Daniels and ask for a dirty, African American part of town?"

"Oh whatever, Eldritch. I'm not being racist."

He plucked a moth, which was hovering around the light, out of the air above him. He opened his hand to Pinball and gently gave it to her. Her eyes lit up with delight as if he gave her a butterfly.

He patted Pinball on her wig and let out an exhausted sigh. "They have Starbucks in South Central, RJ. According to several local reviews I have deciphered on Yelp, this is the worst Austin has to offer."

I spat near his feet. "Deciphered? Were you on the fucking Latin Yelp site?"

The moth flew out of Pinball's hands. In an attempt to recapture it, Eldritch batted it out of the sky, landing it on the front of my black t-shirt. "I don't understand," he snarled.

I caught the moth. "Of course you don't. You didn't decipher anything. You read some reviews on Yelp. You're not Indiana Jones, dude." The moth sputtered around in my closed hands. Following suit with everything else I touch turning to shit, when I tried to hand it back to Pinball one of its wings fell off. It turned on its side and fell to the ground. It leapt around in a circle, struggling for a second. I decided to step on it and put it out of its misery.

She licked the gap in her front tooth. "Why did you do that?"

"Because it was gonna die." Furthering my statement, I crushed it around under the sole of my boot like a cigarette butt.

Eldritch broke out from the haze of the street light and grabbed me by the arm. "Do not!"

I looked down at the remains of the moth and snickered. "Don't what? It was gonna die. Besides, it was a fucking moth."

Eldritch curled a foggy-eyed Pinball to his side. She turned down her lip in a pout at me. "It's my friend. You shouldn't kill things," she said.

Rather than continue down the path of trying to explain my attempt at mercy for a bug, I began walking away from them.

"Halt!" Eldritch shouted.

I stopped walking.

"You need to answer Paulina," he continued. "You must explain to her why you slew her friend."

I turned to face them and gave Pinball a delicate smile. "I'm sorry, Paulina. I didn't think that the moth was going to make it. So, rather than have it suffer, I put it out of its misery. In my opinion it was the right thing to do. However, we shouldn't kill insects just to kill them. I feel bad and I apologize." I glared at Eldritch. "I didn't realize it was your friend."

Pinball wiped her eyes. "It's okay. It was just a dumb moth." She took her wig off and pointed to small hole under the right side of the bangs. "They eat my hair."

I continued to stare at Eldritch. "Yes, they're rotten fucking insects. Still, you shouldn't kill something because it can no longer fly and therefore be able to eat wigs and clothes. Let's go."

I turned around and continued to walk down Rundberg as I heard Eldritch grunt. They hurried to catch up to me.

As we came up on a strip mall, Pinball rubbed her eyes again. She was tired. I was certain that she hadn't slept well in days and now that she was somewhat comfortable around her abductors, she was letting down her guard.

Eldritch pointed to the center of the mall. "This is what we seek."

"It looks like a mansion compared to the Knuckler's garage," I said.

The sound of a metal pipe knocking on cement sang out from behind the shopping center followed by the emergence of young kid, probably eighteen, in overalls and riding a rusted BMX bike.

I tapped Eldritch on this PVC sleeve. "Are they expecting us?"

"I do not believe so," he scoffed. "Why do you ask?"

"I don't know, because you seem to have called everyone in the area to alert them that we're here." I blew his smoke back in his face. "Remember when I got stomped by that other gang? It sure seemed like they knew who and what I was."

"I disagree with your assumption," he continued. "Maybe you would not have ended up in such a predicament had you not been walking around comatose shouting that you were a vampire."

"That's not the way it happened. At least I don't think that's how it happened."

The kid pumped his pedals furiously as he drifted directly toward us. He got closer to us in a matter of seconds. I looked over his shoulder. Several shadows emerged in front of, and on top of, the plaza.

Eldritch bent down to my ear. "Looks as if the welcoming party hath arrived. This shall be fun."

Right before the dope on the bike was about to crash into me he bunny-hopped sideways, kicking up a little bit of gravel onto my boots. The kid took his foot off the pedal, and, as if he were advertising it, rotated his calf around while he whistled back to his boys. There was a horrific gash from the top of his foot all the way up to the middle of his leg. The leg bones were fully exposed and woven with deteriorated cartilage and muscles. Around the edges of the wound, black skin began regenerating in front of our eyes and suddenly a large chunk of tainted flesh abandoned the lacerated area, much like a snake skin shedding from its host. Eldritch coughed up a little in his mouth.

I surveyed the eaten-away leg a little more. The regenerative process accelerated so quickly that pieces of body were appearing from thin air. I didn't know what kind of vampires these jokers were, but it seemed like they weren't going to be easy to take down. "You might want to get that wound looked at there, dude."

Without missing a beat, he jumped onto the pegs on the front spokes and then hopped again a few times as he stared at Pinball. Eldritch brought her in close to him and tucked her into his vinyl trench coat.

"Is this a member of the gang?" I asked.

Eldritch nodded. "They seem different."

I turned back to the BMX bandit. His eyes were strange; they drooped downwards in the corners like the eyes of a child with fetal alcohol syndrome.

He teetered backwards, then spun the bike into a tail whip and threw himself onto the pedals after the bike completed a three hundred and sixty-degree rotation. He sped back toward the strip mall.

"What the fuck was all that?"

Eldritch put both his arms across his front, shielding Pinball in his coat. "I suspect he was a runner."

"Not the guy," I whimpered. "That fucking huge gash on his leg that was rejuvenating right in front of us. Are these guys more advanced than us?"

"Not that I am aware of. I have never seen anything like that, either."

A muffled voice came from inside the trench coat. "That was gross."

I turned back to the mall. The BMX kid stopped short of going inside to talk to the central figure, who I deduced was their leader. A street light flickered on, revealing an entire gang in beat up overalls.

"Who are these guys, Eldritch?"

"They go by the name the Real McCoys. They are a lesser gang in the hierarchy of the Austin underworld, but I figured they could relay a message up through the ranks, eventually reaching Rodderick."

I started whispering as to not scare Pinball. "These guys are small time? I find that hard to believe. You saw that leg. That wasn't vampire healing."

"Although I agree with the astonishing rapidity that his leg was healing," he flicked a mosquito off his shoulder, "I do not believe we will have a problem with these young men."

"Way to practice what you preach. I put the moth out of its misery for a reason; you just killed that bug." I raised my voice. "You hear that, Paulina? Eldritch just killed a defenseless mosquito."

Pinball squirmed inside his jacket. "I hate skeeters," she said. "They're itchy."

The McCoys began walking toward us.

"Are these pricks gonna sing 'Come on Eileen'?"

Eldritch raised his eyebrow and pondered my question. He then looked at the approaching McCoys in their overalls. He sneered. "Indeed. Dexy and his Midnight Runners. Well played."

Pinball poked her head out from his jacket. "Mister Eldritch, why are those boys dressed like that?"

"Yeah, *Mister* Eldritch. Why are these terrifying freaks dressed like that?"

He looked down to his stomach. "I imagine it is because they are all on the same team."

She put her hand on her head to guard her wig from falling off and bent her head back to talk to him. "Like a soccer team?"

"Yes, Little One. Exactly like a soccer team." He lightly pushed her head back inside the jacket.

I started whispering again. "Who do they play for, fucking Transylvania? This is a bad idea, Eldritch. This is the single worst idea other than—" I nodded to his trench coat stuffed with Pinball.

The leader stopped about twenty feet in front of us and the rest halted behind him. I could see the entire gang now. All of them had huge open wounds all over their bodies. They were all reconstructing and rolling their heads around, ripping at their own skin and shaking.

"Who are y'all?" the scrawny, greasy leader asked. The right side of his face was eaten away and you could see his teeth and gums move as he spoke. Skin started self-grafting and building over the open area, filling in and covering the rot.

Eldritch cleared his throat. "We are from Los Angeles."

The Tooth Fairy took a step closer and then turned to the horde of zombies behind him. "Y'all hear that? These here people are from Hollyweird. Look like a bunch of pretty boys."

A toadie from the back who seemed preoccupied with his exposed arm bone chimed in, "Maybe them is actors."

"Actors? More like faggots." The leader laughed.

A member near the toadie pushed him, showing his approval. Out of nowhere, the toadie jumped on his chum and began raging on his face with the open arm bone. "I tol' you. Never touch me again." The guy on the bottom laughed as his nose became more and more concave with every stroke of the pummeling.

"Stop, you dumb fuckers," the leader ordered.

The rest of the gang started laughing and jittering around like a troop of rabid monkeys. The kid on the BMX bike continued to perform tricks on his bike around the scuffle. At one point, he was bunny-hopping to the beat of his own frenzied laughter.

I glanced at Eldritch, trying to keep my eyes on the leader. "This is insane."

The leader stepped to me. "You got somethin' funny to say there, homo actor boy?"

I extended my hand to shake. "I'm RJ."

He looked at the hand, confused. "Name's 'miley."

I chuckled under my breath and tried not to make eye contact with Eldritch.

The McCoy faked a shake and pulled his hand away, then ran it through his filthy hair.

"Miley?" I said, ignoring his attempt to disrespect me. "Like Miley Cyrus?"

He smiled and pointed to the few teeth left in his mouth. I figured he was laughing *with* me. Who am I to say that naming yourself after a pop star is lame? I was named after a pack of cigarettes.

I put my hand back up to shake. "Nice to meet you, Miley."

He remained still, not accepting my introduction. Then, he pointed to a smiley face pin on of the straps of his overalls. "Said the name's 'miley."

I grabbed his wrist to shake his hand this time. As he pulled it away, his rotten skin pulled from the bone like he was shedding. I planted my hand into his. "And I said, 'Nice to meet you, Miley'."

Eldritch kicked at my boot. "Smiley," he whispered.

The leader spit into his hand as if to cleanse himself of my city boy stench. He nodded his head toward Eldritch.

We all waited a few seconds. A dog barked in the distance. One of the other McCoys sneezed. I almost started whistling when I just burst out, "Is it fucking Miley or Smiley?"

He pulled out a blood-filled syringe and injected it into his hand. "Sa. My. Lee." As quickly as he pulled out the needle, the flesh on his palm began melting off. For a split second, before the restoring began, I could see his eye through his hand. He giggled and shook his head like he had just taken a huge piss. Then, his eyes beamed open and he started wheezing.

"Can I ask you what kind of drugs you all are taking, Sa-miley? You're freaking me the fuck out."

He looked back at the gang and shook his head. "You ain't never seen Sunshine, boy?" He pointed at one of the other McCoys. "Show him."

The kid, maybe fifteen years old, pulled another blood-filled syringe from the front pocket of his overalls and injected it into his cheek. Like the leader, the entire outside of his face vanished, revealing his jaw. His teeth clicked together, showing the hinge near his ear as he spoke. "Like moonshine, but Sunshine. Makes you feel like yer burnin' up in the sun and then like yer flying to the moon."

Eldritch and I both froze, not wanting to continue to look but not able to turn away, either.

I slapped Eldritch on the back. "Okay, then. We can go now."

Eldritch opened his right hand and extended the talons. "What is in this drug?"

The leader turned back around. "I dunno. Bath salts, meth, Krokodil."

"Krokodil." I laughed. "Isn't that Russia's flesh-eating drug?"

He nodded but I wasn't sure if he knew or was just starting the nods.

The Nods. Ask if it has heroin in it.

"Does it have any heroin in it?"

"I already tol' you what's in it. Bath salts, meth and Krokodil."

"Krokodil," I repeated, talking to him and assuring The Gooch. "I've never known anyone dumb enough to take that shit."

Oblivious to the fact that I just called him and the rest of the Midnight

Runners a bunch of nitwits, he got back in my face. "Hey, motherfucker. You a commie? This shit was made in the U.S.A. This is the greatest thing in the world. Why don't you leave, boy? We don't want no actors and fairies on McCoy turf."

I looked around. There wasn't much of anything on their turf other than the abandoned strip mall I imagined they called their clubhouse.

Eldritch stepped between us. He was right before. We wouldn't have any trouble with these jokers. He reached his hand out to introduce himself to the leader. "Hello, good sir." The leader showed Eldritch his recently contaminated hand. "Sorry." Eldritch put down his hand and covered his front with his forearm. Then, he reached out with the other. "I am Eldritch."

The leader stared at him. "Those sure are some funny clothes you got on, Hollywood boy." He surveyed the trench coat. "I wanna get me one of them. Look like *The Matrix*."

"Eldritch, you should give this fine fellow your coat. It does look like *The Matrix*, or at least, a coat seen in *The Matrix*," I said before I remembered that Pinball was tucked away.

Pinball peered out from inside the coat for a second and immediately retreated back in after seeing Smiley.

"Well, what do we have here?" He cackled. "Come on out little girl and let me have a look at you."

"That is why we have come. We are seeking assistance from the Real McCoys to get a message to a Mr. Stephan Rodderick."

The leader remained fixed on the moving child in the coat. "Who?" he asked.

"Stephan Rodderick," Eldritch continued as he crossed both his arms over Pinball. "Is he not the leader of this Austin crime organization?"

"You mean that gay boy from them vampire movies?" the BMX kid chimed in.

"Yep. That's him," I said.

The leader side-stepped back to me. "So. The gay one does talk."

"What?" I asked confused. "I thought we were all gay and I was literally just speaking to you a moment ago." I looked over his shoulder and noticed that all the McCoys were checking out *The Matrix* jacket. It wasn't the coat they were interested in, however; they wanted the little creature inside.

I snapped my fingers at the leader who had somehow managed to lose focus on our conversation in a split second. "Do you know Rodderick or not?"

He took a pack of chew out of the front pocket on his overalls and put it inside of his cheek. "You'd be smart not to snap them pretty fingers in front of my face." He sucked a bunch of juice from the chew and then spit the refuse on my pants.

Eldritch pushed me back. The time bomb was about to go off. "We do not want trouble, sir."

"Well, boy." The leader pressed on the chew inside his mouth. "You found trouble. We outnumber you Hollywood fairies fifty to one."

I stepped in front of Eldritch now in an attempt to keep Pinball out of harm's way. "Look, ass stain. Your math is way off and I assure you that you don't want to fuck with us. Can you please relay the message to Rodderick?"

He spit again, barely missing my leg again. "Who?"

"God dammit. The fucking actor, dude."

"Why would I know some actor fella? Maybe y'all should go back to Hollyweird if you wanna find you an actor." He turned back to his gang for a laugh. Unfortunately for him, they were all now completely puzzled as to where they were and what we were all talking about. One guy chuckled but got something stuck in his throat. Probably a tooth.

I grabbed Smiley by his hand, snapped his arm backwards and pressed him down to his knees on the ground. It sounded cooler than it actually was. He was in such a fog that he stumbled around. "Ask the rest," I insisted as he finally started to feel the pain of the break. "Do you..." I continued.

He craned his neck back to look at me. He was terrified. "Do you..." he repeated after me.

I slapped the chew out of his mouth with my free hand. "Don't talk to me, jackass. I don't fucking know the guy." I pointed to the rest of the McCoys. "Talk to them."

He turned back to his gang. They stood around, each spinning and convulsing to a different song in their heads. "Do you know," he started. I cranked the arm again. "Owwww!" he belted out. "Do you know the actor from *The Matrix*?"

"Not the actor from *The Matrix*, asshole. Stephan Rodderick. He's the actor from the *Nightshayde* vampire movies."

The BMX kid yelled out, "Keanu Reeves!"

One of the other McCoys kind of agreed. "Yeah Stephan Rodderick is the guy from *The Matrix*."

I threw the leader to the ground. "Jesus fucking Christ, Eldritch, are you fucking kidding me with these guys? They might as well be a soccer team. They are so low on the totem pole and so fried they don't even know who they run drugs for. This is, without a doubt, the creepiest and shittiest gang ever."

I mushed the leader's face into the asphalt with the heel of my boot.

"Who gives you the drugs? Do you sell it as well or is that asking too much for a gang to sell drugs?"

I released my boot from the back of his head so he could speak. "Yeah, we sell it. We sell ice, too."

"Then, who takes a fucking cut? Where do you get it? Where do you buy it?"

"We take kids," he said. "Off the street and trade them to this gang for the drugs. That's where the money is in Austin. Taking kids."

No wonder they were so interested in Pinball. I kicked him in the face. "Kids? What does a gang need with kids?"

He sat up and started licking his hand. "I don't know. They fuck 'em, I gather."

"They fuck kids. Great." I brushed his body sauce off of my hands. "Where is this gang and how can we speak with them?"

He began hyperventilating. As his breathing slowed he managed to squeak, "Y'all can find them over on Sixth Street."

I kicked some gravel at him. "What's their name?"

He coughed into his unhealed hand. "The Sixth Street Skulls."

I rubbed my temples. "Really? The Sixth Street Skulls. That's their name?"

"Whose name?"

IX

REJECTED

"Well, they were fun," I joked, slapping Eldritch on the trench coat where his ass was. "I certainly hope that the Sixth Street Skulls are as insightful and pleasant as the Real McCoys." I fired up a cigarette. Eldritch batted it down.

I bent to pick it up. "What the fuck, Eldritch? That was my last blood-dipped smoke." Before I got to it, he smooshed it under the toe of his boot.

He bent his head sideways and signaled toward Pinball, who was holding on to his hand for dear life. He grinned and out of the side of his mouth he said, "No smoking."

I put my arm out in front of our pilgrimage and then bent down to Pinball. "You don't mind if I smoke, do you?"

She pulled away from me and pushed her face into Eldritch's leg.

I scurried over to the crushed butt and picked it up. It wasn't salvageable. "Dammit." I tossed it away. I went to Pinball and turned her around. Her wig tilted off its axis. As I straightened it out, I took a calmer tone. "Pinball, do you mind if I smoke and do drugs?"

She grinned. "Drugs are bad an' so is smoking. My daddy had to smoke outside when I didn't feel good."

I looked up to Eldritch. He closed his eyes and shook his head.

My attention turned back to Pinball. "We're outside right now though. So, if I did still have a cigarette, you would approve, right?"

She yawned and licked her lips. "But I don' feel good."

Eldritch turned her around toward him. "Can you sit down right here while Uncle RJ and I have a talk?"

She stomped her feet and sat on the curb. "He's not even my real uncle. My real uncle wouldn' a kilt my daddy."

Eldritch walked me to the corner.

I put out my hand. "So, give me a clove or whatever you smoke, asshole."

He clutched my balls and my trembling hands latched onto his wrists. "Listen, you pathetic, selfish little goblin, do not smoke in front of Paulina and stop calling her Pinball. I am not sure how riddled with drugs your brain is, but she was called that by a predator; a predator that disguised himself as her father. She is diseased and we kidnapped her. Remember, it was your idea to go there and execute her parents. She is not to be treated like a dog, as you treated her sister. *Her sister*, who is dead as well because you allowed a human into our world."

I jumped back from his grip. "Oh, eat shit. I just wanted a smoke."

"She is sick, RJ. She has cancer. We need to get her to Rodderick."

I massaged my pelvis. "She *had* cancer. That doesn't give you a pass to grab my dick."

"I fear that she is still sick."

"But you don't know do you, Eldritch? You know as much about her and her disease as I do: nothing. The only time I've ever dealt with cancer is drinking some poor sick gang banger's infected blood. It doesn't qualify me as a doctor."

He placed his palm over his face. "Start acting serious. This is a serious matter. This is not a joke to be tossed around between a bunch of heroin addicts at a garage."

He was right. I backed down.

"Owwww," Pinball cried out. "My stomach hurts, Mr. Eldritch."

"Can you hear her cries?" He started whispering. "She is in a massive amount of pain."

"She's probably hungry. When was the last time you fed her anything besides bullshit?"

He looked behind me and stared down the street.

I waved my hand in front of his face. "Drug store. Let's get her some drugs."

He unfolded one of his steel talons in front of his lips. "Shhhhhh."

I turned my head slowly. I hadn't heard anything or anyone on the streets around us. "I don't see anything."

He pointed to an alley two blocks away. "Right there."

"What?" I squinted and tried to focus on what he was pointing to. "I don't see anything."

He flicked his talon. "I see the front tire of a bike."

"Who cares if there is some kid on a bike back there?"

He walked back to Pinball, bending down and leading her to her feet. She dropped the rock as he tugged her away from me.

I ran up to them. "Why do you care if some kid is on a bike?"

He cupped his hands over her ears and whispered, "You phlegmatic nincompoop, we are obviously being followed by the McCoys."

"Give me a break. Those clowns don't have the balls to track us. Why would they? They told us to go talk to the Skulls."

He picked up his pace. "That tire. I am certain it is the boy who was performing for us."

"Who cares, I could decimate those idiots with or without your help." I turned and hollered toward the alley. "Hey, BMX Bandit! Go tell your boy Miley to leave us the fuck alone." I waited for a response and saw a little movement back by the alley. "That's what I thought, you phlegmatic nincompoop."

Eldritch let out a huge sigh.

I caught up to them. "Don't worry about it, guys. They won't attack us. They had their chance." In an attempt to join the buddy system, I grabbed onto Pinball's hand and doubled my pace to keep up. She looked up at me. "Don't worry. We are going to get some medicine it'll make you feel better. Maybe Eldritch will let Uncle RJ get some cigarettes, too."

She tugged loose from my grip. "Your hand is cold."

"Well, I *am* dead," I said under my breath. "And he's dead, too."

She suddenly let go of Eldritch too and doubled over, grabbing her belly. "Owwwwww!" she howled.

Eldritch just shook his head.

"So, it's settled, then?" I asked. "Right, Eldritch?"

"Yes," he said. "We will go to get some medicine for Paulina. Then, we will go talk to our new friends, the Sixth Street Skulls."

Although I was happy that I got my way, I decided to further lighten the mood. "No, that's not what I was talking about."

Eldritch tucked his hair over his ear. "Then what is it you are talking about?"

I laughed. "I wanted to make sure that we were all on the same page about you lying about being raised by wolves, becoming the leader of their pack and even ever being in Canada."

He broke Eldritch character and started laughing with me. "You are a fucking asshole."

Pinball stood up straight and took our hands, relocking the chain between the three of us.

We stood between the pharmacy and some insurance office.

I smoothed my palm upward against the brick. "How are we going to get in?"

Eldritch unlocked his talons on both hands. "I suggest we climb."

I looked up the side of the two-story pharmacy. "You're kidding, right?" I clenched Pinball's hand and raised it. "Are we going to leave her down here?"

"I'm hungry," she said, tapping on the top part of her arm.

SO AM I.

I pulled away as soon as I realized I was being a little rough. "Sorry." I looked around for a solution, then pointed to an area on the side of the store. "Maybe we can build her a fort with those empty boxes." I knew it was important that we got the kid medication, though I'm not going to lie and say that I didn't also want some of my own meds. But I needed to think of the kid. Even though I thought she was just hungry and scared, Eldritch insisted that she was sick. My cravings were strictly secondary.

Eldritch placed both his hands on the wall and determined the plausibility of the climb and then looked at my box-fort idea. "We are not leaving her down here."

"I'm hungry," she grumbled again.

Eldritch rushed over to her. "Yes, I know, Paulina." He grabbed a pack of gummy bears out of a small satchel—not a purse—slung around his side. "Open up," he said.

She opened her mouth and stuck out her tongue. Eldritch dropped one of the bears on it and she swallowed with a joyful gulp. "Gimme another," she said. "Another white one!"

Eldritch looked through the bag of bears. "Ahhhhh," he said triumphantly. "Here you are, a white gummy bear."

Pinball stuck her tongue out even further this time. Once again, she opened wide and Eldritch placed the bear on her tongue. She swallowed and smiled. I made a mental note that she loved white gummy bears.

I slouched over to Eldritch and muttered, "Are you sure she should be eating those? You know, her *condition* and all."

"That's diabetes, stupid face," Pinball squawked.

Eldritch mimicked my concern and patted her on her wig. "You know, 'her condition and all.'" They both started laughing.

I turned away. "Jesus, assholes. Like I'm a doctor. Sugar can't be good for a kid, whether she *had* cancer or not."

Their laughter stopped. "Be a little more sensitive, RJ," Eldritch warned in his best concerned parent tone.

I bored my hand into my pocket and returned with a crumpled-up packet of Combos. "Yummm," I declared as I managed to sift through the bag to find a full treat amongst the crumbs. "Open your mouth."

Pinball extended her neck and sniffed the Combo. "Ewwww. It smells like farts."

Eldritch grabbed it out of my hand and inspected it. I tried to pluck it back but he outmaneuvered me.

"It doesn't smell like farts. It's a treat," I assured them.

He sniffed it. "You will not give this child a canine treat." His crushed the Combo into bits, then and blew the dust in my face.

I vented the cloud as I coughed. "It's not a Snausage, shithead. It's a fucking Combo. And I'm sure it's way healthier than a piece of candy."

Pinball plugged her nose. "Yep. Smells like farts." Then burst into fits of laughter.

I shoved the Combos back into my pocket. "Nice, dude. Calm her down. She doesn't seem sick to me."

Eldritch patted her wig. and put his finger to his lips in a playful shush gesture and Pinball stopped laughing. She smiled at him, much like the way Bait smiled at me.

He pointed over to a discarded milk crate. "Go sit down over there, Little One, while Uncle RJ and I discuss."

She scratched her foot into the dust left over from the Combo and stomped over to the crate. As she was turning it over to sit on it, she groaned. "Stupid jerk. Not even my uncle. Kilt my parents." She plopped down on the milk crate and then screamed, *"Not even my uncle!"*

Eldritch rushed to her side. "Shhhh, Little One." He brushed the wig's badly cut bangs out of her eyes. "It is going to be okay."

She rattled her head back and forth. *"He kilt my mommy!"*

Eldritch covered her mouth, careful not to cut her face with his appliances. "Shhhhhhh." He bent down to her and released his hand. Tears were streaming down her cheeks. "He sent your parents to a better place because they were dangerous to you in our world."

You bet I did.

"We are going to get you a new home with loving parents as soon as we speak to the movie man," he continued.

Her voice muffled. "I hate the movie man! I hate vampires!" Slowly starting to hyperventilate, she turned toward me, and belted out, *"I hate Uncle RJ!"*

Eldritch opened his hand again and a white gummy bear stood on his palm. She didn't acknowledge that she saw it. Her gentle eyes had changed to scorching coals.

Wishing that we had gotten past all this, I turned around and pretended to survey the brick wall on the side of drug store. I might have knocked on the stone and ran my index finger though the lines of cement that held the wall together. I was afraid to turn around. I imagined her stare melting the little white gummy bear in Eldritch's palm.

He whispered, "RJ is a good man, Little One. He did what he felt was necessary. It might not have been right, but I assure you that we will get you to safety. He loved your sister very much. He tried to save her. I was there."

I heard the entire gummy bear bag exchange hands. She sounded surprised. "He did?"

I punched my finger through the mortar in the wall. There was no reason for me to be jealous of Eldritch and Pinball's budding friendship, but I couldn't help being annoyed since I already explained all of this to her.

I looked thought the hole I made. It seemed like there was a small crawl space and some wooden studs that were covered by plywood, leading to plaster and paint on the other side.

Still reluctant to turn around and look at Pinball, I pressed my eyes to the hole and evaluated an important discovery. I called Eldritch over. "Hey, big man, can you come over here really quick?"

"I am going to go speak with RJ," he relayed to her. "Stay right here." He paused for a second. "I bet you cannot eat all of these treats before I get back."

"I bet I can," she delightedly fired back.

"I bet you cannot, Little One."

"I bet I can!"

I was exhausted by the baby talk. "Nighttime's wasting," I reminded Eldritch.

I heard the sound of his trench coat skimming the pavement as he got to his feet. "Right you are, RJ."

Pinball whispered, "I bet I can."

He whispered back, "I bet you cannot."

Without raising my voice, I pulled my eye away from the wall and said, "For the love of God. Who cares?"

Eldritch wrapped his patent leather arm around me. "You need not worry. She will come around."

I ignored his encouragement and stuck my finger back in the hole. I grabbed onto the inside of the brick and started pulling out chunks. "You see this?" I started plugging my fingers into the growing hole around the mortar. When I got all four digits into the hole, I pressed my thumb against the face of the brick and started wiggling it loose.

Eldritch bent in for a closer look. "See what?"

I shook the brick loose and held it up. "Rather than scale this wall, which I won't be able to do and you probably won't be able to do with a fifty-pound child on your back, we should just tear down this wall."

He looked at the brick. "That is insanity."

Pinball squawked behind us. "Hey! Look at me! I'm a fireman."

Eldritch put up his hand and said, "Just a second," but didn't turn around to look at her.

I blew into the hole to clear the dust. "Why is it insane? Look in there. We won't trip any alarms if we go directly through the wall."

"You can sit down here and tear away at the wall to your hearts content. As you said, nighttime's wasting."

Pinball started wooing like a siren and, "Hey, I'm a fireman."

I added some huff to my voice. "Just a minute, *Little One*."

Eldritch cleared his throat. "Do not mock me in front of the child."

"Well, you better start climbing, Spidey." I turned away from him and started shaking loosed the next brick. "I'm going through the wall."

The train on his coat swept my calves as he turned to collect Pinball. However, I didn't hear him move any further. He cleared his throat again. This time to get my attention.

I pulled the next brick out of the wall and threw it over my head as I turned around. "What? I thought, you were going to—"

We both stood still, dumbfounded.

Just above the milk crate, Pinball was swinging around on a ladder that was bolted to the wall on the side of an insurance building.

I looked up. There was roughly a fifty-foot gap between the buildings. "Do you think you can make that jump with her on your shoulders?"

Eldritch glared at me, then pulled Pinball off the ladder and hoisted her onto his back. "Wrap your arms around my neck and hold tight," he told her as he grabbed onto the sixth or seventh rung and started scaling the ladder. He turned back to me but her wig was blocking his face. "I will pull you up over the ledge when I get to the top, RJ."

I grabbed onto the same rung where he started his ascension. "I'm pretty sure I can handle it."

Eldritch reached the top and grabbed the lip of the building, dropping his legs from the ladder as he used his hands to propel himself onto the roof. He also managed to kick some clods of dirt off of his boots, letting it rain down onto my face. I spit it out of my mouth. "*P-tew*."

"Are you okay down there, RJ?" They tried to muffle their giggles. "Might you reconsider breaking in through the wall?"

I reached the top as I scrubbed the dirt off of my tongue. I pulled myself over the lip. "I'm good, you cunt," I added as I hopped onto the tarred, flat summit.

Eldritch was bent over, whispering to Pinball, sizing up the physics of his jump with his arm extended. As if she had any idea what physics were, much less Victorian era physics.

I cracked my neck, back-stepped to the far edge of the building and got a running start. "Don't talk about it, just jump." I hurdled over the inner lip, easily cleared the gap and successfully landed on top of the drug store. The fleshy side of my hands eased my momentum and my boots skidded to a stop. As I stood upright, I added, "Do you want me to come back and get the kid? You seem a little reluctant to make the jump."

"Do not mind him. He is a *culus magnificis*." Eldritch tried to whisper behind his hand.

I pointed to my right ear. "I have super hearing, too. Remember? I don't know what that means, but I'm pretty sure it wasn't nice." I walked to the edge of the pharmacy, directly across from him. "Just throw her across to me," I suggested.

He picked Pinball up and returned her to the piggyback position. "That will not happen." Not afraid that anything could go wrong on the back of her gallant swashbuckler, Pinball closed her eyes and rested her head next to his. He didn't bother to back up like I did. Rather, he took a handful of long strides toward the lip and made his jump. The moon sparkled on his PVC duster. Almost as if he had the wind gliding him across the Grand Canyon, his collar blew up as the shadows deepened his cheekbones.

As overly-flamboyant as that might sound, that was exactly what it looked like. Although I had never seen them, I couldn't help but think Stephan Rodderick should have taken a backseat to Eldritch in those *Nightshayde* movies. He was absolutely the epitome of the vampire you would find in a teen girl's dreams. It kind of made me sick, but by the same token in light doses it was pretty bitchin'.

He landed with his feet planted firmly and crouched into a three-point stance. "We have arrived, Little One." Pinball rubbed her eyes. He lowered her to the ground by bending his arm as she dismounted.

Pinball looked back at the roof of the insurance company. "Again!" she badgered. She opened her hand to reveal the smushed white gummy bears. She took one out of the bag and handed it to Eldritch.

He put out his palm to receive the gift. "Thank you for holding on to these. I knew you would keep them safe. White is my favorite flavor, too."

"Hey, racists!" I called over to them. "Here is our entrance." I bent over and knocked on a black, wooden trap door.

Eldritch straightened his trench coat and brushed his hair out of his face. "Do not be daft." He grabbed Pinball's hand and walked toward me.

I kicked the door with my heel. "What's wrong with this? Not white enough for you?"

He shoved me to the side. "There must be another way in."

"Why?" I asked. "What's wrong with this?"

"Is it not obvious?" He walked around the roof, looking under and into everything ranging from air conditioning ducts to discarded boxes. "It is, after all, a pharmacy."

Not wanting to wait it out, I shoved my fingers through the wood and lifted the door like a bowling ball. The lock snapped from the latch inside and thumped down the stairs. No alarm sounded. "Too late now."

Eldritch clomped back to me, shaking his disapproving finger. "*You! Sir!*"

I flipped the door open. "Look." I pointed into the hole. "No alarm and there's a staircase. Christ, they might as well have sent an invitation to be robbed."

He bit his tongue and looked in to the stairway. "Hmmmm. It was still an extremely impulsive and irresponsible move."

I ignored him and ducked into the hole. "There's a door here. I'm going to open it."

Eldritch remained quiet. He was probably hesitant to come downstairs after me because, as always, he was anticipating me making a misstep.

I closed my eyes so he couldn't see me sweat and turned the handle on the door. *Click.* No lock. I pressed my hand against the door in front of my face and pushed it open. No alarm. And I was inside the pharmacy portion of the store.

I hollered back, "Fuck you, pussy!"

"Indeed." He shrugged, then led Pinball down the stairs after me. He had her fingers lifted as if he were presenting her to aristocrats at a ball. I tried to ignore it. It was so fucking stupid and foppy.

"I'm going to hit the head then start looking around the front." I crossed through the aisles and reached a glass observation window that separated the actual drugs from the sundries. I looked to my left to see a small, sliding window where prescriptions were administered. A metal door was next to the window.

I heard Pinball trying to be as quiet as possible. "Why's he like that?" she asked.

"He does not understand."

I thought about Bait again, pushing through the metal door, then slammed it behind me. I was glad that even with my super-vampo-hearing I wouldn't be able to hear anything from either of them for at least a half hour.

You're iN A drug store.

Not now, Gooch. Please, not now.

X

INFESTED

Being a vampire didn't include night vision, but the moon provided enough dim light so I could sift through the latest delicious flavors of Combos. I threw one of each into a Dora the Explorer backpack that I found on the side of the toy aisle. I took a few steps sideways and luckily came across several different bags of gummy bears, gummy worms and gummy rings. I would have sifted through each bag and casted aside the candies that weren't white but I didn't want to be accused of leading a child down a path to neo-Nazism. I also threw some trail mix, nuts and beef jerky into the backpack. Collectively, it was probably the worst shit for a meal replacement... especially for a sick and starving ten-year-old kid.

As I was making my way over to the refrigerator and snagged another backpack for Lunchables and junk, something caught my eye near the end cap of the shampoo aisle. *Cotton balls.*

NOW YOU'RE THINKIN'.

I glanced back at the pharmacy and saw Eldritch's big shadow cross the window, but that was all. He was pretty stern about me not getting high before we got Pinball into the actor's care, but I couldn't fight it any longer.

I ripped open a bag of cotton balls and shoved them into my jeans, under my nuts. Even if he did frisk me, he would never check *that* pocket.

I wasn't going to find any heroin in the pharmacy but thankfully Oxycodone, a great post-chemotherapy narcotic, would be. They didn't call it "hillbilly heroin" for nothing. I had done Oxy several times when I was desperate, even though it didn't quite pack the same punch or satisfy The Gooch. But it was an opiate, so it scratched that junkie itch, even if it didn't relieve it fully. I don't know why the cotton balls turned on that lightbulb in my brain, but yeah, this was going to be a win-win situation for everyone.

I looked down and started counting with my fingers what I needed. Before I readied a mental list of all tools that I needed to have my post-traumatic pharmaceutical therapy, Eldritch called out. "We may require syringes!"

I threw the backpack in the air, dumping the treats all over the floor. "*Jesus fucking Christ!*" I knew I never should have taken my eyes off the pharmacy.

I looked up and he was talking to me through the sliding window. Eldritch was always silently sneaking around and catching me with my pants down.

"Why are you restless?"

I dropped to the floor and started putting everything back in the bag. "I'm not restless, asshole. It's dark in here and I am trying to get the girl more candy and food. It's obvious she's hungry."

He yelled to me again, as if there were a thousand other people in the store swallowing up his voice. "You need not worry about more candy. We need syringes."

"Quiet down. Haven't you ever robbed a store before?" Knowing better than to fight the first thing on my list to medicate myself, I added, "Why do we need syringes?"

"The Little One and I are having a difficultly locating pain reliving medication in a tablet form. I searched my telephone and found some comparable liquid pain relievers. We will need a syringe to administer such elixirs, should we uncover any."

"They don't sell them in the front of the store."

He waved me away and rolled his eyes. "Of course they do."

I whizzed a bag of gummy rings at him.

He closed the window as the candy smacked into it. Then he reopened the window and blew a long strand of hair out of his face. "Why must you fight against everything?"

"I'm not fighting everything. Here are the facts." I put up my fist and started ticking off my experience. "Number one, I'm a heroin addict. Number two, I was born this way. Number three, I'm old. Number four, if I could walk into a pharmacy and steal syringes, I would have figured that out ages ago."

He stroked his chin. "Hmmmm. What do you suggest?"

Then, miraculously, something caught my eye. "Sixty-Second Clinic." I pointed to a sign.

"What is that?" he said as he tried to get a bird's eye view of the sign.

Unfortunately for him, his head was too big to fit through the little window. "I am not familiar."

I jogged over to a small hallway. There was a sign above it that indicated the pharmacy was also a walk-in clinic. When I reached the WELCOME door, I lowered my shoulder and powered through it, destroying the hinges and collapsing the wood plank to the ground in front of me. I stepped onto the door as if I had conquered a foreign land and quickly started rummaging through drawers. I found a lot more cotton balls, tongue depressors and giant Q-tips. I looked into the lower cabinets and low and behold... syringes.

Hello.

"I got some," I yelled back into the store.

He didn't respond.

"I said, I got some." As I walked back through my path of destruction, I shoved one of the syringes deep into my left boot, making sure the needle cap was tightly screwed on. When I was positive that I had it hidden well enough, I peered my head around the corner.

"Eldritch?" I stepped back out into the store. "Buddy?" I back-stepped so I could see the front of the window. I saw him standing there, reading off of his phone.

I opened up my hand and showed him a bundle of ten or so syringes. "Look, I found them."

He closed the window and then headed back into the enclosed room.

So I had syringes and cotton; I needed to find some kind of safety pin or paper clip to stir the mixture around. I walked over to the home utilities aisle and sure enough, right next to the sewing kits and shoe polish were safety pins. I tore open the plastic container and grabbed three, slipping them into my pocket.

The door window opened again and I bolted upright.

Eldritch studied me, then said, "The sun is coming soon. We do not even know where we are going to shelter ourselves this day. Please stop playing pass the slipper and come help us find Paulina the medication she needs."

I grinned. "What the fuck is pass the slipper?"

He slammed the window shut again.

My finger shook as I surveyed the Rx shelves. My eyes were tired and strained from the darkness of the store. I was also dehydrated and completely burnt out. The habit of rubbing my eyes was only making things worse.

"RJ?" Eldritch whispered from a couple of aisles in the back. "Have you found anything yet?"

I squinted. "I'm having a difficult time seeing anything." I didn't want to alert him that I was beginning to feel the hunger for heroin. I figured it best that he stayed in the dark, thinking that my body was continuing to break down all the poor man and angel dust that wasn't so easily metabolizing inside of me. My insides were all contorted from the different flavors of shit and they made my shaking and withdrawal more about desperation than weakness. A kid in a candy store? More like a street rat in an outhouse. I needed to be on top of my murdering game. The Gooch tried to keep me alert.

A weak vampire is a dead vampire.

I dragged my fingernail across the ribbed plastic top of a bottle. "I can't see shit!"

Eldritch's flashlight suddenly beamed into my eyes from the end of the aisle. I jumped, startled by the brightness and then lifted my hand in from of me as a shield. "Come on, dude."

He dropped the light to his side, grabbed Pinball's hand and headed toward me.

"Jesus, Eldritch."

He put his finger under my chin and studied my pupils. "Are you able-bodied? You seem extremely rattled and agitated."

"I'm rattled." I flicked his finger away. "In the past few days, I have been through an obstacle course of lunacy."

He continued to study my eyes.

I blinked several times and rolled my eyes around. "I'm fine. We just need to get the kid her meds and then drop her off at this dude's house."

"We will still require the aid of the Sixth Street Skulls," he reminded me.

"And what happens if this other gang has no idea who he is either?" I spit on my fingers a little bit and rubbed it across my eyelashes. "We could just dump her outside the fire station."

Eldritch shushed me as he signaled toward Pinball. Thankfully, she was yawning and not paying attention to our conversation. He pulled her toward him and adjusted her wig. "We agreed," he declared.

My eyes were really starting to hurt. The power of the flashlight in my eyes right after I had been squinting for a half hour didn't agree with my vision. "Why is that? The fire station is a get out of jail free card. Druggy mothers do it every day. It's pretty close to what my piece of shit rock star mother did for me."

A tired and cranky Pinball batted away his hand from her head. "Leave it alone," she said.

He continued. "That is exactly what I worry about."

I shook the bottle of pills in my hand. "I'm not following."

"Simply put, I do not know how saturated The Cloth and their alliances are entrenched into the Austin police and fire departments."

"Goddammit, Eldritch!" I tossed the bottle behind my head. "How fucking deep does this thing go? That priest back in L.A. who kidnapped me, Fat Mac, told me that there are vamps and churches involved in this thing everywhere, but he never said anything about there being several chapters of The Cloth. Are they like the Freemasons?"

He tucked Pinball to his side, covering one of her ears with his hip and the other with his palm. "I suspect that we are being policed in all cities."

I shook my finger in his face. "This is ridiculous."

He handed me a flashlight and headed back to his aisle with Pinball latched onto the strap of his jacket. I wanted to wink at her but she turned away too quickly. Probably for the best; old men who kill parents and then wink are creeps.

I tapped the power button on the light. I was supposed to find oxycodone or, if couldn't locate that, I was looking for any other opioid.

DON't forget About me.

I stood in front of a wall of different chemical compounds. It was overwhelming for someone like me whose knowledge of drugs was limited to what was cut with baby laxatives or aspirin before I sold it. In my race to find the narcotics first, I came to the realization that everything in front of me was pre-mixed. I shot the flashlight around to survey the room under the observation window and saw a bunch of crates filled with drugs prepared for pickup. I ran over, licked my fingers and started flipping through the envelopes.

In the first crate, I finally came across a prescription for OxyContin, as well as Percocet. They were, for my purposes, the same thing. I ripped open the envelope on the Oxy and stuffed it into the front of my pants, where it slid down to the top of my boot. I shifted and it slipped between my sock and the lip of the leather. I placed the Percocet on the counter for Pinball.

ONe for Her. ONe for me.

I shoved my open envelope under the crate to hide it and then went back to flipping thought the scripts as quickly as possible. I heard Eldritch and Pinball making their way to the end of their aisle.

More.

I had been judging their progress by listening to Eldritch's squeaking creepers. It was a great way to track their movement.

Hurry.

I proceeded to the next crate. I started flipping through them faster, and I was in luck. I found another envelope with Acetaminophen, another pain reliever from the royal opioid family.

"Excellent idea, RJ," Eldritch acknowledged. He was directly behind me. I looked up to the top crate. I saw the corner of my hidden envelope sticking out. Hopefully, he couldn't see it from his perspective above me.

I pointed to the Percocet on the counter and then handed him the Acetaminophen. "Yeah," I began. "This is what I've found so far. Not a goldmine, but not bad either." I returned to flipping through the envelopes so he wouldn't see the deception in my eyes. I knew he would most likely resort to frisking me if I didn't appear busy and helpful.

"This isn't exactly what we are looking for, RJ," he pointed out after reading the contents of the envelopes.

I scratched the side of my face and continued to sift through the third crate. "It is what it is. I guess most people pick up their meds the same day they turn in their prescription."

Thankfully, I found another oxy envelope near the end of the crate. I turned it around over the back of my head so he could see it.

Eldritch yanked the package out of my hand. "Indeed."

I shuffled around some more to make sure that my bottle was fully secured and undetectable. "Well, at least we got something." I straightened out and yawned as I stood up. I brushed off my pants and I looked at him, waiting for his approval.

He once again surveyed all three of my gifts and then down to Pinball. "Are you positive that this is all?"

I put up my hands.

Eldritch handed Pinball the envelopes. "Here you are, Little One." He unstrapped his satchel from around his shoulder and laid it next to her feet. "Please put them inside this bag."

He patted her on the head and then turned to face me as I handed her the Dora the Explorer backpack.

Eldritch scratched his chin and continued to fixate on my eyes.

I put my arms up in the air. "What? Are you going to frisk me now, officer?"

In a split second, he plunged his hand at my pelvis and slid it against my nuts, around my ass and then down my legs. He didn't bother to look down. If I was hiding something in that area, he would have discovered it right away. I looked down at him molesting me and Pinball caught my eye. Her mouth fell open as the backpack fell out of her hands.

"M-M-Mister Eldritch," she stuttered and her tremoring finger pointed behind me.

"Are the bags inside my bag?" he asked.

"*Mister Eldritch!*" she screamed.

Eldritch let go of me and we spun around to the front of the pharmacy. There were quivering shadows on the other side of the bulletproof glass that separated the store from drugs.

Shaking and starting to hyperventilate, Pinball lifted up her flashlight. At first, the light beamed back into my eyes off the glass, and I reached to veil my face from the blinding glare. Eldritch smacked the light from her hand, picked her and the knapsack up, and secured her on his shoulders.

As I put my hand down, I saw a sea of ragged overalls leading to the spastic and jarring zombified faces of the McCoys. Their shadows were hyena convulsions throughout the store. Front and center on the other side of the glass was Smiley. He winked at me as the rest raised their pickaxes, shovels, bats, sickles, and whatever other farm tools they had armed themselves with.

Smiley took a step toward the glass and started giggling. His foul teeth and gums were exposed all the way up to his eyes. One of them was nearly unlatched from his face, bubbled and moseying, bouncing off his rotted cheekbone as he laughed. He vomited blood into his hand. With his finger, he drew a smiley face in blood and teeth on the glass. He beamed from ear to ear, the Sunshine drug devouring all the skin on the lower half of his face. Bloody bone and a checkerboard between teeth and missing teeth were all that remained.

Eldritch bent down and grabbed his satchel and then instantly jumped toward the exit in back. I stood still, shocked, when all of the McCoys rushed in toward the glass and started beating on it with their farmhand weaponry. Within seconds, a siren wailed and a red security light began whirling near the entrance. I dodged sideways on my left ankle and reached to lock the security door. I wasn't as much securing us from the pounding threat as giving us a few more seconds to escape. My mind scrambled to make sure I had all the key ingredients to get high hidden on me. Cotton. Syringe. Oxy. I always have a lighter. I didn't get a spoon.

Eldritch rushed back to grab me. Pinball shrieked like any kid would, drowning out the sound of the alarm system. Tears, spit, and snot gushed from her face. She hyperventilated and mashed her whole upper body into Eldritch's shoulder.

I slapped Eldritch away. "Go, motherfucker!"

He hesitated when one of the hillbilly demons struck the glass with a digging tool. It stuck into the barrier, which began splintering in every direction. As he pulled it out, the wood handle came loose from the metal spade. Five McCoys that were riding on the shoulders of five others followed up and started pounding around and on the spade with sledgehammers. As the plastic glass boundary split everywhere, large chunks started falling to the ground, nearly slicing the top of my foot off. An opening in the middle of the glass grew into a gigantic hole and it ushered in a mildew death stench.

Fuck the spoon.

I spiraled left and headed toward the exit. Not that it would do any good, but I threw one of the shelves to the ground behind me to buy a few seconds' lead. Then, like a dumb teenage girl running from a slasher movie slayer, I slipped on Pinball's flashlight and tumbled forward. My nose slammed into the linoleum below and blood gushed into my mouth. My heart jumped into my throat.

Get it together, RJ, I told myself. *These guys are a bunch of stupid, fucking hicks.* Truth be told, they may have only been an army of roaches, but I was a one-legged ant at the moment.

Trying to ignore the absolute horror closing in on me, I tried to get back to my feet only to have my right pant leg snag on a sharp piece of metal. Like an idiot, I turned around to see the McCoys lifting and launching each other up to the hole like they were in a mosh pit. From all sides, they packed into the opening and tore at the hole. Flesh from their arms and legs tugged loose and slipped from their bones. They didn't seem to care if they lost body parts. They were filthy, rabid insects, and they were hungry.

I tugged on my jeans and somehow managed to rip them loose directly below my knee. I pushed myself up and shot toward the back.

"The girl is going with *The Matrix* one," Smiley yelled.

I continued to drop the shelves on the left and right behind me. Pills and powders filled the air. As I turned a corner into the stock room, I saw the tail from Eldritch's trench coat flap through a door in back. I picked up the pace by taking longer strides. The sounds of pill bottles popping open and being crushed by the McCoys's work boots let me know that the collapsed shelves served more as trampolines than interference. I heard their wheezing as they bit their tongues off and swallowed.

"She's mine, y'all dumbfucks," one of them hollered.

They wanted Pinball.

"I'm gonna get her and fuck 'er good," another returned. "*He* din't say we couln't fuck 'er. He just said we coun't kill 'er."

I closed in on the door. The sign above it read: NO EXIT. ROOF ACCESS ONLY.

I shoved the door open and jumped onto the fourth step. Although I didn't have any time to reflect, I couldn't help but find it weird that these assholes didn't have any interest in looting the pharmacy. They just wanted Pinball.

As I stubbed my toe on the sixth stair, the Oxy fell out of my untied boot. I turned to see the prescription bottle descending like a slinky back toward hell.

GO bAcK.

I tumbled backward after the Oxy. I crashed into the bottom of the stairwell on my back, my legs pushing the door back open.

Halfway to unconsciousness, I felt all around the floor. I found the bottle and looked up to see the first of the predators breaking around the corner. I desperately reached toward the knob on the slowly closing door, not wanting to see the sadistic roach advancing. I licked at the cartilage from my nasal septum that became unglued when I fell on my face, only to realize that I was breathing so hard that I was hissing wildly. With blood bursting through the middle of my face like a busted water gun, I prepared myself for battle.

"I found the gay one," he hollered back to the rest of the clan. He tore off the straps on his overalls, revealing his ribcage bursting through the sores that were bullseyes for his Sunshine abuse.

I embedded my fingernails into the flashlight, the thick, ribbed plastic crunching in my hand. As he launched himself into the stairwell, I grabbed him by his throat and heaved him over my head, back against the staircase above me. I got to my feet and finally managed to pull the security door shut. He lifted his head off of the stairs, leaving parts of his face merged into the crevasses of the wood. I bashed the flashlight into his skull rapidly until I saw his brain popping through.

The bare feet of the rest of the McCoys slipping and sliding toward me thundered on the other side of the door. Without giving it a second thought, I lifted my victim's head back by his oily hair and wrenched the front of his face onto the doorknob as if he were a door hanger. Making sure the door was secured from the cyclone on the other side, I broke all his bones backward between the first step and the bottom of the door. Before I had the chance enjoy my handiwork, hoes, pitchforks, machetes, and bats started beating against the door. I shoved the pill bottle into the back of my jeans, securing it inside the top of my ass crack, and rushed for the roof.

I peered my head out from the roof's trap door, only to be face-to-shoe with Eldritch's patent leather Frankenstein boots. For the first time, I was happy to see his shitty fashion statements. I pulled myself through the exit and then kicked the hatch closed. Eldritch dropped two cinder blocks on top of the hatch.

I cupped my hands around my mouth and yelled, "Yeah, you pig-fucking dirt farmers," and then stretched my neck back, hoping to see Eldritch and Pinball giving me a smile and a thumbs up.

The world slowed.

Eldritch reached his arms over his shoulders, locking Pinball onto his body. He licked his finger and whispered, "Run, RJ." He took flight and jumped to the roof of the insurance building next door. I looked beyond his launch point and realized that the roaches were crawling over the side of the building, like they burst out of a nest after some kid kicked in the wall of a condemned house. Lead by the BMX kid, three were already sprinting toward me with their eyes bulging from their faces. They seemed to be moving so quickly that their skin was disintegrating with every step they took.

I clutched onto another cinder block by my feet as I noticed a fist punching through the trap door. I stomped on the door as I slung the block at the leader closest to me. He curled sideways, evading it as it hammered into the chest of the dipshit behind him. His chest imploded as he was launched from the top of the building.

With the BMX bandit on my heels, I bolted for the edge. As soon as I reached it, I jumped and spread my legs like I was walking in the sky in an attempt to clear the gravel filled back lot below. On my way down, I latched on to a flimsy tree limb that slowed my momentum but still broke, dropping me on the rocks I was trying to avoid. The ground tore two layers of skin off my exposed knee and one layer off my covered one.

I imagined that the McRoaches would be defeated on the edge of the building, swearing at each about who was to blame for my dashing escape, but I was wrong. The BMX bandit and another hurled themselves off the building like lemmings.

I tried to kick up dirt and get out of there when the bandit dropped onto my ankle, tripping me. He crept up my back. The feeling of this insect touching me caused goose flesh on my arms. I flipped him over my back, mashed his face into the gravel, and plunged my bloody knee into his chest. Quickly, I unscrewed his head, completely demolishing his neck. The head rolled sideways like he was made of rubber as his body squirted out one last shot of diarrhea.

"Get outta here! *Now!*" one of the McCoys screeched from the roof. I figured they were spooked by my amazing feat of strength until an intense melody of automatic gunfire erupted. The few McCoys who were on my tail stopped in their tracks and looked back to the symphony of their brothers being annihilated. The McRoaches were no longer interested in me, so I started running. Without warning, the entire pharmacy went up with a huge explosion, vaulting flaming figures off of the roof.

As I reached the far tree line behind the demolished store, I turned around one more time to see the living zombies who followed me off the roof gunned down by a legion of assassins in cowboy hats. I jumped through the foliage as I grabbed the Oxy from my ass crack and shook it like a maraca.

"Fan out, y'all. There are more around here," one of the exterminators screamed into a bullhorn.

X1

EXHAUSTED

It's a cliché.

Like many times before, I was a vampire racing against the clock to beat my pending doom at the hands of the blazing sun. Rather than stick around to be mutilated, or worse, captured by the Minutemen like the McCoys, I just ran, desperate for refuge. These clichéd tropes reminded me that time was up at dawn. I wouldn't burst into flames or anything, but it would hurt and I had already managed to destroy my nose and scrape most of the flesh off my knees.

I was sure that Austin hadn't wised up to the tags that we painted on safe houses around L.A. But since the last time I went into one of those places I ended up sucking some hook-handed psycho's cock, I figured maybe that was for the best. We aren't charitable or helpful beings. Finding a place to duck out was much more difficult than you would imagine as cities don't offer homeless people many options to come in from the cold, the rain, the snow, or—as in my case—the sun.

I managed to make my way to a subdivision just outside of downtown Austin called Allendale. It was a straight shot from the world's nicest hood on the east side of Austin. As if I even knew when sunrise was, I looked at my burner phone. Luckily, I was able to hang onto it while being hunted by the McCoys. The goose flesh still hasn't faded from my body ,even though that first beam of light was peeking through the openings between the buildings downtown and making me sweat.

I swung my head back and forth as I ran down a cul-de-sac. I didn't want to invade someone's home because I was too exhausted to kill anyone, and knowing my shit luck, I would have broken into some yokel's kiddie porn studio and end up with a face full of assault rifle. Hiding in a garage was never a great idea, either. It was only a few hours away from the daily work grind. The last thing I wanted—besides sucking on the barrel of a pedophile's gun—would be to fall asleep in the bed of some good ol' boy's pickup so he could parade me around town, directly into the sunlight. I figured I was being honest with myself, and at the risk of making wild generalizations of Texans, I had no interest in testing the limits of southern hospitality to a smelly junky.

I reached the end of the dead end and saw around fifteen similar houses with multiple acres each and relatively long driveways. As I tried to rub the fatigue off my face, I began playing eeny, meeny, miny, moe. All the houses looked the same, so it was beginning to look like a crap shoot for which suburban house was to be my shelter. As I opened my eyes to see the morning's red clouds beyond the tree line, I spotted a bumper sticker on a pickup truck. It read, MY KID SELLS DRUGS TO YOUR HONOR STUDENT.

Bingo. I bet they have heroin.

"Nirvana," I whispered to myself.

In the yard, backed into a tree line, I saw several trailers. On one a blue tarp looked to be covering two jet skis, and I deducted that since it was a weekday, no one would be going to the lake to shred. At least I hoped.

As a ray of light grazed my mutilated nasal cavity, I picked up the pace and hopscotched to the front yard of the house undetected.

I heard a garage door opening next door. "See y'all later," someone yelled.

I lost my balance a little and hit the ground hard, knees first.

"Fuck me."

The drying blood worked as an adhesive and tore away from the denim, taking with it the knee skin that had already healed. Not wanting to stand back upright, I started crawling across the yard toward the trailer. With every knee step, I felt pebbles and twigs piercing the wounds in the middle of my legs, especially the right one. When I reached the plastic, blue oasis, I peeped underneath. As I thought, under the tarp were two rednecked-out neon green Kawasaki water cycles. One of them had a separate, fitted cover, which I immediately decided would be used to wrap around my face if the tarp didn't do a good enough job sheltering me. Between the two jet skis, there was this nice little area where I could stretch out and hopefully get some sleep while I waited out the daylight. It all seemed like an adequate hotel where I could lay low for the day.

I tried to cover my nose with my hand as I rolled my head around and then slid into the gap sideways. Shockingly the owners left a puffy life jacket on the trailer as well. Sure, it smelled like mold and it was nowhere near as comfortable as a pillow but, hey, things were going my way for once. As I tossed around in the gap, I remembered Pinball and Eldritch launching off the drug store roof and hoped that they found shelter as well.

I patted my nose to see if the flesh was starting to come back together and then said, "Oh, fuck him." I didn't even know if Eldritch had an aversion to the sun that wasn't self-diagnosed. Stupid vampire. All of us are so lame. Not even really alive. Created in a lab. Abortions. My real concern should have been whether or not the Minutemen gunned his ass down and captured Pinball. I couldn't even imagine what kind of lab they used to create cretins like the McCoys in. The best thing for everyone seemed to be to get that Sunshine disease off the streets before it crossed over into Austin hipster scene and started being mass produced in the Texas toilet: Mexico.

I untied the jet ski cover, ripped open a small breathing hole, wrapping it around my face. It felt weird on my fucked-up nose but the tarp seemed to be thick enough to protect me from the sun when I needed it. I took it off and rested my head on the life jacket. The tweets of birds bringing Austin to life became relaxing and I quickly dozed off. I had hoped to get twelve to fourteen hours of much deserved sleep.

⚔

I was awakened about an hour or two later when the occupants of the house started carrying on about some bullshit.

"We got a big weekend drop, bro," one said in a thick southern accent. The other snorted. "You know it, bro."

I heard two hands high five. "Text me when you get done with work."

"Awwwwww yeah, bro. I can't even believe I have to work today."

Second high five. Maybe, just maybe, the douchebags in Texas were the same as douchebags everywhere else in the world.

A hand leaned against the tarp, resting on the back of one of the jet ski seats. "What did you do with that babe?" he asked.

I felt my nose and rolled my eyes. It was pretty close to a full heal. Too bad I had been stricken with a brutal headache all of a sudden.

The other chuckled as he leaned on the other side of the tarp, on to the other back of the other jet ski seat. "Dumped her ass by the interstate." Seriously. They must have been standing close to each other in the exact same stance.

"No shit?"

"Nah. I got her a cab at like three. Kissed her on the cheek."

"Did you fuck her?"

74

The other dude inhaled and took his resting hand off the tarp. "Fuckin' A right."

The other bro's hand left the tarp and the final high five followed. Chivalry. High fives. Possible fist bumps. These are all my favorite ingredients when screening potential friends.

I looked at the clock on my phone. I still had no signal and I realized that these two baboons had just wasted three minutes of my super hearing. Wrapping things up, I imagined them throwing up a couple of shakas and saying *taste* a couple of times before slamming themselves into their pickups and leaving for work.

On my phone display, there was a notification that I had a text from Eldritch. It said:

Battery drained. Safe.

I responded:

Safe. Need sleep. Charge phone.

I pushed send even though I couldn't get a signal.

The good news was that they averted any conflict with the Minutemen and that they made it somewhere out of sight and out of light. Satisfied, I put the phone up on the seat of the jet ski to my right. Then I re-fluffed my life jacket pillow and shut my eyes. I was confident that I would be awaken by the sun-setting breeze and the smell of the night coming to life.

The coarseness of whiskers brushed my cheek. I shooed them away. Nothing was going to wake me up from my dry out slumber. Besides, it seemed like minutes before that, my ears were being assaulted by the twanging air horns of the Austin High Fivers Club. I felt the whiskers again and I heard something sniffing me. *Rodent.*

My eyes beamed open as I licked the roof of my mouth. I was face-to-face with an opossum who was using its front legs to prop itself onto one of the jet ski's footboards. I didn't how long it had been observing me but I knew I had invaded its home.

I curled my index finger like a puppet to talk to it. "Hey there, buddy."

It inched a little closer and sniffed again. Then it batted his eyelashes over its black, little eyes. I pulled back a little. For the most part, domestic animals liked vampires because we gave off a scent like we're dead. I had never really rolled the dice with other animals, outside of the rats I that used to consume and get high off of on Skid Row. Rats weren't dangerous—outside of transmitting plagues and disease—in that they were easy to catch and never really fought. The fact of the matter was that

I had never seen an opossum up close. Even though it looked cute enough, I tried to limit my movement, as well as quiet my voice.

I squinted my left eye and continued my puppetry. "Is this your house, little buddy?"

It ducked down and then got on its hind legs to sniff my moving finger. It was so close that I started to get concerned so I backed up as far as I could and pressed my spine against the jet ski behind me. I steadied my finger as it seemed to be more interested in it than my face.

I let out a calming breath. "I'm not here to mess up your stuff."

A pencil thin ray of sunlight zipped through an eyelet on the tarp, reminding me that my best-case scenario was to have my new friend quickly learn the meaning of the word *share*. It turned around to look behind it and then turned back to lick some blood off my finger. I felt the mushed bag of Combos in my pocket. Perhaps a nice peace offering would make my check-in go a little easier.

I shuffled my free hand down slowly toward it. The snacks crunched around onto the floor of the trailer as I attempted to maneuver my hips enough to get into my pocket. I accidentally bumped into the jet ski supporting my back a little harder than I would have liked, sending my precious bottle of Oxy clanking and shaking from the top of my thigh onto the metal trailer. In the moment, I shushed the bottle as I tried to grab and silence it with the hand extended to the critter.

That was when all fucking hell broke loose.

The opossum curled its nose, scrunched back its head and let out an enormous "*Hsssssssss!*" Unlike a rat, this wingless bat had inch-long knives for teeth. The top of its tongue rolled around its mouth like a semi-translucent cavern. The varmint was hungry, and Combos were not going to satisfy it. I stared at the blue tarp approximately three and a half feet from my face. A light blue circle in the center of the tarp told me that the sun was directly overhead. I was trapped.

I looked at the bottle of Oxy and then into the eyes of the opossum.

Let's get high.

"Hey, little buckaroo."

As I jammed the pill bottle back into my pocket and shot my back straight, I snatched some dock rope from the seat of the jet ski behind me. I heard my phone fall off onto the outside rim of the trailer.

Without batting its eyes again or hissing, the opossum let out a fierce rumble and leapt onto my face. I didn't realize it until it started burrowing those claws into my cheeks that this little asshole had crazy monkey hands.

I made the second strike. I grabbed it under its arms and pushed my fingers into its armpits. Feeling the pain, it started to loosen the grip on my face. Unfortunately for me, a claw that had bored into my temple was stuck. Stuck to my face and in pain, the agitated mega-rat began snipping at the tip of my nose with the short bridge of Chiclet teeth in front of its snout. Then, by focusing all its weight into its mid-section, it unhooked its claw from my head. Able to move around more freely, it sunk its fangs into my thumb.

I dropped the animal, slicing my thumb right down the center. "Motherfucker!" I cried.

I shoved my thumb into my mouth to suck in the blood. It might as well have filled the fresh wound with lighter fluid. I snapped it back out and captured the opossum's paw. I bent it backwards, and as I snapped it, I felt it go limp. The creature's hisses and growls turned to squeals as I did the same to its other arm. With my free hand, I began securing the opossum to the fiberglass gas tank. It squirmed for a bit but I had officially gotten the upper hand as I started hog-tying it to the tank and around the handlebars with the dock rope.

"That's right. You're gonna get me high."

I had secured it on its stomach with its legs pinned to the tank. It let out a last squeal and then went silent. I blew into its face to see if it was playing 'possum. It sneezed back.

I managed to nab one of the bricks outside from under the tarp. It was a great thing that the homeowners went to work or school, because the commotion going on with the opossum and the fact that my head was now propping up the tarp like a teepee were both red flags that screamed TRESPASSER. I started mashing up the Oxy.

I looked over at the opossum as I pushed the brick onto the pills. "You don't have an Amex, do you?" It sniffed twice and then went back to pretending it was dead. I pried open the seat compartment on the jet ski slightly and dug through some suntan lotion, the keys to the vehicle on what felt like a floaty keychain and some condoms until I hit pay dirt: a laminated boating license. I pulled it out as I noticed the opossum sneakily gnawing on the rope. I blew in its face again. Its eyes closed.

I put the license under the small beam of light coming through the eyehole and squinted to see the shit-eating grin of the face behind my high-fiving cowboy. "Cody Walker, huh? Well, Cody, you will be preparing my opiates today." I sat with my legs around my drugs and began cutting and sifting the powder with the license.

Pleased with myself and happy with the results, I looked around for my tools. The nabbed syringe from the Sixty-Second Clinic. Check. I tapped on my left front pocket. Sweet, my lighter was still there. I drew my finger across the fuel lever and up came a flame. Check on fire. Finally, I dug into my pants and pulled out the cotton that I stashed under my balls.

Check. It was a little moist but that didn't really matter. I had everything.

SPOON.

I forgot the fucking spoon. Dammit.

I put the tools on the seat of the jet ski and crawled toward the rear of the trailer, feeling around on the ground, hoping to find something—anything—to replace the important final utensil. No luck. I crawled back to the compartment on the opossum's vehicle and dragged my hand from front-to-back and side-to-side. There was nothing in there but a moldy, stinky ass wetsuit that some moron hadn't hung out to dry.

I coughed from inhaling the airborne bacteria. "Fuck me!" Nearly defeated, I returned to my little seat in the middle of the trailer.

I looked at the opossum. "Any ideas?" I waited for an answer, briefly. "Of course not."

Hurry uP.

I was getting twitchy and I scratched at my arms. The Gooch wanted results. I looked to the back of the trailer again and then I covered every inch of the ground with my palms down. There had to be something. When I reached the end and I was seconds away from slapping myself in the face, my fingertips caught something, the solid chrome tailpipe of the jet ski. My dead heart skipped a beat. It was a relatively thin chrome pipe. Thankfully, it didn't have any black powder coating on it.

I quickly crept back to the mid-section of the trailer and delicately swept the Oxy onto the face of the boating license, making sure as little as possible remained on the floor. Then I put the syringe in my mouth and held the lighter under my chin.

When I reached the rear of the trailer this time, I bent up the license into the exhaust and poured the Oxy inside. My mission was to spread it evenly into a thin coat near the center of the cylinder. I tied the brick to another piece of dock rope that was intended to tie the tarp onto the trailer and then shoved it off the tailgate, giving me a little air duct to expel smoke while I was cooking. I didn't want to overwhelm myself with the fumes from the butane lighter and the burning narcotic. Without letting my body fall into the sunlight, I twisted around the trunk of the jet ski so I could light the pipe from underneath and watch the cook as it dissolved. To keep my dinner from getting thick and lumpy, I pulled one of the safety pins out of my pocket.

I fired up the lighter under the pipe and began moving the Oxy powder around with the pin. It took a while but through trial and error my feast turned to a syrup as it began bubbling. Once I got it to a nice consistency, I freed up my stirring hand and nabbed one of the cotton balls sitting in my lap. Using a combination of my teeth and my fingers, I tore off a light piece and lightly rolled it to the size of Junior Mint. As the caramelized mound became less dense and dirty looking, I place my little cotton ball in the center. Instantaneously, the cotton absorbed the creamy contents of the chrome pipe. I dropped the lighter and licked my lips.

I cracked my neck, inhaled and pushed the needle into the center of my goop. As I sucked the Oxy into the barrel with the plunger, I let out a huge breath of relief and scratched my hair. I looked over at the opossum. It squirmed around a little. I knew it was in pain. I filled the syringe to the brim and then squirted out any air that might have made its way into the mixture.

As I started to make my way back toward the center of the trailer, I closed my eyes. To me, humans were much easier to kill and use are paraphernalia than animals. Humans had big mouths.

I hated my conscious. It was always in a tug of war with The Gooch. The funny thing being that The Gooch never made its way into my delightful dreams. Hell when I slept. Hell when I was awake.

When I reached the critter, I opened my eyes, lifted the needle back and sunk it directly into where I imagined an opossum's heart would be. Almost immediately, the rodent's body started to reject the drug. It desperately tried to break loose of the rope as its broken arms dangled around. It began going into cardiac arrest when I pulled the needle out and pushed its head to the side to secure myself from the piercing fangs. I closed my eyes again and then dug my face directly into its chest cavity. At first the taste was one hundred percent gamey vermin, but by the time I chewed my way through its ribcage into its heart, the taste was eclipsed by the delicious opiates at the center.

After less than ten seconds, the struggle ended. I snapped its neck to make sure it didn't suffer any more than it had to and I tumbled backward into the jet ski with a palm full of guts. In the middle of losing my motor skills, I grabbed the life vest and tried to cover my prey. I missed and the vest bounced back into my lap. I sat there for a few minutes, shoving innards into my mouth catching my head from collapsing into slumber several times before I finally started to nod off. And then, I heard several small rattles and clicks. Before my eyelids closed and everything went black, six little pink noses crawled and bumped from their slumber. I threw up on myself and fell into hibernation as the orphaned babies desperately fought to slip under what was left of their mother to feed.

I woke up hours later when it was dark and realized what I had done.
To be honest, I didn't know how old the babies were and I didn't know
how long they needed to be fed by their mother. While I slept, a few of
them managed to slip under their mother's back. Opossums are, after all,
marsupials, and they keep warm inside a pocket on their mother's belly.
Since she was cold and dead and not able to feed, I tried to collect them
all and warm them inside the compartment on the non-moldy jet ski. I tore
my life vest pillow into pieces and built the best nest that I could.

My ears picked up prowling steps close to the trailer. The steps were
so faint, so carefully orchestrated, that they sounded like the pitter-patter
of a light rain on leaves. I closed the improvised opossum nest inside the
console but left it open just enough so the babies wouldn't suffocate. I sat
still, quickly realizing that whatever animals were surrounding me outside
smelled the remains of the opossums' mother that had been baking under
a tarp in the hot Texas sun for hours. I scooted on my ass toward the back
of the trailer and cut the dock rope that was tied to the brick. No need to
give any creature easy access.

I shuffled back to the center and pulled my legs to my chest. It
occurred to me that I was still relatively close to downtown Austin. How
could it be that a pack of animals would make it so close to civilization?

Before I arrived at an answer, several snouts bumped up against and
starting tearing at the tarp. The beasts started to yap. They were dogs. I
started karate chopping and kicking in every direction. I looked back to
the jet ski compartment that housed the orphans. The mongrels smelled
the mother, but they would end up wanting the babies.

Reluctantly getting back into action and riding out the final few drips of my high, I rolled back to the front, dragging the tarp from under the bricks. When I was right on the edge, I grabbed onto the hitch and launched myself off the trailer. I dug my feet into the grass, stood strong and readied my body for the pending strike. As if nearly having my eyeballs removed from my head by the opossum mother earlier that day wasn't enough man versus wild for the day, now I had to fight off a gang of beasts.

I clenched my fists and bent my arms forward. The first of the four Pit Bulls jumped onto the jet ski and ripped the dead mother from the seat. It shook the skeletal remains around in its jaws, trying to get at any meat that remained. As the two closest hounds sketchily prowled to size me up on both sides, the fourth leapt onto the seat of the other jet ski, clicking the compartment shut. He lowered his muzzle, sniffed at the little treats inside and started pawing at the seat cushion. The hair on his shoulders all the way down to his tail raised as he squealed a little to report his frustration. His brother on jet ski tossed the mother's bones to my feet. The dog on top of the babies started slashing into the seat cover with his teeth and his brother joining in on getting to the delightful center.

The twins walked back and forth like they were skinheads. They never took their eyes off of me. Rather, they yipped at each other as if they were having a conversation about how they were going to take me down. Their conversation ended and before I had the opportunity to secure my position, the twins both catapulted themselves at me.

The dog on my left jumped toward my top as the other took my legs, tripping me up. I smacked onto the ground and immediately threw my arms over my head like I was in a hockey fight. The heavier of the two bit into my side below my ribcage. I rolled on top of him, trapping his snout under the weight of my chest. As the other bit into my leg, I hammer-fisted him between the eyes, causing him to lose his balance and slump back on his hind legs. I nabbed the dog under me and cradled his neck as I mashed him into my forearm. He snapped at my cock as his dizzy, chicken shit of a brother got his bearings back.

Before the hound I was wrestling with had the chance to bite my pork and beans off, I snatched him up by the loose skin under his chin and, as I got to my feet, I lifted him up over my head and threw him back toward the cul-de-sac. He yelped as his butt crunched into a big rock on the side of the driveway. Obviously bruised, he started licking at his hind quarters.

The dizzy dog bolted toward me, growling. I flopped onto my back to brace myself and as soon as he was on top of me, I boxed his ears with my knees, pulled back my fist and struck him three times on the nose. He became unsteady and went limp in my lap and started panting as his eyes jerked around looking for an exit. I released him, he kicked his paws into the air and then staggered to his brother, who was still licking himself by the rock. He nudged his brother and they both scampered away toward the tree line on the other side of the house.

The two on the trailer continued to bite, thrash, lick, and paw at the jet ski compartment. I started running around the trailer in circles, howling and creating commotion like an insane person. I picked up a brick and threw it at them. Luckily, they took this as my last warning and started rushing to join the rest.

"That's right, motherfuckers! Get outta here!"

One of them stopped in their tracks as the other continued. He turned around to look back at me. He stuck out his tongue and panted a bit as he wagged his tail. When I realized that he wasn't going to give up on eating the delicious babies, they came together, regrouped and immediately began charging me.

BAM!

BAM!

BAM!

All four turned one hundred and eighty degrees, falling over their own speed and fled back toward the tree line. My head bobbled around on top of my neck. The two owners of the jet ski trailer were running toward me, clanging on pots and pans. All of the dogs escaped and hid out of sight. One of them managed to escape with the remains of the mother opossum. They were most likely going to pass out if they shared that meal that was filled with drugs.

I pulled a long strand of fabric from my severed right pant leg and sat down on the tailgate of the trailer. I clinched my body and pulled up my ragged shirt to look at the bite wound below my ribs. The two men stopped in front of me and whispered to each other.

I picked a tooth out of my side and flicked it into the grass. I put up my hand as to acknowledge peace. "Thanks."

If the opossum and the Oxy had given me any strength at all, it was completely depleted by that point. I took several deep breaths and closed my eyes to relax and collect my simple little thoughts for a minute. I opened them up and casually looked back at the nest I constructed for the babies. It looked as if the pack had penetrated the seat cushion enough to give them air. The refreshment of the moonlight pulsated my eyes as I closed them again. The slap, slap of two pairs of flip flops inched closer to me.

My head fell to my chest. *Please don't be vampires. Please don't be vampires. Please don't be vampires.*

"Hey, bro," one of them said. "What the fuck?"

I looked at them but didn't respond and rubbed my eyes with my thumbs.

"He's talking to you," the other spat as he kicked at one of my boots.

"Yeah, bro." I recognized him as Cody Walker from the license.

I continued to remain silent. Before I could let them know that I didn't appreciate being kicked, a pistol cocked. I dropped my hands off of my face and opened my right eye. I sniffed up some blood that was trickling from my reformed nostrils. "You have a gun?"

I opened my other eye to see Cody's pal turn the six-shooter sideways. The chamber was loaded.

"Fuck yeah, I got a gun, bro," he boasted as he kicked at my other boot. "Answer me. What the fuck?"

I lifted my tattered shirt to reveal the bite marks. "If you had a gun this whole time, why didn't you help me with the dogs when they were tearing me to fucking shreds?"

Walker stepped forward. "We don't want any cops around here. Those are my guard dogs."

The friend laughed and slapped Cody on the back. "Word up, bro," he shouted louder than any gun. His face was beat red and his nostrils flared wide and narrowed about ten times.

Hello, cocaine.

I rose up. "Look guys. I don't want any trouble."

Cody sized me up. "Well, you found it. You trying to steal our sleds?"

I stepped closer to him. "Sleds?"

The other dude stepped between us. "Yeah, douche. The fucking jet skis." He pointed to the trailer behind me. "They're totally ruined, old man." A light powder dusted his nose hairs. If they had coke, then they might have heroin. If they had heroin, then I could probably get into their house and steal it. Maybe I'd kill them for kicking my boots and yelling at me.

"No, bro," I said, attempting to communicate in their language. "I wasn't trying to steal your jet skis. I was out all day getting wasted and I got lost." I pulled out the rest of the Oxy and shook the bottle. "I did too much of these kickers."

He popped the collar on his Polo knit shirt and pulled up his board shorts. "Whatcha got there? Penicillin?"

Cody followed suit and also pulled up his same brand, different colored board shorts. They were both laughing in unison. "Yeah, Penicillin. Do you have the sniffles or something?" A fist bump followed.

I tossed the friend the bottle. "It's OxyContin, guys."

Cody intercepted the bottle and signaled for his friend to ease up. He read the side of the bottle and tossed it back to me.

The gunman un-cocked his firearm and tucked it into the back of his shorts. "Hey," he said. "Sorry about that." He hesitated but then started to extend his hand.

I reached toward him. "Yeah, man. I was stumbling down your street when I passed out on your trailer. Then, your dogs attacked me. Think I was too wasted to realize where I was when I woke up."

He curled his fingers back from the shake and walked past me. Concern grew in his tone as he circled the trailer. "Fuck, bro."

"Is she there, Braxton?" Cody pushed me aside as he also started analyzing the trailer. "There's blood everywhere."

"Wait, is who there?" I asked.

Braxton spun around hysterical. "Possie. It was our pet opossum. She just had babies. Goddammit!"

I played dumb. "They got her. I'm not sure where the babies are."

"Bullshit. Those dogs are terrified of her, bro." Cody hopped up on the trailer and immediately noticed the demolished seat cushion. He flipped it open. "They're here. It looks like Possie built them a special nest inside the jet ski to keep them safe. Man is she smart."

Even though it was ridiculous to consider that an opossum could open the compartment under the seat of a jet ski, tear up a life vest and create a bed inside and then carefully move each of her babies into it, I didn't take credit.

"Braxton," he yelled. "Go get a small box out of the garage."

Braxton did as he was told and sprinted toward the garage.

"What can I do?" I asked.

"Get up here and help me."

I walked up onto the trailer and he started delicately handing me the babies one-by-one. "Cradle them together," he insisted.

Braxton came running back and headed toward original nest.

The babies remained asleep, despite all the commotion. "Have you guys done this type of thing before?"

Concurrently, they both responded *yes* as if saving opossums was everyone's civic duty.

Cody placed the last baby into my arms and pet it on the head. "Bro, you reek. Are you, like, homeless or something?" He looked into my eyes out of concern, although I figured he was way more concerned about the baby opossums than me.

I tried to deflect attention away from me and to Braxton. "Is that nest ready?"

He ripped off his Lake Travis embroidered knit top—as if it was in his way—and slobbered. "I'm going as fast as I can, bro."

Cody grabbed me by the back of my shirt and walked me slowly around to the side. Then, he started plucking the opossums out of my arms and cautiously planted them into the box nest. He picked up the box and race-walked like he was in a picnic egg run over to one of the pickup trucks. He opened the passenger's side door, pulled up the seat and gently laid the box onto the backseat.

Braxton ran to the truck and handed Cody his gun. "Keep this," he said. He then walked to the driver's side, cranked on the ignition, slammed the door and rolled down the window. "Call Whitley and tell her what's going on, bro." Then, he spun the truck around and peeled out of the gravel driveway.

Cody and I stood there watching the taillights disappear.

"Who's Whitley?" I asked.

"Oh right," he returned. "You fucking smell, bro." He pulled his phone out of his back pocket, unlocked it and searched for her name.

Phone. That's right. My phone fell off the trailer. I walked away from him and acted like I was studying the damage.

He snapped his fingers at me and pointed to the ground in front of him.

I raised my eyebrows and nodded back as I stepped on my phone. I bent down and picked it up to show him that I wasn't up to no good. He nodded back in approval as if my retrieving my phone was something that needed to be sanctioned.

I walked back to the tailgate of the trailer and took my seat.

He raised the gun back out and walked toward me. "Get up." I raised my arms up and complied. He shook the gun toward the side of the house. "Walk over there."

Even though I thought for a second that he wanted to take me to the side of the house to put a bullet in my head, I decided that these two pussies wouldn't kill anyone. I mouthed *Put the gun away* as he pressed the phone against his ear.

"Oh right." He laid the gun down on the trailer. "Whitley. It's Cody Walker. BroSkiz." He paused for a second. "Oh, yeah, my name comes up." He paused again, most likely to get an earful about being stupid. "Brax is on his way over there." He waited again and then bent over at the side of the house to turn on a spigot. He signaled for me to turn around and he picked up a hose gun. "I don't know if he has your blow with him. Possie was killed by the dogs."

I took off my shirt, lifted my arms and got a whiff of my pits. Damn, this guy wasn't kidding. I smelled awful.

"No, the babies are alive. He's bringing them to you now." The freezing hose water pulsed into my back. "I don't know how you're supposed to get into the rescue. Call the doctor," he responded. "Turn around," he instructed me. "Not you," he told Whitley. He aimed the nozzle at my cock and fired it.

"Careful on my dick," I warned him.

"Oh yeah," he said first and then, "No, I'm not having sex with a guy," to Whitley. "I'm washing down some bum who passed out on one of my trailers." He stepped around me and started fanning water all over my body. Thankfully, he was careful on the wounds. "Brax should be there in like ten minutes. I gotta go." Before he hung up the phone he said, "Fine, the coke is free if you help the babies."

Cody took a final pass at me and then turned off the hose.

I rubbed the water into my body and tried to get all the dirt off the wounds. "So, Whitley is a doctor?"

"Naw, she is some cokehead who works at the Austin Wildlife Rescue. She steals prescription drugs for us and trades them for blow."

I dug into my side with my fingernail and pulled out another tooth particle. "So, does this type of thing happen regularly?"

He scratched his nose. "What?"

I spit out some animal hair. "Your dogs attacking people?"

I don't think he understood the question. It was pretty obvious that these two knuckleheads needed four Pit Bulls to protect something, and the last thing they wanted was someone bitten by one of their dogs and a call to the cops.

"Fuck. You still stink." He headed back to the spigot.

I followed him toward the house and played to the dog bite in my side. "Is there any chance I can use a shower? Clean up this wound and maybe get some clothes."

He waited a second before turning the water back on. "I don't know. You're like all homeless and shit."

I shook the Oxy bottle in my hand. "I'll give you this." I had no intention of giving him my precious opiates and I figured that this could be my ticket inside.

He took his hand off the faucet crank and stood up. "We should wait for Brax to get back."

I pointed to the lacerations on my ribs and my leg. "Come on, man. I need to fix this up."

He pulled the gun back out. "Yeah, okay, bro. But I've got, like, my eye on you."

I started to head toward the door. "Fine. You want to watch me shower?"

He started following me to the front of their house. "No way, bro."

XIII

SAVED

I let the warm water pound against the laceration under my ribs and pissed all over my feet in the shower. My urine was darker than the water and it smelled like the back of a garbage truck. My body felt like it wanted to open up and dump all unmetabolized drugs inside of me down the drain. My spine creaked as I tried to clean in-between my toes. I put my mouth up to the shower head and slurped until I felt full. The water quality in Austin was shockingly sweet, compared to the mud that we Angelinos had become accustomed to during the never-ending droughts.

I was surprised that my host let me take a shower. He was probably scared I would sue him for the dog attack. I also knew that he was no match for me, even with his gun. When he sent me upstairs, he patted me on the back and called me *friend*. I knew he was sucking up to me because his Pit Bull took a chunk out of my side, but it felt nice for once in my life to be called friend, even if it was because I never told him my name. As a matter of fact, *buddy, pal, Mack, guy,* and *dude* all would have sufficed. He had already called me *bro* over a hundred times, so I wasn't interested in hearing that again.

I scrubbed the new bar of soap he unpackaged for me deep over my skin, trying to get rid of the blood and hide from the McCoys, blood and hair from the opossum mother, and pieces of teeth from the pack.

When I was as satisfied as I could be, I took a quick look outside of the shower curtain. I jumped back a bit. He was in there. Fucking creep. Had I gone into hibernation or were my ears filled with water? Was he a vamp? Either that or I didn't even care at that point if a prowler came in and killed me.

"Can I help you?" I asked.

He laid some clothes down on top of the toilet seat, as well as some peroxide and bandages on the sink. "Sorry, bro." He called me *bro* again. I was really hoping for *Mack*.

"Didn't mean to alarm you, just wanted to give you this stuff. Holler if you need anything else."

I looked at the shower caddy. "Do you have that shampoo and conditioner in the same bottle?"

He laughed. "You can take the extra time to use both. Don't worry. I won't shut off the hot water if you take the time you need."

I snorted up some phlegm and spit into the drain. I closed the shower curtain. "You didn't really need to get me new clothes. I like mine just fine."

As he left the bathroom and closed the door, he returned, "I threw those away. They smelled like a dead person."

If he only knew, I thought.

I opened the shower curtain to see if the Oxy was still on the sink where I left it. I was quick to suspect a switcheroo when he dropped off the bandages. It was still there. I opened up the bottle and checked the contents. Since I had never met a nice person, I always suspected the worst from everyone. So far, this guy wasn't giving me any reason to think he was after me "Lucky Harms".

I took his suggestion and completely cleaned and conditioned my hair. When I was satisfied that it was less gross than usual, I turned off the facet and stepped out of the shower on to a nice, warm and thick shower rug. I sunk my feet into it, enjoying the moment. It might have been the first time something that nice had touched my bare feet. The only shower mat that I had at my old house was ratty and was pitched as soon as Bait had an abortion all over it. Awful shit.

I picked up the jeans. Size thirty-two. There wasn't a bunch of cheesy stitching on the back pockets and they weren't wangster baggy. They were just the way I liked them. I don't know why, but I sniffed them. The denim smelled clean, almost new, so I slipped them on. Then, I grabbed the shirt—that fucking shirt—and observed it. I hadn't noticed when I shimmied on the jeans that it was a tie-dye. I shook it out and read *Keep Austin Weird* in big white letters across the front. I folded it back up nicely and put it back on top of the toilet.

I walked over to the door, opened it and yelled downstairs to my new friend. "Hey, Mack," I called out as I smirked.

"Yeah, bro," he shouted back. "Name's Cody."

"Is this, like, the only shirt you have?"

He paused for a second. "I think so. I don't want the blood on your side to seep through and jack up my good shirts."

I took a look at the bite wound from the dogs. It was nearly healed at that point. "Right," I muttered to myself. I closed the door, locked it and walked back to the sink. "Gotta make this look legit," I whispered.

He had seen the size of the wound when he washed me off with the hose. I didn't need the peroxide, but I poured some down the sink to not raise any eyebrows and then firmly planted an extra-large adhesive bandage horizontally from back to front.

It's not so much that I was trying to trick him as it was a narcotics thing. They make you feel guilty even when you weren't really doing anything wrong. Sure, I had done a lot of things wrong to this guy already, like killing his pet opossum, but he seemed to want to help me. I was injured and needed shelter and he was the closest thing to a do-gooder that I had ever met. And it was pretty clear he didn't want any cops sniffing around his place.

I shook the shirt open in front of me again. "Keep Austin Weird," I read aloud this time. I smelled it as I had with the jeans. Smelled the same. Good. Probably should have smelled weird. After a few seconds debating whether or not I wanted to wear it, I pulled it over my head and looked at myself in the mirror.

"Man. This shirt is lame as shit," I gulped as I rolled my eyes sideways to check out my bloodshot level.

Before I left the bathroom to formally introduce myself, I opened the mirror in front of me and scoured the medicine cabinet. Tylenol. Q-Tips. Extra toothbrush. Crotch spray. Nothing that was any use to me. The Gooch stayed quiet for the time being.

He pointed to my chest as I sat down at the kitchen table. "Now that's a cool shirt, bro," he joked. Then, as if I hadn't already seen it, he nodded his eyes to his hand, where his six-shooter was resting on the table.

"Ah, yeah. Totally bitchin'," I said acknowledging that he was armed. "Thanks."

His fingernail flicked against the trigger. "You're welcome." I expected him to raise the gun at me and take a couple of shots. He was on to me. Luckily, he pushed the gun off to the edge of the table. "Ha. I'm just fucking with you." He extended his hand to shake. "I'm Cody," he said.

"Arnold Babar," I fired back at him.

His fingers retracted before our hands met. A little grin slipped out of the corner of his mouth. "Two B's?"

Right before I was about to engage in the whole routine, I bit my lip. "You've seen *Fletch*, huh?"

"Of course, bro." His hand deliberated midway between my hand and the gun.

I reached further toward him to sway the decision. "Look, man. My name's RJ." I closed one of my eyes, realizing how ridiculous my name was. "RJ Reynolds." It sounded a hell of a lot more badass when I was fourteen and living on the streets. Like my existence, my name made me cringe and my skin shiver.

"Like that's any more real than Arnold Babar." He met my hand in the middle of the table and shook it. "You from Austin, RJ?"

I released my grip and pointed to the tie-dye. "Of course. Don't all locals wear these?"

He turned his head sideways, still unsure of how the meeting was going. "My mom loves Austin. She doesn't get it."

If I had a mother story to share, other than the story of my mom aborting me into the hands of The Cloth, I would have told it. Instead, I simply said, "Moms. Right? Can't live with 'em. Whores."

He took a drag off of a giant eCig. "I don't know about that, bro."

"Which?"

He tilted his head back and blew out a gigantic cloud of bakery flavored vapor. "That moms are whores."

"Mine was."

He scratched at the grip of the gun. "Mine wasn't."

"Must be an L.A. thing. I'm from L.A.," I admitted.

"Really?" He looked me up and down, trying to sniff the rat out of me. "Yeah, I can see that. You look like an L.A. guy."

We sat in silence, waiting to find something that we had in common when I realized that my phone wasn't in my jeans. I stood up and patted at my pockets. "Phone?" I said.

"Your phone was broken." He pointed over to the counter next to a TV that was on mute. "I took the SIM card out and put in my old phone."

I walked over to the charging outlet. It was a nice phone. Maybe a little too nice.

"Don't worry," he continued. "It's untraceable and jailbroken."

I put the phone down.

He took another pull off his vape. "It'll be charged in like two hours and then you can split. I put some money inside the case." He coughed a little and then blew out another cloud.

I looked toward a window. It was night out still. I could have made a break for it and maybe taken, at most, six bullets to the back. "What do you want? Sex? Do you want mouth sex?" I asked, becoming strangely

90

hysterical.

He re-gripped the gun. "The real question is what do *you* want, L.A. boy."

Even though I didn't have to, I put my hands up. "I don't want anything."

He swung the barrel of the gun upward. "Lift the shirt up."

I rolled my fingers around the bottom hem of the shirt. "Why?"

He lifted the barrel again and then stood up. "I just need to be sure of something."

I slowly scrunched the shirt up to the bandage. "Where's your friend?"

Pointed the barrel at my head. "Braxton? Oh, he's kind of my bitch. He doesn't live here. I'm sure he went over to Whitley's house afterward and they're probably on a bender."

I pointed to the bottom of the bandage.

He gripped the gun handle with both hands. "All the way. All the way up," he insisted. "I'm not dicking around here, bro."

I pulled the side of the shirt to my armpit. "What's going on, Cody?"

He quoted *Fletch* again. "It's nothing of a sexual nature, I assure you."

If I wasn't in the South. If I knew this guy any further than I could throw him. If I had any idea where I was. Then, I would have played along. I slowly peeled the bandage back and revealed the nearly healed bite mark. I ripped off the bandage completely and shrugged my shoulders. I rolled the bandage up into a ball and tossed it underhand onto the kitchen table. "I guess the wound wasn't as bad as we thought."

"You can put the shirt down." He waved the gun down and returned to his seat. "So, I guess you're here to take my drugs? A new gang tries to take control of the coke in Austin and just cuts me out. You know, that's bullshit, bro." He tapped the gun against his head. "Stupid. I shouldn't have made that deal." He took the tank off his vape and started refilling it with a dropper. "It's in the garage. Take it."

I unraveled the shirt and tucked the front into my jeans. "Take what?"

He screwed the tank back onto his battery. "My coke." He pointed to a door that I guessed led to the garage and his stash. "Fucking new L.A. vampire gang comes to town, pushes out the local businesses. Fucking L.A. posers."

I looked to the garage and then back to the kitchen table. "So, you know about vampires?"

"No shit, bro. You took on a pack of guard dogs less than an hour ago and you don't have a scratch on you."

I studied his defeated face and asked point blank. "So, you're a dealer?"

"Cut the game. We both know why you're here. Please don't kill me or whatever. I can't call the cops on you. I let you in so you wouldn't call the cops on me."

"I am a vampire," I confessed. "I'm not here to take your cocaine. I'm a heroin vampire." I realized how stupid that sounded and immediately retracted it. "Look, we're not really vampires. We're kind of like gangs of walking, homeless abortions."

He flipped his vape over in his hand. "Not according to the Austin vampires. Or all the L.A. gangs who come here for South by Southwest every year."

"What the fuck are you talking about? Every year?"

"Certain L.A. gangs come out here every year to hear bands and get fucked up." He waited a beat and then asked, "Are you going to take the coke or not?"

I snapped my fingers in front of his eyes. "Step back a second. I am the leader—was the leader—of an L.A. gang. I was never invited to come out here."

"I don't know what to tell you, bro."

"So, do you know Stephan Rodderick?"

He shrugged and looked down to his placemat. "I've met him a few times. Kinda full of shit."

I got excited and looked at the phone. "But he is kind of the leader, right? You can take me to him." I needed to get this information to Eldritch as soon as possible. The thought of redeeming myself in the face of so many fuck ups was exciting.

"RJ, I never deal with any of them. I'm the distributor."

I walked back over to the phone and turned it on. "You said some gang moved to Austin and took over. Who the fuck are they?"

"They call themselves the BBP."

I gripped the phone tightly, almost demolishing it in my hand and stared at the black screen. "Preppy assholes? All dress the same? They look like they just got shit out of a country club?"

"Yeah, that's them." He sighed. "They don't really fit in around Austin but they're constantly here. I think they moved here."

Suddenly, the stars aligned just as the screen on my phone lit up. Linnwood Perry was the only person in Los Angeles who talked regularly about how great Austin was. Everything that had happened to me, to L.A. vampire drug kingpin King Cobra, and to Bait all lead back to the night Linnwood Perry arrived at my door.

As the illustrious leader of the Blue Blooded Perrys, he sent me and my former best friend Dez to take care of a snitch in his gang who was working with the cops to get rid of vampires. We were supposed to intercept a bunch of coke that the snitch stole from Linnwood and Cobra.

Long story short, Dez and I brutally murdered the rat and the two cops he was working with, and the coke turned out to be heroin. Since Dez and I are vampires, we're automatically stupid. We took the heroin and put it back on the streets under King Cobra's nose. It was a set-up from the second Perry gave us the marching orders, and Cobra knew it was heroin the entire time. He also knew that we would take it.

It may have seemed like a lucky coincidence but at the end of the day, drug dealers follow users. They always end up swimming together in the same shit, just in different toilets.

I'm safe. Just found out Linwood Perry was here with his boys.
I pressed send on the phone.

"So let me get this straight." I pointed to the fleet of jet skis in the three-car garage. "You take the innards out of the jet skis and fill them with coke?" I taped my hand on one of the neon noses. "How much can you fit in one of these?"

Cody's eyes lit up as he shot me a wink. "About forty pounds, bro." He opened one of the engine covers, revealing the guts. "Everything inside was taken out and replaced with these. He pulled out a pound bag that was tightly bound in brown shipping paper and tossed it to me. "Try it," he said.

I peeled off the husk, revealing the white gold. "Do you have any blood?"

"Oh, yeah. I always forget about vampires." He walked over to a wok bench that sat beneath an enormous seventy-inch TV. But rather than common tools like hammers, screwdrivers and drills, it housed sifters, scales and cutting boards. A different kind of work bench.

He lifted his hand like an outfielder. "Throw me that."

Not gonna help.

"You got any heroin?" I asked on behalf of The Gooch.

"Heroin? Hell no. Heroin addicts are poor and never pay their tabs."

I rewrapped the bag and launched it to him. My mouth started to get wet but my body reminded me that cocaine was only going to infect that itch and make me crave heroin more. "You don't have to do this."

He caught the package. "Why not?"

"I don't know," I questioned my judgment and wiped the spittle out of the corners of my mouth. "I'm kind of putting you out. Besides, I don't think that I need any blow right now."

He tore into the package, grabbed a coffee mug off the workbench and headed toward a mini fridge in the corner. "You'll want to do this." He opened up the fridge and pulled out a plastic gallon bottle filled with what appeared to be blood.

"Is it human?" I asked as I tried to look over his shoulder as he poured some blood into the mug.

"It's great coke," he said as he topped off the mug.

"Not the blow. The blood. Is it human?"

"Of course. The gang that used to run coke around Austin robs blood banks. They always make sure I'm stocked for times when I get new product." He put a paper towel over the top of the mug and put it in a microwave on top of the fridge. Before starting it up, he asked, "How long?"

"I don't know." I put my finger to my temple. Deep thoughts. "Maybe thirty. Just make it warm enough so it doesn't taste like Clamato. How hot is a body?"

"How am I supposed to know that? Different vampires like different temperatures." He pushed start on the microwave. "Thirty seconds should be fine."

That was a really long thirty seconds, so I had time to walk over to him and watch the countdown.

The microwave beeped and he took out the mug. "Dip your finger in. Make sure it's okay."

I did and pulled it out quick. "It's a little hot."

"Good," he noted as he walked back to the cutting board, put the mug down and then shook out some chunky powder out of the bag. "I still need to cut the Charlie."

"Not too much," I said.

He started chopping the blow with a razor blade. "I'm not an amateur. I've been giving y'all samples for years, bro."

I started to get the itch. Seeing any powder being cut up, whether it was coke or heroin, made my legs feel like dancing, even if I couldn't stand. If I were human and didn't have the vampire erectile dysfunction, I would have gotten a boner.

When he was happy with his mincing and sifting, he grabbed the mug and put it under then end of the cutting board. Then he swept the powder into the mug.

"Let it absorb," I proposed anxiously.

He smiled back at me and grabbed a screwdriver. "Of course." With the blade, he stirred my milkshake.

"Kind of like Alka-Seltzer, huh? We do it a bit differently in Los Angeles." The L.A. way was more a show of power than anything else. It was definitely a rush to lure some pimps, thieves, or scumbags into a dark alley, fill their arms with heroin, rip the arms off, and then drink the warm blood mixed with the drugs out of their knuckles. Of course, it was always more bravado than necessary.

"You like the news?" He picked up a remote and turned on the enormous TV.

I stood on my toes to get a comprehensive view of the treat. "Yeah, the news is fine." I rubbed at my arms. "How long have you been a dealer?"

He surfed through the channels. "I'm not a dealer. I'm the distributor."

I walked over by him. "What's the difference?"

He stopped punching the channel up button and tossed the remote onto the work bench. "I get the product and I deliver it to the dealers."

"That is kind of the dealer of the dealers." I reached out for the mug.

He grabbed my hand. "It's not ready yet, bro."

"Okay, okay, okay," I chattered, trying to relax.

He flipped his thumbs back toward his chest, pointing out the Lake Travis tank top. "My real job is owning a jet ski rental business at Lake Travis."

I pointed to the TV. "And, that pays for all of this? You live in a fucking mansion."

"Of course not, bro. The coke pays—" he opened his arms, "—for all of this."

I liked my lips and stepped a little bit closer to him. "So, the rental business is just a front?"

"No shit." He tapped on the side of the mug. "This is good to go."

I nabbed the mug out of his hand like I was running a marathon and grabbing a bottle of water. "Tell me more." I didn't want him to think that I was using the ins and outs of his coke racket as background noise, but it was and I was really only interested in his drugs. I mean, he was my bro, right?

"So, we take eight trucks down to the lake with two jet skis on each trailer the second Saturday of every month. We put fourteen of those jet skis in the water."

I took a gulp out of the mug. Delicious. "Cool." I tried to pay attention. I ran my fingers through my shampooed and conditioned hair as I licked a little blood off the mug's rim.

"The other one we leave in the parking lot, locked down." He turned and went back to cutting up more coke. His steady hand flip-flopped the powder back and forth with the razor. He smoothed it out and then quickly separated it into four small lines. Then, instead of sucking them into his nose, he destroyed the perfectly constructed bumps and started over again. "The dealers then drive up in a pickup that they took the month before, drop it next to our rental hut and then jump in the new pickup truck that we leave in the parking lot."

I did the math in my head and took a larger sip of the blood and coke. "So, wait, you move eighty pounds of blow a week?"

With his free hand, he shot me a shaka. "Yeah, bro. Killer, right?"

"Are you fucking kidding me?" I licked blood off of my teeth and pushed it into my gums for a freeze.

"Not at all." He picked up the remote again with the shaka hand and started changing channels.

"No fucking way! That's like a million bucks a month."

"Yeah. But it's not every month, bro." He stopped at a channel and turned up the volume. "Summer and Spring Break rock. Fall and winter suck. This week is a bust for me. Someone intercepted the drop and took the drugs. I figure it's the BBP trying to move in to Austin."

I shot-gunned the rest of the mug and threw my head back to feel the gift coat my throat and enter my bloodstream. I gargled a little bit and sucked the rest of the gum reserve in through my teeth. "Still. I never cleared anything like that. I don't think all the gangs in L.A. made that kind of money." The news report caught my ear.

"The parents were left in the living room of the house, both dismembered. If you have any information on Paulina Jenkins..."

I looked up at the TV and brushed at my gums with my finger. There was a picture of Pinball that I guessed was taken of her when was undergoing chemotherapy. She was in a hospital bed with a bowed hat pulled tightly over her bald head.

"...please contact your local authorities. How's it going over there, Melissa?"

The newscast split to two screens. A reporter in front of Pinball's parents' house stood in front of some yellow police tape.

"Things are tense, Don. If Paulina Jenkins sounds familiar, you might remember a campaign in Peoria to raise money for her chemotherapy."

The other reporter responded.

"Yes. She is a brave young girl. Has her sister turned up yet?"

Two pictures flashed in between them. A picture of Pinball on her bike and younger Bait in a pair of waffle glasses with her arms crossed like an eighties rapper. The words AMBER ALERT faded in below the photographs in red.

"If you have been following this tragic story, the sister, Bailia Jenkins, has been missing for over a year and is presumed dead."

Cody's eyes were glued to the television, like mine. "This is so fucked up, bro."

I handed Cody the mug. "Can I get another one?"

He took it from my hand and headed back to the fridge. "It's pretty pure cocaine," he said, "but I guess you can have a little more."

He was right about the quality. My throat reverberated, sending vibrations out from my chest, through my pelvis and armpits, all the way to my toes and my fingers. I felt like I could shoot lightning from my hands. "This coke is amazing!"

He turned up the volume and opened the fridge again.

"*Are there any leads or suspects, and does the Peoria Police Department believe the two cases are related?*"

"Of course they're related," Cody guessed. He poured the blood into the mug and then closed the door.

"*A few people said they saw a strange car in the neighborhood last week when the killings and abduction occurred.*"

The other reporter interrupted her. "*Although no make or model was given, one underage witness said he saw this.*"

The reporter on the scene held up a kid's drawing. The newscaster from the station said, "*Can you pull in on that? I can't see it.*"

The camera pulled in on the drawing. It looked like a classic hot rod with flames on the side.

Cody grabbed the mug out of the microwave and started to walk back to the bench. "Looks like a Hot Wheels car."

The reporter on the scene responded. "*Although it may seem silly that a murderer and a kidnapper would drive such an unmistakable automobile, several adult witnesses also claim to have seen something strange.*"

Goddammit, Eldritch, I thought.

"*Melissa, did anyone see anyone around the car?*"

The AMBER ALERT text stayed on the screen but the photographs of Pinball and Bait disappeared. They were replaced by an artist's sketch.

"*Several people in the neighborhood have seen strange activity and this unknown male has been seen around the trailer park area for the past month.*"

Thankfully, the sketch looked nothing like Eldritch or me. He was fat with rat eyes. If I had seen that guy around the neighborhood, I would have called the cops immediately. He might not have been involved in the abduction of Bait and Pinball, but chances were pretty solid that he was a pedophile.

Cody pointed at the TV. "Nice, mullet, bro."

"*Thanks for the update, Melissa.*"

"*Thanks, Don. I will keep you updated as this story continues to unfold.*"

The screen returned to the studio as Melissa was replaced by the police sketch. Don recapped the details.

"He is a Caucasian or Hispanic male, around two hundred and fifty pounds, between five-foot-five and five-foot-ten. If anyone has seen this suspect please call the Peoria Police Department or your local authorities at—"

Cody muted the TV and then brushed my second helping into my mug. "Jesus. What kind of dirtball kills a family and then steals their kids?"

"It was only one kid," I corrected him.

"But the other girl was missing, too."

I didn't share any more intel with him at first. I felt sweat beading up all over my body. To not make him suspicious, I walked back over to one of the gutted jet skis and had another look. Then, I finally said, "It was probably the kids' real father."

"The father is dead, bro."

I changed the subject. I was leading on that I knew more about the case than I should have. "Why don't you have a line?"

He waved me away. "No. I'm in The Program, bro."

I stood up from the jet ski. "The Program? Are you like CIA or something?"

"What? No." He picked up the pound of coke and started wrapping it back up. "I'm in Narcotics Anonymous. How could I be in the CIA? Look at all this coke." When he was satisfied that the package was re-wrapped properly, he walked back over to me and handed me the mug.

"Narcotics Anonymous?" I grabbed the mug. "Cocaine isn't a narcotic."

"RJ, what the fuck are you talking about, bro?"

My eyelashes batted in double time as I took a sip of the new mixture. The cocaine was unbelievably pure and strong. "Are you a fucking narc? Only narcs don't know the difference between narcotics and other drugs."

Unfazed by my paranoid turn, he walked back over to the open jet ski and tucked the bag back in. "Maybe you're the narc, bro."

I put up my fist. "I'm not a narc. It wouldn't make any sense for me to be a narc, either. I'm a fucking vampire."

Cody pulled his vape out of his front pocket. "You said you weren't really a vampire."

"I'm not. I'm like—" I wiped sweat off my forehead with my wrist. "I'm like a fiend or like a walking abortion." I sucked down the rest of the drink.

"Whatever," he said, dismissing me. He walked over to a brown leather couch on the other side of the garage and sat down, pointing to a matching recliner next to it. "Come sit down, bro. You don't look so good."

I went back to the cutting board. "Fuck, man." Strangely, I already forgot that I drank all the blow that he cut up. Then, I paced around the garage, evaluating all the jet skis. Evaluated is putting it lightly. I might have been circling them like a buzzard. "Yeah, man." I shook my head again with my tongue out. "This business of yours is awesome. Fucking brilliant!" I bent over to try and get a good look at the operation. "Can you open this one up for me?"

He didn't respond. Instead, he turned on another huge TV on the coffee table in the center of his garage living room.

"Yo! You got another TV out here, Mack?" I tried to flatter him. "Shit, son." I have no idea why but when I got really wired and the world was spinning, I started talking street. "That's what's up, right?"

In an attempt to drown out my lunacy, he cranked up the volume again. "I think you need to relax, bro. I remember the first time I did coke."

I slid in between jet skis and made my way over to him. Thankfully, he wasn't watching me. For all intents and purposes, I was doing a clumsy version of the *Thriller* dance. "What does that mean, homie?" I sat down on the recliner.

"It means you're spazzin' out, bro." He clicked open a soda. "That's why I stopped doing coke."

I folded my legs under my butt. "Oh, that's right. Big man. You're a quitter."

He lifted the remote and muted the new TV. He opened his mouth to speak and then my new phone vibrated in my back pocket, sending me to my feet. I stood on the chair, fumbling to get the phone out of my pocket. I looked at the screen for a second. The words were all jumbled around. I thumped my finger against it. It didn't do anything. "Oh, shit," I shouted. "Fucking screen is upside down." I turned it around. "Please swipe to unlock? Okay, master. Whatever." I laughed to myself as I looked to the couch.

Cody yawned and turned the TV back up. "You want some water or something?"

"Naaaaaa, I'm all good." I clicked the text icon. "Nice!" There was a message from Eldritch. I read it aloud: "We are elated you are safe. We are as well."

I read what I originally texted him because I couldn't remember what I had written. "Oh, that's right." I typed back.

Did you know that the BBP is here? Let's fucking kill those fucking assholes.

I looked over at Cody again. He was steadily pressing the up and down buttons. I looked at the TV. He was browsing the guide.

"Hey, bro!" I tried speaking his language. Apparently, he didn't understand street. "Can you arrange a meeting with the BBP, bro? I totally hate those pricks. They framed me and got a lot of my friends killed, bro. You gotta help me out here, bro."

I cracked my neck on either side. Then I strutted back to the work bench and looked down at the cutting board. Once again, I remembered that I already did all the coke that Cody prepared for me. "Fuck!" I picked up the plastic board by the handle and hurled it at the garage door.

"Come on, bro." Cody got to his feet and turned off the second TV. "What's wrong with you?" He walked to the front side of the garage and picked the board up. "Why don't you go into the front yard and start yelling that you're all coked out?"

I flicked my tongue against the inside of front teeth and changed up my lingo a smidge. "That sounds killer, bruh."

He whizzed the cutting board at me like it was a throwing star. "I'm being sarcastic, *bruh*."

The board hit me square in the shin. I grabbed my leg. "That might have hurt if I wasn't a vampire. Can we meet up with the BBP or no?" I lifted one of my hands to gauge interest. "Yes?" Then, I lift the other, sliding it up and down as if the answer was on a scale between likely or never going to happen. "Orrrrrrrrr no?"

Cody walked past me, stretching his arm behind his back. "I'm not sure if that's a great idea."

I caught him by the strap of his tank top. "Please. You gotta help me out."

He pulled away as his tank top ripped a little. "I don't really know them that well. Besides, bro, they are in the middle of this, like, turf war—"

I let go of him. "Haaaaa. Turf war." I was really close to breaking into a turf war routine a la *West Side Story*, but before I started snapping my fingers, I decided to put my hands in my pockets. "I can handle them." I felt around in the new jeans. The pockets felt like they were filled with felt. "Hey, did I thank you for these jeans, bro? They're totally epic."

Cody reached the door and clicked off two of the three garage lights. "Go to bed," he suggested. "I'll see what I can do." He pointed to the corner. "There are couple of bloody steaks in the fridge that Brax and I were gonna grill. Enjoy."

He shut the door and locked it behind him.

I yelled back. "As if I can't kick that door down."

"Please don't," his muffled voice returned.

I looked at the phone. It was locked again. "Swipe to unlock," I read. I walked over the fridge and opened it. I took the steaks off the plate one-by-one started sucking the blood out of them.

Perry dabbles in Heroin.

I clicked on the message icon on the phone and then wrote:

Bro. Eldritch. We are TOTALLY going to start a turf war with the Perrys. IN AUSTIN! I'm so pumped. I wanna do like push-ups to prepare.

New message.

You're in pretty good shape, so you should be fine. Me? Probably not in as good of shape. You've seen me fight though, bro. I'm fucking tight as shit and mean as a fucking badger, bro.

New message.

Pound 4 pound, I can fist fuck the hell out of any of those pussies. You know it. YOU FUCKING KNOW ME, BRO! All about being a badass. Fuckin' A.

New message.

I used to run a gang. A badass gang. I was the leader. This is gonna be awesome, bro. Me and you. Perrys. Battle of the century. Several gladiators enter the ring. Two exit. RJ Reynolds and fucking BJ Eldritch.

New message.

That would be dope. Me RJ. You BJ. Fucking blow job all over their faces, bro. Totally in the zone. Totally ready to light fucking Austin on fire, bro. We should sell tickets. Fucking FIRE!

New message.

Better call the Austin Fire Department because the kid is hot, bro. Man, this thing is hard to type on. It doesn't matter. I am gonna take that fucker's head and just smash it into a million pieces.

New message.

Imagine Linnwood's smug fucking face when I am like totally scalping him. Bring matches and gas or something. I'm gonna rip off the top of his head and light his brain on fire, bro.

I sat down on the couch and turned the TV on.

It's gonna be a Towering Inferno, bro and I'm gonna be OJ. OJ Reynolds. Fucking crazy ass murderer and shit. Hatchet to the fucking skull, bro. Just like OJ.

New message.

Fucking Motorhead, bro. Ace of Spades. We should bring a deck of cards and take all the aces of spades out of the deck. I think there is like 10. One for each Perry.

New message.

How many are there? Perrys? We take the cards and light that shit on fire, bro. Throw them on their fucking graves. Gambit in the fucking house versus the fire department.

I let out a huge breath of relief. It was going to be amazing. At least, whatever gibberish I pounded into the phone sounded like it was going to be amazing at that time.

I watched two hours of *Golden Girls* and the entire time I was eyeballing the jet skis packed tightly with love and care. I checked the phone for a response from Eldritch about every five or six seconds. Then I made the mistake of turning on the news again.

Melissa in Peoria showed the child's sketch of the hot rod drawn with crayon flames on the side.

"We believe the suspect or suspects have made their way to Texas."

I looked back over at the open jet ski and pulled a blanket over my legs from the arm rest of the leather couch.

As I start to doze off, the phone buzzed with a response from Eldritch. *Go to bed.* ☹

XIV

RECRUITED

For someone who was a callous monster like me, I certainly had an unpleasant conscious that seemed to creep in on me whenever I closed my eyes. And since I didn't have any heroin, I couldn't block it out. Maybe it was the blaring reminder that I killed Pinball's parents and kidnapped her that played out on the TV as white noise as I slept. I was never one to believe that any premonitions or higher powers were real, but I couldn't help but think that someone was trying to tell me something.

I was in the gymnasium again. The scumbag gymnasium from St. Matthews. The shithole where I was born. Rather than the "healing circle" that plagued me from my other dreams, there were two rows of chairs sitting across from each other. Staring at me from the other side were Bait, Pinball, and two members of my L.A. gang, the Knucklers, Tahoe and Pico. All but Pinball were dead. Standing between the two rows was a headless King Cobra—the vamp who was once my greatest enemy but ended up being closer than a brother at the time of his death. Cobra was holding a mic that didn't make any noises other than feedback. By my side were traitor Dez, and that cunt junkie hole, The Habit. Next to her, Smiley Cyrus and a few more McCoys. My conscious had put me in really shitty company. Two of the McCoys were whispering into each other's ears and snickering as their body parts fell from their torsos as if they had leprosy.

The Catholic leader of The Cloth, Father McAteer, was across the room one second and then sitting right beside me the next, bumping into me as he tried desperately to find a vein in his arm. When he did find it, he tilted his head back, plugged his nose, and inhaled through his mouth. I turned away, but I immediately felt sludge on my leg. He laughed as his skin, followed by his bones, melted onto the chair, leaving only his clerical collar. A syringe laid in the goop that used to be him.

Nightmare Dez kicked my foot. "That was pretty dope, huh?" He picked up the syringe and started pricking it into my legs. "This is the new cut. Whoop whoop!"

I waved him away and didn't answer.

The Habit lifted-up her nun outfit and pointed to the headless King Cobra. Her pussy was talking. "He doesn't have a head anymore because of you."

I turned to hear what, if anything, Cobra had to say. He waved his hands like he was talking, but the mic continued to only transmit a distorted whine. Behind him on a blackboard, "The Program" was spray-painted in huge red letters. Suddenly, over the distorted PA system in the gym, I heard, "If you or a loved one was diagnosed with Mesothelioma, you may be entitled to financial compensation."

The TV news had infiltrated my dream.

My attention turned to Bait and Pinball who were dangling their feet down from chairs that were bigger than all the others. "I hate you," Bait said in Pinball's voice. "You kilt my parents." A skinnier, taller Eldritch walked up behind both of them and used his hands to reach behind their ears as if he were a magician producing a coin. In a matter of seconds, he pulled back his hands revealing fistfuls of white gummy bears. Both children's faces lit up.

Eldritch stared into my eyes. "He gave my mother cancer, Little Ones." He then grabbed Pinball by her wig. "He gave you cancer. He is cancer."

Dez moved in closer to share my chair with me. My ass teetered on the edge, his brown teeth scratched at my face as he spoke. "Dunk that doughnut. Am I right? Dunk that doughnut." It was our call to arms whenever we subdued a pimp or a creep. It meant it was time to inject heroin into their arms before we ripped the appendages off and enjoyed getting high.

Cobra walked over and stood in front of us when I realized that the chair was free again. Dez disappeared, but he left the syringe in my lap. I held it up and looked into the barrel. There was something moving around inside. I looked more closely. It was filled with hundreds of miniature baby opossums. As they had when they unsuccessfully attempted to feed and get warmth from their dead mother, they squirmed around inside the sleeve. Their eyes were closed and they warped around each other to stay alive. In an attempt to release them from their captivity, I smashed down on the plunger. Nothing came out.

"RJ Reynolds, as I live and breathe," Cobra's voice called out, reverberating from all around. I looked up. When he was alive, he would say that to me, letting me know that I was in deep shit. His armless and legless torso was now nailed to the blackboard. His killer, The Habit, stood behind him and pointed to a strap on dildo that she revealed by throwing her robe over her shoulder like a matador wearing a cape.

She smiled. "Dag nabbit!" she yelled in her pre-teen television voice. A crowd of derelicts and misfits lined up behind her to take a swing at the fallen king. One-by-one, they took their turn fucking him in the ass. Cobra didn't speak anymore at all and eventually, he disappeared.

"My name is Dirt and I'm an addict," Cody said as he took Cobra's place on a chair.

Dez returned and he was now sitting in my lap. "That was pretty dope, huh?" he repeated. He snapped at my face with his toothless mouth. I shoved his face away and threw him across the room. He slumped into the corner and again said, "That was pretty dope, huh?"

I got up from my seat to walk over to him, not sure if I was going to apologize to him or kill him, but when I reached the other line of chairs, Bait grabbed my arm.

"That's the father of my baby," she said. I looked down and she was holding Possie, the mother possum, who was wrapped up in the same brown paper that Cody used to wrap his cocaine.

Then, at the front of the gymnasium, Melissa On Location appeared. She was holding a long gameshow host microphone in her hand. "The girl is Paulina Jenkins, who you might remember from a report last year when her parents pleaded with the public to support a lawsuit against the Peoria Cancer Institute. According to the suit, the Peoria Cancer Institute administered chemotherapy treatments without their consent. The case never went to trial but neighbors have told us that the sick little girl's parents continued to shave Paulina's head long after the cancer was undetected in the ten-year-old's body."

Reporting From The Studio Don appeared next to her. "That is unsubstantiated, correct, Melissa?"

Melissa's head popped out of Don's shirt. "There have been no confirmed reports whether any of these allegations are factual or not."

Don shoved her back inside of him and asked, "Do we have any leads on the suspect or suspects?"

"Not yet, Don," she responded but didn't appear. A projected image of the artist's rendition of the kidnapper lit up behind Don. "The suspect is a white male, five-foot-five to five-foot-ten. He is heavy set and has long brown hair."

I walked up to the reporters and was suddenly in front of Pinball's parents' trailer. The crude drawing of the hot rod was projected against the doublewide's decaying vinyl siding. As I walked toward the door, Don followed me and started talking with Melissa's voice. "A neighborhood child drew this picture to show the police a suspicious car that was spotted in the neighborhood."

Another Don appeared on my right side. "Do the Peoria police have any leads on this automobile?" He pushed the microphone in my face.

The Don on my left was then Melissa. "No one else saw this type of car but reports have come in about a pickup truck. That seems to be a better lead than a drawing that isn't a real make or model."

I swung my head from right to left, trying to keep time with the banter. The McCoys were lined up on either side of my path, beyond Don and Melissa. They twirled and swung their weapons around as they had back at the pharmacy.

Don shoved the mic in my eye. "Did anyone happen to get a license plate?"

"Unfortunately, no."

Melissa disappeared. Don moved in front of me blocking the entrance to the trailer and said, "If you have any information on the abduction of Paulina Jenkins or the murder of her parents, Ronald and Billy Jenkins, please contact the Peoria Police Department at—"

I felt the flicking of fingers on my ear.

"Wake up, bro."

I shooed the voice and fingers away. "Let me sleep."

It's four," the voice continued.

I massaged different parts of my body and stretched my legs over the end of the couch. The all-over ache felt like someone had pulled my skin off and had taken a hammer to my old bones and muscles. "Fuck off." I didn't open my eyes. "Turn off the TV."

I heard flip flops walk away from me. They stopped. "Where's the remote?"

I dug around under the blanket that half covered me. "I don't know."

The flip flops clicked away a little more and I heard the TV shut down. "It's off. Get up."

Then, he proceeded to walk across the garage. I heard the tops of the one of the jet skis close. "I'm surprised you didn't try and snort all my blow."

I opened my right eye. "What do you want, Cody?"

"It's four." He flip-flopped back over to me. "Like four p.m."

I picked up the can of a Lone Star that I had been drinking, crushed it and threw it at him. "We sleep late. Sunlight is *no bueno, amigo*."

"Yeah, I know bro." He caught the can and walked it over to the proper recycling bin. "Your buddies are awake. I shot Linnwood Perry a text."

I planted my forehead into my hand. "Yeah? What did that punk ass say?"

He smirked. "He said that he was glad I contacted him and that he wanted to adjust our arrangement."

I swung my body around and put my feet on the rug of the makeshift living room. "So he thinks he's Darth Vader now? What does that mean?"

"It means he wants to meet with me, bro. Today. I told you that he wanted to cut a deal with me."

I grunted, trying to get to my feet. "You didn't say anything about me being in Austin, did you?" That didn't work so I sat back down. I dug around between to cushions on the couch and found the new phone. No more messages from Eldritch since the message about going to bed. "Do you have any more blood? And coffee? Bloody coffee? I feel like shit."

He walked back to the fridge and opened it. He moved some stuff around on the shelves. "I think I can mix something up for you."

I reached toward the table and seized the bottle of Oxy. "No more coke. It gives me bad dreams." I lobbed the bottle to him. "This will make them go away."

"Vampires dream?" he scoffed as he bobbled the bottle and then caught it.

"Of course we dream." I scratched my forehead. "I was dreaming about all sorts of awful shit."

He put a new mug in the microwave. "We need to get ready. I'm supposed to meet him in an hour at some parking structure."

I used my hand as a visor and looked toward the side door. "Still too early for me to go out there."

"Oh, yeah. I got you covered, bro." Not wasting any time, he headed back into the house and returned almost immediately with a ski mask. "You can use this." Then he threw me some sunscreen. "And this."

I studied both articles in my hands. "Why do you have a ski mask in Texas?"

"It snows here. Anyway, Braxton and I used to rob liquor stores before I joined The Program. We hit ten in one week," he bragged. "I kept this one to remember the good old days. You know, before I ran a business and all." He threw me a hoodie. It was bright red and again it said '*eep Austin Weird* across the chest.

I threw it back to him. "Not a chance."

"Your call, bro." He started folding it up. "I just went down the gas station and bought it."

"Why?" I moaned. "Why in the fuck would you purposely go buy me that shit?"

"Look, bro. I'm trying to help you get revenge or whatever. Quit being a dick."

I fully stretched out my body and yawned again. My back popped. "Are you fucking with me?" I tilted my head. "Seriously, why are you fucking with me?"

The buzzer on the microwave went off and he pulled out the mug. "I'm not fucking with you. I wanted to get you something to cover your arms." He tossed the sweatshirt back on the couch.

"And you couldn't have just gotten a shirt that didn't say anything on it." I covered the sweatshirt with the blanket.

"They only had these and some shirts that said 'Don't Mess With Texas' and 'She's Weird' with an arrow pointing off the shirt." He walked back to the cutting board and started mashing up the Oxy.

"'Don't Mess With Texas' would have been fine," I concluded.

He turned around to look at me. "But you're not a Texan, bro. Besides, they only had kid sizes." When he was satisfied with his mash, he started chopping up the narcs.

I was becoming increasingly impatient with my host. My eyes—and everything behind them—were pounding. "Just get that shit ready, please." I bent over and pulled on the jeans by my feet. "When do we have to meet them again?"

He swept and sifted the powder as he had before, this time a little bit more eloquently. "In an hour, bro," he said as he dumped the drugs into the mug.

I got up to meet him half way near the jet skis. My body felt like it was a burrito filled with the dried-up remnants of several different kinds of drugs that gave my organs, bones, and muscles an eviction notice.

He handed the mug to me. "You should probably pound this."

I let my tongue dangle into the cup. "Not bad."

He didn't respond. Instead, he pointed back to the couch and said, "Grab your gear. The sun isn't going to set until like seven-thirty."

I sat back down on the couch and pulled on my new Texan outfit. Then I reluctantly put the ski mask and the sunscreen in my back pocket. I picked up my phone, unlocked and messaged Eldritch.

We're gonna go meet Linnwood at a parking garage in an hour. He doesn't know we're coming.

The phone buzzed back almost immediately.

Not a good idea.

I ignored him and sent another text.

I'll send you the address. Be there. Maybe tie the kid up wherever you're hiding out.

He waited a bit to think about it.

☹. Did you sleep?

I responded.

Yes.

It was apparent that he knew I was on something the night before, but if I didn't allude to my texts, maybe he'd forget about it. I responded one last time.

I'm gonna go take a shower.

XV.

ENLISTED

I turned the music down in Cody's truck as he pulled out of his driveway. "Dude, what is this dreadful noise?" I rubbed my head through the knitted face mask. I always detested listening to anyone else's music in cars. It made me want to punch a hole in the windshield.

He turned it back up. "Totally bluegrass, bro."

"Bluegrass?" I picked up his phone and started scrolling through his music. "Don't you have any punk rock?"

He grabbed the phone back. "Punk rock? Ha! No one listens to that trash anymore."

We were headed directly west into the setting sun, so I pulled down the sun visor and covered my eyes. "You Austin poser."

"Me? The poser?" He patted me on the chest to remind me how he'd dressed me. "How old are you, anyway? The only people who still listen to punk rock around here are ancient."

I slapped his hand away. "I'm old. I was born in a laboratory inside of a Catholic church. My mom died before I was alive, and I lived on the streets since I was a teen."

He turned the banjo music back up and wiggled his thumb. "Didn't really ask for your life story, bro. Live in the moment. Forget the mistakes you've made in the past and be glad you're still alive."

"Not alive." I put my head down and let the covered crown of my head take the brunt of the late afternoon sun.

I saw him take his hands off the wheel and do some air-banjoing. He then started brush drumming on his knees. "All I'm saying, bro, is that you should live for today. Admit you have a problem."

"Did you learn all that bullshit in The Program?"

He put his hands back on the wheel to straighten out the truck. When he was satisfied, he began playing an upright bass, then a fiddle and then back to brush drumming on the dashboard. "Yeah, I've learned a lot from The Program. One day, I ended up in a ditch, naked with dicks drawn all over my face. My mom came and found me and took me right to rehab. I have never looked back."

Growing more bored than annoyed with his preaching, I decided to cut him off at the pass and end the sobriety discussion. "I'm a vampire. I was born addicted to drugs. I never knew my mom because she died before I was *stillborn*. So, not only did I not have anyone to pick me up in her solid gold Rolls Royce, I didn't have any money for rehab. End of story."

He gripped the steering wheel and started humming along with the lead singer's high-pitched wailing. "I thought you said you weren't really vampires."

I accidentally rubbed some threads from my mask into my eye. "We're not. We just don't have a name."

"How about addicts, bro?" he fired back. "Or maybe junkies? How about fiends?"

I turned the radio off. "You're giving me a headache, Cody." I turned the focus back to him. "You have a lot of fucking nerve, you hypocrite. You must run the biggest cocaine enterprise in the South."

He started strumming. "I would never have made it where I am without The Program, bro. It's transformed me into the business man I am today."

At the risk of baking my eyes in the sun, I lifted my head and stared at him. "It wasn't a compliment. Do you know why I ended up at your house?"

"No."

"Because I surveyed all the houses on your cul-de-sac and decided on yours because you're so fucking stupid that you have a bumper sticker on your car that says, MY KID SELLS DRUGS TO YOUR HONOR STUDENT."

He smirked. "Yeah, it's a good one."

"You *are* a drug dealer, dude. Fuck. How stupid are you? And guess what. You're no better than me. You're a sober drug dealer."

"Distributor."

"It's the same fucking thing! You have two huge TVs in a garage that is filled with pounds and pounds of cocaine. Said garage is attached to your mansion paid for from getting kids hooked on drugs. Something, I might add, you advertise on the bumper of your truck."

"Look, bro. I don't know where all this hostility is coming from." He returned to the upright bass and swayed his head back and forth to the beat.

"I don't deal to any kids because I just distribute the drugs to the dealers. Think of me as the car maker and the people who I sell the drugs to as dealerships."

I exhaled and slowed things down. "You don't make the coke, idiot. You're the dealership and they are car salesmen."

He patted me on the thigh. "Sweet, bro. I own the dealerships. Tell me a drug addict who owns a bunch of car dealerships?"

"I'm sure there are several." I back-stepped. "Wait? What? No, you misunderstood me." I literally started banging my head against the dashboard. It felt kind of good to be knocking the pain out of my head. "The whole point of this pointless conversation was to show you that you're the problem. Whether you're sober or not, you aren't a do-gooder because you sell drugs. Those drugs wind up in the hands of kids. Kids take drugs and get all fucked up and then have abortions that turn into vampires... who then sell drugs."

"Yeah, I guess you sell drugs to kids, too." He turned out of his neighborhood onto a busier street. "You're a drug dealer and a drug addict. I've seen it before in myself. I saw a little bit of the old me in you last night, bro. It brought back some really bad memories. I almost drew dicks all over your face."

"If you would have drawn a dick on my face, I would have ripped off your actual dick and shoved it in your mouth. Look, Cody, I don't want to get into a conversation about who between the two of us has slightly higher morals." I aimed the vent toward me face. I was beginning to sweat under the ski mask. "You're lucky. I could have killed you the second that you let me into your house and not thought twice about it."

"And you're a killer."

"I'm sure someone has died from all the millions of dollars' worth of cocaine that you have *distributed* onto the streets." The wool ski mask started to itch on my face. "You can sit here on your fucking throne all at day and try to get me to praise you for being sober. I don't care. I can't be sober. I need drugs and blood to survive. If I quit—"

He picked up his phone and switched songs. "How would you know what would happen if you quit? You've never even given it a shot, bro."

"I can't. I need it."

"Who says?" he began. "Do you have some voices in your head telling you that you need to use drugs?"

"As a matter of fact, I do."

"That's your addiction talking to you, bro."

"I call it The Gooch."

He looked at me sideways. "You mean like on that TV show, *Scrubs*?"

"*Scrubs*? What the fuck is that?" I licked around my flakey dry mouth, making it worse. "It's like The Gooch from *Diff'rent Strokes*, dude. He was Arnold's arch enemy."

"It's addiction. I'm sure you only hear it when you're going through withdrawal. I was in treatment with a bunch of junkies. They all said the same thing, bro. All you need to do is confront The Gooch and you're on your way to a better life."

"I'm just fine, Cody."

"You keep telling yourself that. Or, better yet, have The Gooch keep telling you that."

I wanted to cover my ears to shut out him and his horrendous music but that would have meant that the things he was saying were ringing true. He was a ridiculous piece of Texas trash. Probably literally fell off a turnip truck. More likely his parents were these rich oil tycoons who ass fucked him with a silver spoon. "How about this? We stop talking for a while," I finally said.

For the next fifteen minutes, I sat with my head down and endured his excruciating snake handler music. One thing was for sure, it was better than listening to his uninformed sermons about what it was like to be me.

At the first measure of the third or fourth or fifth uninterrupted banjo-pickin', finger lickin' song, he pulled into an alley. An umbrella of shade filled the car and I lifted me head.

I scratched my face under the mask. "Are we here?"

He dropped a business card in my lap. "Yeah, we're here. Go through that door and take the stairs to the sixth floor."

I picked up the card. It had a jet ski printed on it and it said: *Cody Walker. CEO. BROSKIZ.* Below that, his phone number 1-855-BROSKIZ was listed. "Thanks for the ride, and everything else, Cody."

He put out his hand to shake. "My number is also in the contacts on your phone. You know. If you want to talk to someone or you're in trouble."

"I appreciate everything you've done for me," I added as I shook his hand.

"Remember, I'm here if you need me" He winked. "I'm concerned about you. Next time you talk to The Gooch, tell him I said 'hello'."

I didn't respond again, but I waved him away as his truck backed out of the alley, giving me one last look at the bumper sticker that brought me and Cody Walker together. As I made my way through the door, I dropped his card in a garbage can and made my way up the stairs.

"BROSKIZ. With a Z," I said to myself as I shook my head in disbelief.

XVI

REUNITED

On the sixth floor of the garage, I tapped my heel against a cement pylon, wanting desperately to take the wool mask off my face. However, my plan was to walk out of the shadows, then slip off the mask, revealing that I was Linnwood Perry's old nemesis from Los Angeles. So it had to remain on. The reveal might have been a little dramatic—on the sixth floor of a nine-floor parking garage near sundown—but the payoff of Eldritch and I mashing what was left of the Blue Blooded Perrys into pieces deserved some theatrics.

I looked at my phone. Eldritch still hadn't responded since I suggested that he tie Pinball up or stuff her in a closet. He had to have wanted this payback just as badly as I did. Not only did the Perrys fuck me over, they also got Eldritch involved. Well, technically that was me, but this vengeance was for the greater good. I actually enlisted Eldritch to help get the stolen heroin back onto the streets.

It wasn't even for the greater good. It was stupid and a lot of people died because we took the heroin. If anyone was to blame for that it was clearly Linnwood Perry and Dez. Linnwood constructed the double-cross with King Cobra and Dez double-crossed King Cobra. I decided that everything could be traced back to Linnwood because he is where it began.

Maybe it was the leftover buss of blow giving my muscles, but I felt like a fucking badass. I backed my foot up against the cylinder I was leaning against and lit a grit. Even though I decided—after coming down—that I wasn't going light them up with gas and matches or throw flaming playing cards on their graves, I was going to fuck them up. Wipe them out.

I looked at the lock screen on my phone. Jesus. It was close to seven.

No Eldritch? No BBP?

The elevator light *dinged* as someone exited onto the other side of the garage. I shook the coke twitches out of my calves and forearms, counted to ten and then re-took my stance. This time I leaned against a black muscle car, careful not to set off the alarm. I dug into my nose and scraped some dried boogers off the edges.

It was a false alarm. Just some sap getting off work for the day.

I rolled up the ski mask on the top of my head and took another drag from the cigarette. "Evening." I saluted him. I must have looked pretty shady because he didn't respond and rushed to get into his car.

He slowed as he drove by and rolled down his window. "Get out of here, you creep." He gave me the finger.

"Piss off, asshole," I hollered as I tried to flick the rest of my smoke into his car. He peeled away and the lit cigarette got a twisted around and singed my hand.

I tapped on the phone with my thumb.

Besides a few cars with more day workers that passed by me in the garage, it seemed to be empty. At seven thirty I sat down and decided to give it ten more minutes. I would have sucked on a few more Oxy pills, but that would have made me slow and less hungry.

I texted Eldritch again.

Where are you?

It wasn't like him to not respond to me if he knew I was walking into a possible situation—especially with a gang as dangerous as the BBP. More so, it wasn't like him not to want to hear himself talk or think. Him not responding, to me, meant something was wrong.

I'm getting kind of worried. About you. Also about me. I didn't get wasted before coming here so, yeah. Here at the old garage. Some prick almost drove over my foot and called me a creep. Must have been freaked out by the ski mask that I'm wearing.

I decided that joking around with him might get him to respond.

What are you wearing?

For a split second, I noticed that he might be responding because a little word bubble with three dots appeared at the bottom of our conversation. Then it disappeared.

C'mon. You know you want it. You want all of this good shit.

I pulled the camera away from my face, snapped a picture and sent it.

You like that shit? Check this out.

I maneuvered my body so I could fit the phone down my pants and took a picture of my dick. I pulled it out, approved it, then sent it.

Again, I saw the little word bubble appear. I'm sure he thought me too much of a philistine to figure out good dick pic techniques.

The bubble disappeared again.

I know you're there, Eldritch. Fucking answer me.

No bubble.

If you and the kid are in trouble, you need to tell me where you are.

It was time to call it, I decided. I hadn't concluded whether Cody wanted to get rid of me because I was a liability around his drugs, whether Eldritch and Pinball were in trouble, if the BBP were uninterested in "altering their deal", or a combination of the three, but I knew that I was sick of waiting. At the risk of believing that I was wronging Bait, I realized that it was time to start leaning toward the alternative to getting rid of Pinball. I didn't mean to think crass thoughts, but if this Rodderick guy wasn't going to respond to any of our communications, Eldritch and I needed to decide. Being a ward of the state was a much better fate than being the mascot for two drug addict abortions who likened themselves to supernatural creatures. I hated to think about it, but maybe we could hand her over to the Minutemen. I never had parents. I lacked the ability to understand any connection to anything besides drugs and Bait. Difficult decisions needed to be made.

And then, in the middle of my bombshell, I heard the rattling engine of an antique car a few floors down. It had to be them.

I scrambled to get back into position by taking my stance against the muscle car and pulling the ski mask that was drenched inside over my face. After I lit the last cigarette from the pack that Cody happily blood-dipped for me, I crossed my arms. I needed to be aloof, so I dug one of the tips of my boots into the cement.

A vintage Mercedes Benz limousine rounded the corner onto level six of the parking garage. The engine made an old fashion tinkering sound instead of purring like a modern stretch. All the windows were blacked out, but knowing the Perrys for as long as I had, there was no question as to whether it was them or not. I never knew how these other gangs—or Eldritch for that matter—got their hands on all such cool vehicles and costumes and shit. I had taken the bus since I was on the street and I wore the same gross jeans and ripped up t-shirts every day.

I held my ground. There was no telling how many Perrys were in the car. Things would have gone so much smoother had Eldritch showed up. The limo spun in sideways and chugged to a stop about twenty feet in front of me. My phone buzzed, but I didn't look at it. The Perrys were here.

The engine cut and the thumping music inside stopped. The driver-side door opened and out marched their prim and proper chauffeur. My eyes slid sideways in his direction. He was suited in a black tuxedo and patent leather cap that had a checkered band around the middle. The hat covered his blonde shelf haircut that made him instantly recognizable as a

Perry or Perry apple polisher. It also made him a dead ringer—with the outfit and the hair—for Watts from *Some Kind of Wonderful*. I hid my mouth behind my hand and giggled. "Haaa. Watts."

He walked around to the other side of the car and opened the two back doors. Then, as a proper servant should, he stepped aside. One-by-one, five almost identically dressed Perry's stepped out of the car. They all had on tennis sweaters, some over oxfords, some lightly tossed over their shoulders and one wrapped around a waist, covering the backside of a pair of loud, checker-patterned madras golfing slacks. One of them stretched and yawned as his neighbor swatted him on the chest and pointed in my direction.

After the driver was sure that they were all standing outside, he closed the door. Then, he stepped toward the front passenger side door and opened it. He faced me with his arms behind his back as the glorious Linnwood Perry set his white leather tennis shoes on the floor of the garage and crouched under the car's doorway. He didn't immediately look in my direction. Instead, he headed back to his disciples. He walked to the Perry wearing the gaudy pants and straightened out the collar on his shirt. Linnwood patted his friend on the cheek, revealing that he had a set of spike brass knuckles on his right hand.

As I casually lifted my boot out of the cement, I turned to face them. I curled my fingers in and out, preparing for a beat down.

He walked down the line of his boys. He stopped at the last one and turned him around, lifting up the back of his sweater. Making sure I could see it, he pulled out a handgun. "You're a good kid," Linn told him as he unlocked the clip from the gun, checked it to make sure it was loaded.

I continued to crimp my fingers and then started bobbing my head back in forth like a boxer.

Linnwood pounded the clip back into the handle of the gun and turned toward me.

I guess I had spent too much time preparing my stance for when they showed up because I didn't have any idea what I was going to do.

"So, Mr. Cody Walker. The BROSKI," he stated as he twirled the gun on his finger. "We're here. Why?"

The posse continued giggling and swatting each other. Linnwood remained serious. He waved the gun behind his head. The other five silenced. The driver remained emotionless.

I searched for what to say, but before I decided on anything, he continued. "You know my time at South by Southwest is very valuable to me."

I nodded my head up and down and grunted out, "Yeah, bro."

He chuckled a bit and turned to his sidekicks. "Then, what am I doing here?"

I didn't respond again.

One of the others called out, "Why are you wearing a ski mask?"

I started lifting the mask off my face when another said, "Bitchin' Mustang. Where did you get it?"

"Now, now, boys. I'm sure *Cody* here has something important to tell us." Linnwood pointed the gun at my head. "Isn't that right, *Cody*?"

With the ski mask resting halfway up to my nose, I opened my mouth to begin the big reveal but something didn't feel right.

He beat me to words again. "Before you take off your silly mask, I want you to know that I could blow your worthless little head off right now. I mean, you are human, after all. We could just eat you here and now."

Three more pulled out guns and instantaneously cocked them. Sure, they were acting like typical chicken shit Perrys, but I always wondered why more vampire gangs didn't carry guns. Like the McCoys for instance. Those assholes had, like, Garden Weasels and shit.

He smirked. "It seems we have you outnumbered, *Cody*."

I took a step toward them and grabbed the bottom of the mask. Before I lifted it over my face, one of them cried out: "Keep Austin Weird!"

Linnwood stumbled backwards and fell onto the chauffeur. "I can't," he said as he broke into hysterics. "I can't fucking do this anymore. This is too classic."

My stance went limp as I finally pulled the mask off my face. I looked at my phone. Eldritch texted me back.

Alas, I cannot come.

Linnwood lifted his beat red face off of the shoulder of his driver, who had broken character to join in the party. He paused for a second and looked me up and down. He looked back at the rest. "Oh my goodness, boys. It's our old friend from Los Angeles, RJ Reynolds. But I thought we were here to meet Cody Walker, the jet ski king. What kind of black magic is this?" He waited a beat and then unable to contain his laughter, erupted, yelling, "Keep Austin Weird!" The thunder of all seven Perrys echoed through every level of the parking garage.

I tugged the sweatshirt over my head, threw it onto the car and inflated my chest, prepared for a fight.

"You had better make this quick," Linnwood insisted, still giggling. "I'm sure you have a lot more canvassing to do today in your quest to 'Keep Austin Weird'."

"Goddammit, Cody!" I yelled as I tore the back spoiler off of the Mustang and lifted it over my shoulder.

Trying to contain himself, Linn stood upright and tucked his gun into his belt. He put up his hands to surrender. "Is this any way to greet an old friend, RJ?" He turned to his boys again and put his finger to his lips. "Shhhhhhh." He twirled back around daintily. "Put the spoiler from your 'stang down. We're here to talk."

I bent the black spoiler behind my head taking aim at his face like a baseball player. "It's not my fucking Mustang, asshole."

He continued to wave a white flag with his hands by pushing his palms toward me. He spoke in a calming voice. "What's this about?"

"You know what this is about. You set me up in L.A. You sent me to kill that rat. Garvin? Davin?"

"Gavin," he corrected me.

I choked up on the spoiler and readied it to swing. I could have taken his head clear off his body. "Yeah. You sent me to kill him. Then, Dez and I took the heroin that was supposed to be coke. You set us up with Cobra."

He walked over to one of his buddies and put out his hand. "That's not the way it went down, friend." The other Perry dropped a cigarette into his palm. Linn started packing it on the face of his watch. "Cobra and everyone else had been trying to push you out of Hancock Park for ages."

"Oh, bullshit, Linn."

He stepped toward me. "Come on, RJ. Put the spoiler down. I didn't set you up. I was being pushed out, too. Besides, it was your brilliant idea to steal the heroin. Everyone knew you would."

"Where were these meetings even taking place?" I let the bumper fall to my side. "Was this the grand council of asshole drug dealers?"

"A junkie is a junkie. A cokehead is a cokehead. I would have done the same thing. I seriously sent you there to kill Gavin. I had no idea that they switched the drugs."

The spoiler fell to the ground and a clanking sound zoomed down the ramp.

"Smart move." He straightened out his sweater. "Like you could have taken all of us out with that spoiler. We all have guns. Besides, we aren't an Austin gang."

I tossed the ski mask aside over by my sweatshirt. "Meaning?"

"We've heard that you have already flattened two of these gangs on your own. Name one gang in L.A. that you could have done that to."

I scratched the hair over my ear but came up empty. "I hadn't thought about it."

He stepped back to his driver, whose arms returned to his back as he straightened up. Linnwood picked a piece of lint off of his jacket and then brushed it a little. "It's because they weren't cut from the same *cloth* as us."

"I don't think I understand."

He put his arm around Watts. "I have been to Austin for SXSW several times. Besides Rodderick, these maggots are all bottom feeders. Nobodies. It pains me to even have to relocate here."

"Why the fuck would you want to move here? You owned Beverly Hills."

"Guess what, RJ? Every L.A. gang was wiped out."

I didn't second guess him because I knew everything he said was true. "What about this Rodderick dude? Eldritch and I have been trying to get ahold of him since we've been here."

He took his arms off the driver. "Really? Why? Do you want his autograph?"

I rung the sweat out of the ski mask in my fist. "Why would I want his autograph, asshole?"

"Do you really want me to answer that?" He pointed to the shirt again and snickered.

I knew better than to tell anyone besides Rodderick about Pinball. Bad memories about Los Angeles and Bait returned. "We have a business proposition for him."

"A business proposition? Hmmmm. Are you sure that's what you want?" He paced in front of his gang. "Fine. I'll text him. But first—" he paused as he stepped over to Watts and brushed off the sleeve of his coat and then reached around to the back of his head, "—let's get high."

He latched onto the driver's hair and smashed his face through the limo window. As the cap fell on the other side of the door, Linnwood sawed through his neck using the newly jagged window glass. The driver's eyes open wide with shock as Perry jerked his jugular vein back and forth. The body trembled and the poor man tried desperately to open a breathing passage before he swallowed his tongue.

I looked at the spoiler because this was a strange turn of events. "You kill your own now?"

Linn laughed as he beat Watts's neck further into the glass. "Oh, God, no. I found this idiot on Craigslist. I told him I could make him a vampire last year."

"Please," Watts begged as his mouth filled with blood and he started drowning internally. Satisfied that he was going to hold on long enough for us to get some of that glorious warm, living heart blood, Linn walked over to one of the boys, who handed him a towel. As three of the other Perrys stretched the arms to keep the driver alive for a few more second, one of them opened the trunk, then opened a duffle bag and finally pulled out a bag of coke. It was wrapped in the same brown paper that the drugs in Cody's garage were wrapped in. He walked over to me and brought me in for a hug.

ASK if he HAS heroin.

"Do you have any junk?" I asked.

Linwood patted me on the back and yelled back to his gang. "Of course not," he whispered in my ear. "Heroin is for gutter people."

I pushed him away. "Thanks, dick."

It didn't take long for me to remember what a ruthless bunch of butchers the BBP were. Guns or not, they would have fucked me up.

XVII

ROLLED

Linnwood and I sat in the stairwell outside the entrance to level six of the parking structure.

"You killed that lap dog of yours, didn't you?"

Against my better judgment and Eldritch's stern speech about right and wrong, I took a slug off Watts's arm. "Dez? No, he ran away like a punk bitch."

"Shit," Linnwood said. "I hated that kid. No one ever wanted to do business with you because that little pussy was always around. Then he would try and get people on board to help take you down."

"Are you kidding me?"

"Nope." Following my lead, Linn picked at Watts's other arm and dumped some coke into the open wound on top. "I know you think I had a lot to do with setting you up, but the truth is that I was just another pawn like you."

"Look where that got us." I raised the arm to cheers. I pointed toward the Perrys who were picking at the rest of the body that was still hanging off of the busted window of the Benz. "Is that all that's left?"

He returned my cheers and we high-fived the two arms in the air. "Of the Perrys? Yeah. The Cloth came at everyone hard. Sangre. Batwangers. Stillettos. Time Pilots. It didn't really matter."

I was responsible for the end of Nomi and the Batwangers, but I kept that book closed. It wasn't so much that I was worried Linn cared about a vampire code like Eldritch as it was that he would think I was working for The Cloth.

"The gangs in L.A. are all but gone," he continued. "So, I packed up the boys. Since we come out here every year for SXSW, I figured we could just come out here and take over the coke scene. As I said, these vamps are soft." He tore into the jugular vein of his arm and peppered on a little more coke. "Whatever happened to that whore junkie that you used to fuck?"

"The Habit?"

"Yeah, that little girl from TV."

"She's the one who killed Cobra. She fucked off somewhere."

"Good riddance to him. He was a shitty leader."

I ignored the comment about Cobra. I felt the coke scratching and ripping its way through my body. Might as well throw some poison ivy on the mosquito bite on top of the chicken pock. "Why does everyone keep talking about South by Southwest like they come here all the time?"

He shoved me and I teetered into the wall next to me. "All of us have been coming here for years. It's pretty much the vampire Mardi Gras."

I pulled myself up straight using the hand rail over my head and started buzzing my tongue in between my teeth. Just like the night before, this crazy stimulant was making me pulsate and shiver. "Wait? What? Quit fucking around. I didn't know that. Fucking weird, dude. Fucking not cool."

"Good coke, huh?" he asked.

"I did a bunch of cock last night at the guy Bromski's house. It's creeper-insane." I slapped my hands against the wall like I was playing bongos.

"Ha!" He spat up a mouthful of blood. "You did a bunch of cock? Ha! Bromski? Good ol' Bromski."

I launched myself off of the wall. "Who's Bromski?"

"I don't know who the hell Bromski is. You just said you sucked his cock. Don't you mean *Broski*?"

"Yeah, that's him." I started hopscotching up and down, from step to step. "He kept trying to tell me that he was just a distributor and not a drug dealer."

"That's how the whole system is set up out here," Linn began. "It's too bad that the gangs are so weak because the system is much better than Cobra's shitshow."

I jumped down to the landing at the bottom of the staircase and yelled back. "Well, how does it work? Enlighten me on the brilliance of Austin."

"Rodderick runs it, but he's a big Hollywood star and all."

The stairwell become smaller and the world moved like a flip book— ten thousand frames a second. I ran up it and panted like an animal. When I reached the top, I leapt onto the other landing like I was hoping onto home plate after hitting a home run. "So?"

"So, he can't be tied back to drug dealing, idiot. He runs all this cancer research and charity nonsense. He's in the public eye constantly."

"Well, then how does he do it?" I asked. I wanted to get as much information about Rodderick as I could.

"The gangs are weak. He rules over them. It works like this." Linnwood put Watts's arm on the top step. "This is Rodderick. He's top of the heap." He pushed the arm back further from the ledge. "Only you can't see him because as far as everyone know, he isn't involved." He put his phone two steps down. "These are his generals. The leader of every gang reports to him and pushes the product to their gangs." He dropped his money clip next to his phone. "Parallel to the generals are the Minutemen. They are kind of like private security. They make sure that the vamps don't get out of control and ensure they do their job."

I sat down again but my body was buzzing harder and harder from the drugs, making it difficult to focus or sit still. "So, it would be like Cobra working with The Cloth?"

"Kind of. Except for the fact that these dudes aren't religious. They are the Austin equivalent to a vigilante border patrol. All they care about is making money and keeping Rodderick in the shadows. They clean up the messes that the vamps cause."

I shook my head like a maraca. "Yeah, I've seen them in action. Where do the gangs fit into this?"

He dug into his pocket and threw a pack of matches down a few steps. "These are the distributors. Like Cody Walker. They deal with the generals very little but they get the drugs to the gang members and the lower gangs. Rather than all the gangs being equals, like L.A., a bigger gang such as the Sixth Street Skulls runs the street and controls gangs like The Real McCoys, The Chaplins and the Rattlers. There are also these dumb human go-betweens who think we can turn them into vampires. They get the drugs, break it up and give it to the gangs." He pointed to the middle of the staircase. "We intercepted Walker's drop after these fools picked up the trailer."

"That was asshole-ish."

"We have to let them know that the BBP is here."

I studied the steps that Linnwood used to show me the hierarchy. "So, where are these gangs?"

He pointed to the bottom of the stairs. "See that piece of toilet paper?" I squinted. "No."

"Exactly. They are so far removed from the top they don't even matter." He put his white leather shoe between the phone and the money clip. "This is where I want to be. I want to be running the generals and not reporting to the fucking Minutemen."

"Does this guy Rodderick even know you? Eldritch knows him but he's not returning calls."

"Eldritch?" he screamed. "That asshole is out here?"

"Well yeah, duh. I told you we were looking for him."

"Tell him that Dracula wants his fucking gear back."

"Shhhhhhh," I insisted as I raised my finger.

"Shhhhhhh, what?"

I waved my hands to quiet him down. "Shut up." I grabbed the blood bong under my armpit and put Watts's hand over his mouth.

We waited for a minute.

"You hear that?" I finally asked.

"Yeah, man." He closed his eyes to concentrate. "Sounds like someone is spraying water on the ramps above us."

"Shhhhhh." I pulled myself to my feet and put my ear through the door into the garage. "Hold this." The arm fell to my side. Common sense told me that I would be able to decipher any sound if it were near me but considering the state I was in, everything sounded like it was in a wind tunnel. "Kinda sounds like someone rolling a steel ball down a sink."

Linnwood jumped to his feet. "Yeah. That's exactly what it sounds like. Eat more coke."

"Why," I responded as I twirled the arm like a baton.

"Eat it," he insisted. "Now!"

I dug my teeth into the center of the arm, trying to get as much cocaine and blood into my body as possible.

He ran into the garage and threw his arm at the other Perrys. "Hey!"

They all looked up to him at the same time. Their faces and proper clothing were drenched in Watts's blood. "Yeah, Linn?"

He waved his arms for silence. "Quiet!" One of them continued to chew on flesh. Impatient, as most coke addicts are. Linnwood booted him in the face. "God dammit," he said. "Fucking shut the fuck up!"

They all turned on their listening caps.

"I don't hear anything," one said.

"Maybe a bunch of dudes are pissing off the roof," another added.

I stumbled over to them, knelt down near the center of their pow wow like a coach going over plays during a time out and took a small dollop of blood and coke from Watts's heart. "Listen closely."

Linnwood reached into the Benz and grabbed his gun.

KURATCH!

A car windshield a floor above us was smashed. The car alarm discharged.

KURTACH!

Another car alarm started blaring.

One of the Perry's whispered, "Maybe it's an earthquake?"

Linnwood took aim around the corner of the ramp coming down toward us. "It's not an earthquake, you idiot."

KURATCH!

I covered my ears. The sounds of multiple alarms bouncing off the walls of the parking structure where clouding my already gridlocked head.

Another windshield was smashed and another alarm when off.

"Get up, you dumbfucks!" Linnwood screamed at his soldiers. "Get your fucking guns out."

The Perrys scrambled to get to their feet. Mimicking their leader, they all cocked their guns and aimed them at the hook in the ramp. Who or whatever was around that corner was camouflaged by a thick concrete wall. The original sound intensified. I realized that it was the sound of several pairs of roller skate bearings spinning at around ten miles per hour.

I started jogging back to the door.

Linnwood shouted and stopped me in my tracks. "Where the fuck are you going, junky?"

I held up my phone. "I forgot my phone."

He shot at my feet, just missing the toe of my left boot. After a little jitterbugging and tap dancing to avoid the bullet, I ran back to the Perrys.

"It's the RTL," one of them yelled.

I was shaken awake in the middle of the ramp by the sound of all the Perry's discharging their pistols.

"Fucking RTL! Fucking RTL! *Fucking RTL!*" Linwood cried.

The blow took further hold of my body. I squeezed my eyes shut and burrowed my nails into my shoulders to try and shock myself out of the buzzies. I blinked my eyes open toward the turn to see ten to twelve massive chicks in roller derby gear take the corner like a flock of Valkyries. They were all assembled in the same, back bent positions with one arm behind them and the other cranking toward us. They fanned out and half of them hunched behind the other half and clutched their hands around the waists, becoming parasites to their hosts. The Perrys frantically unloaded their hardware into the incoming battalion of bitches.

Before I had time to make a run of it, two of them were heading straight at me with no intention of slowing down. The host stood straight up as she started gliding. The parasite squatted further down and let go. As I started to turn and run, the host reached in between her red knee-high striped socks, pulled the parasite through and then fired her like a BB in a slingshot. I completely turned away and pulled my arms over my head as I felt the full force of her helmet collide with the center of my shoulder blades. I turned my head so the side of my face took the brunt of the impact. The good thing was that my teeth didn't spill out on the permanent oil spill where I landed. The bad was that I crushed my jaw near my ear.

"Get off me, you fucking pig," one of the Perry's screamed.

All I could hear was chaos as the car alarms continued to blare and the Perrys continued to shoot their guns and scream. The parasite on top of me started pummeling the back of my head and the exposed side of my face with a wing mirror. The glass crushed under my cheek as I tried to turn my face. I rolled back and forth, making it more difficult for her to connect. Considering the wasted state I was in, it was about all I could do to defend myself.

During one of my evasive twists, I saw Linnwood jump on top of the limousine. Everywhere below him, different members of the BBP were tangled up with one or two of these derby girls. Linn took aim and at close range he blew a hole into one of the derby girl's heads. As she dropped, her roller skates went into opposite directions causing her legs to split. To make sure she stayed down, Linn took a couple extra shots at her.

"Help me," I begged as the host skidded to a stop next to me and began hammering on my ribs with the metal stopper on the front of her skates. Accidentally, she kicked the thigh of the skater on top of me, giving me the opportunity to squirm my way out on the other side. I rolled toward the door to the staircase and eventually pulled myself to my feet using the doorknob. As I caught my breath, the two girls who attacked me split up and started skating in different directions. They crossed each other and started coming for me again. Feeling a burst of energy, I ran away from them down the ramp.

I took the corner going down to level five. One of them was closing in on me. When I heard the bearings of her skates on my heels, I ducked down to her mid-section and disrupted her momentum by lifting her over my head. She flew over me and skidded to a stop on the cement with her face.

The other girl, the parasite, blazed around the corner to join us on level five. This time I was ready for her. She threw the car mirror at me but I sidestepped and it landed in the face of her host.

"You dumb bitch," the host yelped as she tried to stretch loose flesh back onto her face. "Look at my face."

Once again, the parasite tried to jump on me but I was too quick for her. I locked onto her arm with both my hands, spun my body and heaved her into one of the many pylons near me. Her spine snapped in two as soon as she made contact and her rubbery dilapidated body bounced to the ground.

The host started crying as she tried desperately to pick up all the pieces of her face. "What the fuck? What the fuck?"

"We've gotta get outta here!" Linnwood and two more Perrys had rounded the corner to also join me on level five. His face was beat red and drenched in sweat and blood. He took the lead and ran toward mangled face and unloaded four more bullets into her. She slumped over as the thin strips of her face slipped through her hands into her lap. The other two Perrys surrounded the parasite that I catapulted into the pylon. She wasn't moving but they decided to fire several bullets into her head anyway.

Linn grabbed the host by the strap of her helmet and lifted her dead face. "Jesus, RJ. What did you do to this bitch?" he hollered. "You guys. Come look at this. RJ ripped her face off."

The other two walked over. "Get down by her," one of them said as he grabbed his phone out of his pocket. The other bent down by her corpse and the three of them took pictures.

Linnwood pulled his pants down and put his bare ass up to her skinned face. "Open her mouth, if you can find it."

The other two picked up her face and ripped her chin off. Then, Linnwood farted in her mouth. They all broke into a frenzied laughter.

"This is classic," Linnwood said as he tried to contain his laughter. "RJ, you need to get in on this."

I looked back up the ramp to see two more Perrys round the corner. One had a couple of cuts on his face and the other was nursing a pretty bloody wound on his hand.

"Holy shit. Look at the bitch."

"What did you do to her?"

"Hilarious."

They two newcomers ran past me to join their pals at the bottom of the ramp.

"RJ, you gotta get over here and get some pics before we have to split."

I smoothed my hand all over my face. "What the fuck was that?"

"What was what?" Linnwood pulled his pants back up.

I pointed at the host. "What is all this shit?" I pointed at the parasite. "What the fuck?"

"The RTL?" he began as he rolled a cigarette on the dead host's face. He left it there to suck up some more blood and turned to me. "They are— I mean, they *were* some Austin gang called Ride the Lightning." He grabbed the cigarette from the exposed face and flipped it into his mouth. He reached into his pocket but before he lit the butt he said, "Yeah, until tonight, they ran the coke in this town."

"I guess they don't anymore," one of the other Perry's injected.

I started to walk back up to level six.

"You pussy, RJ," Linnwood called after me.

I stopped and turned around. "Pussy? Fuck you. I have been attacked by more of these weird ass gangs over the course of this week than I can even count."

He walked toward me but first turned back to the photo opportunity at the host. "Wrap it up, guys. We gotta get out of here." He ran and caught up to me. "What's your problem?" he put his arm over my shoulder. His gun dangled near my ear.

I didn't turn to him. "Just get that Rodderick dude to meet with me."

"Rodderick? You're kidding, right? I told you that he's in the shadows, dude."

I stopped again and shrugged the gun off of my shoulder. "No. I'm not kidding. I came here to meet you so I could get in touch with him."

"You dumb junkie." He waved his gun at the parasite, whose body was nearly detached into two pieces. "He doesn't want to meet with you."

"Would you just text the guy, please?"

He came in close and pressed his gun sideways against my chest. "Don't you see what we've done? L.A. is gone. This is our new city. I told you that these gangs are soft."

I pushed him away. "Who are you kidding? These gangs aren't soft. They're psychopaths. Have you seen this drug that they are using down here? Sunshine? It's totally nuts." We turned the corner. Pieces of RTL were scattered all around the sixth floor.

"Yeah, look at these bitches. It took us five minutes to dismantle this whole gang. This," he picked up a severed head still inside a helmet. "This is an Austin gang. And, this…" he flapped his hand between our arms, "*This* is an L.A. gang. Hollywood has already taken control of SXSW. We should follow suit and take the streets." He chucked the head up by the limousine.

"Look, Linn, I don't care how you preface the conversation. You can say that you want to talk about an arrangement, but you need to let him know that I need to speak to him."

We reached the car and he moved what was left of Watts to the side. "That prick doesn't know who the fuck you are." He then used his gun to hammer out any leftover glass that was still in the window. He pointed to the back seats of the Benz. "Get in." He yelled down to the rest of the Perrys, who were just turning the corner from level five. "Do any of you losers have the keys to this car?"

One of them fumbled around in his pocket, pulled out some keys and jingled them in front of him. "Got 'em."

As I sat down, I looked at my phone. Eldritch finally responded again. *Sorry I could not meet you.*

I typed.

Where are you?

The rest of the Perrys got into the back of the limo and Linnwood got into the driver's seat. "Where do you need to go?"

The Perry who had the keys sat next to him in front.

Eldritch sent through an address.

Before the suicide doors were closed on either side, I heard the humming engines of several pickups below us.

"Now what?" I grunted.

Linnwood slammed his door closed. "Minutemen. Rodderick must know that the BBP is in town."

XVIII

HUNTED

I slumped against the window and watched a massive pickup truck trying to veer the Perry mobile off the road. "Why are they always on the scene?"

Linnwood leaned forward, keeping his eyes glued on the road. "I told you. They clean up the vampire mess."

I scrunched myself up in the back quarters of the limo and squinted a little bit. In the pickup truck there were two roughnecks, both with cowboy hats. I looked behind us to see three more flatbeds competing for pole position on the other side of our car.

One of the Perrys, who was sitting directly across from me because the backseats faced each other, smashed the window closest to him with his gun.

I swept a few shards of glass off my thigh. As my head continued to swim around in the drug pool, I tried to get a closer look. No vestments. No priest shit. Just cowboys. I looked at Linnwood via the rearview mirror.

Before I opened my mouth, he said, "No. Not Minutemen like the Revolution. Minutemen like border militia."

I leaned forward so he could see my reflection in the mirror. "I was going to say the Minutemen like Mike Watt."

"Nobody in this car knows what the fuck that means." He pounded his foot on to the gas and swerved in front of the pickup next to us. "They capture the vamps who step out of line and drag us across the border. I've heard that they leave us out in the Mexican desert to be killed by the sun."

"Hey." I waved my hand in front of the Perry across from me. "You know Mike Watt, right?"

He turned away from the broken window and glared at me.

I lifted an imaginary microphone in front of my mouth. "D. Boon?"

"Idiot," he hissed and turned back to the window.

Rather than continue yapping on and on about a band they clearly didn't know, I fell back into my seat and crossed my arms. "Idiot," I repeated in my best asshole voice.

The truck on the left pulled slightly in front of us. There were three more Minutemen in the bed with their shotguns raised.

I uncrossed my arms and leapt forward. "Jesus!"

As one of the hunters got a shot off, Linnwood stomped the breaks and twirled the wheel. The two trucks on either side darted in front of us. Instead of ramming into the back of our limousine, the two trucks behind us pivoted around the Benz and spun into the gravel shoulders on either side. One compensated for the jolt but the other toppled over, tossing two passengers into the middle of the street.

Linn threw the car into reverse, trying to run them over. He mashed one of them into the pavement. His amigo held onto his leg and started firing a Colt 45 at our car. Linn curved back and forth trying to hit the injured assassin but quickly gave up, pulled alongside him and blew his brains all over the Texas asphalt. Knowing that time wasn't on our side, he twirled the wheel and hopped over the median in the road to start heading back the other way.

"Give me a fucking gun!" I shouted.

"Bennington," Linnwood barked. "Give him your gun."

Bennington Perry tossed me his gun. Under normal circumstances I would had made fun of his name, but since we were being chased by a lynch mob of unsavory vampire killers, I focused on getting out of another shitty situation by the seat of my pants. Getting left in the Mexican desert didn't sound like a wonderful vacation.

The backseat Perrys and I looked behind us. The three remaining trucks had managed to flip to the other side of the road as well.

"I don't think they are going to let us go," said one of the Perrys.

"Shut up, Lukas," the rest said in unison.

Lukas, I thought. *Lukas. Luke. Oh, shit. Luke Perry.* "You're named after the guy on *90210?*"

He cocked his gun in my face but didn't say anything.

I put my hands up. "I mean… awesome! You're named after the guy from *90210!* I suppose it makes sense considering you guys worked out of Beverly Hills."

"You're goddamn right, it makes sense," he said as he re-focused his attention to the rear of the car.

I looked at the other three Perrys in the car. The dude riding shotgun happened to have curly blond hair. I pointed to him. "Is he Ian Ziering?"

Before anyone could respond, one of the trucks banged into the back of our car, sending Bennington into my lap. Linnwood cut the wheel, but instead of turning around again, he pulled into a gas station. He tugged on the emergency brake and then threw the car into park. He opened his door and charmingly stepped out of the car. "Get out. We fight better on the ground."

As everyone evacuated, the truck that was ramming us quickly pulled into the gas station. Linn took steady aim on their windshield and unloaded a few rounds, taking out the driver. The truck swung to the side of the gas station and all the Perrys fired into the window of the passenger, killing him and two cowboys in the jump seat.

Linnwood rounded the Mercedes, flung open the unlatched trunk and saved the coke-filled duffle bag. Luke split off from him and headed to the truck. He jumped onto the running boards, opened the door and pulled the driver out, throwing him into the door of the women's bathroom on the side of the building. "Bennington, take the station owner!" he said as he put the truck in park.

Bennington flipped Luke a thumbs up and rushed inside the gas station. I sped over to the carjacking scene and heard two gunshots ring out from inside the building. The other Perrys followed me and Linnwood grabbed the dead passenger by what was left of his head and yanked him out of the truck.

"Jump in the back," Linnwood said as he dropped a clip out of his handgun and reloaded with one he had tucked away in the pocket of his shirt under his sweater. "And hold on to this." He handed me the duffle bag.

I looked into the bed and remembered the fate of the two Minutemen out on the street. "I'm not getting in there," I yelled back as Ian Ziering grabbed the bag from me and he and the yet unnamed guest star Perry hopped in.

Bennington ran passed me and smacked me on the back. "Then, stay and die, Knuckler." Ian and the other dude helped him into the truck.

"Get in the back," Linnwood insisted as he fired his gun in the direction of the headlights of the two other trucks that were rapidly approaching.

I hesitated.

"Get in!"

I stepped into the lifted wheel well and onto the tire. Right before Luke Perry punched it and sped out, Ian Ziering grabbed onto my forearm and pulled me onboard.

It was as if we were sitting on the receiving end of a firing line. The passengers in the back of the two remaining Minutemen trucks stood up behind the blazing flood lights and started discharging bullets into our truck bed. One such shot destroyed the back window of our truck. Thankfully, the shrapnel narrowly missed Linnwood. Even more thankfully, it also missed my new best friend Luke Perry. The would-be heartthrob sped back onto the road as we all fired back at the Vamp Rangers. He was a much better driver than Linnwood, but skills didn't really mean anything in a huge truck that was being chased by vampire cleaners.

Somehow, the four of us in the back managed to take out the flood lights. The Minutemen in the backs of both trucks took cover from our barrage. Bennington, who gave me his gun, curled up close to the tailgate and clutched onto the handle from the inside.

"Back the fuck off," Linnwood screamed. "We've already killed half of you twats!"

I emptied my gun and then turned to the cabin and saw him yelling into a CB radio microphone. "Linn, give me a clip."

He didn't hear me so I crawled closer to the cab.

"That's a negative, demon. Y'all are dyin' tonight," one of the Minutemen broadcasted over the radio.

"Linn, give me a clip," I repeated through the broken back window.

Just then, Ian Ziering got to his feet and started shooting into the windshield of one of the trucks. Before he could sit back down and fight from the limited cover of the bed, a rifle shot nailed him in the chest and then another slipped into his forehead and out through the back of his curly head. He crumbled on top of me.

"I don't have any more," Linnwood yelled back through the window. He nudged his head at Ian. "Throw him."

Ian's hand shook to a stop in my lap. "I'm not gonna throw him," I said.

Linnwood handed me his gun. "Use him as a shield. He's fucking dead, you junkie scum."

Listening to Linn, I placed what was left of Ziering's head under my chin and then used the rest of him to cover my body like a blanket.

"That's one," the southern drawl called out again over the receiver. "Why not pull on over and let us send you to hell with a little bit of dignity, boy."

I squinted into the truck on the left after I was sure that I had my Ian Ziering body armor fully sheltering me. I saw the passenger in the truck with the microphone to his mouth and shot from Linnwood's gun.

"You hear me, mother—"

I picked him off and the CB communications went dead.

"Got him," I crowed.

The headlights from the left truck turned off to the side of the road. "They just got Donny," the driver added. "We're done."

"Roger that. We'll get 'em," right truck driver called back. In an attempt to wiggle us off the road, the driver did several elusive maneuvers by faking left, then right, then ramming our bumper.

"You should probably turn around with your friends, motherfucker," Linn yelled into the microphone. "Oh, shit, I forgot to press this button—"

"You pressed the button, idiot," the driver said.

"Fuck you," Linnwood started again. "We've taken out seven of your boys and you've take out one of ours."

In an attempt to brake and disrupt again, Luke Perry slammed on the brakes. The hunters' truck smacked into the tailgate. Bennington was shot into the air but since his hand was entangled between their front bumper and our tailgate, he started to flip over onto their hood. He took a bombardment of bullets that popped him in the air like he was a plastic bag being targeted by an assault rifle from the three gunmen lined up behind the flood lights. Finally, he landed on their hood and both vehicles came to a stop.

Luke and Linn jumped out of our truck as Bennington fell from their hood and onto the ground after his completely severed hand was freed. The snipers in the back of their truck took aim at me and started shooting. Rather than take my chances that none of them would shoot me in the face, I ducked under Ziering. When I heard one of them stop firing and start reloading, I launched the lifeless shell at the Minutemen in back, fully knocking the flood lights off the cab and causing them to take cover. For all they knew, the body could jump back to life at the drop of a dime and consume all of them. I started to exit on the opposite of the vehicle as the random Perry jumped onto the sand below.

The driver clicked the ignition, furiously trying to turn over his truck and retreat. To his chagrin, the passenger in his cab and the gunman in back jumped off the truck.

Finally, his truck turned over, he shifted into reverse and sped away backward down the street.

"Jeb! Where the hell are you going?" one of the gunman shrieked.

"Get back here, ya son of a bitch," the passenger added as he started shooting at his own truck.

Unfortunately for them, Jeb didn't bother to stop and wait for his comrades to run and catch a ride back to Redneck HQ. Rather, the chicken shit cowboy turned around and bumped his horn a few times to signify *see you soon*. One of the four remaining Minutemen turned around to see me, Linnwood, Luke Perry and Random leaning against the smashed-up ass of our truck.

"Run," he advised his associates.

And they ran.

Linnwood put out his hand. "RJ. May I?"

I was doubled over, gasping for air. I lifted my arm up without looking at it and handed the gun to him.

"Thank you." He ejected the clip that I was using from the gun and shoved in another.

"Hey, I thought you said that you were out."

Linn grinned. "I wanted to see if you were strong enough to throw Chadwick."

"Who's Chadwick?" I asked.

Random interrupted. "The guy you were hiding under like a little girl."

I scratched some blood off of my leg. "You mean Ian? Ian Ziering?"

"His name isn't Ian." Linnwood pressed the pistol against my temple. "He was a very old friend of mine."

I shook my drenched hair. "If he was such a good friend, then why did you want me to try and throw him at their truck?"

He pulled the gun away. "He was already dead, asshole."

"How did they even know where we were?" I remembered their appearance at the pharmacy. "How did they know where I was when I got attacked by the McCoys?"

He brought me in closer to him and breathed into my ear. "Jesus, Reynolds. How many times do I have to tell you who these asshole are? They're the cleaners. They sweep up the mess left by things like us."

I pushed him away. "Get off of me. How do they know?"

"Because they work for Rodderick, idiot." He walked to the side of our truck and slapped his hand against the compressed flared fender. "Lukas, get this piece of shit started." And then, he smacked Random on the butt. "Come on."

"You don't want me to come?" I asked.

As he and Random began jogging after the Rangers who retreated on foot he looked at me and answered. "You're useless. Get those two corpses out of the back seats of the cab. Maybe wipe them down."

Luke Perry did as he was told. So did I. After a couple of minutes, I heard some gunfire and a series of southern cries.

XIX

DUMPED

The Golden Aces Hotel was a single level motor lodge on the outskirts of Austin. It was a dump. The faded brown stucco building had rusted air conditioning units dripping a darker brown goo onto wilted potted plants. I imagined that the plants were supposed to camouflage the obvious health code violations, but whatever was in the sludge stunted the growth and killed the greenery. There was a soda machine near Eldritch's door that desperately needed some attention because the lights inside flickered and buzzed. I shoved my hand into my pocket because a soda sounded nice, seeing as how my mouth was so dry.

"Do you guys have any change?" I asked Linnwood, Luke Perry and Random.

"Change?" Linnwood asked. "Why the fuck do you need change? Go get some from Dracula."

"Come on, dude. Give me some change. I want to get a drink. My mouth feels like I've been chewing on a sand-filled cactus."

He whipped out a fat money clip and handed me a fifty-dollar bill through the broken back window of the cab. "Here."

I attempted to hand it back to him. "Do you have anything smaller?"

"Just take the money," he sighed.

"Can you drop me around back?" I didn't want the Perrys to know that Eldritch and I were the kidnappers of Pinball. They would, without thinking twice, kill us and then eat her or rip her into pieces for the fun of it. I doubted there was any reward for Pinball because I killed her parents and no one else except for the cable news channels seemed to care about her. That being said, and as fun as my bonding experience with the West Beverly Hills gangsters was, I knew that they were self-serving lunatics and they could turn on me like a pack of mongooses.

Linnwood took down a bullet of coke and then offered it to me. "Why? Do you need to wake up, too?"

I wisely rejected more drugs. The last thing that I wanted to do was storm into the room, bounce around like a maniac and scare the shit out of Pinball. "I just need to get my head together. Maybe I'll barf and take a dump."

"You're such scum. Have you ever wondered why people hate heroin addicts?" Linn asked as he picked around in his nose. "Why don't you wait to do all that until you get into the room? What? You don't want your boyfriend to smell your stench?"

"I just need to get my shit together, Linn. I've had an exhausting couple of days."

He slapped Luke on the arm. "Do it."

Doing as he was told, Luke Perry shifted the truck into drive and drove slowly. I heard the sound of both rear tires rubbing up against the crushed backend.

We pulled around the back of the Golden Aces near a strip mall that had a Mex-taco restaurant, a liquor store and a beauty salon. The truck came to a stop under a broken street light.

Linnwood pulled out his phone. "What's your number, RJ?"

I pulled out my phone and looked at it. "I don't think I know."

"Fuck, man. Call me." I unlocked my phone and started dialing him as he read off his number. His phone buzzed and he declined answering it.

I stuck my head into the cab. "What, you're not going to answer?"

"No, dummy." He touched the screen and then added me to his contacts. Rather than adding my name, he simply wrote JUNKIE.

I started to get out of the back of the truck and I fist bumped Random Perry. "Nice, Linn." I said. "I appreciate it."

"At least I won't forget who you are," he said. "I'll text you if or when I hear from Rodderick. Don't expect anything to happen."

I flipped up two fingers. "Peace."

As I leapt off and they headed back to wherever they were staying, I heard Luke say, "Hey, don't forget to 'Keep Austin Weird', loser." They all laughed. The three remaining Blue Blooded Perrys were still the three biggest assholes in the world.

"Fuck you, Luke Perry," I said to myself as I took off that terrible shirt and tucked it into my back pocket.

In an attempt to sober up a little, I walked up and down the street, across the parking lots and through the alleys to puke for about an hour. I stopped next to a dumpster to try and squat out a shit but I was constipated. I wasn't looking forward to using a discarded Doritos bag as toilet paper, anyway. Instead, I just coughed up bloody bile and pissed a few times.

The area had a minimal traffic and almost no people, which I'm sure was part of Eldritch's lay low plan. A plane soared by me in the sky above. It was a little closer than I was comfortable with, because I was terrified of flying things. I guessed that I was close to the airport but not a popular route from downtown Austin. We were still in the middle of South by Southwest and I hadn't seen a headlight on either street near me since I had gotten there.

I walked back from the alley and looked at the businesses again in the strip mall. The liquor store was the only business open. I spit on my arms with what little fluid I had left inside of me and then plucked the tie dye from my pocket and started scrubbing all signs of blood off of my arms, chest and stomach. I strutted into the store as a shirtless Texan would and a tinny, distorted bell rang out. Turns out it was actually more of a head shop than a liquor store.

The burnout behind the counter nodded his head. "Zup, brah?" He had a fuzzy brown beard, blended into his long hair that was pulled back into a pony tail. He was wearing a black Big Boys shirt with a giant anarchy symbol on it.

"Sweet." I pointed to his shirt. "I love the Big Boys."

He turned his back and sucked some THC out of a vape pen. "Whatever, dude. I, like, got it at, like, a thrift shop or whatever."

I walked over to the drink fridge, opened it up and grabbed a Gatorade. I closed it and then looked at the fifty in my hand that Linnwood gave me. I reached back in for another bottle. "Yeah, they were a killer hardcore band."

"Hardcore is lame, dude," he said as he puffed out a huge cloud. "Fuckin' poser."

I didn't respond. I walked toward the counter, waving my way through the fog. I stopped at a rack of t-shirts and sifted through them. One said *High As Fuck*. Another said *Legalize Freedom* and had a pot leaf mixed into the lettering. Yet another one said *Natural Born Chiller* and had Darwin's evolutionary progression where a monkey evolved into the silhouette of some guy sitting down smoking a bong. The best shirt had a bootleg version of the Converse Chuck Taylor logo and said *Pot Head All Stars*.

I held up the Chuck Taylor shirt and pointed to the logo. "Do you have any shirts that aren't weed related?"

He ignored me and picked up his phone and started scrolling through music.

"Excuse me." I snapped my fingers.

He rolled his head back as if I was putting him out. "*What?*"

I pointed to the shirt again. "Do you have any non-stoner shirts?"

"You'd like that, wouldn't you, you fuckin' narc?"

"Narc? I just—"

He held up his phone and crushed his thumb into the volume button on the side. He closed his eyes and started waving his head back and forth.

I dropped the shirt on the floor and grabbed the *High As Fuck* shirt. It was black, whereas all the other shirts were green or even more ridiculous. As I was heading to the counter to pay, something caught my eye. It was one of those red, yellow and green Rasta hats with dreadlocks sewn into it. It reminded me of King Cobra. It wasn't very cool, but it was marginally cooler than Pinball's wig.

The dipshit at the counter yelled over whatever shit indie music he was jamming out to. "You gonna buy anything, you fuckin' asshole?"

I wanted to kill him so badly but instead, I held up the hat. "How much is this?"

He turned around and started playing with a Rubik's Cube like he didn't hear me respond to his question.

I reached the counter and I put the hat, the shirt and the two bottles of Gatorade on the glass case that contained every kind of porcelain bowl and bong slider you can imagine, as well as random shit like papers, brass knuckles and zippo lighters. "Hey, man," I said.

He didn't answer, again.

I tried to reach across the display case to tug on his shirt but I couldn't reach him.

"Hey, man," I said again, this time louder.

He spun around tossed the Rubik's Cube into the air. "*What?*"

"Jesus. I've been trying to get your attention." I lifted the Rasta hat up again. "How much is this hat?"

He looked down at my items. "I don't know."

I held up the fifty. "I have money."

He reached out toward the bill. "Let me see that."

I reached in so he could grab it.

He snatched it from my fingers and then held it up to the light. He then shook his head, balled it up and threw it back at me. "It's counterfeit, you fuckin' convict."

I bent over and picked up the money. I uncrumpled it, pulled it out with both hands and then smacked it face down on top of the hat. "It's not counterfeit, shithead. How much is all this crap?"

He looked down at my items and shrugged his shoulders. "How am I supposed to know?"

I grabbed him by his shirt. "Because you work here. That's how you know."

"You smell like you hurled, you fuckin' hobo," he said as he slapped my hand off of his collar.

I started collecting my stuff. "How much?"

"Like fifty bucks, I guess." He tossed a plastic bag at me.

I flicked the money at him. "This should cover it." I put on the shirt and then I packed up the Rasta hat and the two bottles of Gatorade in the bag and headed out of the store.

"Come again," he called out after me.

I resisted the urge to bounce back into the head shop and mutilate the jackass who accused me of being a poser, a convict, a bum, and a narc, among other things. The last thing that I wanted to do was draw any more attention to the cyclone of waste that I had somehow managed to leave in my path since I arrived in Austin. If the Minutemen really wanted to get me, it wouldn't be too difficult to follow my breadcrumb trail of body parts and drugs across the city.

Several times I walked up to the door to Eldritch's room and bent my wrist back to knock. Just as many times, I retreated back to the alley or across the street. I desperately tried to shake the drugs out of my system. I don't really know why. I guess I didn't want him to think that I was out having a good time while he was stuck with the kid.

My jaw clicked a little because it still wasn't fully healed from getting pounded into cement. I sat down next to a dumpster and shoved my finger down my throat, guessing that drugs even though most of the garbage left over from my three-day binge, after my previous three-day binge, were still shimmering around.

Still waiting on that heroin.

I expected that my super metabolism just ate the shit out of all the coke I did back in the garage with Linn, but I didn't feel great and usually puking rattled my bones back to life.

After I was fairly certain that I had rid my body of everything down to the bile, I glanced down at the *High as Fuck* shirt I was wearing. A treasure it was not. But, it was better than the *Keep Austin Weird* shirt that made me the asshole for the better part of the day.

"High as fuck," I said to myself in a burnout voice.

I looked across the street to the motel and sat back down next to the garbage. I figured if I sat there long enough, some sanitation workers would come put me out of my misery. That's really how beaten I felt. I was on a useless crusade to save myself. I kept trying to insist that the entire trip to Austin was to vindicate Bait and Pinball from the predators that they were unfortunate enough to have to call their parents. I beat that into my head over and over again. If I said it enough times, it had to come true. I was doing the right thing. I was the hero. I was the one making the world a better place for children.

But the fact was that every miserable circle and gruesome path lead back to me. And there it was. It was all about me. My horrible decisions and my irresponsible, self-serving mountain of filth. The mountain was stacked high by the bodies of everyone I touched, spoke to, or had any type of contact with. It started with my mother and it was going to end with Pinball.

One of the yarn dreadlocks slithered its way out of the head shop bag. Memories of King Cobra bolted to his bed at The Cloth's church latched on to the ball of guilt building inside me. I was one the one who brought that piece of shit The Habit into our world and she managed to tear it down from the inside. She brought down the leader... or at least the closest thing that we all ever had to a leader. It's a shame that I spent so many years trying to take him down myself, only realizing that he was my closest ally when we had both seemingly reached the end of the road.

I pulled the Rasta hat fully out of the bag and looked at it, placing it on the cement like it was a dead rodent. I didn't want to put it on because my hair was pretty coated in flesh, blood, and drugs.

As if my dreams were going to let me forget, I asked the hat, "I fucked up, huh?"

I don't know if I really expected an answer. I suppose that it would have been nice to get some guidance from somewhere or someone other than The Gooch. I could have deflected the responsibility back to my whore of a mom for not aborting me. The fact that I asked questions of a hat with dreadlocks sewn into it rather than just knocking on Eldritch's motel room door proved that I didn't want to have to answer or explain my actions to anyone.

I picked up the hat and tugged on the elastic base as I made quiet Reggae rhythms. I put the hat over my hand like a puppet. "You're a total scumbag," I said with a Jamaican accent. "What er ya gonna do wit dat little girl?"

After twirling the hat around my finger for a few minutes, I got to my feet and dusted off my jeans. For a few seconds, I debated throwing the hat into the dumpster. Against my better judgment, I dropped it back into the plastic bag and finally headed over to the Golden Aces Hotel to face the music.

I looked at a pile of empty and cheap champagne bottles stacked up outside the door next to Eldritch's room. *Great, we're staying next door to a hooker*, I thought.

Even though the lights were on inside Eldritch's room, I lightly scratched at the door. It was important to seem like I was being considerate. No one answered, so I knocked a little bit with the bottom of my palm. I held my hand over the decomposing air conditioning unit in the window. The synthetic warm breeze felt nice as it curled under my fingernails.

"I am coming," Eldritch called out from behind the door.

I looked down. I wanted to give myself every second that I had to clear the coke rage from my eyes.

I heard the security chain hang and clink against the wood as the door peeped open.

"Look up," he demanded.

"Can I come in?" I asked as I cleared the passages between my gums and teeth with my tongue.

He delicately lifted up my chin with his fingers. "Look up." He then looked at my shirt and sighed.

I closed my eyes.

Then he closed the door, fully unhooked the chain lock and opened it. "Get in and be quiet. The Little One is sleeping."

I dragged myself onto the carpet in the room, trying to avoid eye contact with him.

"Follow me," he said as he led me to the back of the room, toward the bathroom.

As I crossed by her bed, Pinball shuffled around under the covers. I stopped for a second.

Eldritch grabbed me by the shirt and pulled me along. "Come on."

When we reached the sink and vanity area of the room, he pulled closed the sliding door that separated the sleeping and living area from the bathroom. Then he pointed to the toilet. "Sit."

"Here," I said as I sat on the throne and held up the head shop bag.

"What is this?" he asked.

"A gift," I announced. "For her."

He took the bag and looked inside. He sighed again. "Why?"

I continued to look at my feet. "I don't think she likes the wig. I thought maybe this would make her feel cool."

Without responding to the gesture, he dropped the bag in the corner, under a clothes hanger bar on the other side of the sink.

"Look," I started.

Apparently I got some barf on the bag when I was hiding out next to the dumpster, trying to cool down. Eldritch turned on the sink and furiously washed it off his hands.

"Look," I started again. "I'm really shaken up, dude."

He shut off the sink. "Do tell. I am curious where this could possibly lead. I have only heard from you through a series of volatile text messages over the past forty-eight hours."

I scratched my neck. "Well, I was hiding out under a tarp after we separated at the drug store."

He guided my head up and over with his finger again. "I want to see your eyes."

"I got into a fight with a huge opossum. Then, I fought off a pack of guard dogs. After that I met some sober cheeseball who runs all the cocaine in the Southwest through a jet ski rental business." I blinked but looked him straight in the eyes. "Then, I met up with the BBPs and we were attacked by some gang of psycho bitches called the RTL. Apparently, Linnwood thinks he can just take over the coke business in Austin without starting a gang war. Well, that didn't work out."

He turned around and cupped his hands together behind his back. "Is he still among the living?"

"Yeah, he's still alive." I stretched my legs out. The top of the toilet tank behind me shook loose. "Only three Perrys still alive, though."

"Unfortunate," he said as he paced a few steps to the hanger bar.

"I met the Minutemen. They're a fun bunch." I grabbed some toilet paper and stuffed it into my mouth in an attempt to dilute the gross smell of my insides. I threw the conversation back on him. "Any word from Rodderick?"

He side-stepped back to the sink and turned on the water. He then lathered up his hands again and scratched at his skin. "I do not believe that I have his most current number."

I stood up, stretched my arms up to the ceiling and bent my back toward the tub. "I do have some possible good news."

"Do tell." He turned off the water and wiped his hands on a towel. Then he laid the towel on my shoulder.

"Linnwood knows him." I grabbed the towel and wiped my face. It was semi-moist and I could smell hints of the generic cheap motel soup lacing the terrycloth. "He and the Perrys come down here every year for South by Southwest."

"Everyone comes to Austin for South by Southwest."

"So I've heard." I backed up to the toilet and sat down again. "He sent

Rodderick a text. He said he'll give him our message and then get back to me."

Eldritch stepped to the threshold between the vanity room and the bathroom. "Will he betray you?"

"Hard to say." I put my elbows on my knees and rested my cheeks on my hands. My body creaked after every movement. "The catch is that the Perrys just took down Ride the Lightning. Ride the Lightning was running cocaine for Rodderick. Linnwood is starting a war in Austin because he said Los Angeles is over."

His boots turned away from the bathroom and he walked back to the sink. "Yes. I concluded as much. Linnwood has a habit of taking things that do not belong to him."

"I've been thinking, Eldritch."

"You have? That seems amusing to me." For the third time, he turned on the faucet. "It sounds like you just returned from a celebration all over Austin." He chuckled to himself. "RJ has been thinking."

"Fuck you, asshole." I stood up from the toilet and faced him. "I didn't come back here to fight with you."

He grabbed the soap and covered his hands and wrists with froth. "I'm quite surprised you came back at all."

I stood in the bathroom doorway and looked at him in the mirror. "What's that supposed to mean?"

"You know damn well what it means." He slammed his fist on the porcelain sink. "Killing the girl's parents was your idea. But taking the girl was my idea." He flicked a long stand of hair out of his face and stared back into the mirror. "She does not understand our world, RJ."

"That's what I was thinking about." I lightened my tone, reached over and turned off the water. "If we don't hear from Rodderick tomorrow, I think we should hand the girl over to the police or firemen."

"How dare you!" He turned from the mirror and shook the foam off his hands.

I pointed toward the other room, reminding him that Pinball was asleep. "How dare me, what? We need to do something."

"I do not want to betray the trust that I have built with the child. I will not make her a ward of the state. Those people are monsters."

"What the fuck are we? I take that back." I handed him the towel. "What the fuck am I? Surely the authorities are better than me."

He wiped his hands. "Yes, they might be better than *you*."

"You act like I had a choice in what went on over the past few days. Your good friend Rodderick hasn't gotten back to you. I've been attacked by three different gangs since we got here. We need to cut our losses and head home."

145

"Cut our losses? Cut our losses? You are acting like you lost a game." He turned back to the vanity and began sopping up the water overflow from his three hand washings. "Maybe it would be better if *you* returned to L.A. and cut *your* losses."

"I can't get back to L.A., dude. You know that. I'm agreeing with you. If you would stop washing your hands for a second and listen to me, you'd realize that my purpose is to get the girl safe. Safe and away from us."

He stopped drying off the counter but didn't say anything. Instead, he just looked at me in the mirror.

"I was wrong," I admitted. "This whole trip. This whole thing. It's wrong. I know that. Have you seen the news? They aren't far behind us, Eldritch. We either have to get the girl to the actor now or we have to turn ourselves in. I don't care if it's the cops or the fire department. Anyone is better for her than you and me."

"Speak for yourself," he whispered. "I have not seen the news. I do not want the Little One to hear what is happening."

I stepped closer to the mirror. "Why are you resisting this? I am trying to do the right thing. We put the girl in the center of a zombie apocalypse at a drug store."

He starred back. "They are not true zombies."

"They sure as fuck looked like true zombies to me. And let's be honest." I tapped on the soiled drywall. "While you were hiding out in this room, I've been out there on the streets getting batted around like a piñata."

He reached toward the hot water lever.

I slapped his hand away. "How do you pay for this room, anyway? How do you pay for everything?" I put my finger to my chin as if I had solved a crime. "That's right. You have credit cards. You had a family. This vampire thing is only a dress-up game to you."

"You know nothing about me," he insisted. "You know nothing, little man." He spun around and grabbed me by the throat. "The only game here is the one that you started." He lifted me up to his face. "Do we need to go through this again? Do we need to relive these moments constantly where you question my credibility?"

I gasped for air. "I'm not questioning your credibility, *friend*. I am questioning your intent. Why don't we just go leave the girl in the office of the hotel and get in your rental car and be on our merry way?"

He tightened his grip. "As I said before and I will say again, this was all your doing. I led us to Austin because I have a strategy. I have a plan that will enable the girl to have a real life after this."

"And then?" My larynx fought his fingers. "Share the plan."

He let go. "You will sleep in here tonight." He pointed to a pillow and a blanket under the hanger rack. "You will shower and then you will go to sleep."

I coughed and dove under the facet. I twisted open the handle and let the cold water sooth my throat.

He crossed his arms across his chest. "I will share the plan with you in the morning. Hopefully, your collaborator will send a message tomorrow. Please leave your filthy rags on the other side of the door and I will launder this evening." He turned around, slid the door back open and left the room.

As he was closing the door behind him, I heard Pinball ask, "What's going on in there?"

"Nothing, Little One," he responded. "Uncle RJ and I are having a disagreement."

She yawned. "Oh, he's back?"

"Yes. He slayed more evil creatures in your honor."

"Okay."

I took off my clothes, balled them up and set them outside the sliding door. Before I got in the shower, I also put the bag from the head shop outside next to my laundry.

XX

DRAINED

I struggled to fall asleep to the metronome drip of the Golden Aces' facet. I got up several times from the hard floor that was covered by a thin layer of mangy, damp carpet to try and shut it off to no avail. I heard a lot of movement outside in the main living quarters, which I guessed meant that Eldritch was doing my laundry. I knew better than to open the door again to ask any questions. It was better to sleep off my drug-logged body and try again to appeal to his senses in the morning. Finally, after rolling around in my cell, I fell asleep.

I sat alone in the circle. I was in the gymnasium again, but the rest of the band of dreamtime regulars were nowhere to be found. I felt relieved.

Dez entered the meeting and sat down across from me. "He's right, you know. This is your fault."

"I admitted it was my fault," I said.

He walked around and took the seat next to me. "I sure didn't help. Did I?"

I tried not to look at him.

"Ignoring me isn't gonna help you," he said.

I put my fingers in my ears and closed my eyes.

"I said, that's not going to help you."

I looked back across to the other side of the chairs, still trying to avoid talking to Dez. The Cloth leader Fat Mac was sitting across from me now. He had one of the dog collars on that The Cloth used to keep vampires restrained. His arms were where his legs should have been. "He's right, you know," he said as he tried to loosen the collar with one of his feet hands.

"*Adstringo gutter!*" a voice on the other side of me shouted.

The priest winked at me. His head didn't explode.

I turned to my left, where the new voice was coming from. It was The Habit again. The lights flared on in the gymnasium and melted mutant Fat Mac in his chair. The collar spun like a ring on the floor under the chair as my attention returned to the papers.

I kicked the chair over and a waterfall of sludge splashed everywhere. "It's *your* fault. Why didn't you just let us all die? Why did you need to bring us to life?"

"That's not gonna help," Dez said a third time.

I turned to face him. "What happened? What happened, Dez?"

He got up from his chair and walked over to the leftover plasma dripping off Fat Mac's chair. He plucked up a dollop and snorted the priest's remains like they were coke. "What happened when?"

I jumped on top of him from behind and began bashing his face against the dirty linoleum floor. "You know when, you fucking traitor. When you killed Bait." I bashed and bashed and bashed and all he did was laugh until his entire body turned to dust.

The Habit, now dressed in one of her teeny bopper outfits from her show Dag Nabbit, stood over me. She put her hands on my shoulders. "That's not gonna help."

"What's not going to help? I don't understand." I pulled away from her embrace and got back to my feet.

She walked in front of me and I reached toward her face. "You evil piece of trash!" I yelled. I balled up her head in my hand and ripped it from her body. Like Fat Mac's body, her head melted in my hand.

As I shook her goo off, a voice called out from the circle of chairs. "Hey, you, scumbag."

I felt around in the air for the door and then snapped at the voice. "Just a fucking minute!"

"Hey, scumbag. Come on over here and help us."

I looked back to the circle. It was Bait and Pinball's parents.

The mother lifted a giant syringe over her head. "Can you get over here and hold this cunt down?"

I ran over to the circle. The mother knelt next to little girl as she used her knee to nail her to the ground. "Let's get high."

The father pulled a knife out of his back pocket and started combing his greasy comb over. "Yeah, man. Let's get high." Not realizing that he was using a knife to comb his hair, he stared peeling skin from his skull.

I looked at the mother, who started kissing the little girl on the ground.

"I want some of that," the husband said. He handed me the knife. I hadn't noticed that he was naked when I first saw him but as he closed in on the captive, his skin started to shed, revealing a bloody blob. "I want that bitch to suck my balls."

For a minute, I couldn't move. I had to sit there and watch.

He walked over and kicked the wife out of the way. She started hissing as her face morphed between human and opossum features. As he stood over the child and prepared to dip his pelvis onto her, his body liquefied and dripped into a thousand babies who started nibbling on the body. The body didn't move. It just laid there.

The opossum lady laughed. "Worthless piece of shit," she said.

I looked at the knife.

Dez reappeared next to me. "That's not gonna help." He walked over to the girl on the floor. Not paying attention to where he stepped, he squashed the babies. One by one they shrieked. At one point he bent over and picked one up. Like Fat Mac, he turned to me and winked as he took a bite of the baby's face. He bent over next to the mother. "It's not going to help you, RJ. It's not going to help you because you're a fucking waste." He unbuttoned his pants.

The opossum mother started kissing his neck as she hissed at me. "You fucking poser," she said. "You fucking derelict."

Suddenly, I was able to move. I ran at them and pulled the blade back behind my head. When I reached the circle, I started to carefully jump around, trying to avoid the sea of babies that covered the floor. Every other step, I would smash one and it would scream. I would bend over to pick them up, hoping that they could be saved but they would dissolve and drip out of my hands. Furious, I took the knife and began slaughtering Bait and Pinball's mother and father, just like I had in their trailer.

Then, the lights went out.

When, they came up again, I was sitting in the meeting alone.

"It's not going to help you," I told myself.

I felt the metal of Eldritch's grip my throat from behind.

"You're right. Nothing you can do will help," he said. He flipped me over the chair and started strangling me on the floor. I grabbed on to the leg of one of the cheap plastic chairs.

Before I knew it, the naked husband and the opossum mother where on top of me. She pressed her knee into my neck as he started unbuttoning his pants.

"Hey, you, scumbag," she called out.

The husband's skin had returned. He dangled his dick over my face and started dripping cum and blood into my face.

My eyes shot open, bringing me back to the other shitty world that was just marginally better than my nightmares. I got up and shoved a full-sized towel into the sink. The dripping stopped.

My phone buzzed me awake and I uncurled myself from being a ball rolled up under the sink. I always had such lovely dreams. The cracked screen was adhered to my chest. I rarely slept naked but Eldritch insisted that my clothes should be washed.

I peeled the phone from my body. A piece of glass remained attached to my left nipple. Without waiting another second, I yawned and swiped it unlocked.

The message was from Linnwood.

Talked to S-Rod. He wants to meet with you. Alone. He knows who you are.

I texted him back.

Why doesn't he want to meet with Eldritch? I've never even met this fool.

He responded again.

He only wants to meet you. Maybe he doesn't want to draw attention to himself by being seen with a gigantic goth vampire. He did just survive an overdose. The press is all over him.

I held the phone up to the light, trying to read between the cracks and messaged back.

That's weird but it makes sense. Does he want me to come to his compound or something?

I scratched my sack and yawned again.

I could see the three dots blink. Then they stopped.

They started again.

Compound? LOL.

I pulled my foot out from under the paper-thin blanket and started picking at my big toe. I typed:

I don't know. Cobra and the Battlesnakes had a compound. Why would it be so weird for this guy to have a compound? He has a lot of money. Money equals compound.

Finally, he wrote:

Don't be such a dumb junkie. I'll send you the details later and then come pick you up. I'm going to need you to smooth things out for me. You know. After what YOU did to the RTL. Peace.

My knees popped as I pulled myself up to the sink. I put some toothpaste onto a brush that Eldritch left for me and looked into the mirror. My reflection didn't laugh at me. It didn't even seem to want to look at me. Maybe real vampires never saw their reflection in the mirror because they didn't want to see themselves. More likely, they didn't because they didn't fucking exist.

I surveyed my body. The bite mark that the dog took out of my side was completely smoothed over and my jaw was clicked back into place. I pushed on the healed wound with my palm, making sure that nothing fishy was going on inside me. As if I would have known the difference.

I spit out my last mouthful of toothpaste and spotted a disposable razor and some shaving gel on the sink. I turned around and cracked the door into the room a bit. I hid my naked body and pressed my lips between the door and the wall.

"Can I shave?"

I heard a movie blaring from the TV.

No one responded so I asked again, a little louder. "Hey, man. Can I shave?"

In an annoyed tone, Eldritch yelled back, "*Yes!*"

I switched positions with my mouth and my eye. Eldritch was sitting next to Pinball's bed on one of the complimentary chairs provided by the Golden Aces Hotel. "Jesus." I said. "I just wanted to know if I could shave."

"And I said yes." He got up from the chair and walked toward the bathroom.

I shut the door and locked it.

"Unlock the door, RJ." He tugged at the handle on the other side.

"Why? I'm getting ready."

He lightened up a little. "I have your clothes. Against my better—"

I turned back to the vanity, blasted the hot water and filled my hand with shaving gel. "Can't hear you. Just leave them in front of the door." Steam quickly filled the mirror, blurring me out. I hoped the steam could blur out my conscious and The Gooch. Their tug of war was making my body and brain hurt.

"Did you receive any communication from Linnwood Perry?"

I responded with the same short, annoyed tone and covered my face with the gel. "*Yes!*" With my other hand, I wiped a diagonal streak across the mirror.

"And?"

I rubbed the gel all over my face. "And, he wants to meet with me."

He tugged on the door again. "Who wants to meet with you? Linnwood?"

"No. Rodderick." I washed off my hands and then grabbed the razor.

"Open this door." He shook on the handle. "There must be some mistake."

"There's no mistake." I dragged the razor up under my chin and then tapped the hair off of it in the sink. "He doesn't even want to meet with

Linnwood. He said that he knows who I am."

Eldritch let out a large sigh.

I scraped the razor down under my short sideburns. "Oh, what? I'm not cool enough for him to want to meet with me?"

"Would you mind opening the door, RJ?"

"I'm naked, dude." I tapped some more hair off of the razor and then scrubbed at the steam on the mirror again.

"Please, open this door." He rattled the handle again.

"Jesus!" I threw the razor in the sink, unlocked the door and then threw it open, completely exposing myself to the hotel room. "I'm shaving."

Eldritch waved his arms in an attempt to block off the bathroom area from the kid. "Not in front of the Little One." He kicked my clothes into the small room and then slammed the door shut.

I grabbed the razor and finished off the shave with four final strokes. "I kept telling you that I was naked." I turned off the sink and fully wiped off the mirror.

I made a gun with my finger and winked at myself. "It was nice seeing you again, RJ." I said. "What an awful mess you are."

I passed the beds and took a seat at the table in the corner by the door. It was afternoon, but the sun wasn't bursting through the brown curtains. Eldritch sat on the edge of his bed.

He handed me a cigarette case. "Please. Take one."

I took the case and opened it. An overwhelming scent of cherries and cloves swirled into my face. Unsurprisingly, the case was loaded with red filtered and brown wrapped cigarettes. I snapped the case shut and pushed it onto the table. "Gag."

He watched my rejection carefully but refrained from making any comments about disrespect, vampire traditions or any of his other bullshit. Instead, he subtly flared his right nostril and cut to the chase. "Let us return to the topic of Stephan Rodderick."

"I got a text from Linn about an hour ago." I slid down into the chair. "He said that he wanted to meet with me. Alone."

He grabbed the cigarette case. "I suppose the question is why does he refuse to meet with me. Does that seem as perplexing to you as it does to me?"

"Not really," I answered.

I heard a gurgle coming from his stomach. He tried to ignore it but he bent over slightly and covered it with his hand.

"What the hell is that?"

"Umm," he began. "We have only eaten Mexican food since we have been here." He batted his eyelashes in Pinball's direction. "It is all that the Little One will eat."

"Gnarly. Are you gonna be okay?"

"For the time being," he assured me.

"Do you have any regular cigarettes?" I asked as I waved the smell of him away from me.

"I do not. Back to the issue at hand. Have you ever encountered Stephan Rodderick? Maybe you crossed paths at a museum or hostelry?"

Knowing I still wasn't off the hook for the three-day binge and kill orgy, I gave short answers. "I've never met the guy." I counted off with my fingers. "I've never been to a museum. I don't know what a hostelry is."

"A hostelry. An alehouse. A public house."

"A bar?"

"Precisely." He simplified his tone and widen his eyes. "A bar," he said in a breathy voice.

"I've never met him. I've seen the billboards for his lame movies around L.A." I noticed Pinball out of the corner of my eye. She was wearing the Rasta hat. "Hey, Pin... ummm... Paulina." I winked at Eldritch and then looked over to her on the bed. "That sure is a dope hat."

She ran her fingers through the yarn-locks. "Do you really think so?"

"Super cool," I assured her. "Totally hip."

I turned back to Eldritch but noticed her pushing the wig under the covers with her foot.

Eldritch did a double take. "Where did you get that, Little One?"

"I found it in the garbage when I got me a Coke," she told him.

Eldritch turned back to me. He bent his head back and tossed his hair around in an attempt to gloss over the fact that he tried to dump my gift.

I stared at him. "Really?" I asked her. "That was lucky."

"Yeah." She shook her head. "It has dreadlocks on it like One Love in the movies Mr. Eldritch showed me."

Eldritch grabbed the cigarette box and doubled over again as his stomach let out a howl.

I waved my finger at him. "What movies were those?"

"You know, the movies 'bout the vampires. That guy that Mister Eldritch is going to get to save me from you." She jumped on Eldritch's bed, next to him and loudly yelled, "What's his name again? The vampire guy?" She jumped up and down and then finally landed on her butt. "The guy who is gonna save me from Uncle RJ?"

He cupped the bottom of his stomach with both his hands. "Shhhhh,

Little One."

"No, no," I interrupted. "Go on, Mister Eldritch."

Pinball hopped around on her butt and started chanting. "What's his name? What's his name? What's his name? What's his name?" She pointed at the TV.

I turned to look. They were watching one of the crummy *Nightshayde* movies. Rodderick's character was bent over in a forest. He picked up some dirt and sniffed it. Then, he flew into the trees like Peter Pan.

Eldritch pat her on top of the red, yellow, green, and black knitted cap. "Shhhh, Little One." He picked up the remote control and turned the volume down on the TV.

"*But what's his name?*" She grabbed the remote from him.

He looked at me.

I smirked and helped her get to the bottom of the mystery. "Well? We're waiting!"

"L. Byron Nightshayde," he mumbled.

I put my hands behind my ears and stretched them outward. "I'm sorry. I didn't quite get that."

"His name is L. Byron Nightshayde." He flipped a clove into his mouth and then created a fire to light it by snapping his fingers. "Please, Little One." He petted her on the head again and tucked one of the dreads behind her ear. "Let Uncle RJ and I speak."

I pointed to his lit clove. "So, I guess the non-smoking rule has been lifted."

"Booooo," she said. She stood up and leapt from one bed to the other and then summersaulted back to her pillow.

Eldritch reached out to make sure she made the journey safely but must have unlocked something in his bowels. He looked down to his stomach and then up at me. He lifted his index finger, signifying one minute and then, embarrassed, he shuffled into the bathroom. "I will be back, Little One."

Paulina didn't pay attention to him. Rather, she turned the volume back up on her movie.

I looked back at the TV. I didn't know what to say to her.

The girl character from the movie was in the middle of this weird six-pointed star inside of this sacrificial temple or something. Once again, Rodderick twirled to the ground, after collapsing the ceiling onto a bunch of thousand-year-old vampires in Victorian garb and the like.

"*What are you doing here?*" she asked.

"*These beings are my blood. You are my soul.*"

"What's her name?" I said, trying to break the ice with Paulina.

Her eyes were glued to the screen. "Her name is Hamster Fist Rose."

I laughed a little. "Hamster Fist? That's kind of a weird name."

Eldritch yelled out from the bathroom. "It's Amethyst Rose."

"I like Hamster Fist better," I told her.

She smiled back at me.

Without making any jarring motions, I dragged my chair over next to her bed. "I don't know if you can understand this…"

She put her finger over her lips. "Shhhh."

"Oh, yeah, cool." I turned back to the film. This was a great way to get him to connect with her.

Rodderick's character, which by this point I had finally concluded was named L. Byron Nightshayde, was standing across from the girl character, which I had also concluded was name Amethyst Rose. He was caressing her cheek with the back of his hand. A tear fell onto his skin and he started glimmering.

"*I shouldn't cry,*" she said.

"*What is… cry?*" he said back.

"Haaaaaaa!" I burst out. "'What is cry?' Priceless."

"Shhhhhh," Paulina reminded me.

"It's just—"

She lifted the remote and paused the film. "It's just, what?"

"Well, this guy has been alive for hundreds of years, right?"

"I dunno."

"He's not a robot. He knows what the fuck crying is."

Eldritch pounded on the wall. "Language, RJ."

I turned the chair around so I was facing her. "Do you like this movie, Paulina?"

"I guess," she said.

"You know that vampires aren't like that in real life, right?"

"But Mister Eldritch tol' me that he was real and I was gonna go live with him in a mansion."

"Yeah, sure." I struggled to connect with her. "I mean, he's real, right. But there are other kinds of vampires." I ran my fingers through my hair. "Like me."

She put the remote down next to her leg. I bent forward and she hid behind the Rasta wig. It was a trait that I remembered seeing in her older sister when she'd hide behind her hair.

I took a breath. "I promise you that I want to do the right thing here. Do you understand that?"

She shook her head and bit into one of the dreadlocks. "No."

"It was a really bad thing that I did to your parents. I want to do the right thing here and I want to get you to safety. Please trust me that I would have done anything for your sister."

"Then why is she dead too?"

I scratched at my leg and then my arms. "I can't answer that." I looked at her bedspread. "It's just... it's just that... I'm kinda busted."

"Mister Eldritch says you're a druggie."

"And he's right." I looked around the room for words. A puppet show with my dreams coming from one hand and The Gooch coming from the other wouldn't make any sense to a child. "I don't know how to explain me."

She reached for the remote.

I delicately put my hand over hers. "Have you ever had a pet that you can't stop playing with?"

"I hated my dog. He was meaners."

"Yeah. Sure. He was pretty mean." I looked around the room again. "What about a toy? Have you ever had a toy that you couldn't stop playing with no matter who told you that you should put it down?"

"I din't have no toys," she whispered. "After Bailia left me, I would always go in her room and play with her toys every day. I wanted her to come back so my daddy would stop bein' mean to me. Daddy found out an' threw all them toys away. I wasn't allowed to go in her room no more."

I lifted my hand off of hers and put the remote back in her hand. "I didn't have any toys, either. We're gonna get you some toys. I promise."

I turned my chair back around to watch Rodderick's movie. After what seemed like an eternity of seeing how perfect L. Byron Nightshayde's counterfeit vampire life was, Eldritch flushed the toilet and reentered the room.

"I do not recommend anyone go in there," he said, as he winked at me and patted me on the shoulder.

Paulina giggled.

"Look, Eldritch," I whispered. "We need to clear the air now. I don't care what the fuck you're telling her about me. I know that the truth is much worse. I'm sorry for leaving and I'm sorry for getting wasted. I did fight an opossum. I did fight a pack of guard dogs and I did end up in the middle of a coke war between the Perrys and the roller chicks."

"Ride the Lightning," he said, correcting me. "I know them well." He glanced over at Pinball and began whispering. "On one such occasion, the leader, Darla Destruction, and I shared a bottle of absinthe said to contain the blood of Vlad the Impaler."

I started whispering as well. Mocking him. "Oh. La-dee-da. I didn't realize you were such good friends with all the gangs in Austin," I sighed. "She got her fucking face ripped off and Linnwood farted in her dead mouth and took selfies."

He bowed his head. "Unfortunate. She was a great friend."

"So, the chicks—what was there name again?"

"Ride the Lightning."

"Ride the Lighting. Sorry. The all-girl gang named after the Metallica album."

He inhaled the clove. "It was actually a passage from the Stephen King's *The Stand*."

"Fine. They are named after a passage from a Stephen King story." I waved the smoke back in his face. "My point is, I got caught up in the moment. I was hiding out and I was being an asshole. I did a bunch of oxy that I cooked inside the exhaust of a jet ski. I snorted a bunch of coke the night I sent you all those texts. I also did a bunch of coke with Linnwood yesterday."

He turned to Pinball, who was settled back into the world of *Nightshayde*. "We need to make this right, RJ," he said.

"I know that. I want to do the right thing here. It was a mistake, okay?" I tilted my forehead across the room. "It was my mistake. I know that I can't get Bait back. I know that I can't go back in time and fix everything that I fucked up."

He turned back to me. "Her parents were monsters. You did not do the right thing, but you will do the right thing."

I reached out to take a drag from his cigarette. "Do you accept my apology?"

"I do." He took another puff and handed it over to me. "However, the plan has changed. If Stephan will only speak to you, then we need to not make room for error. The Little One's life depends on it."

"What's the plan?" I took a drag of the clove and sucked it down to my lungs.

Eldritch reached out. "Don't inhale."

The powerful clove smoke tore into my lungs and was immediately rejected. I started to cough. "Then why do you smoke these?" Rather than flick it back in his face, like I normally would have done if I wasn't pleading for forgiveness, I handed it back. "What's the point?"

"Smells like cherries," Pinball deduced as she pinched her nose. "I hate cherries."

Eldritch mashed out the clove on the table. "Sorry, Little One."

I tried to hack the taste of the cigarette out of my throat. "Do you have any water?"

Eldritch reached behind him into a disposable Styrofoam cooler and grabbed a bottle. He handed it to me.

"What's the plan?" I asked again as I took a swig.

He pulled his chair closer to mine. "We... I mean, you... need to convince Stephan to take the Little One. He owns his own research foundation for children's cancer."

"Why is this so complicated?" I moaned. "And, why do I have to be the dog in this plan?"

"You are doing the right thing, of course," he returned. "I rushed to your side and saved your life on several occasions. The girl goes to Rodderick and we return to Los Angeles."

"Yeah." I pulled my chair closer. "I mean, I figured we'd just leave the kid with him and he would be a hero for saving her. Have him make up some story about how he was filling up his car at a gas station and saw her in the back of van or something."

He stroked his chin. "I am not sure we need to go that deep into the story."

"Well, then we'll let him come up with the story. Linnwood told me that he is laying low because the paparazzi is camped out in front of his compound."

He tilted his head. "I am not sure he has a compound."

I weighed the options with my hands. "Compound. Mansion. Who cares?"

"I think he has a ranch. A mid-century ranch."

"Fine," I said. "The press is camped out by his ranch because he just OD'd. I will go meet with him—"

"At the ranch?"

"No, he doesn't want to meet at his place because he doesn't want anyone coming in or out. He is probably going to have to sneak out."

"Then where are you meeting him? On the set of his movie, I imagine." He nodded his head.

"Don't be stupid." I grabbed my shirt and pulled it out so he could read *High as Fuck* written across the front. "If this guy is laying low, the last thing he wants is someone who is so obviously a drug dealer that he advertises it hanging around with him. I don't know where he wants to meet. Linnwood just said that he wanted to meet with me. I'm not sure but I think that Linn is making it seem that I am the middle man in their dispute."

He grabbed on to my knees. "Are you mad? That does not concern you?"

"Should it?"

XXI
ENLISTED

"Look, asshole," I said as I grabbed a pack of Dunhills out of the center console of the Perry Boys' latest rental car, a BMW. "It kind of seems like you're setting me up again."

Linnwood looked in the rearview mirror, downshifted and then gunned it in front of a bus. "What now?" He chomped on gum.

I pulled my seatbelt around my body and secured it into the latch. I wasn't going to fall so easily for him playing my friend again. "You fucking heard me."

He squished my thigh with his hand and slowed down. "Actually, I really didn't hear you. What was that?" The bus's headlights pounded the passenger mirror, blinding me.

"I said it seems like you're setting me up again."

"Ha!" He used the steering wheel to turn up the volume on the stereo. "I thought we went through that. I knew nothing about Cobra's plan. Besides, you're the one who stole the heroin, stupid."

"I'm not even talking about that." I lit the cigarette and rolled down the window. Dunhills were gross but they were a zillion times better than Eldritch's cherry turds. At least they were pre-bloodied—obviously bloodied by the chump who owned the car we were driving around town in. "You're setting me up right now."

"Look, RJ. I didn't set you up in L.A. Sure, I was glad to see that you got fucked over, but I was just as much a pawn in the game as you were." He pushed the volume button on the wheel again and turned the volume up another decibel. "Check this out." He closed his eyes and then cut back in front of the bus that was now trying to pass him on the left. Avoiding my question, he twitched around to whatever horrible psy-trance song he was playing. "Can you feel that bass all over your body?"

"Why are you playing stupid?" Instead of blowing smoke out the window, I blew it in his face. "Eldritch and I both know why you're introducing me to this guy. I don't need him to kill me. I really need his help." I continued to conceal the Paulina situation from him.

He swerved back into the right lane, cutting off another car that laid on its horn. "Just enjoy the song."

"Quit driving like a dick and answer my question. Are you setting me up?"

"That depends on what you mean by setting up." He rolled down his window and waved the bus to pass him on the left.

"Fuck you. You know what I mean." I looked out the passenger window to see the school bus—which I noticed had a big metal six attached to the grill—starting to pick up speed to pass us.

"Watch this." He continued to wave it past. I couldn't see inside because it was so much higher than our car and the driver had his brights on. When the front bumper reached the middle of our car, Linnwood hit the gas again and passed it. He cut it off so tightly this time that the bus wobbled and almost drove across the center lane into oncoming traffic. "Classic," he said.

I dug my fingers into the sides of my seat. "It's not classic, you jackass. What if there are a bunch of kids in there?"

"Oh Lord. Give me a break. Like you care." Linnwood started swerving back and forth between lanes to the beat of his dreadful song. "You should open a school for kids. You seem to care so much about humans."

"I do care." I eased my clamp on the seat. "Do we really want to draw a bunch of attention to ourselves right now?"

He grabbed a forty out of the backseat and twisted the cap. "Hey, can you light me a cigarette?"

I took a cig out of the Dunhill pack and jumpstarted it with mine. "Here," I said as I handed it to him. "So, back to our conversation. Why are you trying to set me up?"

"Look, RJ..." He took a huge pull off the bottle. I could see that it was half full of blood. "I'm not really setting you up. I need you to smooth things over for me. That way, you and I can be in business together in Austin. Close your eyes and think about it. Coke and heroin are big business in this town. It would be like the Crips and the Bloods going into business with each other."

"What a load of shit. *That* sounds like a set up." I flicked my cigarette out the window and used my hand to block the bus headlights in my side mirror. "Why don't you just go talk to this dude yourself? I have other things I need to talk to him about."

He pulled into the right lane, this time using a turn signal. "Are you trying to cut me out?"

"Cut you out of what? I don't even like this shitty town. I'm not interested in setting up shop in Austin. This is the drug war you started."

"You were there, too. You killed two of those bitches, RJ."

"Oh my God. Would you stop trying to justify this?" I grabbed the pack of Dunhills again and pointed back to myself with my thumb. "I'm right here next to you. What if this Rodderick guy tries to send you a message by cutting off my hands or something?"

"Why don't you have another cigarette, you mooch."

"I will." I lit the cigarette. "Is this guy even like us? All that I know is that he's a dumb actor in movies about vampires and he has a heroin problem."

"I don't know if he's a real vampire." He took a drink. "I've only met him three times at South by Southwest parties."

I remembered the gangs that I had come face to face with since being in Austin. "Couldn't you just tell?"

"Tell how?" he asked. "Do we smell different than humans to you?"

I let my hand down from blocking the headlights and took a drag. "It's pretty easy to tell who we are."

"How?"

"I don't know. If I run into someone who is really fucking stupid who is trying to kill me." I tugged on his tennis sweater. "And they are wearing some equally fucking ridiculous costume." I pointed at him. "That's a vampire."

He slowed down. "I take offense to that."

"Why? You're obviously trying to get me killed by sending me in to 'smooth over' your bullshit. This isn't L.A. anymore. If I didn't need to talk to this guy, I'd just kill you right now."

"Big talk, Reynolds." He laughed. "You've had your chance at the title several times."

"What title?" I put my hand back up to block the bus's high beams that were now flashing between high and low.

"You know what title." He turned up the shitty music again, trying to drown me out.

"Oh yeah," I joked. "The World Championship of Cunts. You certainly have that crown."

"Do you want me to just leave you out here?" He reached into the backseat and pulled out a crumpled piece of paper. "Find your own way."

The bus caught up and hovered at a safe distance behind us.

"What's this?"

162

"It's a flyer. This is where Rodderick wants to meet you. Just say the word and I'll let you get there yourself."

As I opened it up I glanced into the sideview mirror. "Why don't you just let the bus pass us?"

"Because I'm a cunt," he responded.

"He suggested this?" I looked at the flyer. It was for some South by Southwest Bluegrass showcase featuring a band called Clyde Craft and the Whiskey Brothers. "Are you kidding me? Fucking bluegrass?"

"I suggested it, asshole." He took another pull off the forty. "I didn't want you to walk into a bad situation. I wanted you two to meet with a bunch of other people around. You know, in the interest of coming together on neutral ground. He isn't going to chop off your hands in front of his adoring fans. He has a new movie coming out in a month. It's the final film in the *Nightshayde* series. I guess you can throw away your little theories that I'm trying to set you up."

Remembering that Rodderick had just OD'd, I said, "I thought he couldn't even be seen in public."

"I guess he thinks that this meeting is pretty important, dumbass. Don't fuck it up. Remember the stairs? This is our chance, man. We can be the on top of the money clip and the phone."

"I don't even remember where the money clip and phone were."

"You junkie, RJ."

The bus let out three friendly honks.

Coming to the end of patience, I made the mistake of asking, "Why couldn't you have found a punk rock show?"

"Punk rock? Are you being serious?" He twirled his fingers to the trance song he was blasting. "No one listens to punk rock anymore."

"You're still setting me up to take a hit for you. All this 'We're All in the Same Gang' bullshit isn't fooling me for a second."

"I'm trying to do you a solid here." He waved the bus around again. "All that junk in your body is making you paranoid."

"Excuse me, fuckshit." I helped him out by also waving the bus past by pointing left with my thumb out the window. "Coke is the paranoia drug. Heroin is the guilt drug."

THANKS for remembering me.

"Go around!" he screamed out the window.

The bus picked up speed. The moon glimmered off the metal Olde English six on the grill.

"Why is this bus still keeping pace with you?" I dug into the seat again. "Something isn't right."

"What do you mean?" He looked into his driver's side mirror. "Watch

163

this." He took a last gulp out of the forty bottle. "Cheers," he said, lifting the bottle. Then, without warning, he lobbed the bottle out the window. Almost instantly, the glass smashed into the front window of the bus.

"Fuck off," he screamed as he gave them the finger. The bus swerved again and turned sideways. Another car swerved into the guardrail behind us trying to avoid the bus.

"Gun it, bitch. Get us out of here." I turned around to see a bunch of dark figures get off the bus. "I don't think that was a bus full of students."

He stomped on the accelerator. "Paranoid junky."

Linnwood spun a U-turn and slowed up to the club. "You're welcome." He dug into his pocket and pulled out some money.

"For what?" I unbuckled my seatbelt. "Almost getting me killed before Rodderick has his chance?"

He tossed the money into my lap. "Yeah, the bus full of little kids is going to kill us."

"For the hundredth time, those weren't kids. It was a gang."

"You loser. Get out." He pointed to the marque in front of the club. It read SXSW BLUEGRASS SHOWCASE. "You asked me to get you some face time with Rodderick and I did that. If you don't want to put in a good word for me, then fine."

I pulled the latch on the door. "There it is. That's exactly what I'm talking about. This is all about you and your fight with RTL. You know what your problem is, Linn?"

"What now?"

"You just can't do a favor for someone without wanting to get them to do all your dirty shit for you." I started to step out of the car.

"You're one to talk. Who cares about those fucking human kids on that bus?"

"Fuck off!" I slammed the door shut. "They weren't kids."

He bit into his Dunhill. "What is it with you and little girls, anyway?"

I rested my hands on the open window frame and bent over. "What does that mean?" How could he know about Paulina?

"I think you know." He spat the cigarette at me and hit gas.

I lifted my arms, avoiding getting the frame slamming into the sides of my hands.

"What does that mean?" I yelled as he sped away. I walked into the middle of street, hoping that he'd turn around and try to run me down, but he took a right a block after the club.

Something continued to not feel right about my meeting with Rodderick, and Linnwood's comment about little girls only heightened my unease.

I walked to the entrance of The Settler's Inn and was met by a plump bearded guy in a coonskin cap and a leather vest who was sitting on a stool. The rickety old seat growled as he made the slightest movements. It looked like it was going to give at any second.

He put up his hand to signify that he wanted to see my ID. "Y'all havin' a little fight with your boyfriend tonight, slim?"

I patted my jeans and came up empty. "I forgot my license."

"Must be because you're 'High as Fuck'." He pointed to my shirt. "No drugs in the club."

"I don't have any on me."

"Turn around," he said as he waved his finger in a circle. Then, he cleared his throat. Guessing by the intensity and length of the hack and the wheeze that followed it, he was in a race with the stool to see which would die first. "What's that in your back pocket?"

"It's the flyer for this show." I pulled out the yellow piece of paper and showed him.

He refused to fully stand up from the stool, even though it was barely supporting only the top of his ass. "You got drugs wrapped in there, son?"

I stepped toward him and handed it to him. "Here." God forbid he reached out and took it from me. He did bend in slightly, pulling the cowboy shirt he had on under his vest tight to his body. The shirt ruffled around his mid-section, revealing bits and pieces of his hairy gut and stretch marks.

He read the flyer, then handed it back to me. He tried to better adjust his rear on the stool. "I can't let you in without your ID." He took his curly hair out of its pony tail and ran his fingers through it. Then he rewrapped the elastic around it. "Them's the rules, boy."

"Look," I finally said, pointing to my face. "Do I look like I'm under twenty-one?"

He stuck his neck out and squinted.

"Well?" I asked.

He didn't say anything. He just looked at my face.

I pointed to the flyer. "It says, 'twenty dollars'."

He unfolded his arms and grabbed the flyer and then looked at me again. "Sure does."

"How about I give you forty," I held up two twenties. "And we call it a night, huh, buddy?"

He stared at the money and then looked at his watch. "Yeah, I can't wait to get off tonight."

Without thinking, I decided to play friendly with this hick. "I heard that."

He closed his eyes and began swaying his head.

I kicked the toe of my boot into a crack in the cement and dug out a cigarette butt. All of a sudden I heard a banjo from inside the club.

"Sounds like Clyde is getting started." He opened a bag of chew between his legs. "He's gonna play at my BBQ, you know."

"I'd really like to go check him out."

"Can you ask him if he'll play at my BBQ?" he asked.

"I thought you said he already was."

He ignored me. Instead, he opened up his vest, revealing two, poorly rolled joints in the front pocket of his shirt. "You wanna get high?"

I put both my hands in my front pockets. "I thought that no drugs were allowed in the club."

"No drugs are allowed *in* the club." He pulled out one of the joints that was bent from being cramped into a miniature pocket that was dwarfed by my new friend's boobs.

"How about sixty bucks? Will sixty bucks get me into the club?"

He laughed. Then, he hacked. He sneezed. He got so excited that he dropped the warped joint. His boot stopped taping as he tried to catch it. Although, it rested on the top of the boot for a second, he made a slight movement that caused it to roll right off. We both looked under the stool at the doob on the ground. Using his forearm, he mopped up some of the drool caused by his frenzy. I looked back at the joint. I heard him cough again and then spit back on the wall. That was followed by a slow gasp that sounded like a zeppelin being deflated. There wasn't a chance that he was going to try and pick up the joint.

"Do you... ummmm... want me to get that?"

He nodded his head up and down, causing creases in his short neck, around his ears.

I got on my hands and knees and reached under the stool, plucking the sad little joint off the ground. "Here it is," I said. I brushed off a little bit of dirt and then straightened it out with my fingers. "Good as new." I handed it back to him.

He might have let out a sign of relief or maybe he was still deflating. He took the joint, reopened his vest and put it back into his front pocket. "Maybe I should wait until I get off work."

I smiled and patted him on the shoulder. "Can I go in now?"

"Sure, buddy." He clicked the hand tally counter attached to his wrist by and elastic wrist coil. "Free of charge."

I walked to the door and turned to shoot him a salute. "I'll ask Clyde if he'll play your BBQ."

"He doesn't like you gays," he responded.

XXII
SEDUCED

I plugged my ears with my fingers and looked around the inside of The Settler's Inn. The banjo picking and fiddle screeching felt like someone was throwing bricks at my skull. Bass-heavy tunes—like Linnwood's music—were calming to my over-sensitive vampire ears and body compared to this.

"Go around back, gramps," a green and blue haired chick covered in tattoos instructed.

I took my finger out of my right ear. "What?"

She pressed a stamp on my hand. "The band is out back, old man. Two-for-one Lynchburg Lemonades."

"Old man?" I flicked ear wax at her.

She rolled her eyes. "Yeah, you fossil." She used a mirror app on her phone to pick a piece of lettuce out of her front teeth. "Get your fingers out of your ears and enjoy the tunes."

"Hardcore." I pointed at her hair.

"Hardcore sucks."

Being an asshole from Los Angeles, I had become very aware of trendsters trying to out-cool each other. I was no stranger to playing the "I know more fresh shit than you" game. I had rolled my eyes daily at followers, pretenders and posers. That was *my* thing. However, it seemed that the citizens of Austin took this art to intergalactic levels. If something came from someone else's mouth, it was automatically deemed lame by their "everyone is fringe" society. Every day must have been a chore to decide what the next dope music genre, fashion trend or sociological school of thought was on deck. Thankfully, I wasn't dumb enough to announce that I was from L.A. It was, after all, the poser capital of the universe in the mind of Austinites; therefore, super lame.

I didn't want to walk into another painful conversation like the ones I had with the head shop burnout or that lonely, sad doorman, so I simply shot her a thumbs up and said, "Thank you."

She returned my gesture with a peace sign. "Deuces."

Satisfied that was the most cordial invitation that I was going to get into the club, I walked toward the curtain. The noises of Clyde Craft and the Whiskey Brothers grew louder. I crossed the threshold of the curtain and walked into a world of beards, beanies, and blue-collar beers. I took a few steps and almost instantly shit my pants when some jackass in cords and a ripped-up cardigan loudly whistled his approval to Clyde and the boys.

He saw me looking at him and pointed to my shirt, then mimed smoking pot with his whistling fingers. *High as Fuck*, he mouthed.

"Right on," one of his buddies added.

Three girls started a conversation next to me. They all had the same extra-black hair dye, tattoos and piercings look, making me think of Joan Jett. However, as a collective they represented tall and lanky, short and stubby, and finally big and burly. They looked like action figures that represented different female body types, just with the same paint job. I noticed that they were passing a joint between them. I guessed that they hadn't gotten the strict instructions from the bouncer outside that drugs weren't allowed *in* the club.

"It's him," Slim Jett said as she pointed to the far corner of the patio.

"Are you sure?" Jumbo Jett responded.

"He's hot," Shorty Jett added.

I walked over to them. "Who are you all talking about?"

Jumbo flipped her hair. "Not interested."

"Ewwww," Slim said.

Shorty stood on her tiptoes and continued to look across the room.

I licked my lips. "I just wanted to know if you were talking about Stephan Rodderick. I'm supposed to meet him here."

Shorty looked me up and down. "Star fucker." She exhaled a huge cloud of pot.

"Fan boy," Jumbo said.

Slim Jett walked away.

The others followed.

"I love rock 'n' roll, too," I hollered at them.

Slim Jett flipped me off without turning around.

A bouncer walked over to me.

"Let's be cool, man. The ladies are here to see the band."

"Copy that." I shot him a peace sign like the hostess in the front room.

"Deuces."

He walked over the bar and said something to the pigtailed and overly-bearded bartender. He pointed at me and then signaled *keep an eye on that guy* with his fingers and his eyes.

I waved back and clinched my teeth together for a big smile.

The bartender started to wave back as if he'd just made a new friend when the bouncer slapped his hand down. A glass broke across the room and the bouncer left the bar to check it out. The bartender pointed to his own shirt and then to me. *Me too*, he mouthed. He bent down behind the bar and then returned with a Tall Boy can of Schlitz. He put it on the bar.

I walked over and grabbed it. "Thanks man," I said.

As the fiddle squealed on the stage, nearly crippling me, he put out his hand. "Ten bucks."

I reached into my pocket and threw a bill at him. "Keep the change."

He lifted the bill to the light. "There's no change here. You gave me a ten."

I grabbed the bill back and exchanged it for a twenty.

He took it, put it in his pocket and said, "Thanks."

I waited for a second and then asked, "Where's the change?"

"You told me to keep the change."

"That was when I gave you the ten."

"There was no change for the ten."

I took a barstool. "Fine. Keep the change." The bartender left to serve other douchebags and I turned toward where the girls were pointing. Even though they didn't seem like the star struck-types, Rodderick was famous. I'll bet they were surprised to see him out and about at a bar so soon after the story of his overdose came out.

I surveyed the bar. I can't imagine that Rodderick would have stood me up, especially since I had to answer for all of Linnwood's stupid mistakes in a city where he hadn't earned respect.

I didn't see him but then again, I only had a vague picture in my head of what he looked like that I saw on billboards all over L.A.

The bartender came back. "You lookin' for someone?"

"Funny you should ask," I said. "Is Stephan here?"

"Stephan who?" He flipped up a bottle of whiskey out from the cooler behind the bar.

"You know. That actor from those vampire movies. Stephan Rodderick. I'm supposed to meet him."

Surprisingly, he gave me a straight answer and pointed across the patio. "See him?"

"I think so." I looked in the direction he was pointing. "What's he wearing?"

"Black cowboy shirt."

I looked around the bar. Ninety percent of the bar was wearing black cowboy shirts. "Little help. I don't see him."

He reached over the bar. "See that girl dancing with the flowers in her hair?"

I looked over. Some hippie was spinning around near the middle of the dance floor.

"Yeah, for sure."

"Now look just to the right and you can see the back of his head."

Squinting again, I saw a black-haired head bobbing around attached to a black cowboy shirt with red roses around the collar. "Got him." I put out my hand to shake the bartender's. "Thanks buddy."

He walked away. "Have a good time, stalker."

And to think, I thought, *I'd met someone in Austin who wasn't a complete asshole.*

I tapped the bar with my palm and headed over to Rodderick. I didn't feel like a dead man walking. Rodderick chose The Settler's Inn for a reason. I pumped myself up. If he did indeed know who I was, then he also knew that I was a complete badass. I clenched my fists, moved my shoulders around and then rubbed them with my hand like I was entering a boxing ring. I needed to assure myself that he didn't want to start a conflict with what was left of Los Angeles. I supposed that if he wanted confirmation of my ruthlessness that I could take total credit for spreading RTL all over the parking lot. Even though it would be less than a half-truth, he could choose to believe me or Linnwood. Linnwood, of course, being the punk trying to move in on his territory.

I reached his table and tapped him on the shoulder. "Stephan?"

He turned his head, smiling and gave me a "just a minute" signal with his finger. He had black bobbed hair with one white streak lock that hung over his large horn-rimmed Ray Bans. His face was perfectly chiseled behind the glasses. His nose was long and thin, leading to his plump lips. His long feminine eyelashes blinked over his crisp green eyes as he passively entertained one of his fans.

Then, he turned back to a conversation that he was having with the short Joan Jett chick.

"Like I was saying." She shot me a rude stare. "*Into the Darkness* was the first book I read in the *Nightshayde* series."

He cupped his hands over hers. "But that was the third book."

Her gloom and doom facade was instantly washed away by the excitement of the mesmerized tweenager still lingering inside her after all these years. "I know, right? Anyway, I made my mom take me to a bookstore that night and buy me all the rest of the books. I didn't sleep all weekend."

"Well, *the author* thanks you."

She turned her hands over to connect better with his greatness. "But *you* were L. Byron. I know you've heard this before, but you were born to be him."

I stretched my shoulders again and cracked my neck, then placed my right hand over my left near my crotch. I wanted desperately to plug my fingers in my ears, but I didn't want to come off as uncool.

"You better be there for the final movie next month," he said as he tickled the inside of her hand.

"As if I'd miss it, Stephan." Her eyes lit up. "Can I call you Stephan?"

"Call me Steph," he said. "That's what my closest friends call me."

She started giggling, almost convulsing. It was as if he just jammed his fist into her ass and licked her neck.

I looked across the bar and saw Jumbo and Slim enviously looking on. I smiled at them as I continued to pump myself up. Slim gave me the finger again.

Rodderick saw it and he turned back to me. "Just another minute."

"I have seen every one of the movies at the midnight showing on opening night," she confessed. "I know it seems stupid, but I really feel connected to you. Since I read that first book, I've felt like I'm Amethyst Rose."

"Hamster Fist Rose," I joked.

She looked at me again and snarled. "Loser."

Furthering his connection, he slid his hands up her forearms. "It's not stupid," he said. "The thing is—"

Tears started to well up inside of her heavy-lined eyes as if she thought he was going to propose to her. She swallowed as her eyes shimmered, becoming wider and wider every second that he hung on that beat.

"The thing is that you're more beautiful than Amethyst."

She blurted into nervous laughter that couldn't be registered by a Richter scale. I was starting to think that Steph was truly a traditional vampire. He had this girl completely under his spell. I guessed that if I looked at the seat of the chair she was sitting in that it was drenched.

She took her hands from his caress and pulled back the collar on her shirt. "Will you sign my neck?"

He pulled his head back and looked at me dumbfounded. "Should I sign her neck?"

I think I was also under his black magic spell. I didn't respond.

"RJ?" he asked again.

He knew my name!

He knew my name!

"Should I sign her neck?"

I froze.

He turned back to Short Stack. "It seems as if my friend RJ here is just as taken with your beauty as I am."

She looked at me and grunted. Switching channels from a prince taking off his shirt to a pig taking a dump didn't agree with her. "Perv," she said.

He stood up and took off his cowboy shirt, revealing a wife beater underneath. While wrapping the sleeves around his waist, he pulled a Sharpie out of his leather pants. "Oh, come now." He handed me a beanie. "Can you hold this, buddy?"

"Sure," I said. I wanted to call him Steph but I didn't think that I had established myself as one of his friends yet.

He moseyed around the picnic table to the moonshine jug beat of Clyde Craft and the Whiskey Brothers and took the cap off of the pen, putting it in his mouth. "What's your name?"

"Shelby." She closed her eyes, sensually shifting her pink-streaked hair off of her neck and ran her tongue around her lips in a circle.

Rodderick bent over and slowly wrote his name between a neck tattoo of a sheriff's star and flower. "I don't usually do this, Shelby."

She exhaled like she was about to have an orgasm, seemingly feeling every stroke of the pen from the tips of her hair to the ends of her toenails. After he was finished signing, he kissed the spot where he signed. Shorty's body seized. After a pause, she reached out to touch his abs but he had already turned around and headed back to his seat. Jumbo and Slim giggled from across the bar. They should have been so lucky.

Stephan sat back down. "I'm sorry to cut our talk short, Shelby—"

She opened her eyes and frowned like a baby.

He put out his hand to say farewell. "But, unfortunately my friend RJ and I have a lot to talk about."

She continued to sit across from him, enchanted. "I wanted to tell you that we—" she pointed to the other Jetts, who waved. "Well, we hope you're doing okay."

He scratched at the light stubble on his cheek. "Don't believe everything you read, Shelby. I'm going to be fine."

He was right. For someone who had just OD'd on heroin, he sure looked like a million bucks. He was going to be fine.

Shelby got up from her dream encounter and blew Stephan a kiss. He caught it in his hand and then blew it in front of his face. She walked back to her crew in a daze. They lit up in excitement.

He pointed across the table. "Take a seat, RJ."

I sighed. "Do I have to sit over there?"

He signaled to my pal, the bartender, by holding up two fingers. "Why do you ask that?"

I pumped my fists again, playing it cool. "Because I don't want to go sit in a bucket of Shelby's pussy juice."

"Hilarious." He placed some earplugs in the middle of the table. "I guess my sources were correct about you. Take a seat."

I walked across the table from him and wiped my hand on the bench. It was dry. I think. I sat down, grabbed the ear plugs and quickly put them in my ears. Anything that would help ease my bluegrass-induced headache would have been perceived as an olive branch at that point.

He put out his hand. "Nice to meet you, RJ."

I returned the gesture and shook his hand. "Nice to meet you, too. Thanks for the plugs."

"No worries. I know how intense this type of music can be to our ears."

I pointed to the Jetts, who were still whispering and giggling. "Does that happen to you all time? Chicks ask you to sign their bodies?"

"Yeah. They're mostly pigs like that one. I like them a little younger, if you know what I mean."

I looked at Shelby. She couldn't have been over twenty-five.

He winked at me. "You know what I mean."

"Ummmm, I think I do." I flicked at my knee under the table. "I don't mean to be a dick, but are you a molester?"

He waved my assumption away. "Oh, God no. Why would you ask that?"

"Forget it. My bad." I didn't want to let on that I was there screening him to be Pinball's temporary guardian. "You told me that you liked them younger." Eldritch vouched for this guy and I had to believe that he knew what was the right thing to do.

The waitress in short blue jorts came over and dropped off two bottles of beer. "Here you go. As you ordered them, Steph."

I looked at the bottles. They were dark and I smelled warm blood mixed with the hops. I picked it up and turned it sideways, making sure I wasn't imagining things. "How did you do that?"

He took a drink. "Do what?"

"How did you get them to put blood in the beer?" I took a drink, as well. It was awesome.

"This is my bar." He smirked. "They brew the house beer to my standards."

I licked some fermented blood off my chin. "I thought this place was Linnwood's idea."

"Right," he began. "I told him to have you meet me here. He said he was sending you in good faith."

174

"So, you're not pissed about the RTL situation?"

"Why would I be?" He looked genuinely confused. "I want to recruit the BBP to run the coke in Austin and they got rid of the RTL. I hated those bitches. Always skimming off the top. They were worst drug dealers in Austin and they didn't even really work for me."

"What about the Chaplins? The McCoys?"

He crossed his hands on the table and moved in closer. "What about them?"

"I'm the one who took them out." I stopped flicking my knee. I puffed up my shoulders.

"Good. You did me another favor." He twirled the Sharpie with his fingers. "Those losers did nothing good for me. Bottom of the food chain, RJ. Bottom of the food chain."

"Eldritch told me—"

"Eldritch? Ha. Gimme a break. That tool is out here? Hilarious." He tapped his chest and quieted down further. "Do you think that someone in my position would bother myself with a weird theater fag and a bunch of inbred, zombie scumbags?"

"I don't know. That's the way it was run in Los Angeles. All vampires worked for Cobra. All vampires had different assigned zones where they could deal and kill."

He opened up his arms. "Look around you. Does this look like L.A.?"

I looked around. Two hipsters were sharing a small ceramic bowl and blowing smoke into each other's faces. "Kind of."

"Look." He took a hard rip off of his beer. He sounded angry. "I don't know what you've heard about me, but I'm a celebrity and I am also a businessman."

"Are you a vampire?"

"Oh, come on. You and I both know that neither of us are vampires. Are we the same? Yes. But I know what we really are."

"I know what we are, too."

"I'm guessing you got a peek at the record's room before you burned down the church?"

My toes curled up inside my boots. "How do you know about that?"

"I know everything about *us*." He grinned. "I also know that you didn't take out the McCoys. The Minutemen did."

"How? Were you there?"

"I know it because everyone in Austin works for me."

I pushed out the bench to stand up.

He lowered his hands. "Sit down, RJ."

I hesitated and then returned to my seat. "The Minutemen are like The Cloth, asshole. They want to exterminate all of us."

"Let me guess." He rested his head on his hand. "Eldritch told you that."

I didn't respond.

"They work for me. They are my private security. They help me keep order around my city."

"They would have killed me if I hadn't gotten away."

He mocked shooting himself in the head with his finger. "Maybe they should have. No one was told that you were coming to Austin. We knew that the Perrys were here. We know that most of the L.A. gangs come out here for South by Southwest. You, on the other hand, have never been here. I only know of you because I know The Habit."

There she was. Always showing up in my life when I needed her least. I put my hands on the edge of the table and began breaking off the wood.

"Calm down." He laughed again. "I worked with that wasted piece of shit when I guest starred on her show. She shows up every once and a while looking for work."

I continued to break off pieces of wood.

"I was a teenager. After she got all fucked up on heroin, the bitch tried to burn down the set of the first *Nightshayde* movie when I didn't get her a reading for the part of Amethyst Rose. Then, she tried to go to the tabloids with a story that I was a real vampire."

I let go of the table. Chunks of wood dropped onto my feet and splinters bent into my palms.

"I told her that if she left me alone that I wouldn't go to the cops."

I found my voice. "Why didn't you just kill her?"

"I don't know. I liked to fuck her. You know, feel superior to her. When I was on her show, she bossed everyone around and treated people like they were beneath her. On the day when I had a line on the show, she took the director aside and told him that I looked like a Guido. She made them shave my head."

"She killed Cobra."

"Good," he said. "I guess she finally did something right."

"Look, motherfucker." I leaned in, trying to remain cool. "He was my friend."

"Really? King Cobra was your friend?" He lifted his fingers and ordered two more beers. "That asshole didn't have any friends. He'd come down here with his gang, try and boss us around and act like he owned the city. One time, he went into one of my clubs and killed two of my friends for not sucking his dick. Then, when we tried to get his wasted ass out, the Snakes shot the place up. He always called me 'Dracula's little sister'."

I bit my lip and nodded my head as if I understood. Truth be told, the nickname was pretty good. Classic Cobra.

His passionate rant continued. "He never, *ever* showed me the respect that I deserved even though his empire was turning to shit and mine was turning to gold. Austin is the real deal. I only go to Hollywood to collect checks. Fucking bitch city."

I was homing in on a common theme with Rodderick. He thrived on respect and money. That's all he cared about.

He kicked his beer up sideways and poured a little into his mouth. Then, he swished it around in his mouth for a bit before swallowing. "Why are we *really* here?"

I was unsure about Rodderick. Everything he said made sense, but I needed to be sure that he was going to take care of Pinball. I also wanted to be sure that he wasn't going to turn Eldritch and I over to The Cloth or the Minutemen. "L.A. is over," I said, picking a splinter out of the middle of my right hand. "I want to work for you. I want in to Austin."

"Why do you think I want anything to do with you? What can you give me that I can't get from Linnwood Perry or the Skulls or the Minutemen? You're out of your element, RJ. Go back to Los Angeles and start something new. People listen to you. You ran your own gang. Go start a new one with the rest of the leftover Cali street trash."

"There's nothing left in Los Angeles except The Cloth."

The waitress delivered our second round of beers.

"This should cover it?" He handed her a hundred dollar bill and a gram of what appeared to be the cleanest, purest horse that I had ever seen. My face followed the bag from his hand to her pocket. I might have been drooling. My skin veins itched.

JACKPOT!

She stroked his chin. "Thanks, Stephan."

"Bottoms up," he said and started chugging his second beer.

I followed his lead, not knowing if he was going to take me up on my offer or not. When we finished, we both slammed our bottles on the picnic table.

He looked deep into my eyes, trying to see deception. "It's amazing," he said.

I opened my eyes wide and shook my head. "What's amazing?"

"That heroin." He pointed to the waitress, who immediately headed to the back room. "It's the best heroin in the world. Nothing synthetic about it. I am reluctant to even call it junk."

The best heroin in the world.

"Okay."

"You wanna get high, RJ?"

My body felt relaxed all of a sudden as if I finally close to scratching the itch. "I'm kind of living on the street, Stephan," I said as the taste of cotton candy filled my mouth. I wanted to get high so badly.

"We can go to my house." He got up and waved me to follow him. "And, please, call me Steph."

XXIII
SPOILED

I stood in shock in front of Rodderick's beaten up, nineteen-forties Chevy truck. I heard the *Back to the Future* music in my head. I desperately wanted to pump my fist and sigh like Marty did when he saw his new pickup in the garage at the end of the film. Rather than make I dick out of myself, though, I just asked, "This is yours?"

He jumped into the driver's seat. "Pretty dope, huh? I found it at a scrap yard and I've been trying to rebuild it for years now."

The huge wheel wells bulged out behind the withered grill that was missing the old school Chevrolet logo above it. Even though I guessed that it was originally a turquoise color because it had matching wheels, it had more rusted-through holes than fresh paint. Some of the holes were plugged with Bondo, while some remained naturally deteriorated, exposing some of the classic mechanics of its vintage construction. If I were to ever steal enough money to buy a car, I think that truck would be my dream. Like I told Paulina back at the hotel, I never had any toys. I had a pretty rad record collection once but I found them all in a dumpster. What I didn't find there, I stole.

After several turns of the key, the engine started. It puttered and clicked and made pinging noises like a World War II prop plane preparing for battle. The left headlight clicked on and off like there were loose wires inside. There was no way that this truck was street legal, but that was one of the perks of being a star.

I slapped the hood. "Are you gonna put a blower on this thing?" It was a trick question.

"Do I look like I'm into rockabilly?" he scoffed. "If ever get this fucker in shape, I'm not going to trick it out."

I nodded. *Good answer.*

"Besides, I have a strict policy against pompadours and chain wallets," he added as he closed his door.

Even better answer.

I walked around to the back and looked in the bed. It was filled with some wood planks and saw dust. It looked like Rodderick was trying to build a teak liner for it. I was glad that he wasn't going to ghetto it out with flames and a bright metallic paint job. I was also relieved that it wasn't filled with vampires. The last thing that I wanted to happen was some fucking asshole popping up the second we started driving to strangle me.

He opened the passenger door form the inside because it was missing a door handle. "Come on, man. Get in."

The old hinges creaked as I fully opened it up. If I was shocked that this dude had such great taste from the outside of the truck, I nearly fell into a coma when I saw the interior. I pressed on the vinyl turquois and white-striped bench that matched the wheels. "Fuck, dude."

"As you can see, I've spent a little more time on the interior than the exterior." He patted the seat.

I put my foot inside the truck then hesitated. "I don't want to mess it up."

He slapped the seat again. "Just get in."

Carefully, I slipped into the truck. The dashboard and insides of the door had all been replaced, undented, recovered, and repainted to the truck's original glory. The round speedometers polished chrome vents made it seem like we were sitting in the belly of a refinished, vintage appliance. Calling it a sweet toy was an understatement.

He grabbed tightly on to the humongous steering wheel and cranked the stick into reverse. "Close the door, RJ. That heroin isn't getting in our bodies any quicker with you jerking off all over my ride."

"Sorry. I've just never been in something this old and cool before."

He stomped on the gas pedal and we were off. "I'm sure you want to hear something better than that bluegrass shit," he said as he flicked open a pack of Marlboros.

"Pre-bloodied?" I asked.

"Of course."

I grabbed one as pushed in the cigarette lighter on the console. "That thing works?" I asked.

"Totally works." He grabbed a smoke from the pack. It wasn't easy to find."

"I'm sure."

After about a minute, the lighter popped out. I snatched it up and lit his cigarette, then mine.

He took a drag and then blew smoke out of the side of his mouth. "What about music?"

I looked at the original radio in the dash. "Are there any good stations in Austin?"

"Not really." He fiddled with a touchscreen in the center of the steering wheel. I blew smoke out of the crack in my window and raised my eyebrow.

"Oh, come on, man." He laughed. "It's the original steering wheel. It just has some renovations." He took his eyes off the road. "You like country and western, right?"

I laughed as well. "Fuck you. I don't listen to that garbage."

"Let me guess." He scrolled through the bands. "Let's take it back to the old school."

"Salvation" by Rancid came on. Rodderick seemed pretty cool; granted, he was younger than me. I smiled and acted like I was into it by tapping my hand on my thigh.

"Diamond rings," he sang along as he strummed some power chords on the top of the steering wheel. Because I knew the song, I mouthed the words along with him. At the end of the day, he was being a very courteous host, even though I didn't mind Rancid but hardly thought that they qualified as "old school." Besides, his choice of driving music was significantly better than Cody's bluegrass or Linnwood's trance. That said something about him. He was listening to Rancid because he liked them, not because he wanted approval from his sheep back at The Settler's Inn.

I looked out at the road in front of us. The damaged headlight on his side of the truck went completely out. He twisted both of them on and off a few times, using the trigger next to his left knee.

"Oh well," he finally decided. "I'll have to look at that tomorrow."

"Aren't you worried about getting pulled over?"

He laughed. "Who do you think I am, RJ? The cops don't care what I do."

I sighed. "Let's not get carried away here."

"Think about it. I don't mean to boast but I do a lot for this community. I brought the filming of the *Nightshayde* movies here from Vancouver. I renovated a bunch of buildings and turned them into new clubs and businesses. I helped build a cancer research and prevention institute."

Half-kiddingly, I added to his list. "You sell drugs, employ gang members and you're a walking corpse."

He hit the turn signal and used both hands to complete a left turn. "As long as the money is going towards good, can't I justify it?"

He made a valid point.

"Let me ask you a question," he said.

"Shoot."

"Do you care if the losers you sell drugs to die or not?" He took his cigarette out of his mouth. "Do you care if the pimps or criminals that you use to get high are off the streets? And before you answer that, I know that's how it's done in L.A."

"How is it done here any differently?" I tried to justify my massive body count. "We are what we are. Bottom and top of the food chain."

"My point is that I give back to humanity after I take from it." He stalled. "And believe me, I take what I want."

Rodderick was turning out to be more and more like me, but I still wasn't satisfied with his story. "I bet you had parents and a great childhood, as well."

"Fuck you, asshole." He snatched his beanie out of his back pocket and put it on. "My parents were self-made. They gave me things because they didn't have anything."

"Then how did you make it this far? You know, as a vampire?"

"I'm not a fucking vampire. I only play one in the movies." He turned the music back up.

Rodderick was hiding something. Unless Austin truly was a lawless city of weirdoes, it didn't make sense that the police just let him come and go as he pleased. "Did you convince the cops that you could turn them into vampires?"

His face started to turn red. "You can't turn people into vampires!"

I clinched my fists. "No shit. I just want to know how you get away with all this." I turned the conversation back on him, trying not to reveal my hand. "Don't act noble. If I'm going to work for you, I need to know how the game works in Austin."

"Let it go, RJ. I didn't meet with you so I could confess all my sins and tell you my life story. You don't need to know anything about me."

"Here, I'll help you out." I sat up. "My name is RJ Reynolds. I'm a walking abortion sucked out of a prostitute who was addicted to heroin. I named myself off a pack of cigarettes that another thing like me gave me in the alley that I was dumped in after I was brought to life by a combination of heroin and illegal steroids. These steroids gave me super strength and hearing. I can't go in the light. I need drugs and blood to live. Until a few weeks ago, I figured I was a vampire. I lived on the streets of Los Angeles my whole life. I ate rats for blood and stole to feed my habit since I was able to walk. I never had a family other than the other outsiders I was in a L.A. gang called the Knucklers. Well, I ran that gang. I think that they're all dead now. They were all killed by the same group of anti-abortionist, churchgoing assholes who brought them to life."

He flicked the turn signal on again as if he hadn't heard a word I said.

"Well, I can tell you that you're about to have the best heroin you've ever had in your life. I also have a big surprise for you."

"Oh, I love surprises. I don't think I've had enough since I've been in your town." I tried not to sound pissed that he ignored my life story. "So, you make the shit yourself?"

"You could say that. The cancer institute acts as a front for my lab. I make everything that hits the streets out here."

I ashed my cigarette. "So, you don't actually care about humanity and cancer and all that shit you were bragging about earlier?"

"I wasn't bragging," he mumbled. "I was telling you how I game the system. I've helped plenty of needy children through the disease. When you taste this junk, you'll understand."

"Understand what?"

"That I can help other people and then help myself. I'm an addict, too. So, please don't hand me your sob story. To be frank, I don't care about your struggles in life before today. I just want to make your life better starting tomorrow."

"Why?"

"I told you that I had a surprise for you," he said as he pulled up to a fortress-like gate that covered in shrubs.

I looked around the compound. He was far more loaded than I could ever have imagined. "I thought that reporters were surrounding your place."

"Most of them left this morning." He rolled down his window and punched some numbers onto a keypad. "Besides, this is the secret entrance to the compound. My PR team pointed them in a different direction." He looked at me and smiled. "I'm sorry, man. I don't want to come off as a braggart."

I returned the smile and sized him up. He didn't look a whole lot tougher than me, but he sure was in better shape and better looking than me.

It had been a long time since I had heard "Salvation". To be honest, it was a pretty cool song and if my memory served correctly, Rancid's guitarist was from the UK Subs and had something to do with Agnostic Front. So, maybe there was an element of old school punk in their music. I kicked my feet back and enjoyed the end of the song as we pulled around to the back of the compound.

Rodderick threw the keys to the pickup on the counter as we entered his house through the back. "Do you want a beer or some whiskey?" he asked as he crossed me by the center island in the middle of the massive kitchen and then headed to the stainless steel, four-doored refrigerator.

I pulled out a barstool at the island and took a seat. "Can I have both? It hasn't been a great week."

"Sure." He laughed. "I know how you feel. Last summer, when we were shooting the final *Nightshayde* film, it was like twenty-hour shoot days, every day. Speaking of which." He touched the screen on his phone. Two gigantic TVs turned on, across the kitchen from each other. He pointed at one in my eye line. "Check it out."

I looked forward toward the screen and saw a car driving up a hill in the rain. I think it was like the Pacific Northwest or something gross like that. The film cut to a shot of a young gothy-type girl looking out the window of a rainy pick-up truck. The screen went black and Rodderick's name faded in, followed by the title, *Nightshayde*.

"I've got these monitors in every room of the house," he bragged. "Watching my films helps better my craft."

Ironic, I thought: a vampire who loved looking at himself.

He touched his phone screen again and turned up the volume. It boomed throughout the entire house.

"It never rained like this in New Mexico and I certainly didn't pack the right outfits for Portland. My momma always told me that I wore the wrong thing. She would constantly ask things like, 'Why are you wearing shorts, Amethyst? It's snowing,' or 'Why are you wearing a flannel shirt, Amethyst? We're at the beach.' That was my mom. She's not with me any longer. She's with God. That's why I had to go live with my dad."

"Hamster Fist." I laughed, remembering Paulina.

Rodderick remained fixated on the screen. "What did you say? It's *Amethyst*, you moron. Amethyst Rose. She's my lover in the films."

A man got out of a pickup truck that looked a lot like Rodderick's. *Scrap yard, huh?* He walked to the back and grabbed a bag out of the bed. The girl got out to join him.

"It ain't much, Amethyst." He pointed at a log cabin. *"I made a room for you that was my office."*

The girl grabbed another bag. *"Anything will be better than sleeping by mom's side while she faded away."*

The man dropped his bag and lifted his finger to deliver a stern message. *"Your mother was a good woman."*

The girl's face started welling up. *"Then, why did you leave us?"* she finally screamed and then ran into the cabin.

"Just what I need. A teenager," the dad said in an almost inappropriate tone.

Rodderick closed the door to the fridge and walked back toward me, eventually handing me a beer.

I took the beer and cheersed him. "I don't mean to sound like a dick, but is this—" I pointed to the screens, "—the big surprise?"

"You're not being a dick." He cheersed me back and took a sip.

"Then what's the surprise? Why did you agree to meet with me to begin with?"

He rubbed the bridge of his nose and he muted the compound's sound system. "When I found out that you were in Austin, I… umm… I wanted to thank you."

"Thank me? You already thanked me for taking care of the McCoys and the RTL."

"Not that. I wanted to thank you for making me who I am."

I backwashed into my bottle, causing it to overflow with head. "I don't understand."

"You're not making this easy for me." He walked back to the pantry, grabbed a roll of paper towels, and threw them to me. "Clean that up, please."

I started cleaning the foam off of the side of the island and the floor.

"What did Father McAteer tell you back at St. Matthews, RJ? About why you're alive."

"I don't know. He told me the church rounded up a bunch of hookers and street people. They didn't want them to have abortions. They kept us alive because of the church's stance on abortion. And they dumped us on the street for whatever insane reason."

"That's half the story," he said.

"Still not following." I paused sopping up the beer.

"It wasn't the church's decision to bring you to life. It wasn't the church's decision in any of the cities. I brought you here to thank you, RJ. Well," he paused. "Not you only."

I nodded my head and half smiled. I felt a tug at my arm. I tried to brush it off. I guessed that The Gooch wanted to see how the rich and famous lived as well. Either that, or he could feel my heart speeding up.

He took another sip of his beer and took off his beanie. "This is hard, so bear with me." He started pacing around me. "I had cancer when I was young." He started to cry. I think. "I was almost DOA just like you and your kind."

"I thought we were the same."

"Not entirely." He patted under his eyes with his knit cap. I didn't see any tears. I guess he wasn't a great actor after all. "My parents heard about some experimental treatment. I became part of that program. I became what I am because of you. You and the rest of your kind were brought to life and kept in the basement of that church through a pharmaceutical research project."

Something flicked at my ears a few times. I waved it away. "That's not true."

"I'm afraid it is true. The church became a farm to grow organs and bone marrow and stem cells for kids with cancer."

His words, the truth, burned me like he had just thrown acid in my face.

He tapped on his stomach. "There's probably some of you inside me."

"Wait. Back up." I tossed the balled-up towels on the bar. "Fat Mac told me that he put us out on the street because it was an act of God that we were alive or something like that."

"Total transparency, RJ. He went against the investors who paid to grow you by leaving you on the street. He was supposed to dispose of your bodies when you reached a certain age. He did the wrong thing."

I felt a scratch on the back of my neck. I swatted at it like it was a gnat. "So, I'm the wrong thing?" I grabbed a bottle of whiskey by the neck off of the bar and held it up to his face.

"No, no, no," he said, stepping back. "I wanted to thank you for my life. My parents thank you for my life." He pointed back to the TV. "Look at all I've achieved. Look at all *we've* achieved. You're here now, right? You're alive."

My veins growled and a swarm of legs crept all over my skin as if The Gooch had dumped an ant farm down the back of my jeans.

"So, you think that bringing me here and saying thank you is going to make us straight?" I turned the bottle back over and set it down. No matter how I felt about what he was saying, I was there for Paulina. Her dream of toys tugged me back to the reason I was there.

"I don't mean to offend you or sound indifferent to you saving my life. I just wanted you to know that I appreciate it." He grinned. The tears, if there ever were any, dried up pretty quickly.

I looked around his kitchen and thought about the alley where I grew up. I didn't know how to respond.

He untwisted the top on the whiskey and poured three shots. "Linnwood is on his way here. I want you both to work for me. I want to make this—" he waved his hand between us, "—right."

"I'm not sure if that's okay." I felt pricks underneath my toenails. The Gooch wanted his fix. I grabbed the shot out of his hand and slammed it down.

"Well, unfortunately I can't really give you time to think about it. C'mon, man. This is your dream. Linnwod running the coke and you running the heroin in Austin."

"Austin sucks. I can't wait to get out of here." I wet dog shook the whiskey down.

"You're part of my gang now, RJ," he said as he took his shot.

My nostrils flared. "You don't want to *play* gangster with me, homeboy."

His arrogance sucked all the air out of the room. He put up his hands and twiddled his fingers, mocking me. "Oooo. Fucking L.A. badass." He put his fist out to bump.

"What the fuck, dude?" I smacked his hand.

He stepped into my face as he lifted up the whiskey bottle and took a swig. "I don't think it's fair, either. That's why I'm doing this to pay it forward."

Then he suddenly threw the whiskey bottle across the kitchen and it exploded against a cabinet. "Bitch! You're a guest in my fucking palace and I just thanked you for my life. That simple. You don't have to do anything." He put up his fingers and started counting. "I had cancer. My parents had money. It went away. I have powers. I'm stinking rich. Every little fucking girl in the world wants my dick inside of them." He pressed his open palm toward my face. "I love heroin. So, let's go get high."

I sat back down on the barstool and swiveled it back toward the island, where I rested my beer.

"You don't even know the scope of my operation. This isn't a club for a bunch of homeless people. This is the big time. Everything you've ever wanted. Think about it. I'm giving you a magnificent gift."

My body felt warm like I had a fever. It could have been because I was angry that this little, rich prick just added another bleak chapter to my life, but it was more likely that I just wanted to curl up next to my favorite pillow.

HeROiN!

The tugging started again. "How do you know what I want? You haven't even asked me why I wanted to meet with you. It wasn't to be your mule. That's what Linn wants. I came here to smooth shit over for him. I came because Eldritch—"

"*That* fucking loser. He is the biggest failure I've ever met. This guy dressed in all his stupid vampire clothes had such a boner for me that he got my cell number off of a call sheet that we used on the set of the second *Nightshayde* movie. He seemed cool at first but then he started stalking me. I stopped answering his calls and texts. Guy blows up my phone. It's annoying."

I turned my empty beer bottle on its side and started spinning it around on the counter. I stared at it, trying to block The Gooch. I was there for

Paulina. I wasn't there to get high. "So, you did get his texts when we first got to Austin?"

He paused for a second.

"No, I don't think so." He looked at the ceiling as if he was trying to remember. "What texts?"

"Eldritch sent you a bunch of texts when we got here."

"I told you I changed my number."

I stopped the bottle from spinning and pointed it at him. "No, you didn't."

"Well, I did," he insisted. "Why are we even talking about him?" He turned away from me and headed back to the fridge. "You want another beer?"

Even after drinking the beer and the whiskey my mouth was dry. I was hungry. More hungry than usual. I desperately wanted to follow him and get high and then just kill him. The bottle stopped spinning, letting it back in.

The world's best heroin.

The thought of it began clouding my mind and The Gooch was taking the opportunity to ambush me.

The itch was becoming unbearable. I was so close to scratching, but I was sick of hearing about how great this guy had it. How *he* got the life. How *he* got the fame.

He sighed as he handed me another beer. "I guess you're jonesing, huh?"

"What makes you think that?"

He opened a cabinet drawer on the side of the island and pulled out a spoon. "Because you're sweating and you're swatting at the air like there are bugs in here." He put the spoon in front of me.

The world's best heroin.

"I'm not a meth addict. I'm not swatting at shit." I wiped my face with the balled-up towels that I used to clean the floor. They smelled.

"Gross, you pig. Use a new towel." He handed me the roll again.

I knocked it over. "I'm good."

"I hope you know that if I decided to let you in, you can't be using all my product. That's why King Cobra's small-time shit went out of business."

"Look, Mack. I don't want to be in business with you. I'm here for Perry." I groaned. I was becoming delirious. Was it right for me to want to play with my toys before I got Paulina hers? I don't think Eldritch would see a problem with that as long as I got done what needed to get done. Back at the hotel, he had winked at me and patted me on the shoulder.

"Fuck off, you L.A. trash." Stephan walked out of the kitchen. "Do you want me to call you a cab? Or do you just want to leave with Perry before we even get this agreement started?"

I wanted to just rip him limb from limb but The Gooch kept saying one thing and one thing only.

The world's best heroin.

"If you want to get high, follow me."

Blindly, I stepped down off the stool and started following him like he was the Pied Piper. Little did I know that I was still going to have to endure at least fifteen more minutes of his gratuitous bragging before I even saw any product.

Upon exiting the kitchen, we entered into the colossal foyer area. It was less gaudy than the solid-gold snake entrance to the Battlesnakes's compound, but it was disgusting, nonetheless. It looked like the designers at IKEA teamed up with Hot Topic and started mass-producing the least cool items from Eldritch's loft and lacquered everything with brush metal spray paint.

"Do you know what Rodderick means?" he asked as he pointed to several street art pieces that lined the floor around the factory fabricated pseudo-Gothic staircase.

Everything was becoming a blur. I couldn't even understand what the fuck he was yapping about.

He pointed to a painting of a crown and a family crest at the top of the stairs. I had seen this a thousand times in films where assholes would point to paintings or statues and overanalyze how it represents their power. "Stephan is a French word that means crown. Likewise, Rodderick comes from the Germans and it means 'famous power'." He stopped for a second and looked deep into the painting, only taking his eyes off of it to make sure that I was understand the veiled message.

The world's best heroin.

I bobbed my head. "What about that junk, dude? Come on. Fuck!"

Tug. Tug. Tug.

He looked at the painting one last time and let out a small gasp. Then, he started walking across the last leg of the foyer, down a hall, toward two large doors.

He paused and reflected. "I have been around the world. The thing is that I have seen the strangest things right here in America."

Flick. Flick. Flick.

I followed him down the hall, panting like a starving dog. The street art ended and framed posters from all of his vampire movies decorated the walls. I stopped at one, all it said was…

The world's best heroin.

I closed my eyes, trying to do anything to drive away from The Gooch's trap.

He walked up to the two large doors and opened one up. "After you," he said, bowing and inviting me in by rolling his hand like a medieval squire.

This dude was becoming weirder by the second.

scratch. scratch. scratch.

I pulled at the flesh on my arms. "Are we there yet?'"

He winked at me at he looked up from his bowing stance. "We shall see, won't we?"

"There's heroin in that room, right?"

The world's best heroin.

"Among other things." He stood up, brushed off his shirt and lifted one of his eyebrows.

"Is it fucking in there or not?"

He opened the doors and I ran inside, frantic for the feast. He started flipping on the lights and all the electronic devices, one by one from his phone. The room was filled with all his toys. All his fucking toys. A pool table. Huge TVs. Leather sofas and chairs. Video games. Action figures. Dolls. Trucks. Race cars. This was a pedophile's playroom.

"And this is where I bring the little human girls," he whispered.

He hit the touchscreen on his phone again and the volume his film, playing from ten different colossal TVs thundered so loudly that it felt like we were in the front row at a Slayer concert.

I stopped.

The world's best heroin?

Out of nowhere, I heard bumpers coming alive as he hit the last switch on the phone. In the corner of the gigantic room, almost hidden in the dark, I saw something illuminate that clawed me back from the sweats and the fevers and the itch. It was a *Nightshayde* pinball machine.

"Fuck you, Gooch," I said aloud.

"What did you call me?"

I dug my feet into the floor and curled my fingers into fists. "I thought you said you weren't a child molester."

"What was that?"

"You fucking heard me."

He tossed his phone down on the couch. "I don't think I did, asshole."

I pointed to an overflowing toy chest. "What is all this?"

"C'mon, bro. It isn't wrong if they want it."

"Fuck you. Fuck your 'thank you'. Fuck your operation. And fuck your 'World's Best Heroin'."

He looked at me dumbfounded and then shoved me. "Prick."

I grabbed a glass sitting on one of the bars and whizzed it at one of the TVs. It demolished the screen right as Amethyst Rose was dramatically looking at her reflection in a swamp.

I hocked up a loogie and spit it on the wood floor between us. "Let's go, Hamster Fist."

Rodderick hurdled himself on top of me, crashing me through a glass table. "You want to know how bad a hamster fist hurts, you ungrateful piece of shit?" He bomb-fisted me in the face twenty times. "Why are you here, RJ? Why the fuck are you in my town, bitch?"

As I twisted my face to avoid the slaughter, glass tugged away at my right cheek all the way up to my tear ducts, almost yanking my eye out of my face. I spit blood back at him and managed to break the iron frame from the table behind my head. I put it up as a shield in front of my nose, so he moved on to punching me in the throat and the chest. I bulldozed the steel frame under his chin and got on top of him.

"I want to leave," I screamed.

His throat was tight under the frame and he gasped for air. He picked up a die-cast fire engine next to him and slammed it into the side of my face. I got dizzy and let up on the choke hold enough for him to get to his feet. I fell forward onto my hands, trying to click the pain out of my jaw, which was dislocated again.

He danced around me and kicked me several times in the back of the head. I melted onto the floor. I don't know what he got next, it felt like a wrench, but he pounded it onto the back of my neck until everything went black.

XXIV
RESCUED

I was awakened by the feeling of my teeth being dragged across the gravel on the driveway to Rodderick's back entrance. Unlike every other time that I had passed out or gone to sleep since arriving in Austin, I didn't dream. It might have had something to do with the fact that Rodderick had beaten me so profusely that my brain wasn't working. The guy handed me my ass.

As I tried to come back to the world of the "living," I spit some chips and dirt out of my mouth. "Where...?"

Rodderick grabbed me by the hair and pulled me toward him. "Shut the fuck up!" He bounced my face into the headlight on a car. It zapped into the pusing, healing sore that the table had torn into my cheek. The headlight cover fell off and the light illuminated the veins in my eyelid. Rather than help me to my feet, he let me fall forward. I wasn't off the hook though, because he walked back a few steps and then punted me in the face, nearly knocking me unconscious again. I flipped onto my back and felt something broken in my back pocket pierce my ass cheek. I felt around. The phone that Cody gave me was demolished from the melee.

I was disorientated because my right eye was glowing from the light and my left eye was swollen over. At least I was mending. I laid there, waiting for him to finish me off. He mumbled something but it just came out as a garbled mess.

I heard a car door open and shut. Footsteps crunched the gravel and stopped.

"Hey, man. Are you going to pay to get that fixed?"

He stood up and kicked some rocks. Not at Rodderick. At me.

"I certainly hope you're not talking to me, Perry," Rodderick shouted back.

"Of course I'm not talking to you," Linnwood returned.

"What took you so goddamn long to get here?"

"I was at a titty club. I didn't get your message because there was no signal until I went to take a piss."

A hand wrapped around the front of my neck and brought me to my knees. "Get this piece of shit out of here."

"I'm not taking him anywhere," Linnwood said.

"My ass you aren't, dickhead. I knocked him out over twenty minutes ago, so I want him out of here before he heals and decides to jump me again. Fucking psychotic junkie."

Linnwood walked closer to us and slapped me on the back of the head. Rocks fell off of my face as he asked, "What the hell am I supposed to do with him? I thought we were gonna talk business."

"There is no business between you and me. Put this piece of shit in your car and take him back to Los Angeles. Neither of you are welcome in Austin anymore."

"Yo, dude," Linnwood started to grovel. "What did I do?"

"You brought this scumbag to me. You told me he would be my 'guy'. Trust me, this isn't my guy. Not yesterday. Not today. And, not tomorrow." He bent down to my ear. "You're lucky I'm not going to kill you, RJ. I tried to thank you and give you the opportunity of your shitty life and you repay me by trashing my house."

"Wait, wait, wait," Linnwood began as he got behind me to lift me up from under my arms. "This has to be a misunderstanding. Let's all go inside and check out the damage. I can help RJ pay you back."

Rodderick pushed Linnwood and I slipped out of his hands. "What are you going to pay me with? The coke that you stole from me?"

"Stephan. Brother. You know I was bringing that back to you. It's all in the trunk.... At least what's left of it."

Rodderick walked toward the back of the car but not before spitting on me. "Open the trunk, pussy."

My eyes started to creep open but I still couldn't get to my feet.

Linnwood clicked the fob to the BMW and the trunk opened. "See. Right there in the bag."

A flood light lit up the back of the car. Rodderick rested the duffle bag on the back of the car and zipped it open. He sifted through it, grunted a few times and then closed the it. "How much did you and your other dickless friends steal from me?"

Linnwood didn't answer.

"That's what I figured. Go back to L.A. and send me food stamps or however you dirty scumbags pay for things. I just want you the fuck out of here." He heaved the bag onto the stoop by his backdoor. "And no, you won't be getting any parting gifts."

"Wait," Linnwood said as he pointed at me. "This dude doesn't speak for me."

Rodderick walked back over to me. I cowered, expecting another blow to the head. "If he didn't speak for you, then why did you send him here?" He picked me up by the back of the shirt. "Open the door."

Linnwood, thinking that he still had an opportunity to salvage his position in Austin, did as he was told. "Can we talk about this?"

"Fuck you," Rodderick said as he stuffed me head first into the car.

I rolled around and sat down in the passenger seat. They both slammed the door shut.

Perry's voice became desperate and he started to beg. "Look, I'll kill him for you. I'll do whatever."

I wobbled around in the passenger's seat and pointed at my ear. *Super hearing*, I mouthed.

Neither of them were paying attention.

As Linnwood approached him to plead his case, Rodderick spun him around. He crowbarred his arm behind him and smacked his face onto the hood of the car. Then, after he elbowed him between the shoulder blades, he let him go and walked back to the door.

"Get out of here, trash," he said as he picked up the case, entered the house and turned off the porch light.

There was no music on in Linnwood's stolen car and all he did was grumble to himself. I would have said something sooner, but my face hadn't fully healed yet and it hurt.

"I'm sorry," I said after about ten minutes of no conversation.

"Oh, so you can talk. I was hoping that Rodderick pulled your fucking tongue out of your face."

I licked my fingers and started wiping a crusty mass of blood off of my chin. The pus my on cheek was hardening over the cut from the table. "Hey, man," I returned quietly.

He threw the car into gear and started accelerating. Out of the corner of my eye, I noticed him staring at me. "Looks like that went well, dick," he whispered.

I didn't respond.

I could hear the car humming as he shifted gears and the brakes pumping every time he hit a stop sign. For the next twenty-five excruciating minutes, he didn't say a word to me. Instead, he kept his eyes forward, adjusted his seat and grunted.

After one severely intense groan, he pushed a button under the stereo, causing the convertible top to retract. "It's hot in here."

I finally asked, "You okay?"

"No, I'm not okay. You're a loser, RJ," he said. "You just fucked up everything for me in Austin. You just fucked up everything for *you* in Austin."

We passed a sign for the Austin-Bergstrom International Airport. I knew we were getting close to The Golden Aces. "I didn't want anything to do with Austin, Linn."

He swung into the right lane. "I sure hope you enjoyed yourself. I hope that his heroin was the best thing you've ever put into that derelict body of yours."

"I didn't get high," I finally said. "Rodderick is scumbag. I want nothing to do with him."

"Your only mission in meeting with him was to get us in his group. Remember the money clip and the phone? Remember the generals? About an hour ago, that was us."

"He fucks little kids and I think that he uses their blood to make his drugs."

"So?" he said. 'Who fucking cares? It's us versus them, RJ. It's vampires versus humans. I don't care how old they are. We need to get high to stay alive."

I didn't tell him the truth about vampires like us. I probably should have.

A car honked and cut him off. "Jesus," he shouted. "Learn how to drive, asshole."

"You're driving pretty slow," I pointed out.

"Thanks," he spat. "I didn't know you were a fucking expert on driving. You're definitely not an expert on business or survival."

"Just sayin'."

"Don't say anything, junkie." He hammered his fist on the center console. "What exactly was the point of all that?"

I reached for his Dunhills. "I told you that I didn't want to smooth things out for you."

He smacked my hand. "You haven't earned cigarettes, asshole."

"Fine." I cracked my neck. It was still tingling from whatever object Rodderick hammered it with.

"That's what happens when you send a vagrant to do your work for you," he continued. "To think, I was trying to do you a favor. I actually thought you could see the big picture here. The big picture didn't involve you getting into a fight with our ticket back to the game. The big picture didn't involve you getting so wasted that you didn't even know who you were talking to. Remember Cobra?"

I nodded.

"Good," he huffed. "Too bad you didn't remember him an hour ago. Rodderick is that piece of shit times a million. For fuck's sake, RJ. I was so close. *We* were so close."

"I already said that I'm sorry I fucked things up."

He grabbed the Dunhills. "That's all you ever are. Sorry. You're just sorry."

As I looked off to the side of the road, Linnwood crossed over into the left lane and passed some guy trying desperately to conceal his last road-Coke of the night.

"What happened, anyway?" he mumbled.

I sighed and pried my eyes open with my fingers. "He took me into some gross romper room to get high. It's where he brings kids to fuck them and kill them. I'm not cool with that."

He bent forward toward the windshield so he could light his cigarette. "And you couldn't just be cool?"

"He kept saying all this shit to me about how much better he was than me." I pulled some of his smoke into my blood-crusted nostrils.

"Dear Lord. Suck it up. He is better than you." Linn rubbed his hand down my cheek like he was wiping his ass. "He's definitely stronger than you."

"Can you let it go? I don't want to do business with him."

"I'm not ever going to let this go," he insisted.

A pair of headlights blazed into my side mirror. I put up my hand to shield my eyes. "It's done, Linn. You might as well go beg him to let you in yourself this time. I want nothing to do with this city. I want nothing to do with him."

"Right. As if I'm going to go beg him to take me into his organization after you just took a dump on his life's work. What? Am I going to bring him some gift? 'Here, Mr. Movie Star. Here's a gift for you. I know that you have all the drugs and fame you could possibly want, but here's a quarter sack of weed.' Fuck that. I've got nothing he could possibly want."

"It's your problem now," I reminded him. "It was your problem to begin with. I didn't tell you to try and kick your way into his gangs."

"Go around, you little fucking girl!" he snapped at the headlights. Then, he whispered to himself. "Little girl."

With those words, I remembered that he had said something about a little girl back at The Settler's Inn. *Jesus!* As everything dropped into slow motion, I heard him roll his window down all the way. "Go around."

"What did you say?" I looked at him. He was blocking his eyes from the driver's side mirror.

"I told this fucking little girl behind me to go around!"

He waved his arm furiously outside the window.

"What did you just say about a girl?"

He dismissed the question. "I called this bitch a little girl." He flicked his cigarette out the window. "*Go the fuck around!*"

I turned around. I couldn't see a thing behind us beside two huge headlights. "What do you know about the girl?"

"What are you talking about?"

I forced his head out the car. "What do you know about the little girl, Linnwood?"

He struggled to pull himself back into the car and stay in his lane. "Relax," he huffed and I pushed his lips up into his nose.

I saw the lights in his rearview mirror getting closer.

He took his hands off the steering wheel and shoved me into the door on my side of the car. "Get off me."

"How do you know about the little girl with cancer?"

He massaged his face. "Fuck you, punkass."

I turned around again to see the headlights closing in on us, and I saw the familiar chrome six on the front of the bus from earlier that night blast to the left and gun it. Everything became crystal clear.

I pried open the glove compartment and grabbed both of his guns. "Fuck us."

He ignored what was happening behind him and slapped me in the face. "What's wrong with you? Don't touch my hardware, bitch."

I slumped forward as the bus pulled up to Linnwood's side of the car. The Sixth Street Skulls.

In every window there was an eerie face, tattooed and painted like a sugar skull from *Dia de los Muertos*, the Day of the Dead. They all had weapons. One of them bounced a bat off his hand. Another pulled a chain tightly in his mouth and bit into it with his steel teeth. The third cut across his face with a machete and flicked at a pin connected to a grenade on his chest. Blood slid into his mouth and he spat at us.

"Jesus, Linn! Get us the fuck out of here."

The next window caught up to us. The forth Skull smiled as he held up an Uzi and then tapped it on his half-open school bus window.

Linnwood turned around to see the Skull taking aim at his head. "Shit!" he cried as he used both his feet to stomp on the brakes. The bus flew by us but not before the gunman got off a few shots that ripped into the hood and my side of our car. We fishtailed around and the bus continued ahead of us.

I pointed to an off ramp. "Take that exit. Now."

He downshifted and spun back toward the exit. "What the fuck was that?" he yelled. "What did you get us into?"

He was breathing uncontrollably so I tugged the wheel toward the ramp.

"That was the Sixth Street Skulls, dumbass," I screamed at him. "That's Rodderick's gang."

Smoke started to emerge from the hood. Apparently, a few of the bullets hit the engine.

He continued to scream. "We're fucking dead!"

When we reached the bottom of the ramp, our car started to sputter. I looked behind us. There was long streak of fluid, making it all too easy to track us down.

Linnwood blew threw a stop sign and turned left to go under the freeway.

"You didn't tell Rodderick where I was staying? Please tell me that you didn't tell him where we were staying."

"No. I didn't say shit."

"Get us to the hotel. *Get us to the fucking hotel!*"

I grabbed the phone that Cody gave me out of my pocket and tried to turn it on. No luck. It had been completely destroyed during the fight with Rodderick.

Linnwood took a right but didn't respond. Near the gas gage, a red light flared on and started beeping.

"What's the name of the hotel?" I yelled again as I tossed the phone out of the car.

"Golden Aces," he finally shouted. "I know how to get there."

"Are you sure?"

"Yes." He insisted as he pumped the brakes and flipped a bitch at a turnaround. "I've been there like three times now."

"Are you sure you know where you're going?"

"Yes!"

And then, as if things couldn't possibly get any shittier, the BMW clunked and we slowed to a crawl under the freeway.

I slammed my fists onto the dashboard. "Fuck! Start the car."

Linnwood pushed the start button. Nothing happened.

"Start the car, Linnwood,"

He pushed the button again with his thumb. "I'm trying. It won't turnover."

The sound of Reggaeton music being played over the bus's antique speaker thundered in the distance.

"Do you have your foot on the brakes?"

"Fuck. My foot was on the gas," he realized.

I gripped his knee. "Put it on the brakes!"

The music got louder.

"Hurry up, man."

Linnwood repeatedly pushed the starter but it wouldn't turn over.

The blaring, tinny music stabbed my brain through my ears. I turned around and saw the headlights of Skulls's bus take a left two blocks away. It slowly rolled toward us.

"You gotta start the car," I begged him. "They're coming."

He turned to see the bus. Piss filled his pants as he furiously drilled his foot onto the brake pedal.

I grabbed him by the back of the head. "Please, Linnwood. Slow down. Press your foot on the pedal and hold it down. Don't bang on the button."

A tear streamed down his cheek. "Do you want to do this, RJ?"

I turned to look back. The bus came to a stop about a block away. I could feel my heart pushing the blood around in my body as it tried to escape my skin.

I tried to calm him. "Slow down."

He closed his eyes and dropped his foot onto the brakes. Then, he slowly pressed the button. The alternator turned over and the car purred. He pushed the gas a few times and wiped the long tear off of his face with the back of his hand.

Behind us, the Skulls poured out of the windows of the bus. In the darkness, I could see nothing other than the shadows of the bodies and their brightly painted faces. A few of them took the lead and started walking towards our car.

"Let's go!" I yelled.

Linnwood dropped the clutch in gear and punched it.

The car sputtered out.

"Fuck," he shrieked.

Horror fell over his face and we both turned around again to see the Skulls start to pick up their pace as the music hit the fast-rapping chorus.

"RJ Reynolds," one of them sang. "*Queremos comer usted!*"

"What does that mean?"

I released the magazine in the gun and checked it. It was loaded. "It means they're coming to eat me." I shoved it back in the gun spun around in my chair. I put my knees on the seat and started unloading the gun at them. They jumped around like skeleton marionettes, laughing when bullets made contact with their bodies.

Linnwood started to turn around in his seat as well. He fired off a couple of rounds.

I grabbed him by his hair and dragged him back so he was facing forward again. "What are you doing? Start the fucking car."

The Skulls reached a spot on the road that was two streetlights away from us. I could see them. They were about thirty deep, a lot more than I thought. The leader put up his hands, holding back his gang. They stopped but continued to shake and rattle around with their assorted weapons.

The leader walked to the center of the pack and called out in a thick Spanglish accent. "I guess we're playing with guns now, RJ Reynolds?" Without warning, he slung a machine gun from under his arm and then resumed his stalking, randomly firing in my direction to the beat of the Reggaeton song thumping behind him.

As I ducked down and slid knees first onto the floor, I felt the engine turn over.

I looked up and over to Linnwood, who was dropping in and out of shock. "Please drive," I pled with him. "I don't want to be eaten."

Linn shoved the shifter into first gear and then sped away.

"Hopefully, we can make it more than ten feet," he whimpered.

The rattling of several guns rang out as fire filled the Austin skyline with light behind us. Linnwood's BMW puttered and grinded from gear to gear.

I stayed on the floor and tried to catch my breath, knowing the fight was far from over.

I clutched his dick. "You wormy little fucker."

"Let go!" he squeaked.

"You piece of shit." I pointed the gun at his head. "This is the second time you set me up."

He slipped his hand under my palm removing it from his crotch. "I said stop!"

I pressed the gun against his temple. "Linnwood, I'm going to blow your head off."

"They were going to kill me, too." He looked into the rearview again.

A sickness came over my body as I pulled the gun away and rested it in my lap. The taste of the withdrawal started climbing back up my throat, only to freeze midway, choking me. The Gooch was making his move again. If I had felt empty, useless, disgusting, or evil before that moment, those feelings and thoughts were merely the self-loathing whimpers of a narcissist. I held both my hands over my stomach. It compressed like it was shrinking around a bunch of thumbtacks and razor blades. My heart thumped through my right ear, making me dizzy and drunk. The bitter cold that engulfed me and lumped in my throat made me want to shove the pistol in my mouth and end the trail of torture that followed me around.

The car stammered and backfired as the leaking engine seized up. Linnwood turned the wheel and sailed onto the shoulder. I looked behind us. It seemed as if we had managed to shake the Skulls as I couldn't hear the music or see the bus anywhere. About three hundred yards up the road from us, I saw the familiar blinking sign for the Golden Aces Hotel.

Gagging, I opened the door and fell out of the car. Not being a real human didn't make anything better. My legs weren't working with my brain and I had a hard time getting back to my feet. I dragged myself in the direction of the hotel.

"Do you need help?" Linnwood asked as he quickly gathered all his shit from the car, knowing he had no choice but to ditch it.

"Get the fuck away from me," I slurred as I pointed the gun at him again.

"Why are you fucking pointing that at me? I didn't do it."

I rolled sideways into a bush beyond the shoulder.

Linnwood got out of the car and shoved his other gun into the back of his pants. He walked over to me and extended his hand.

"Get the fuck away from me!" I cried. "You were trying to set me up. You always try to set me up." I rocketed out of the bush and began limp-running toward the Golden Aces. "Get the fuck out of here. Go save yourself. It's what you do best."

"This isn't over, Reynolds," he yelled out after me. "You fucking junkie! Rodderick is never going to let us live now. Just give me the little girl. If that's really his thing, he might forgive me."

I turned around to see Linnwood keeping up with me. My legs throbbed and I started feeling like I hadn't slept in weeks. "I knew you were trying to fuck me," I yelled back again. "You can kill me, but there is no way you can get by Eldritch."

He stopped responding.

When I reached the head shop plaza, I picked up the pace. I rounded the corner into the Golden Aces parking lot and flattened my body into the door as I rattled the doorknob.

No one came to answer. Eldritch must have been in the shitter again. I looked behind me. I didn't see Linnwood.

The Gooch, who was lodged in my throat, started to move to my brain. I started thumping on the door.

Still, no one answered.

I kicked the door open and stepped into the hotel room. No Eldritch. I only saw the Rasta wig peaking up behind Pinball's bed.

And then, I heard a hollowed-out bottle crush me over the head. Blood started to trickle into my eyes and I turned around to see Linnwood standing behind me with his arm cocked back with a second champagne bottle left in front of the hooker's door next to us. He smashed it into my face and everything went black.

I was only out for a second or two. I felt one of Eldritch's creepers smash in my back as he ran toward the door. "Little One?" he screamed.

I heard car tires squeal from the parking lot outside. I opened my eyes and blurrily saw Eldritch unsheathe his sword. "Paulina!"

I pressed my hand into a pile of broken glass and then used the bed to pick myself up. I headed outside to see Eldritch's rental car swerving away from us down the street. Eldritch reached the middle of the road as he watched the car escape. He looked back, but before he could take flight to chase the car, he jumped out of the way and rolled back into the parking lot. The distorted sounds of the tin can speaker of the Sixth Street Skulls blew past the hotel as the bus nearly ran him down. Gun fire zipped out of the windows. Eldritch spun under a car to avoid getting picked off.

"Who is in the car?" he sputtered as he appeared on the other side of his shield.

TAKE A BREATH, RJ!

I felt blood run from the back of my head onto my spine, and fear crept through my body. Not wanting to relive a situation like Bait's death, I went after the bus. "It's Linnwood," I said as I ran past him. There were no more wiseass comments. The only thing left to do was fight.

I felt like I was running in mud. My body wasn't healing as fast as I would have liked it to, but I punched it into overdrive rather than fall back and accept defeat. Thankfully, the Skulls's ancient bus was weighed down by the gang inside. As I got close, I looked for something to grab onto. Eldritch sped past me and jumped onto the back. His arms smashed through one of the rear windows and used the opening to lift himself up. He quickly scaled up the back like a salamander on a wall and rolled onto the top. Gunfire erupted through both back windows, barely missing him.

There was only a small bumper on the back of the bus. Somehow, I managed to jump high enough to secure my hands on the jagged edges of both of the broken windows, and I shifted my feet outward to stabilized myself. I ducked down but the gunfire was no longer coming out toward me. The Skulls were aiming for Eldritch by shooting their guns through the roof.

I peered inside to see several painted and tatted bangers slithering on their backs out of the side windows. The center of the bus's left wall was packed with a full arsenal of weapons from the floor to the roof.

The gunfire aimed at the roof ceased and it was time for me to make my move to the top and help Eldritch. I hopped onto one of the black covers on top of the left side taillight and stepped onto the backdoor latch. To my surprise, it wasn't locked and it sprung open, throwing me off balance and leaving me dangling off the back of the bus like a fishing lure.

One of the Skulls near the backseat ran toward me with a meat cleaver. He took a swing, slicing off a thin layer of skin where the Pit Bull had taken a bite out of me. One of his cohorts inched up behind him and stretched out a few feet of razor wire. The bus driver slammed on the brakes, most likely trying to jolt Eldritch from the top. I swung outward and the back door crashed shut beside me, knocking the meat cleaver Skull back into the razor wire and on top of his buddy.

"*Cabrón,*" the one on the bottom yelled.

Without warning, the bus driver hit the gas and both of the them rolled around and got tangled up in the razor wire. Accidentally, the meat cleaver sunk into the chest of the dumb fucker who took a sliver of flesh out of the side of my stomach. I heard a bunch of grenades roll toward the back.

The sides of the top of the bus were rounded down. While I desperately felt around for something to grip, two Skulls flew over my head and smacked face first onto the street behind us. Eldritch wasn't taking any prisoners. Although the Skulls were packing a full arsenal, no gun, knife, hatchet, machete, or man was a match for Eldritch's frenzy. He became a deranged wrecking ball when he wanted to and unlike me or any other vampire I had ever met, he could turn his maniacal carnage on and off like a shark smelling blood in the water.

I tried to pierce the metal on top with my fingers so I could pull myself up when the bus hit a bump. I held onto the taillight cover and looked back inside the bus. Many of the Skulls had exited through the windows to join Eldritch on top, but one near the middle lifted his gun and started firing it at me. I swung to the side again as my hands started to slip. Two more of members of the gang rolled off of the top. One screamed as he splatted on the pavement. The other didn't have a head.

The Skull inside didn't let up. He walked toward the rear and continued to try and mow me down with his gun. My right bicep took a few bullets and flopped to my side. When that didn't work, he hurled a grenade through the back window, hoping it would make contact with my chest. In the heat of battle, he forgot to pull the pin. I managed to catch it with my throbbing free arm and I locked my thumb inside the pin.

"Goddammit!" Blood streamed from my arm in the wind gusting from the back of the bus. I tried to lift it back up to the top off the bus but it twitched and shivered like it was out of juice.

When I was about to give up and join the growing number of Skulls as roadkill, Eldritch's taloned hand grabbed my wrist. Unfortunately, it wasn't to save me from falling off. He snapped me over his head like a dodgeball, dislocating the shoulder attached to my bullet-filled arm and launched me into three Skulls who had made their way to the top. Somehow, I managed to hold onto the grenade.

My body spun sideways as I collided with them, knocking them over the front. As two of them spun under the front of the bus, one of them grabbed onto my boot as I slipped down the hood and snagged my crotch onto a metal stand that supported two round mirrors on top of the wheel well. Tears burst out of my eyes. I spit up a mouthful of bloody barf at the Skull who became hysterical as he seized handfuls of my calves and thighs like he was climbing rungs on a ladder. I pulled my right leg loose, retracted it back and mashed it into his skull-tattooed face. He turned his face sideways as he managed to snag the one of the mirror frames.

I hammered away at his nose with the heel of my boot. "Get off, bitch!" I yelled. "Get the fuck off me." A burning pain ran from my dead arm into my chest and pushed needles into my heart. As I looked for something to cling to, screws from the frame started popping out and I slid further down the front of the wheel well. I caught the inside of the Skull's chin on the metal six emblem on the grill.

"No me mates! No me mates," he begged as his voice became garbled from blood filling his mouth.

I pulled my boot back on and stamped the tread into his chin, ripping his bottom jaw off his face. His tongue dangled as he looked down in horror at what remained above his neck. The mirror frame came loose and he spiraled over the front of the grill, ending up pressed under the tires of the bus.

I pushed myself up to the hood before I slipped to my death as well and hooked my limp arm around the side mirror. Before I had the opportunity to try and rejoin Eldritch on top, the bus door flung open and the same gunman who filled my arm with bullets clicked a magazine into his gun and started firing aimlessly around the corner of the door.

I kicked my feet up and let go of the mirror. I started slithering on my stomach across the hood. He rolled around the outside of the door. He smiled as he pointed the barrel directly between my eyes. The bus hit another bump and his aim was thrown off. He shot right through the front of the windshield. Bullets chopped through the driver's forehead, exposing his brain. His head slumped onto the steering wheel.

"Eldritch, jump off," I shouted over the music. "We're gonna crash."

The Skull tried to get back inside the bus to take the wheel, but he was thrown to the side and onto the road. The bus jerked left and started heading for the other side of the street. I shook my arm as I slid back down the opposite side. I flipped the pin out of the grenade and chucked it through the window. Without waiting another second, I bounced my feet on top of the wheel well again and launched myself off. I rolled onto the cement, further crunching my disabled arm. Bullets kicked up gravel into my face, and I rushed to the side of the street, looking for cover anywhere. The bus skidded into oncoming traffic and flipped onto the side of the road. It toppled over and immediately exploded.

Deaf to the wailing of the powder keg death trap that charred the rest of his gang, one of the lucky Skulls who managed to jump out of a window before the crash walked toward me. "*Queremos comer usted*, RJ Reynolds."

I hadn't realized it before, but he was the leader who sang to me from my first encounter with the Skulls under the freeway pass.

He pressed the gun against his hip and finger fucked the trigger hole. "And now, you die," he snorted.

Just when I was expecting to be filled with lead, Eldritch flew down from above, lifted his sword and bisected the leader from the top of his head all the way down to his pelvis. Eldritch landed on the ground behind him and opened him up like a door. As he walked through the remains and the two sides of the Skull's body timbered sideways, organs and guts sagged and squirted to the ground.

A car spun to a stop behind him. Not realizing what exactly was going down, the driver got out. "Are you okay, man?" he yelled.

Not speaking, Eldritch turned around and stepped through the leftovers of the Skull's leader. He put his sword back into its sheath. Still silent, he grabbed the bystander by the throat and tossed him away from his car like a dishrag. I propped myself up and ran to the car as Eldritch got in. I knew he wasn't going to wait for me so I jumped into the car and slammed the door, hoping that he wasn't going to assassinate me the second he knew I was going with him.

He pulled the seat back, making room for his long legs. "Get the fuck out, RJ."

He didn't speak in his normal flowery language. At that point, I imagined that he only cared about one thing: saving Paulina.

"You can't do this alone, Eldritch," I said. "I didn't get high. I swear."

Without continuing the conversation, he threw the car in drive and put the pedal to the metal.

The owner of the car yelled, apparently after he landed next to the remains of the Skull leader. "Oh my God! Oh my God!"

Eldritch handed me his sword. "Do you know how to get to his house?"

"I... ummmm..."

A text popped up on his phone. He grabbed it quickly, read it and turned it off. "It does not matter." He accelerated and pointed in front of us down the road. A car took a right onto the freeway ramp. "There is my rental car."

I put the sword in my lap. "He lives in West Lake Hills."

He nodded and followed Linnwood Perry onto the highway.

I rubbed my throbbing arm and started picking bullets out of my skin. "I deserved that."

He refused to look at me. "You deserved what?"

"I deserved being thrown on top of the bus." I pulled a bullet out and flicked it out the window.

"You deserve death, RJ."

"I didn't know he was going to take the girl. I didn't know any of this until minutes before I got back to the room. Rodderick beat the shit out of me. He's a child molester, Eldritch. Did you know that?"

He clinched his fist. "That is not true."

I leaned toward him and showed him the healing scar on the side of my face. "Oh, really? He took me into his kiddie dungeon and I got pissed off at him. So, he kicked the shit out of me. I'm not sure, but I think that he only gets high with kid's blood."

His phone buzzed again. He ignored it. "Outrageous. Why would someone in his position do such a thing?"

"Like I know. He's a fucking twisted asshole. He wanted to meet with me to thank me."

"Thank you? Thank you for what?"

And then it hit me. "I think you know, Eldritch."

"I do not."

"You're like him, aren't you? You aren't like me or Linnwod or Dez or Cobra. You're some rich prick who got a second chance at life."

"I still do not know what you are referring to. I have told you several times that I'm not like you."

"I wasn't an abortion brought to life by the church. I was an abortion brought to life as an organ donor. All of us were. We're not vampires. We're not fiends. Were the product of some pharmaceutical company. Fat Mac freed us when he was supposed to destroy us."

"I honestly do not know what you are speaking about."

I rolled my fingers around the handle of the sword.

He looked at my hand and shook his head. "Not a good idea."

I let go.

"Unfortunately, I have no reason to believe your tales. You have not been reliable and you have chosen to use drugs when our mission has been clear since we got here. That is why I had my friends checking up on you."

"Friends? What are you talking about?" I grabbed my shoulder and massaged it carefully before quickly snapping it back into place. Even though I wanted to cry out, I grinded my teeth and closed my eyes instead.

He grabbed the sword off my lap and threw it into the backseat. "The Chaplins and Ride the Lightning. I sent them to look for you on the streets of Austin and at the garage."

"Are you fucking kidding me? They almost killed me."

"That was not the intention. They were sent to look for you. I warned you in the desert. No more drugs. You attacked the Chaplins and I had no idea that the Perrys took the RTL's cocaine. You were in the wrong place at the wrong time."

Tears streamed down my cheeks. The pain spread to the entire right side of my body and cramped my toes. "You piece of shit."

He tapped his talons on the wheel.

I sneezed into my hand and then lifted my finger, asking for a second. I sneezed again. "I was your dog this whole time. You know why you didn't know any of this shit about Rodderick? Because you've got your head so far up his ass that you can't see anything. It turns out that you are the one who put Pinball in danger."

"*Paulina!*" he exploded. "The little girl's name is Paulina. I did everything that I did because I was concerned about you. Do you understand that? I—"

"You asshole. What? Did you think that Rodderick was going to give you a role in his next movie if you helped him get his career back on track? Big hero you are, Eldritch."

"Evidentially, you do not know me. I wanted to help the girl. You chose to play."

"I get it. I fucked up. You care. I was wrong to involve Linnwood. He must have seen Paulina through the window of our hotel or heard us talking to her one of the times he dropped me off. Either that or he was staking me out. I own that, Eldritch. I have to own the fact that he took her because he wants to give Rodderick something he doesn't have. And if she dies, I have the life of another kid on my conscious. All that said, you have to own that you put us all in danger."

He took his hands off of the wheel and tied his long hair in back. "Why did you bring the Perry back to the room if you knew that they wanted the girl?"

"I didn't know until right before he took her. The Skulls chased us back to the hotel and they tried to kill him, too. He was pissed off at me for blowing his deal with Rodderick."

"His deal?"

"Linnwood wants to run coke in Austin." I lowered my head. "He thought I was going to meet Rodderick to smooth things out for him and what's left of the Perrys. Well, Rodderick took me back to his place and that's where things got all fucked up."

"I will take responsibility," he finally said. "You were right. We should have handed the girl over to the authorities."

His phone buzzed again.

"Who's texting you," I asked, feeling that we had both accepted responsibility for a series of *really* bad ideas.

"Back up," he said.

"Anyone I know?"

"We shall see."

XXV
INVADED

He pulled into the main entrance to West Lake Hills and started the upward climb to Rodderick's compound at the top.

"Pull back," I told Eldritch, remembering the way. "I know how to get in there."

"Are there still people outside the front gate?" Eldritch turned off the headlights on our car.

"He told me that the paparazzi stopped coming by the compound yesterday. Besides," I reminded him, "it's too early for them to be there."

He pulled a clove out of his cigarette case. "How many entrances to the *ranch* are there?"

"There's the main entrance at the front gate and then there's a private entrance in the rear. Linnwood will be going in the back. We should go over the side wall and take them by surprise."

He lit the clove. "Obviously."

When we got close to the top of the hill, he pulled to the side of the road.

"Are you ready?"

He nodded and reached into the backseat for his sword. "Promise me this."

"Yeah?"

"Promise me that if we save Paulina, that no matter what else happens, that you will take her to the authorities."

I nodded my head and bit my top lip. "We can't let her die like her sister, Eldritch. I can't erase my mistakes, but I can make this right."

We both got out of the car and started huffing it up the hill.

I pointed to the compound that was hidden behind a wall twenty feet high, camouflaged by shrubs. "It's up there to the right."

"Does he have any security detail on the grounds?" he asked.

I stretched my injured arm behind my back. The feeling was returning and although it was nowhere near one hundred percent, it would have to do. "There will be some Minutemen and maybe what's left of the Skulls on the grounds. I'm sure he also has cameras everywhere."

He secured his sword on his back and waved me to follow him as he trotted up to the wall.

I joined him and tugged on the bushes. "The Minutemen clean up his messes. It has something to do with keeping him out of trouble."

"Interesting," he said as he continued to survey the area.

I tugged on the shrubbery again. There was no way it was going to hold either of us if we climbed it.

He dug his hands in and began scaling the wall.

"Eldritch?" I coughed. "I'm not going to be able to get up that wall." I pointed at my arm.

He looked down to me. "I will meet you around at the back gate."

I remained close to the wall and started shuffling towards the back. "How the fuck am I going to get in there?" I whispered.

"We will figure it out," he returned, hearing me.

I carefully timed my movement because there were several security cameras patrolling the outer wall. Even though I was pretty sure Rodderick knew we were there to crash his party, there was an outside chance that we could get in there undetected. When I reached the corner of the front side wall, I noticed some flood lights that lit up the long dirt road that lead to the back. So, I strayed from the cover of the wall and trailed off to the tree line that followed the long dirt road that lead to the back gate. It amazed to me how big his compound was from the outside. No one in Los Angeles had a place this big.

BOOM!
BOOM!
BOOM!

A big gun started discharging and echoing through the trees. Our cover was blown. I started running toward the back gate, which I immediately noticed was open.

The back gate started to close. The gunfire alerted Rodderick and whomever was guarding the compound that we had arrived. I slid sideways through the gate right before it closed and saw Eldritch's rental car sitting in the driveway.

"Kill him!" one of the security guards yelled into a headset. He wasn't talking about me. I tripled my speed, and undetected, I cannonballed myself into him. The force of my body knocked his gun out of his hand. I got him on his back and I pressed my fingers into his eye sockets. I felt his tears and blood flow into my fingernails. He whimpered a bit but I instantly cut off his voice when I drilled my teeth into his jugular vein. There it was. Warm food.

CRASH!

I looked to my left and saw the tail of Eldritch's jacket zip through a window. Two more guards ran around the corner of the house near his entrance and started firing aimlessly into the house. They didn't notice me, so I left my meal twitching on the ground and bolted around the garage to get to the pool area.

"Fucking asshole," I said as I looked into the garage and saw the pickup truck next to a Ferrari and a Lamborghini. *"Fucking asshole!"*

I took the corner full speed and reached a six-foot steel fence that surrounded the pool. Knowing that I couldn't jump over it, I barreled right through it, upending it and pulling the stakes from the concrete in the ground. Not being slowed, I closed my eyes and leapt through the gigantic bay window that overlooked the pool. Glass crashed all around me but I didn't let up. Gunfire rang out across the house and I followed the sound. It was coming from the foyer at the front of the house. I rushed to get there.

As soon as I ran in, a bullet flew by my head. Eldritch was in the middle of five Minutemen. He spun in a circle, decapitating two of them as bullets ripped into his torso. I ran to his aid, tearing off one of the guard's arms and then firing the gun that was in that hand into two others. One dropped to the ground and Eldritch struck the other down with his sword.

He grabbed the one that had dropped by his hair. "Where is the girl?" he shouted. "Where is Rodderick?"

"I don't know," the final guard sputtered. "Please don't kill me."

I started to head to the playroom.

"Where is Rodderick?" Eldritch screamed again.

"We're here for him, too. We're here for him—"

Eldritch put him out of his misery by piercing his brain with his katana and then pulling it up, releasing the brain from his head.

I pulled the gun from the arm and entered the dungeon. The lights were off and another one of the *Nightshayde* films played on all the screens. I looked at one of them for a second and caught Rodderick kissing Hamster Fist.

"*I am addicted to your human blood, my love,*" he said.

"Rodderick?" I shot up all the screens in the room. "Where the fuck are you?"

"He is here," Eldritch called out calmly from the foyer.

I walked back down the hall. Eldritch was standing at the bottom of the winding staircase pointing his blood dripping sword up the stairs. He stepped onto the first stair.

"Don't take another step," Rodderick commanded from the top of the staircase.

I turned the corner to see Rodderick standing at the top of the stairs with Linnwood hiding in the shadows behind him. Linnwood's smirk lit up his face as he fired up a Dunhill.

"Dude." Rodderick waved his hand, trying to loft the smoke back at the preppy killer. "Don't smoke in my house."

Linnwood's smirk wiped off his face and he took the smoke out of his mouth and looked for a place to extinguish it.

"Put it out, you twat," Rodderick snorted.

"Okay," Linnwood agreed as he walked over to the top of the banister.

Rodderick shoved him. "Don't you fucking dare put that out on the wood."

Linnwood looked puzzled. "Then, where should I put it out?"

"On your fucking tongue, Perry."

Eldritch glared at me quickly and then tried to take another step.

"What did I just say, Eldritch?" Rodderick lifted a gun. "Put the dumb sword away."

Eldritch dropped the sword. "Where is the girl, Stephan?"

I walked to the bottom of the stairs and stood next to Eldritch.

"The loser is back," Rodderick chuckled. "Why didn't I kill you?"

I dropped my gun next to Eldritch's sword and kicked a headless Minuteman out of my way. "Just give us the girl. We know you haven't killed her yet."

"Killed her yet?" He nudged Linnwood in the ribs. "I'm not gonna kill her."

Eldritch chimed in. "Then what do you want with her? Do you want her blood?"

"I don't want her. Perry brought her here. Besides, I can't do anything with cancer blood. I'll probably just fuck her and then give her over to the Skulls to sell her in Mexico."

Linnwood dropped back into the shadows on top of the stairs and curled his lip.

Blood dripped out of the side of Eldritch's mouth as he started growling.

I looked around the foyer without moving my head, trying to figure out a way to get to Rodderick. The only way up was the stairs. The chandelier was out of my reach, and if I jumped up at anything, he would just pick me off with his gun.

Rodderick ran his fingers through his hair. "I'm going to make you watch me fuck her, too."

"Come on, man," I shouted back.

He just laughed.

I started to bluff, trying to buy Eldritch a minute to figure out a plan. "The girl has cancer, Rodderick. Just give her to us or—"

"Or what?" He stepped down on to the staircase but kept the gun on Eldritch.

"*Demon!*" Eldritch roared as he kicked up his sword and started rushing up the stairs.

Eldritch managed to make it a quarter of the way up the stairs before Rodderick opened fire, filling him with bullets and knocking him on his back to the foyer tile.

"*Stay down, Eldritch,*" Rodderick shrieked.

Eldritch's blade fell out of his hand as he tried desperately to plug the holes in his chest with his hands. I bent down to help him out but he pushed me away.

Rodderick shot him in the foot, just playing with him at this point. "Linnwood, get some pictures of this with your phone. I want to remember this moment when I'm massaging the peach fuzz on the little girl's head while I destroy her asshole."

"Oh my God!" I cried.

"These little girls worship me. I'm doing them a favor, *homeboy*. I'm inside of them and then they are inside of me." He turned and started making his way back up the stairs.

I grasped Eldritch's left hand. It was completely coated in his blood.

Out of nowhere, five shotgun blasts blew the huge doors to the compound open behind us.

Eldritch dragged himself to the corner of the staircase. He winked at me and signaled to his sword. Then, he slumped over and coughed up a bunch of blood.

Call it divine intervention.

Call it the twist to end all twists.

Call it the next most fucked up thing that could possibly happen.

Rodderick stepped sideways as one of the doorknobs sailed by his head. "What the fuck now?"

Linnwood pulled his gun out of the back of his pants. "What's this shit?"

As the smoke lifted outside the door, several figures stepped into the light. Some had priest collars and others had cowboy hats. Many of them held leashes, tugging back on a mixed bag of horribles. McCoys. Perrys. Chaplins. RTLs. Six Street Skulls. There were even a few Battlesnakes and Batwangers. Some I'd seen before. Some were new faces. All of them had skin decomposing and hanging off their bodies. Their eyes were glossed over or rolled back into their heads. Their mouths barked and snarled. One of the Chaplins gnawed away at his tongue as his head buzzed. A McCoy next to him moaned and started snapping at his chin, trying to catch the blood splashing out into the room. The Chaplin tugged at the leash's collar around his neck and almost instantly, his head detonated into the delighted face of the McCoy and his teammate next to him.

His Minuteman handler dropped the leash. "Fuck," he whined as the lifeless and headless body fell to the ground.

All of them were slaves to the zombie drug Sunshine, and they were starving for meat. Apparently, The Cloth and the Minutemen built themselves an obedient army of vampires: The Brotherhood of Evil Fucking Druggies.

One of the Minutemen walked to the front of the pack as the others fought to restrain their dogs. One of them stung his servant with a cattle prod, only making it rattle around and claw into its own face.

"Give us the girl, Rodderick," the Minutemen leader demanded.

I gripped tightly onto Eldritch's sword in one hand and my new gun in the other. In no world was this going to end happy. I signaled for Eldritch to make his way back. He pushed himself behind the staircase, leaving a smudged trail of blood.

Rodderick waved his gun. "What are you talking about? How dare you come into my house."

"It's over, son," the leader continued. "Give us the little girl and none of this ever happened."

I got to my feet, steadied myself and pulled back the sword. "Give them the girl," I pleaded.

Linnwood staggered and pulled another gun out of the back of his pants.

"Jesus," Rodderick scoffed. He fired his gun, piercing the Minutemen leader in the head. "Fuck you."

"What are you doing?" Linnwood cried as he retreated to the rooms at the back of the house.

The leader fell back onto a restrained Battlesnake who tore his head off and instantly began chomping on his face. Several other Sunshine-filled monsters stretched their leashes to the breaking point as they dug into the corpse with their fingers and teeth.

"Let them go!" one of the priests commanded.

I turned to see that Eldritch had made it out of the foyer and then immediately sped toward the stairs. Rodderick started following Linnwood toward the bedrooms. He shot several times into the pack, knocking a few of the zombies and their masters off their feet. It wasn't enough though, because as soon as I started up the stairs, the rabid army of the dead were unleashed.

One tripped me up right before I reached the top and started digging its fingers into my ankle. I turned to see the recently decomposed face of Luke Perry grinning. The intensity of his craving caused his teeth to crumble in his mouth. He was so desperate to get me that his fingernails peeled off as they scraped into my leg bone. I kicked furiously to escape and saw the twenty or so others running on their hands and feet like dogs up the stairs behind him.

I sliced Luke's hand off with Eldritch's sword, but that just freed him up to go for my face. Unable to control his blood lust, he impaled himself on the tip of the sword. I kicked him away and turned to follow Rodderick and Linnwood. He fell back with the sword lodged in his ribcage and the other demons instantly tore him into pieces.

I heard Linnwood yell down the long corridor that had closed doors every ten steps or so. "Jesus fucking Christ."

SMASH!

Someone jumped through a window.

Galloping and scratching on the hardwood floors boomed off the walls behind me. I wanted to check to see if the doors were locked, but if I even stopped for a second, I feared that they would catch up to me and devour me before I had the chance to close my eyes. I turned my gun backward and popped off a few rounds as I saw a small light coming from one of the rooms at the end of the hall. It was obviously Rodderick and Linnwood's escape.

I burst through the door and didn't stop. The broken window called to me from the far side of Rodderick's master bedroom.

Before I jumped, I remembered that Paulina was somewhere in the house. I screeched to a halt.

A bunch of the monsters sprung into the room. I shot what was left of my bullets into three of their heads near the doorway.

One of the creatures pounced into the bedroom. As it jumped at me, I avoided contact and threw my gun at it. Instantly, three more stampeded into the room. One of them had Eldritch's sword and it ran at me with it pointed forward like a tusk. I jumped over onto Rodderick's bed and it just barely missed lancing me. It spun back to me as the other two headed toward the window, jumping through. One of the creature's heads half exploded from a faulty collar, and it fell onto a giant shard of glass still secured into the window pane.

As if these things could understand anything anymore, I pleaded with it. "I'm not the one you want."

It was a Chaplin. It spastically wheezed and choked as it tried to lift Eldritch's sword behind its head. Its makeup melted all over what was left of his face and ran into its mouth. Even if it wanted to talk, it couldn't. Its tongue hung out of a hole in the side of its face. It was missing two fingers on both hands and the one that wasn't desperately trying to grab me flopped around, barely attached at its wrist. A blood vessel popped in its eye and it started crying blood. As if it recognized me, it glared at my face and turned its head.

"I'm not the one you want," I repeated.

It grunted as it slowed down and started to step toward me. It was unable to support the weight of the sword so it fell back and clanged on the floor. As if a bell had gone off, it was that instant that I noticed an irritated burn all around his neck under The Cloth's restraint collar.

The collar. The fucking death collar. Just like the collars that The Cloth used to get King Cobra and I to do their bidding.

"Adstringo gutter?" I whispered, unsure.

The busted blood vessel in its eye started to surge muck all over the place. It closed its eyes and smiled as the force of the explosives contained in its neck mushroomed its head all over the room. I turned my head so I didn't get any Sunshine or PCP in my mouth. It collapsed, fell to its knees and then tumbled forward. The top of its body was opened up like a cavern filled with the few bones and organs that were left inside.

I jumped off the bed, snatched the handle of the sword and looked down the hallway. Twenty or so former gang members rolled over each other, up and down the walls. They slobbered blood onto the destroyed floorboards that splintered at their hands and feet. Body parts shot out behind them as the force of their hunt spun up a hurricane of carnage.

I dug the tip of the sword into the floor and took off toward the center of anarchy. The sword tore into the wood until I got a few feet away from them. I pulled it in to my side and bored it into the head of the monster at the front. All of the others jumped toward me and just as I felt the teeth of a former RTL chick dig into my shoulder, I screamed the magic words again.

"Adstringo gutter!"

Teeth, eyeballs, skull fragments, bones, tissue… it all filled the hallway like confetti at a parade.

"Adstringo gutter!" I continued to yell.

One of the beasts, most likely subdued with a faulty collar, hobbled away from me, whimpering like an abused puppy toward the stairs.

"Run away, motherfucker!" I shouted after him.

Without sparing another second, I started kicking the doors open down the hall. "Paulina?" I yelled as I ran circles through every room on the second floor, checking bathrooms, closets and under beds. "Paulina? Where are you?"

Gunfire rang out in the backyard from the pool area.

"Mister Eldritch! Help me!" Paulina shrieked. It was coming from outside.

I grabbed tight onto the sword and beelined it back to the master bedroom. Without hesitating, I jumped through the window. I closed my eyes as I made contact with the glassy pool below.

As I sank to the bottom, I saw several other bodies enter the water. I sprung off the pool bottom and tried to thrust myself to the surface. The sword fell from my grip as one of the zombies grabbed onto my torso. It snapped at my face and his mouth filled with water. The other dug its teeth into my thigh and dragged me back to the floor of the pool.

I opened my mouth and yelled, "*Adstringo gutter*," but the sound was muted by the water and air bubbles. I grabbed onto the ears of the dog trying to bite my nose off and started slamming my forehead into its face. The decay of its face broke off and was whisked into my nose, causing me to cough and suck a bunch of water into my nose and lungs. He pushed himself away from me and drifted toward the top. I began pummeling the second one rapidly on top of his head, cracking his skull open. Skin from his entire body liquefied and filled the water. Like his friend, he drifted away from me but not before he tore a piece of my thigh off.

"Mister Eldritch!" Paulina screeched again from outside the pool.

I pushed myself toward her cries. I couldn't let her die. I couldn't let her be killed by the world that I brought her to.

When I reached the stairs, I hugged the chrome bar and lifted myself out of the pool. As I gasped for air, I crumbled onto the leg that water monster had taken a patch out of. I looked back at the sword that glistened at the bottom of the pool then looked around the backyard.

Rodderick and Perry stood near an outdoor bar. Rodderick had his hands around Paulina's throat. Surrounding him were The Cloth, the Minutemen and what was left of the zombie pack.

"Okay. Okay." Rodderick laughed. "I'll give you the girl." He shoved her away. Paulina looked at me and then at the unexpected guests.

I stumbled on to the deck, trying to cover my wound and waved my hand toward my chest. "Come here, Paulina."

"Are we done now?" Rodderick continued to laugh. "Is this shit done, you ungrateful fucking peasants?"

Linnwood stepped away from him again.

"Where are you going, pussy?" Rodderick shot twice, bringing him to the ground. Perry crawled to a tree and cowered, guarding his face with his hands.

Paulina looked over to The Cloth and the Minutemen who stood behind a thinned-out pack of beasties.

"*Adstringo gutter!*" I shouted across the pool. Horror came over all the human faces in the horde as they covered their bodies to avoid being bombarded by flying napalm that was their slaves' heads.

"That's right, assholes. I know your password. The Cloth used me, too. I returned the favor by burning down one of you research centers."

Paulina, terrified, ran to me and hugged my leg. I patted her bald head and pushed her face-first into my leg.

Rodderick started clapping. "Good job, idiots, you just got beat by a homeless drug addict. Why do I even pay you?"

One of The Cloth members brushed face and gunk off of his vestment. "Stephan. We are going to need you to come with us."

Paulina shivered at my side and wept.

"Come with you?" Rodderick snickered. "Come with you? Where? To the building that I pay for? I fucking own you. You watch. I'm going to go inside, make a phone call and then you can march—" he pointed at Paulina, "—*that* bald, little fucking mutant up to my room so I can shove my dick in her mouth and then chew on her eyes. That way, I don't have to hear or see her cry anymore."

I pushed my hands on either side of her head to cover her ears.

As Rodderick started to laugh uncontrollably, Steel talons enveloped his head as a black mass rose up behind him.

"Incorrect." Eldritch pulled the razors back, opening Rodderick's face in eight different slices.

Rodderick tried to turn around but his skull pushed through segmented skin flaps like a blooming flower.

The army across the deck from me raised their guns.

"Oh, God!" Rodderick wheezed as his entire body flared into seizures. Shocked by the cold wind blowing under his skin onto bare bone, he tried to reach up to put his face back together. "*My face!*"

Before he got the chance to touch the boyish looks that sold millions of movie tickets, Eldritch wrapped his arms around Rodderick's torso and then snapped his hands ablaze. A mix of both of their hair caught fire almost immediately. Rodderick tried to shake from side to side and drag Eldritch to the pool to dowse the growing hellfire that was the both of them.

"Eldritch, no!" I begged.

Paulina struggled to get out of my grip. I held on to her tightly. "Mister Eldritch!" she screamed. Her mouth was muffled by my jeans that covered her mouth. I felt tears rolling from her face onto the exposed parts of my legs, all the way down into my boots.

Eldritch stood tall as both of them were quickly clothed in fire.

"Fire!" one of The Minutemen yelled.

Then, without another word from Eldritch or Rodderick, the firing squad filled them with holes.

As they both fell like a towering inferno, I closed my eyes and continued to restrain Paulina. "Mister Eldritch!" she shouted into my leg. She stopped struggling and started bawling.

For over a minute, I refused to open my eyes. The smell of burnt hair and flesh mixed with the overpowering fumes of chlorine and pool chemicals.

Several guns cocked and magazines were refreshed in front of me.

"Give us the girl," one of them commanded.

Knowing that it was what Eldritch would have wanted, I let her go.

"He said give us the girl," another repeated.

I opened my eyes and looked down to see Paulina's reddened and soaked eyes staring up at me. Snot covered her face from her nose being pressed tightly against my leg.

"You need to go with them, Little One," I said, echoing Eldritch.

I looked over to The Cloth and Minutemen soldiers. They all had their guns raised and pointed at my head.

"I don' wanna to go with them," she whined. "He tol' me, Uncle RJ. He tol' me that you were my sister's friend." She tugged at the bottom of what was left of my *High as Fuck* shirt. "Mister Eldritch told me that you tried to bring her home to me."

I coughed a little, trying to conceal my quivering lip. The smoke from Eldritch and Rodderick swirled around the trees as the flames started to engulf a chaise lounge and then two pool chairs. I bent down so I could be at the same level as her. "He lied to you," I confessed. "Uncle RJ isn't your uncle."

She pushed me back onto my butt. "I don' wanna to go with them."

I rocked myself back up and lifted my arms to surrender. "Uncle RJ is a very bad man."

One of the Minutemen steadied his gun on me and then picked her up from behind and threw her over his shoulder. She kicked her legs and beat her fists against the soldier's bulletproof vest. "I don' wanna go! I don' wanna go."

"I'm sorry," I said.

I dropped my head and prepared to finally die when Linnwood Perry's screaming drowned out Paulina's.

"Don't put that collar on me," he sniveled. "I'm not one of your bitches."

As I too felt one of the collars lock around my neck and then the force of clubs and rifle stocks pounding me into the pool deck, I heard him cry out one last time. "Get up and fight, RJ! I didn't know that the girl had cancer. I was doing it for *us*."

When I didn't respond, he simply said, "You fucking junkie piece of shit."

XXVI

BURIED

"Are they cleaning it up all day again?" a voice said.

"Yeah, just be sure your loud mouth doesn't say anything. The Rangers locked down all of West Hills two days ago. All the neighbors heard the guns and called 911," another voice responded. "They're pissed that they can't get back to their houses."

Two fucking days.

"The press is still lined up at the main entrance," the first voice returned.

"What were they told?"

"The only thing they were told is that a body was found at the actor's house."

"How are we going to get all those bodies out of there?"

"Good thing we brought those vans with us."

I felt my head and face, which were covered in bumps. I still had the collar around my neck. I was under a blanket in the back seat of an SUV. But for some reason, I was still alive.

"That little girl doesn't realize it but she just hit the lottery."

"Yeah, if she sticks to the story, we'll all make some money."

"That's why that piece of shit is still alive back there."

"How much do you think Rodderick is worth?"

"They said on the news when he OD'd the other week that he was worth like two hundred mil."

"No shit? My kids love those movies. The first thing I'm gonna do when I get home is rip those posters of him off the walls in their bedrooms."

"They'll rip them off the walls themselves. I'm sure the fact he was a kid killer and child molester will make your girls never want to see a vampire movie again."

I sat up in the seat and knocked my head into the barrel of a rifle.

"Stay down, motherfucker," one of them yelled.

Sunlight shined through little holes in the blanket. I did as I was told.

"Did you know he was doing that shit? The kid stuff?"

"Fuck no. Do you think I would work for him? I have two little girls of my own."

"I hear you. Hey, pull up over there."

The truck pulled to the side of the road.

"Watch him."

The driver's side door opened and then closed. Then the back door next to me opened.

"Get out," the driver said. "Don't be stupid."

I didn't move, unsure if they were taking me out to assassinate me or not.

He shoved his gun into my chest. "I said get out."

I lifted myself up, making sure that I remained covered by the blanket.

"Come help me, I've got him."

The passenger got out of the truck too and opened the door behind his seat. He pressed his gun into the back of my head. "I'll come in behind him as he gets out," he said.

As I was pulled by my shoulders out of the backseat, my head started spinning.

"Can you believe this guy can even get up?"

"No shit. We beat the piss out of him."

"I'm talking about the tranqs we've pounded him with every time he's twitched since the fight. I've beat these monsters for hours and they don't stay down."

"It has something to do with them metabolizing drugs or having no blood in their bodies or something."

The passenger used his rifle to push me out of the truck.

My feet hit the gravel and my legs buckled. The driver caught me through the blanket and held me up. "You gotta do better than that, Mack," he laughed.

I steadied myself as the passenger exited the truck, closed the door behind us and took my left arm. The driver grabbed my right.

"Where are we going?" I finally asked.

"Don't talk," the driver insisted.

"Pretty crazy couple of days, huh?"

"'Keep Austin Weird'."

"No shit. 'Keep Austin Weird'."

We walked through some grass and sand and then down a hill. I tried to keep pace with them but then gave up and let them drag me. Even though I didn't really feel like I deserved to live and was expecting my send off at any second, I didn't want to run to death.

"How about those priest assholes?"

"Oh, they were okay. Saved our asses."

"Not really. Our vampires saved our asses."

The driver nudged me in the ribs. "This one sure wrecked those freaks, huh?"

"Where did you learn that?" the passenger asked as he nudged me too. I understood the question but didn't respond.

"Maybe he was an altar boy."

"*Adstringo gutter!*" the driver shouted.

I stopped and my body froze up. I let out a breath and waited for the collar to tighten and detonate my head.

"Psyche!" The passenger laughed and flicked me on the neck. "Good thing we had the older collars. The last thing we want is his head all over the place."

They both broke into hysterics as they pulled me to resume our journey. We continued to walk straight when we reached the bottom of the hill. Sweat started beading up all over my face. The thin blanket was no match for the sun.

"You got the phone?"

"Yeah, I got it right here."

"Couldn't we just kill him after?"

"Why fucking bother? We're getting paid to do what the girl wants. Besides, he's just another druggie vampire being dumped across the border." He slapped me on the head. "Say hi to all of your friends."

"I guess you're right. I just hate the fact that I gotta go look for a job again."

"Back to security for me."

"Yeah, I'm gonna take some time off. I'm done with this."

The driver tightened his grip on my arm. "There it is. Up there."

"Finally. I feel like we've been coming out here all morning."

"Would you rather be back at Rodderick's house cleaning up that mess?"

"No, sir."

The foul smell of sewage intensified all around us and the driver pushed me to the ground. My forehead knocked into the side of a piece of metal and my knees plunged into a shallow stream of water.

A gun banged into the back of my head. "Crawl forward," the passenger said.

I stayed under the blanket but felt the sun's power soften as things became dark as I scurried forward into a cylinder.

"Okay, turn around."

I rolled over and sat on my ass.

"Lift up the blanket."

The wet blanket slipped off me and balled up in my lap. I tried to adjust my eyes to the sunlight to see my captors but they were nothing more than blurry figures in cowboy hats.

"Take this," the driver said as he handed me a phone.

I grabbed the phone with one hand as I rubbed my eyes, trying again to get a look at them.

"What's this for?" I asked.

"Unlock it."

I brought the phone under my chin and looked down. Then, with my thumb, I unlocked it.

"Call that first number when we're gone. It's your lucky fucking day, scumbag."

I looked at the screen. The Texas number was proceeded by two zeros and all the language on the screen was in Spanish.

The driver shoved his gun into the tunnel. "Do you understand?"

I looked up and shielded my eyes from the dripping water. "No."

"The little girl saved you."

The passenger swatted the driver. "Let's go."

They both turned around and I watched as they jogged back up the hill.

"Who was the big guy, anyway?" one of them asked.

"Some priest's kid," the other laughed.

After several minutes, I heard the SUV start and I pressed the call button under the number. After two rings, the phone answered but no one spoke.

"Hello?" I finally said.

"Who is this?" a man's voice on the other end asked.

"This is RJ. RJ Reynolds."

"Are you alive?"

"Yes."

"Did the men leave you?"

"Yes."

"Are they going to come back?"

"I don't think so."

I heard some shuffling on the other end and what sounded like a little girl whispering. She said, "You know I only like the white gummy bears."

No one spoke for a bit.

"I'm alive, Paulina!" I yelled. "Do what they say."

A familiar voice softly shushed the girl.

I waited a beat and let the sound of the other voice register.

"Eldritch?" I whispered. "Is that you?"

Then they hung up.

I stared at the phone for a bit and listened to the dial tone, until finally the speaker started barking loudly. It echoed all the way down the drainage pipe behind me and rang in my ears like the fiddle of that shitty, allegedly homophobic bluegrass band. I wanted to get up. I wanted to walk outside into the sun and burn my body into a hard coyote turd on the Mexican sand. But, I just sat on my wet ass and put my face in my hands.

Looks like we Aren't getting high for A loooooooNg time.

"*Leave me alone!*" I screamed and I smashed my fist into the curved wall of the cement pipe, completely bloodying and shattering my knuckles.

I took a second look at the hand. The fingers went limp and pieces of bone snowed down from the open gashes. I licked the blood flow and spit the bone fragments out.

That hand would never be one hundred percent again, I decided.

And then, I looked at the screen again and dialed the only other phone number that I knew. I was sure to add "00" to the beginning of the number. It was obvious to me that I wasn't in Austin anymore.

00-1-855-BROSKIZ.

It rang.

It rang twice.

It rang three times.

Finally, someone picked up.

"BroSkiz, your number one jet ski rental choice for Lake Travis and Austin," the voice cheered.

I cleared my throat. "I'm in a ditch. In Mexico."

Cody yawned loudly into the phone. "Hilarious. You got dicks on your face?"

KNUCKLER
COMING SOON

ABOUT THE AUTHOR

For more than 20 years, Drew Stepek has written, produced, and directed for the publishing, online and entertainment industries. Drew has worked for Film Threat, Sci-Fi Universe, Wild Cartoon Kingdom, *The Tonight Show with Jay Leno, Late Night with Conan O'Brien, Saturday Night Live, The Profiler, The Pretender, Buffy the Vampire Slayer,* and ESPN.

In the past ten years, the author ventured into creative directing and ideation roles involving entertainment and technology marketing for Davie Brown Entertainment and Straight Up Technologies. In 2012, Stepek took a position as the Head of Branded Entertainment for Machinima. He has also been a Creative Director at AwesomenessTV.

Born in Royal Oak, Michigan, Drew moved around a bit as a young man and finally found his home base in Hollywood, California in 1994. Drew attended Rollins College in Winter Park, Florida. His first novel Godless (ISBN# 0978602498) was released 666 (June 6th, 2006) and has since captured a strong underground following.

Currently, Stepek is working on the sequels to *Knuckle Supper* and *Knuckle Balled.*

Where the addiction began

DREW STEPEK

Knuckle Supper

THE ULTIMATE GUTTER FIX EDITION

Lloyd Kaufman
Bentley Little
Kristopher Triana
Shane McKenzie
Alistair Rennie
Jack Ketchum
Ryan Harding
Edward Lee
John McNee

AND MANY MORE...

YOU'LL LAUGH...YOU'LL CRY...YOU'LL VOMIT
DON'T SAY WE DIDN'T WARN YOU.

"Take one part Sid Vicious, one part H.P. Lovecraft and shake.
Throw in a dash of the thrill kill thug life and you have *Mother's Boys.*"

~ David C. Hayes, author of *Cannibal Fat Camp*

Available through Blood Bound Books
www.bloodboundbooks.net

Made in the USA
Columbia, SC
27 December 2017